RAVE REVIEWS FOR *UNVEILED* AND JENNI LICATA!

"A great ride, a great read."

—Tess Mallory, author of *Jewels of Time*

"A delicious blend of intrigue, suspicion, betrayal, and sensual romance."

—Sheryl Horst for *The Romance Reviewer*

"Stylish and witty. I enjoyed every word!"

—Julia Quinn, author of *How to Marry a Marquis*

LONGING REVEALED

Alex's thumb brushed across the fullness of Tori's lips, quelling her words. She shivered against her will and felt her stomach drop to the vicinity of her toes. Rational thought evaporated into the night.

"I've saved you," he said softly. "Twice."

The soft claim took her aback and raised a question for which she had no answer. "Aye," she whispered. She held her breath and dared to look at him, to let him see her confusion. "But I don't know why."

He went still, gazing into her eyes. "Don't you?" His free hand came up from the folds of his cloak. Tori watched it draw near with a fascination that she found both compelling and frightening at once. "Don't you really?"

His hands cradled her face and he closed the inches between them. Tori held her breath as his fingers traced the heights and valleys of her face, feeling every sense she possessed come alive for the first time. Gloriously so. And when he, with the barest of pressures, urged her mouth upward to meet his, she couldn't find the will to stop him.

Unveiled

Jenni Licata

LEISURE BOOKS NEW YORK CITY

For Matthew, Joshua, and Caleb for being so patient with a mom who was just a little . . . different.

But most importantly for Steven, who rarely complained about burned meals and always encouraged me onward with unflagging faith. I love you.

Leisure Entertainment Service Co., Inc. (LESCO Distribution Group)

A LESCO Edition

Published by special arrangement with Dorchester Publishing Co., Inc.

Printed in the United States of America.

ACKNOWLEDGMENTS

I'd like to convey my appreciation for a few very special people who had some effect on the evolution of *Unveiled:*

Liz Flaherty, Tina Runge, and Judith Palmer (a.k.a. the GMTA'ers), the best friends and best critique group a writer could hope for.

Kathy Gonya, best friend extraordinaire and also a wonderful reader in her own right. I affectionately call her "Eagle Eyes."

The late, great Anne Douglas Bayless, a tough old bird who never failed to encourage me to stick with it. Always by her side was Betty Balog. Betty, thanks for believing in me from the beginning.

Roberta Brown, who brought me wondrous good luck in 1998.

Last but not least, my family—you all know who you are.

Unveiled

Chapter One

February 1712
London, England

She had returned. Just as he'd expected.

Alexandre Rawlings, Earl of Carlton, watched the pale figure cross the crowded ballroom. A hint of a smile tugged at his lips. Aye, she had returned—not that there had ever been a doubt in his mind. It was his destiny to find the woman in white again.

Like a will-o'-the-wisp, the young woman drifted among the fashionable throng who'd assembled at St. James Palace by invitation of Queen Anne. Held in honor of Prince Eugene of Hanover, the glittering reception had dulled when the queen retired after the operatic festivities. The nobles were left to gossip, trade flirtations, and resist boredom until the time they could gracefully take their leave.

The woman gave notice to none of them. Tall and willow slender, she slipped through the crush untouched, as though the shimmering fabric of her gown magically shielded her from the chaos. Enthralled, Alex followed her passage with his gaze. Though an elaborate periwig concealed her hair, though her features were hidden behind a silver demi-mask, a certainty formed in his mind.

Alors, she was magnificent.

It was the mask that intrigued him most. That and her aspect. With her chin held high, she turned her head to and fro, as if searching for something—or someone. As she moved across the polished marble floor toward the open doors on the opposite side, she seemed oblivious to the whispers and scandalized gasps that trailed after her passage.

"That woman! Can you believe her audacity?"

The familiar voice sounded in his ear, interrupting his preoccupation. With a frown, Alex glanced down at the voluptuous woman who had claimed his arm all evening long, and his bed even longer. Baroness Elizabeth Rowan, his eager mistress for the past seven months.

Too eager. *Seven months, ye gods.* Lately it had seemed more akin to seven years.

Alex gazed at her. "Aye," he said in his raspy voice. The tightness in his throat exaggerated the natural grating of his voice, enough to make him wince at the coarse sound of it. He'd had years to regret the duel that had left him with half the voice of a normal man—years to regret many things, including the recklessness of his youth. "She's quite intriguing, don't you think?"

Bess gave a haughty sniff, but craned her head to better view the woman in white. "Her gown is quite modish, true. But to wear a mask to a reception given by the queen? *Or* a dance for the Duke of Hamilton, *or* a ball by Lady Margaret? 'Tis just not done—" She tossed back her wig-covered head, and the diamond earrings he had given her swung wildly against her neck. "Not by a woman of *quality.* Yet she has been seen at all these and more in the past three weeks. Costumed in precisely the same manner."

She arched a brow and leaned back, satisfied. Alex got the impression that he was meant to understand her meaning without question. He raised his gaze to the open doors through which the mysterious woman had disappeared. Quality? He couldn't agree with her more. Her quality was obvious.

"Jealous, Bess?" he murmured, amused.

"Should I be?" Green eyes narrowed in suspicion. She leaned closer to him with a whisper, "They say she's a spy—mayhap even French!"

Ah, yes. It was no secret that the fashionable of London loved a good intrigue, and the woman in white did not disappoint them. In the weeks since her first appearance, she'd been cast as a notorious French spy, *La Fantôme;* a murderess seeking the lover who'd betrayed her; even a pirate queen. Still her true purpose remained shrouded.

Abruptly, Bess' demeanor softened. Moving closer, she rubbed her body against him, the soft cushion of her breasts gliding along his forearm in an unspoken invitation.

Months ago, her bold seductions would have had him burning with desire. Now he could only wonder at the absence of temptation. Had he really once fancied himself in love with her? Lust certainly had a way of blinding young fools.

Spreading her fan wide, Bess used it as a shield from prying eyes and stretched on tiptoe to breathe a laugh into his ear. Her teeth grazed his earlobe. "Trying to bait me, are you, Alex? Ah, but we both know that I am the expert at that."

That and so many other things. Having met half the men who had known her bed before him, and having experienced her expertise firsthand, Alex was wont to agree with her. But, by the gods, perhaps an expert was no longer what he wanted.

His gaze drifted once again to the yawning doors. Just now, temptation led along a path of mystery to a prize in virginal white. If only he had the time to follow.

Pressing a manicured finger along his jaw, Bess drew his attention back to her. "Have I competition, milord?"

Her voice reflected concern, but her eyes showed a confident gleam—Bess well knew her effect on men. "Why, my dear Bess, what woman could possibly compete with you?"

The baroness smiled and gave a full-throated purr. "Hmmm, that's good. Very good. You know how I hate disloyalty. But then, you know how I reward faithfulness, too." The fan artfully shifted position. Bold as a cat demanding attention, Bess captured his hand and drew it to her full breast, molding it firmly along the smooth curve. She locked her gaze with his. "Have you any suggestions?"

Alex shifted in discomfort. "Bess—"

Her eyes shone like liquid glass. "My scandalous Devil Lord. Would you not like to escape the festivities?"

Devil Lord. How he hated that ridiculous nickname. A personal gift from the gossips in his reckless youth. Like *La Fantôme,* he had been the object of their attentions often enough. And how very like Bess to remind him of it. No doubt she found it dangerous and appealing.

With an uncustomary thankfulness for duty, Alex shrugged away from her. "Nay, I cannot."

"Nay?" She touched her tongue to her lip, moistening it. Her gaze swept his body. "I would make it worth your while."

Heedless of the amused regard of several witnesses nearby, she placed her hand on his chest. Alex grabbed her wrist and halted her progress, feeling too much like cornered prey for his own comfort. "Not now, Bess."

She snatched her hand away. "Not now? Cannot?" Her voice rose dangerously as she mimicked him. Pride and fury turned her eyes hard. "I think *will not* seems more likely."

Alex cursed his luck as several pairs of eyes swung in

their direction. Ah, his loving mistress. She cared naught that all of London would know of their disagreement on the morrow. Though she meant for her demands to cow him, they had quite the opposite effect.

Muttering under his breath, he spun around, dragging her by the wrist behind him. Not until they had quit the assembly hall for the privacy of a dim corridor did he release her.

"Ah, so this was your plan, milord."

Exasperated, Alex leaned a hand against the stone wall and glared at her. "By the gods, you're a stubborn wench!"

She arched an auburn brow. "Persistent, aye. Stubborn? Let's just say I know what I want. And right now I've a hunger for you, Alex." She moved against him and slid her hands up his chest, locking them about his neck. "Come, milord. Do you not ache for pleasure?"

Time was running out, and an appointment with the queen could not be put off. Alex gritted his teeth. "I'll meet you at Rowan House later. I have business to attend to."

Bess tilted her head and assessed him carefully. "Just what sort of business?"

"You may be my mistress, Bess, but my business is my own." He pulled her hands from him and stepped away. "'Tis none of your concern."

Tightening her lips, Bess crossed her arms beneath her breasts. "Beast. Just be sure you are there before dawn. Or you may find your place has been taken." She tossed her head and minced away, swinging her hips in a brazen challenge.

Alex watched her go, more amazed than ever by her selfish demands. It was just such behavior that made his blood run cold.

Shaking himself from his black mood, he pulled his watch from his pocket and freed the tiny catch. The queen expected him at midnight. That left him little more than fifteen minutes to navigate the unfamiliar corridors between the grand hall and her private chambers, and even less time to prepare himself. Tension gathered between his shoulder blades. What could the queen possibly want of him?

Alex squared his shoulders and set off down the hall, remembering the strange little man who had delivered the summons that afternoon. The messenger had avowed ignorance of the queen's purpose, yet he'd presented himself wearing an ill-fitting wig and a false beard. It had obviously been a disguise.

Unease sharpened his senses and made his heart beat with heavy thuds. Alex quickened his step. The sooner this meeting was over, the better.

Heedful of the messenger's caution for discretion, he followed the directions he had committed to memory. Between candles placed at wide intervals, shadows claimed the hallway. It occurred to him that *La Fantôme,* though a flesh-and-blood woman, should likely be quite at home in such eerie surroundings. Where had she gone?

At the second cross passage, Alex turned to the right. Here not a single candle lit the way and full darkness cloaked the corridor, forcing him to feel his way along the wall. His toe caught on a loose floorboard, and he stumbled.

"Bloody hell!" His voice exploded in the vast silence, unnerving him. Alex shook his head at his uncustomary jumpiness and wondered if the absence of candles was a sign of Anne's frugality or just her way of striking him humble.

Another turn. Ahead should be the servants' stairs. This hall was brighter than the others, thanks to a pool of light spilling from an open door near the end of the passageway. He approached the entrance on quiet footsteps, fully meaning to pass it by and allow the occupants their privacy. Yet even as he broached the golden circle, something within drew his gaze. He stopped and peered inside.

It was *La Fantôme* he noticed first. Absorbing the light from the fire in the hearth, her dress and skin appeared more warm gold than cool silver . . . and she looked decidedly free of earthly bounds. Not a phantom, Alex decided. An angel.

His gaze lowered. At her feet lay a man. Buried to the hilt, a dagger protruded from his chest.

Alex knew the man. Even without the wig and false beard, the stout body and pocked cheeks betrayed his identity. The queen's messenger was now a corpse. "*Sacrebleu.*"

At the rasp of his voice, the woman turned her head slowly toward him. "He is dead."

So calm. So matter-of-fact. Yet Alex was certain he heard a slight tremor in her sparse words. The woman blinked several times, but seemed unable to look away from the body. Stepping gingerly around the pool of spreading crimson, Alex knelt by the man's head. Bloodshot brown eyes stared sightlessly up at him. A touch at the man's neck verified the woman's claim.

Alex transfixed her with a hard stare as he rose to his feet. "Madame, what do you here?"

Her gaze flew to his. Her eyes looked wild, fearful, for the first time since he'd walked into the room. "I?" She touched her fingers to her breast, sounding surprised that he should ask. "My presence here is none of your concern, sirrah."

"A man has been murdered. Pray tell me why I shouldn't be concerned."

" 'Twas not I who killed him. I happened here only moments ago. I swear it."

She was telling the truth, Alex suspected. A great deal of blood had pooled beneath the man. He had been killed long before he'd seen her at the reception. Also, her gown attested to her innocence. Not a speck of blood marred the perfect white surface of the cloth.

Her elaborate mask hid much of her face from him, but

her skin was deathly pale and her full lips trembled before she remembered to clamp them together. The motion drew his attention to a tiny mole at the corner of her mouth. Not a patch, but a true mark of beauty he found intriguingly lovely. He wondered if she was as young as she appeared.

There was only one way to find out. "Take off your mask."

The woman crossed her arms across her breasts and shook her head once, hard. "Nay."

"I would know that you speak the truth, madame. I would see it on your face." Alex stretched out a finger to touch the corner of the mask.

She flinched and ducked aside. "Nay," she said in a choked voice. "You must believe me, I—" Her breath caught in her throat.

Alex circled around her, placing his bulk between her and the door. "Were you meeting him? Was he your lover, perhaps?"

Her mouth, lovely and soft, fell open. "How dare you!"

Alex steeled himself against her physical appeal and resolved to learn the facts. "I dare anything I please. Tell me the truth."

"I just did. I know nothing of this man. No more than you. Now, if you please, I would like to leave."

She tried to push past him. Alex grabbed her wrist and swung her around. "So you know nothing of the man. Know you who killed him?"

She stared, transfixed, at his hand, then slowly lifted her gaze to his face. "You mistake me, sir. I just told you—"

"You've told me nothing. I don't know your name, nor your purpose for being in this part of the palace."

She wrenched at her arm, but he held it fast. Her fine-boned chin lifted. "For that matter, neither do I know *you,* sir, nor your business here. Mayhap you killed this man yourself and seek to blame another." Her eyes raked him boldly. "You speak French. You may be a spy. Or worse."

"And perhaps you know who murdered this man. Perhaps you're an accomplice."

Tension sang in the air between them, tuned to a fine pitch as they stared at each other. With more strength than he would have guessed that she possessed, the woman strained against his grasp until Alex feared her bones would break, at last forcing him to release her. She stood apart from him, rubbing her wrist.

"What is your name, madame?"

She shook her head, closed her eyes, then opened them again. As he watched, she took one wavering step toward a nearby chair. "I . . . I am not . . . I cannot—" She reached blindly for the chair. Missing it, she swayed on her feet, pressing her hand to her forehead.

Alex rushed forward and slid his arm around her waist. For a moment the woman stiffened as though she meant to refuse him. Then she leaned against him in surrender.

"Thank you, my lord," she whispered. "The shock must have . . . overwhelmed me."

Alex frowned, rebelling against his masculine urge to shelter her. The woman was perhaps no more than a consummate actress, a charlatan bent on escape.

Was she playing him for a fool?

Her scent enveloped him, a mixture of citrus and crushed cloves and some flower he couldn't name. Heady but fresh. Gazing down upon her, he again found cause to wonder about her age. Her skin was fine, as pale and smooth as a child's. The mask and wig taunted him, daring him to brush them aside.

Farther down, small breasts swelled from the low cut of her gown, as enticing as the mark that graced her lips.

He cleared his dry throat. "Are you going to swoon, madame?" he murmured, then grimaced. He sounded like a goat.

The phantom woman laughed once with a hint of wry humor. Color had begun to return to her cheeks. "At a time like this?"

Time. The word jolted through Alex, a lightning-swift reminder of his duty. Not even murder could excuse a delay in an appointment with the queen. Alex touched the woman's chin, trying not to notice the exquisite softness of her skin as he urged her to look at him. "We've not settled things, but I cannot help that now. Give me your name."

She pulled from his arms and smoothed her hands down the front of her gown. " 'Twould hardly be prudent to do so, my lord." She cocked her head to indicate the dead messenger. "I swear to you I know nothing of him, nor his murderer. Should we not alert the guard?"

He shook his head. "I'll take care of that. Have you a coach here?"

She shrugged, unconcerned. Alex fought against a rising tide of frustration. If he left her to her own devices, she could be discovered. Perhaps even wrongly accused. The prospect conjured disturbing images of the Crown's punishments.

"I cannot see you away," he said urgently, "as much as I may wish to. I have business that prevents it."

She shook her head, already gazing toward the door. "I don't require your assistance."

Alex set his jaw. "If you have no carriage, you will use mine."

"I could not possibly—"

" 'Tis a coach and four, with a crest on the door—a wolf grappling a wounded bear. The driver's name is Rorick. Give him this." Alex unhooked his fob and pressed his watch into her hand.

She lifted the watch she wore from the chatelaine that suspended it. It swung back and forth before her. "I already have a watch."

Alex caught a brief glimpse of an engraved griffin and a rose before she tucked the timepiece back among the folds of her skirt. She held his watch out for him to take back.

He shook his head. "Nay. The watch will show my driver you speak the truth. Tell him. He will see you safe."

Puzzlement knitted her brows as she opened her mouth to refuse again. Losing patience, Alex grabbed her by the hand and guided her forcibly to the open door. "Go now, madame. There is no more time."

Without his watch, Alex could only hope that he would make his appointment. Climbing the stairs by threes, he allowed himself one last thought about *La Fantôme.* Would she take advantage of his offer? He had no way of assuring she would do as he'd bidden. He could only wonder as he attended the queen.

"Carlton. You are late, sirrah."

Alex bowed low and knelt before her, lowering his head. "My apologies, Your Majesty. I had some difficulty—"

"Never mind that now, Carlton. You may stand."

Alex straightened. Across a large sitting chamber sat Anne, queen of the united Britain. She looked different from when last he'd seen her, two years prior. Tired. Pale. Drawn. Myriad tiny lines gathered at the corners of her eyes and pinched her mouth. He'd heard word that gout had taken its toll, swelling the queen's body and leaving her in horrible pain. Seeing her now, he could well believe the truth of the statement.

In his mind's eye, he saw again the dead man down the stairs, and he wondered how Anne would react at her courier's murder.

While Alex waited, a plump lady-in-waiting carefully placed a thick robe over her lady's lap, curtsied low when the queen said, "Thank you, Abigail," then disappeared into the next room. But Alex knew instinctively he was not alone with Anne. He was certain her confidante would witness their every word.

The queen peered at him in close assessment. "Know you why we've summoned you here, Carlton?"

Alex shook his head. "Nay, my queen. I must admit, 'tis a puzzle to me."

Anne relaxed against her chair, but her eyes remained watchful. Her fingertips tapped a slow, continuous rhythm on the smoothly curved chair arms. "Allow us to come to the point, then. 'Tis said that there are those who wish us dead, Carlton. Have you perchance heard such a rumor?"

The directness of her approach took him by surprise. "Nay, my queen. I must confess I have little use for rumors." He'd been the subject of them far too often, himself.

Anne inclined her head in appreciation. "And well you do for it. This rumor, however, is of a sort we cannot afford to ignore. Do you understand that?"

Alex frowned, wondering what this had to do with him. "Aye, Your Majesty. But I do not see—"

"And have you heard of the barbarians that assault the streets of this fair city?" Anne interrupted. "Mohocks, they fashion themselves."

"I have read of them, in the *Spectator.* They've caused quite an uproar of late, it seems."

Anne sniffed. The movement flared her nostrils and tightened her thin lips. " 'Tis said they are *gentlemen.* Nobles of our own court!" Her voice rose swiftly, communicating the depth of her sense of betrayal. "That any of you should be involved in such heinous acts of brutality is unacceptable to us."

Uncertainty accompanied suspense in a slow crawl up Alex's spine. Did she think he might be a part of these men? He hastened to agree with her. " 'Tis certainly barbaric, as you say, my queen."

Anne's gaze was fixed upon her own hand. One bejeweled finger traced back and forth along a tiny groove on the chair arm. As her silence lengthened, Alex found his own gaze drawn to that motion. The weighty silence raised gooseflesh along his arms.

When at last she spoke again, her voice was low and

controlled. "They beleaguer the city's watch. They terrify the good people of London, making them fear the dark that descends each night. They vandalize, scandalize, and brutalize the property of good and proper citizens. And now, 'tis said they are the hired mercenaries who will endeavor to take our life. They are the sword our assassins would wield." Her scrutiny snapped upward to snare his concerned gaze. "You have French blood, do you not, Carlton?"

The sudden change in her direction stunned him, and yet at long last, he thought he understood the point of her thrust. "Aye. My beloved mother was a Frenchwoman. But through her marriage to my father, she became a loyal English subject."

Anne's fine eyebrows rose. "Indeed? And where do your loyalties lie, my dear Carlton?"

Without conscious forethought, Alex dropped to one knee and clasped his fist to his chest, bowing his forehead to his clenched hand. "I am your most loyal and faithful subject, Your Majesty," he vowed. "England is my lifeblood, as it was my father's, and his father's before him."

For the third time that evening, Alex mentally cursed his youthful foolishness. The harsh rasping of his voice in his throat conveyed little of the reverence he wished to express. As he awaited her response, his heart began to clamor like a loose shutter in a high wind. The queen obviously suspected him because of his lineage. Whether she also suspected him of being involved with the Mohocks or in the plot against her, he couldn't be certain. His thoughts churned in desperation. How could he convince her of his loyalty?

Sparing him, Anne inclined her head in a regal nod. "Well spoken, Lord Carlton. Such devotion is well received. Please stand." As Alex rose to his feet once more, she continued. "Indeed, we are quite impressed by you, sirrah. You are much more than we had anticipated. We believe you shall do quite nicely."

Wary, Alex froze, scarcely daring to breathe. "Do?"

"Aye. We have a request of you, Carlton." The queen leaned forward in her seat, her eyes keenly measuring his every motion. "We want you to infiltrate this gang of blooded rakes. Become one of them. Learn their ways, their habits, their practices. We would know if the designs on our life are truth or exaggeration." Pale eyes swept over his dark garb. "If your present attire is any indication, you should fit in quite nicely."

Alex frowned. "But I am not a spy, Your Majesty. Surely you have some trusted man who would be better suited—"

"Are you turning us down, Carlton? We might have known you would. You unfortunately appear to be as patriotic as your father. Marrying a *Frenchwoman*—pah!"

The harsh words sent a righteous fury crashing about Alex's ears. From the day he was born, he'd been shunned and tormented by all manner of nobles for the simple reason that his mother was French. The enmity between England and France was too great for tolerance of any measure of disloyalty, no matter how imagined. He was used to it. But to hear his father's morals questioned by the queen herself . . .

If he turned Anne down, it would be the same as betraying England; but worse, it meant the Rawlings name would lay tattered in the ruin of political scandal. Retribution would come, swift and irreversible. His mother, with her fragile sensibilities, would pine away in shame.

He had no choice.

Alex gritted his teeth and bowed low before her. "As you wish it, Your Majesty. My sword is yours to command."

"Very good, my dear Lord Carlton! But it may not be so easy," Anne warned. "Danger will be your constant companion. You must trust no one. No one must know of the arrangements we have made."

"Have plans been laid? I know not any members—"

Anne smiled for the first time since Alex had entered the room. "Ah, Carlton, you surprise me. How quickly you grasp the needs of a situation. 'Tis quite refreshing, we assure you." She paused for breath, then continued. "Our aides have provided a contact for you. Sir Julian Whittendon. He has agreed to assist you in your assimilation into this gang of miscreants."

"Agreed?"

"Young Sir Julian has a taste for gambling, but we fear he sups on the delicacy too often. In exchange for his aid, we agreed to clear his debts . . . and to keep him from Traitor's Gate." She smiled again, a cool, ironic twist of her lips. "We are certain he will be invaluable. You'll find him at the Wolf and Fox tavern in Pickway Street tomorrow afternoon at four of the clock."

Resigned to his fate, Alex hesitated only a moment, clearing his throat. "There is . . . one other thing I must tell you, Your Majesty." Quickly he related the events of the evening, leaving out only the details pertaining to his discovery of the woman in white.

Anne listened carefully to his explanation, but in the end only nodded sadly. "Perhaps now you see the necessity for this bit of subterfuge, Lord Carlton," she said quietly. "Secrecy is our only option, and you will do well to cultivate it yourself in dealing with these monsters."

As Alex turned to leave, the queen's parting words came from behind him, soft but emphatically clear. "You must not fail us in this, Carlton. Your success is of utmost importance to me."

And to all of England. Alex finished the thought for her as he eased on silent feet from the chamber. *Including my future heirs.*

With less difficulty than he'd expected, Alex hurried through the dark to find his driver and cousin, Rorick McDowell. The appointment with Anne had left him much to think on. But as he approached his carriage, anticipation began to build within him at the prospect of seeing the woman in white again.

A voice, rich-timbered with a Scottish burr, stopped his hand in midair as he reached for the polished carriage door.

"Are ye finished for the evening, *lord,* or shall I take ye somewhere else, too?"

Alex swung around, clenched fists instinctively at the ready. "Blast, Rorick!" He released the breath that clotted like blood in his throat, and gave a short laugh. "You nigh startled the wits from me."

The burly Scotsman unraveled from the night shadows. In his dark clothing and black cloak, his cousin seemed almost a part of the night itself. Except for his hair, Alex mused. Red the shade of a foxtail dipped in fire could not be disguised so easily.

"Wits! Hmph. 'T has been a good, long time since there's been any o' that in evidence."

Alex frowned. "From your tone, I take it you are still miffed that I asked you to drive me here tonight."

" 'Twas to ha' been my night off, *lord.* If ye'll remember, I am yer valet, no' a bloody coachman. And ye werena even planning to attend the queen's reception. What happened? Did ye get a sudden itch for yer woman?"

Alex stared at him but held his tongue. His young cousin's unruly manner had been a problem since he'd arrived unexpectedly on his doorstep eight months before. He suspected it was also behind the trouble that had made the man leave his family in Inverness. More than once he'd wondered at the wisdom of giving in to his cousin's insistence to work for him, when he could have simply stayed with him as his guest. The Scotsman's distaste for charity, he supposed. "The reason isn't important. Rorick, I told you, had Burles not come down with a stomach ailment, I would never have asked you."

The tall young man sniffed his displeasure. "Burles is always taking ill. I doona think 'tis a valid excuse."

"Nay?" Alex lifted a dark brow in irritation. "The man

had the trots. I could hardly be stopping every mile for him to rush to the bushes, now could I? Assuming he could find bushes.'' Impatient now, he tried to distract his complaining cousin. ''Come, forget this nonsense. I wish to hear of the woman.''

''Ye're always wanting to hear of a wench.''

''Do not jest at a time like this, Rorick. This was no ordinary wench.'' In his mind's eye, Alex admired again the lovely skin, the full lips, and the delectable mark that graced them . . . not to mention the slender but enticing package she came in. Nay, not a thing about her could be labeled ordinary. ''Where did you take her?''

''Who?''

''*La Fantôme* of course!''

''Ah, the unordinary wench. Sorry, cousin. I didna see anyone who would fit that description.''

''She didn't come to you for protection?''

''Alex, what is this all about? I have seen naught but drunken coachmen and flea-bitten stable lads since ye left me to their mercy earlier this evening.''

Disappointment filtered through him on the heels of realization. He should have expected this. ''A man was murdered in the palace. Away from the celebration. I offered protection to the woman who found the body.''

Rorick stopped and gave him a slow, measuring stare. ''Well, now. Are ye sure she only *found* the body and didna also make it?''

Alex shook his head. ''Nay, she was dressed in white. Were she responsible, the proof would have been obvious for all the world to see. She had not a drop of blood on her.''

Suspicion traced across Rorick's features. ''How came you to be so far from the reception hall? Following the wench, I'll wager.''

''I didn't say we were far from the hall.''

''My mistake,'' Rorick allowed smoothly. ''But I take it my wager was correct. So. Who was she?''

Alex could feel hot blood assaulting his cheeks. "Lord help me, I don't know," he admitted. The next was even harder. "Moreover, she still has my watch."

"Your watch!" Rorick sniggered. "An odd price for a wench."

" 'Twas my intention that she bring it to you! Are you sure you didn't see her? Perhaps she lost her way."

Rorick sobered. "I swear I saw no one else, Alex. Are ye sure the man was dead? If the wench made off with yer watch, 'tis possible the murder was a part of the ploy as well."

A ploy? Was that possible?

The blood arose in Alex's mind, a great, spreading pool of it. The dwindling life of a man. "Nay. 'Twas no mistake. He was most certainly dead."

"Then mayhap she was frightened away. Mayhap she'll set about finding you."

"Perhaps." But how? Formal introductions had not been foremost in their minds. And then there was the small matter of notifying the queen's guard of the body at the palace.

As Rorick settled the carriage into its usual rattling motion, Alex racked his brain, trying to remember whether the woman had given herself away. Any insignificant thing. The silvery pale gown she'd worn was expertly tailored and expensively fitted, but nothing that could be traced to a specific seamstress. The mask? A relic from her great-grandmother's attic, possibly. Her body was tall and slender, with a willowy grace he found enchanting; had he seen her in any garb other than her disguise, he would have recognized it. She did not frequent the London circles.

Something . . . Anything . . .

The watch.

He remembered the glimmer of gold as she swung it back and forth before him, looped from the silver cord and chatelaine at her waist. That was certainly an antique. But it was the design etched into it that he considered now, a griffin, fierce in demeanor, clutching in its sharp talons a single, perfect rose.

He'd seen that emblem before.

"The house of Middleham?" he whispered aloud. And he knew he had his answer.

Grinning broadly, Alex pounded on the roof of the carriage with his fist, signaling for Rorick to slow. As the conveyance crept to a snail's pace, Alex threw open the window and leaned his head out. "I have an idea, Rorick. Take us down Albemarle Street, past Stafford. And hurry!"

Rorick drew his collar up and heaved a long-suffering sigh. "Aye, milord. I will."

With the crack of a whip overhead, the Flemish horses broke into a gallop, clattering over the slick cobblestones toward what Alex suspected was only a simpleton's folly. Street lamps flickered at every tenth house or so but did little to dispense the fog and shadow that seemed to swallow the city like a living, breathing entity.

Turning onto a side street, the horses slowed to a walk. Alex sat, tense and waiting, on the edge of the velvet-upholstered seat, castigating himself for the worst kind of fool. His memory was wrong, the etching on the watch was not part of an emblem at all. Or it belonged to another noble family. Or it was stolen. He shouldn't be wasting his time pursuing the trail of an elusive phantom. He should be planning for the success of his mission on the queen's behalf. He knew that. Yet anticipation rose within him, hot and sweet, with each crossroads they passed.

As they neared the area he had indicated, Alex opened the windows and extinguished the outer coach lamps, not wishing to draw attention to them when they stopped. Only blocks from his own home, Albemarle Street was familiar to him. He needed no light at all to see in his mind the imposing homes, the grand, walled lawns and gardens that lined the fashionable boulevard. Just ahead lay the mansion that most interested him: Maryleborn Court, winter home to the Marquess of Middleham.

A quiet call from above signaled the slowing of the grays. Alex craned his head to see the house through the open gate. The structure was set away from the street, so the details of the architecture were indistinct in the fog. Beyond the fact that the home towered four stories above street level, Alex could see little. At half past one, the windows were shrouded in darkness. All but one. On the third floor a faint light moved, a single candle. Alex squinted into the night, determined to see what he hoped was the truth.

As though the person within sensed his urgent summons, the light moved closer to the window. Alex held his breath as she came into view, the candle illuminating her face. *Alors, La Fantôme.* She stood just before the window with the candle cradled in her hand, still as marble. Though fairly certain she could see neither him nor the coach, he shrank away from the window into the darker center, unwilling to risk recognition. Not yet.

She still wore the ethereal gown from the evening's festivities but had removed the grand periwig. Her own hair drifted softly over her shoulders, long and pale. Blond. She was blond.

Who was she?

His lips curved in a slow, determined smile. Her identity was a mystery . . . but not for long.

Chapter Two

Through the rain-streaked window in her bedchamber, Lady Victoria Wynter stared out into the night, wondering for the hundredth time where her brother was. Tears gathered in her eyes as the horror of the evening returned. For a moment she yielded to them; then, straightening her shoulders, she blinked them back and tucked the thoughts away. She had to be strong, both for herself and for her brother. God knew Charles seemed incapable of such practicalities himself.

She had not anticipated the murder. *That poor man!* Whoever he was, her heart cried out for his immortal soul. Had she known how the evening would end, she would never have gone to St. James to spy on her brother. Ungrateful scoundrel that Charles was, she doubted he would appreciate her concern. Had she any sense, she'd leave him to his drinking and roistering without another thought.

It was her misfortune that she happened to love him.

Tori sighed at her own sentimentality. Aye, she loved him. And she would not stand by while he drank himself into oblivion, just because he yearned for the attention of their absentee father. Left to his own devices, Charles seemed content to destroy any chance he had of ever finding happiness. And she wanted him to be happy. Even if it meant putting aside her own dreams for a time.

She rested her forehead against the glass, grateful for the coolness against her brow. They were silly dreams, anyway. Fanciful, irresponsible, girlish dreams. Highly improper in light of her obligations. It was best to forget them.

A chance movement below dragged her attention away from her musings. Tori cupped her hands around her eyes against the glare from the candle and peered out.

Darkness and a light mist obscured much of the gardens and street, but she could just see the faint outline of a carriage stopped in the gateway.

Tori scowled. Charles, probably. Or worse yet, some of his cronies. Wastrels, the lot of them, and all up to no good. Seven and ten Charles was, and still he'd not learned the meaning of the word *trustworthy.* At times she wondered if he ever would.

For a moment she considered what the occupants of the carriage might do if she stormed from the house to confront them. The image made her grimace. Running through the rain, her hair hanging in strings to her waist, she'd be fortunate if they listened to her complaints at all. They were far more likely to drag her off to Bedlam, laughing.

She backed away from the window and snapped the draperies shut. Charles was an idiot. Why, just a sennight ago the *Spectator* had cautioned citizens against traveling alone after eventide, and yesterday there'd been printed another tale of the much-feared Mohocks, whose favored pastime seemed to be committing barbarous acts against the people of London. She couldn't rid herself of the idea that his friends were somehow involved.

Much worse was the worry that Charles took part himself. It was suspicious that he'd been out the night of each and every attack, dressed all in black, returning only at dawn and refusing to speak to her. Twice he'd returned with blood on his clothes. *Dear God, Charles, what have you gotten yourself into this time?*

Crossing the room, Tori snuffed the candle and climbed onto her bed without a care for the ball gown she still wore. No need to, really, she told herself. It had served its purpose. Now that she'd been seen in it she could hardly wear it again unless in disguise.

She drew her knees up to her chin and stared numbly at the fire that burned low in the grate, trying to ignore the trembling that beset her limbs.

She kept seeing that poor, dead man.

She'd come across the body by chance during her meandering search for Charles. She'd learned enough of his habits to know that his wont was to meet his friends at the grandest social events they could find—the queen's birthday celebration for Prince Eugene certainly qualified. But she hadn't found him. She'd been about to leave altogether when she'd come across the corridor with light spilling from an open door. But it wasn't Charles she'd found. Instead she'd found herself embroiled in a situation far worse than her rebellious brother could possibly provide.

Reaching a hand under her pillow, Tori withdrew the gold watch she'd taken under protest, and cradled it in her palm. The gold warmed swiftly with the heat of her flesh. She ran her thumb over the well-worn finish, smoothing the faint nicks and abrasions on the cover. A man's watch. Sturdy. Blessedly real. Its weight was solid proof she hadn't imagined the whole thing.

Her fingers found the spring catch that released the hinged cover and she flipped it open. An inscription was engraved inside the lid: MY SON, MY WORLD HAS BEEN BLESSED BY YOUR PRESENCE. And above it, three scrolled letters. A. P. R.

It was not a distinctive watch, yet it was obviously well

worn and well loved. Tori couldn't help but wonder about the man who owned it.

Dark, he had been. Dark hair, dark eyes.

Dark purpose?

Who was he, this A. P. R.?

A nobleman. That much was certain, judging from the cloth and the fashionable cut of his garb. A handsome gentleman of title.

Handsome? His face alone could knock the starch from a lady's petticoats. When combined with thick hair, black as a raven's wing, and blue-black eyes as fathomless as the sea at midnight, the effect was devastating. Oh, aye, he was handsome. The starch makers of England could make a fortune from this man.

Tori groaned inwardly as she wondered what he must have thought of her. To be found alone in a room with a man freshly dead was damning, indeed. He likely thought her a murderer. But if so, why did he offer her his protection?

The watch burned into her palm as another possibility struck her. Perhaps he knew the true killer's identity. Perhaps he had seen him. . . .

Perhaps he was the murderer himself.

She didn't want that to be true. Suddenly, vehemently, she didn't want that to be true.

Reminding herself to be practical, Tori brushed aside her questions about the mystery man at the palace and began to unlace her gown. The important thing now was to discover the truth about Charles and his involvement with . . . well, his involvement. She would put away all thoughts of the other man. She would never see him again.

She had to be sure of that.

A loud pounding yanked Tori from the depths of slumber she had at last achieved with the coming of dawn. Groggily, she lifted her head from the pillow and peered, bleary-eyed, around the room.

Bedposts. Bed curtains. Chair. Wardrobe. Early daylight peeping around the edges of the drawn draperies. Cold remnants of a fire in the hearth. Everything seemed in order.

Snuggling back against the goose-down pillow, Tori closed her eyes once more, determined to resume the compelling dreams that had held her in their thrall. Dark dreams lit by a single, summoning presence with soul-piercing dark eyes. Eyes that promised . . . what? And what secrets did that bewitching voice whisper?

The pounding came again, louder this time, more forceful. And again.

Tori opened her eyes in a hurry. Someone seemed determined to beat down the front door. Where in heaven's name was Smythe?

There was no hope for it. Tori sprang from the bed and stumbled as her foot caught in the folds of the gown and whalebone hoops she'd discarded before succumbing to slumber. Kicking free, she ran to the mirror and groaned as she saw the tangled state of her waist-length hair. Downstairs, the pounding resumed.

Seeing no other choice, Tori grabbed her dressing gown from where it lay on the end of her bed, pulled it on over her chemise, corset, and petticoats, and flung open her door.

As she raced down the front stairs, the noise only grew louder, yet to her consternation she saw none of the household staff. Just before she reached the foyer, the casement clock in the withdrawing room began to chime. She counted eight—it was later than she thought. She pulled the door open.

Two men towered over her in the open portal, tall, disheveled, and well grizzled from at least a day's worth of whiskers. Their clothing was rumpled and smudged with dirt. One wore a powdered wig knocked askew beneath a crushed tricorne; the other had lost his hat entirely. Both stared at her without a sound or gesture of greeting.

Tori resisted the impulse to cross her arms over the dressing gown that suddenly felt as thin as gossamer as two sets of eyes traveled the length of her twice over. She lifted her chin in challenge, chafing beneath the heat of embarrassment that crept slowly up her torso. "May I help you?"

The tallest man grunted with a sound of near assent. On cue, the two parted to reveal a third she had not seen behind them.

Her eyes widened at the sight. Remarkably, her brother was still standing, though by the wavering of his stance it was anyone's guess for how long.

"Charles Emerson Wynter!" She gasped. "What on earth!"

To her horror, her beloved younger brother smirked at her, wavered a little more, then belched. Long. And loud.

Tori's control snapped. "Bring him inside. Straight ahead, then to your left at the first door."

Each man took an arm and led Charles inside. Tori followed.

"Charles Wynter, you've been drinking again, and heaven only knows what else," she fussed. "How you can do this to yourself is beyond my comprehension. When will it stop?"

The men dumped her brother unceremoniously on a low settee, then turned to leave.

"Wait!"

Without a word, they turned to face her and waited, staring at her. Tori felt her nerve draining from her beneath the weight of their stony-faced scrutiny. In desperation, she blurted, "Won't you even tell me how long he's been like this? Or where he's been? Or with whom?"

The two shared an amused look, then shrugged. The ogre still sporting his tousled wig answered, "Why, with us, milady. Where else would he have been?"

Roaring laughter trailed behind them as they took their leave. Furious, Tori turned back to her brother. He had closed his eyes and was well on the way to a sound sleep. "Charles! Wake up!"

He squinted up at her through one slitted eye. "Why, hullo, Tori, m'dear. Where'd you come from?"

Tori set her hands on her hips. "I have been home. And you have been drinking. Again."

"I've not!" He hiccuped. And grinned.

"Do not deny it, Charles. You are inebriated beyond comprehension. Besotted beyond words!"

With a wallowing roll, he managed to raise himself to a precarious sitting position. " 'M fine, sis. Really."

Tori rolled her eyes heavenward. "Oh. 'Tis fine you are. How foolish of me to worry!" She began to pace a relentless circle. "What tavern did you frequent this time?"

"I had but a nip. P'raps two. No more."

She halted in front of him, forcing him to tilt his head back in order to meet her gaze. "You, Charles, are hopelessly drunk. Will you be a John-o'-dreams forever?"

Her brother's blue eyes, so often mirrors of her own, widened in surprise. Thinking she had made her point, Tori straightened in satisfaction. But as she watched, his balance gave out and he toppled backward against the settee. His feet flew up. To her horror she saw he wore only one shoe.

A whoop of giggles arose from him as he lay in an undignified heap, trailing off in a stomach-weary sigh. "Why, sis, you wound me. 'M merely befused . . . conmuzzled . . . er, m' mind's a bit muddy, 'tis all. But I'm certain 'm not hopeless." Charles raised himself up on his elbows to peer at her, humor raising the corners of his mouth. " 'M most hopeful of becoming soundly drunk once again."

Much pleased with himself, Charles dropped his head to the upholstery, his laughter rising to the ceiling. Tori surveyed him with a jaundiced eye.

"Once? Once, he says. Hopeless," she pronounced, shaking her head. "You stay, Sir Hopeless. I'll get you some cocoa.'' Assuming that I can find our missing household staff, she amended dourly as she headed toward the rear of the house.

The kitchen was empty when she entered, but the long table where the servants took their meals still contained remnants of the morning meal on dirty plates. The yeasty smell of rising bread met her nose from an enormous bowl on a worktable near the fire. A pot boiled from the hearth, its lid clattering against the opening with the escaping heat.

At the end of the room, the door to the courtyard stood wide open. The sounds that wafted in on the cold air left no question as to the location of her missing servants.

Tori circled the table. Pausing in the open doorway, she was amazed to find every maid, every footman, every stable boy the household possessed congregated about an oddly wrapped bundle on the flagstone. Tightening her dressing gown about her body, she watched.

''You open it, Mr. Smythe,'' urged the youngest stable boy.

Never known for his courage, the thin-nosed butler stepped back. ''I haven't time for this nonsense. We all have duties—''

Mrs. Pertwee, the housekeeper, stepped forward. ''Oh, come now, Mr. Smythe. Ye know ye want to know as much as the rest of us what that is.''

Tori's maid, Phoebe, dropped to her knees beside the bundle, oblivious to the frigid flagstones. Her eyes saucered as though she were bewitched by the bundle's prospect. ''I 'ad a vision last night, I did. Two men on black mounts. The moonlight shined on 'em like they was made o' metal. I opened my window to 'ear their words, but all I could make out was their laughin'.'' She shivered, remembering. ''Satan's henchmen, I swear it. Be careful, Mr. Smythe.''

Several of the maids gasped and made the sign to cast off the evil eye. Mrs. Pertwee urged Phoebe to her feet and, with a swat on the girl's plump rump, shushed them all. " 'Tis only yer dreams again, Phoebe. And as for the rest of ye poltroons, that bundle is like to be some fool's rubbish. Open it, Mr. Smythe."

The much-beleaguered butler sighed. "Very well."

Grimacing, he stooped low and grasped one end of the tied bundle. Slowly he moved it from side to side, as if waiting for the contents to pounce at him. The only response he received was a dull clink. Frowns of puzzlement passed from manservant to maid and on again. Smythe shook it again, harder. A metallic sound could clearly be heard.

" 'Tis gold!" the stable boy cried. "A gift from heaven!"

"For heaven's sake, open it, Smythe!"

Assured that the bundle was not living, Smythe grasped the knot and worked it free. Holding his breath, he inched apart the loose ends. Tori found herself straining to see through the press of bodies around the bundle.

From the disappointed groans, Tori deduced the bundle contained something less than treasure. "What is it, Smythe?" she called.

The butler looked up in surprise. "Oh, 'tis you, milady. It appears we are the brunt of a joke. Or perhaps the recipient of a riddle." He held up the bundle. Within the dirty folds of cloth were brass door knockers. Dozens of them.

Tori frowned. "Where did they come from?"

Smythe shrugged. "I'm sure I don't know, milady. Jamie, the footman, found them here this morning on his way in to breakfast."

Disappointed by the reality of the bounty, several of the servants began to drift back into the warmth of the kitchen. Tori stepped out to let them pass through, shivering with cold. Her eyes found the young footman. "Is this true, Jamie?"

"Aye, milady, 'tis," he answered. His ears and cheeks were red, perhaps with cold, perhaps with embarrassment, but his eyes met hers with ease. Tori felt certain he wasn't lying.

"What shall we do with these, milady?"

Blast. She had no time for this with Charles in such a state, but as mistress of the house, she knew the responsibility fell to her. "Rabble-rousers. I wonder if 'twas the Mohock band again. The *Spectator* has made several mentions of the miscreants this past fortnight."

"Mohocks? Here?" The butler glanced about nervously.

Tori ignored him. " 'Tis our duty to inform the proper authorities. Smythe, you'll have to send someone to deal with that. And around the area as well. Perhaps some of these belong to our neighbors."

Turning back to the kitchen, Tori breathed a sigh of relief. "Mrs. Pertwee, please see that a cup of cocoa is sent to the blue room while I run upstairs to dress. I'm afraid Lord Charles is indisposed."

Though censure shone briefly in the warm brown eyes of the aging woman, she did nothing more than raise an eyebrow and fidget with the great bundle of keys she kept on a sturdy chatelaine. "Aye, milady."

Tori nodded. "Phoebe, I shall need your help, please."

Followed by the young maid, Tori made her way to the front stairs. Before she could set foot upon them, an abrupt knock at the door was matched by a thump and a muffled curse from within the drawing room.

"Blast, what now?" Tori groaned, not caring if she was heard this time. " 'Tis too early for callers. Phoebe, you take care of our visitor while I deal with Charles."

Muttering under her breath, Tori ducked into the drawing room and closed the door. She leaned her back against the paneled wood and made a face as she caught sight of her brother.

The cause of the thump was obvious. Charles had fallen to the floor. Unable to find the balance or the inclination to move again, he lolled upon the carpet, one foot having found a perch on the settee's carved arm, the other pressing treacherously close to a pedestal supporting a small likeness of Zeus. Tori rushed over and caught the stockinged foot before it could dislodge the costly statue.

"Charles, wake up!" She took up the lapels of his coat and shook him.

Charles grunted. "G'way."

Undaunted, Tori stood up and pulled as hard as she could, forcing him to a sitting position. "Charles, you oafish buffoon. If I ever get you through this—"

Her younger brother giggled. He opened his eyes. "If ye want me that bad, Elsie, I c'n try to manage. Just gimme a minute to collect m'self."

"Elsie!" Tori's mouth fell open and she lost her grip. Charles dropped to the floor with a solid *thunk*. "Charles, don't you dare tell me you've been—"

"Owww! Did y' have t'do that?" he complained, rubbing his head. "I vow, Tori, y're a vicious wench."

"And you are irresponsible."

"I was merely jest'n."

"Having fun at my expense, is more like it."

Sullen now, Charles crossed his arms. "I need another drink."

"What you need is hot cocoa, and much of it."

"Excuse me, milady." Phoebe ducked her head inside the door. Her voice was an exaggerated whisper. "A gentleman has requested to see ye."

It would appear her life was destined to be hectic and disordered forever. "I cannot possibly see anyone, Phoebe—"

"Beggin' yer pardon, milady, but 'e says 'e cannot wait."

"Send him away. Give him an excuse. Any excuse."

"But milady—" Phoebe began. "Whoop!"

Her protest ended on a high note as the gentleman in question brushed past her. Tori opened her mouth, but the retort she'd intended to give lodged in her throat, and she felt her heart drop to the vicinity of her toes. Standing across from her, an amused expression on his flawless countenance, stood the dark nobleman of the night just past.

He was staring at her.

Staring—that was an understatement. His eyes roved over her with obvious, unhindered delight. Tori recovered from the shock of seeing him long enough to yank Charles's cloak from the settee and throw it about her shoulders.

The man seemed to share none of her unease. After one last look at Tori, he turned toward Phoebe and smiled. "Do forgive my impertinence—"

The young maid gaped at him, then bobbed in a quick curtsy. "Phoebe, yer lordship," she supplied quickly. " 'Tweren't yer fault, really, I—"

Tori's brows stretched high as she observed the exchange. Phoebe positively glowed—with only one smile from the man! She cleared her throat. "Phoebe, you may go upstairs and ready Lord Charles's room now. I'll follow shortly."

The girl blushed and bit her lip. "O' course, m'lady."

As the plump maid quit the room, Tori steeled herself to speak to the only man who could tie her to the unfortunate death she had witnessed. *But he does not know me! He could not know it was me.* She wrapped the cloak tighter about her and faced him with all the aplomb of a fully clothed woman twice her age.

She hoped.

She pasted a pleasant smile on her face. "I'm afraid you find me a bit at a loss, sir. Have we been introduced?" *Bold devil.* His dark eyes glowed with a knowing good humor.

"I hope you'll forgive me for interrupting your morning peace." His glance flickered briefly over her brother's reclining figure, but returned to her without comment. "Actually, I fear you are mistaken. I'm quite certain we met last night."

At this, Charles raised himself to his elbows. His eyes

narrowed at Tori in suspicion. "I thought y' said you were home last night."

With an inward groan, Tori wished she had never tried to wake her bothersome brother. She presented him her back and hoped her flush of embarrassment was only internal. *A pox on Charles anyway!* "My brother is quite correct, sir. . . ." Tori gave a delicate pause, hoping he would supply her with his name.

"Alexandre Rawlings, Earl of Carlton, my lady. But I'm afraid I must beg to differ. It *was* you I met at the queen's reception last night."

Chapter Three

Carlton. Carlton? Where had she heard that name before?

The nervous churning in her stomach was compounded as much by the determination she heard in his whispery voice as by the question her mind posed. His eyes—so intensely dark!—seemed to pierce her subterfuge with ease. Tori pinned her gaze to the cleft in his chin. "You have me confused with some other person—"

"Nay." The quiet word brooked no denial. "You were there."

Charles laughed merrily and tottered to his feet. "My sisser's bound to give y' a run for your money, Lord Carlton. Best have a drink wi' me to stiffen yer resolve for the race." He walked unsteadily to a low cabinet and withdrew a crystal decanter. "Claret, m'lord? 'Tis French . . . the very best."

"Charles!" Tori knew she was blushing now. She knew not what was worse—that Charles had insulted her, or that he had exposed his weakness to a guest in their house. The earl's scowl spoke volumes of his feelings on the matter.

Her brother only grinned at her. ''Can I not offer a man a drink?''

Tori cast him a withering glare. ''Charles, please leave me with Lord Carlton. I'm sure I can clear this up if only—''

''What? In the state o' dress you're in?'' Charles's mouth dropped open as though he were scandalized; then he closed one eye in a slow wink. ''Nay, I think I shan't miss this. Should prove t'be enlightenin'.''

Fuming inwardly, Tori could say nothing. She turned back to their guest. ''Lord Carlton. What makes you so convinced that it was I you spoke with—last night, did you say?''

Carlton's lips curved. His gaze dropped to her mouth. ''Did you believe I wouldn't recognize you? Your mask didn't conceal everything, my lady.''

''Mask!'' Charles hooted. ''Oh, what would dear ol' Papa say?''

How could she think with her brother spouting inanities? Yet she knew she must remain in control. Ignoring Charles, she summoned her poise. ''Sir, a lady would not present herself in a mask in polite company.''

''But you did, madame.''

As he had the night before, he said it in the French way, and always with that curious, rasping voice. Just the sound of it was enough to raise gooseflesh along her arms. And at that moment, she realized where she'd heard of him before. Carlton, the infamous Devil Lord. Goodness, it was said he—

She lifted her chin, not wanting to betray the recognition. ''My lord, are you questioning my sensibilities?''

''Nay. I only say 'twas you at St. James.''

Exasperated, Tori pressed her lips together, uncertain how to influence such unswayable determination. ''And what proof have you?''

He shrugged. ''None but the conviction of my own eyes, my lady.''

His lack of proof didn't seem to faze him. He knew. Desperate now to convince him, Tori groped for a way, any way. "But if the lady in question wore a mask, what good is such . . . proof?"

Heedless of their drunken but rapt witness, Carlton came to stand before her, and Tori felt the breath squeeze from her lungs. He was no more than a foot away, twelve tiny inches. She could feel the energy of his presence, like heat lightning on a warm spring night. His eyes held all the secrets of the universe in their indigo depths.

His hand came up between them, slowly, irrevocably. Every instinct in her warned her to flee. Determined not to yield to his bullying, Tori steeled herself against the primal unease. But in the end, the choice was not hers. His long, hard fingers stroked the corner of her mouth, and with one gentle touch rendered her incapable of further protest. She'd been bested.

The blasted mark! What folly had caused her to choose the silver demi-mask she'd found to complement her garb over the full vizard? Foolishness. And the devil's kiss had given her away.

Her brother for the moment forgotten, Tori frowned but forced herself to meet his gaze. "My lord?"

His eyes did not appear unkind. "Tell me your name, madame," he murmured.

Tori shook her head. "I will not. I cannot!"

"I know where you live. Your name won't be difficult to unearth."

"I might be a servant here."

His lips curved in a mocking smile. "I think not. Servants don't wear silk. Most certainly not at eight o'clock in the morning." His gaze dropped to travel the length of her. She could feel the heat of his gaze even through the woolen cloak. "Your quality betrays you."

Tori felt heat climb from the high collar of her cloak. She wrapped her arms tighter around her body, until the wool encased her like an Egyptian mummy. Before she could respond, Charles interrupted from his vantage point on the abused settee.

"Her name's Victoria, m'lord Carlton. Lady Victoria Wynter, daughter to the esteemed Marquess of Middleham." Charles grinned hazily at his sister. "Sorry, sis, but the poor man was trying s'hard, I jus' had to help 'im for his trouble. 'Sides, we both know you can take care o' yerself."

His snicker threatened to erupt into full-fledged giggles. For the first time since her brother had returned home that morning, Tori wished he'd drown himself more deeply in his cups. At least then he might be quiet.

The earl seemed well pleased by the intervention. "Now that I have your name, Lady Victoria, perhaps you could tell me what you were doing at St. James last night."

"Yes, Tori, what *were* you doing?" Charles chimed in.

All the ground she had fought to attain was sliding away beneath her feet. And all because Charles couldn't resist the siren call of the cups! Tori stiffened her spine and walked across the room, needing as much distance from them both as possible.

She turned back to fix them with a haughty stare. "As I told you last night, Lord Carlton, my reasons for being at the palace are my own and do not concern you." She walked to the door and held it open. "Please excuse my absence of manners, but I'm afraid I must ask you to leave."

Charles snorted into his cup. "Watch out for ol' Miss Fuss-'n'-Bluster, m'lord. Not quite as obliging as what yer used to with yer baroness."

Cringing inside at the impropriety of broaching the subject of the earl's mistress, Tori cleared her throat. "I'll escort you to the door, my lord—while Charles collects the wits he seems to have lost." She gave her brother a pointed frown that said *I'll deal with you later,* then followed the earl into the hall, closing the door firmly against the barrage of laughter from within.

Carlton paused in the hall. He turned the tricorne in his hands, tracing the edge in a slow way she found most fascinating to watch. "I shall leave for now, Lady Victoria, as you seem to be in the midst of a familial . . . er . . . *situation.* But I feel obliged to tell you this is by no means over."

So. His acquiescence was somewhat less than that. "Are you threatening me, Lord Carlton?"

He met her gaze easily. "Do you feel threatened?"

"Nay. But then, I also feel my actions are none of your business."

"On the contrary, Lady Victoria. A dead man necessitates more than a common degree of accountability."

Tori whirled around to face him. "You know 'twas not I who killed him!"

"And how would I know that, my lady? Until a moment ago I didn't even know your name."

She crossed her arms, her mouth pressed tight in disbelief. "You think me a murderess?"

Carlton hesitated, then shook his head, his gaze never leaving hers. "Nay," he said slowly. "The thought had crossed my mind, I must admit, but . . . I abandoned the notion upon reflection."

"Then why—"

"I am not the person you need to convince."

He meant the queen, of course. If what he intimated was true, her life and her family's reputation were at risk because of her chance encounter. But was this the truth or a lie for his own purpose? Deciding to brazen it out, Tori shook her head. "My reasons are my own. If the queen wishes to question me regarding my actions last night, I will be glad to comply. But I will not air my reasons with you, milord, a stranger."

The earl frowned. "My concern is for you, Lady Victoria. I gladly offer you my protection—"

"As you did last night? To offer me your carriage? And what then were your intentions, once you had me in your clutches?" Tori turned up her nose with a haughty sniff. "A pox on your offer! I'd rather endure the Tower dungeon than yield to the Devil Lord's *protection.*"

He moved in so quickly she had no chance to escape. Suddenly he loomed over her, and the wall pressed against her shoulder blades. Her gaze fixed on the cleft in his chin. Lord, he was tall, so tall that she had to tilt her head back to meet his gaze. Granite hard, his eyes held hers captive against her will. "Careful, madame. The offer was kindly meant—and if I am truly a Devil Lord, I'd think you might wish to oblige me better."

Misgivings fluttered through her breast. She could feel heat emanating from his body, and she could feel its echo rising within herself. It was almost . . . pleasing. Absurd thoughts seemed to accompany the sensation. Thoughts of the curve of his lip. The faint shadow along his jaw where his beard would grow. The way the daylight caught flecks of blue in his nearly black eyes.

The way he looked at her.

Tori swallowed as the flutterings took on a new, frantic pace. "Devils are meant to be disobliged, my lord," she murmured, determined to stand her ground. "For the sake of a woman's soul."

Silence stretched between them, interminable seconds that lengthened into what seemed like hours. Something strange seemed to urge her toward him. Or was it the other way around? Tori held her breath as the distance closed between them, knowing she should stop what was about to happen, but unable to summon the energy necessary to push him away. His lips looked softer, somehow, and almost unbearably sensual—

"Well! Well, I do say."

Tori jumped as Charles's voice registered upon her stunned senses. The earl stepped back quickly.

Charles grinned as he teetered in the doorway, watching them. "Good work, m'lord. Seems the High Lady Fuss-

'n'-Bluster found 'er heart after all, 'nless my eyes d'ceive me.''

Tori cringed and squeezed her eyes shut. She began to count to ten. She made it to four. ''Charles Emerson Wynter—''

''I know, I know. 'Ye're a drunken fool,' '' Charles mimicked in a high falsetto.

Tori gritted her teeth and turned to Alex. ''I beg your forgiveness for my brother's improprieties, Lord Carlton. He's not bad. Just in great need of some . . . reserve.'' She slanted a disparaging glance at her brother. ''And, perhaps, intelligence.''

Charles made a face and clapped a hand over his chest. The movement undermined his balance, and he fell against the door frame. ''Aw, sis. Y' wound me.''

A twitch appeared at the corner of the earl's lips, but he quelled whatever emotion prompted it. ''I'll take my leave of you now, Lady Victoria. You seem to have your hands, er, full.'' He donned his tricorne, lowering it to what she considered a most rakish angle. ''But rest assured . . . I shall return again soon.''

The words held both threat and promise. Tori found herself nodding as he left her home, knowing it was useless to protest. As soon as the door closed, she turned back to her brother.

''Charles, you're a beast. A horrible cad.''

He crossed his arms, and his lips turned down in a pout more befitting a child of ten than a young man of seventeen. ''Me? Y're the one's got yerself into a fancy predicament. 'Twas quite a display, I must say. Given up the Mother Victoria facade, have you?'' he queried sarcastically.

Tori gasped. How could he be so cruel? A flurry of hurt feelings and embarrassment brought a reaction she'd not resorted to in years. Abandoning all claims to maturity, she stalked purposely over to where Charles lounged in the doorway. Raising a slippered foot, she brought it down on his instep. Hard.

"Owww!" Her brother's dramatic cry eased her misery only slightly.

"Bait me, will you? How dare you behave so abominably, Charles? I wouldn't be the least surprised if all of London hears of your improprieties before the day is out."

Tears gathered in her eyes, threatening to spill. Unwilling to let him see her weakness, Tori tried to turn away, but Charles grasped her chin, holding her still.

Emotion warred across his features. Then suddenly his youthful face lost its arrogance. Instantly contrite, he seemed younger, the sweet brother she had known before their mother died. His hand dropped away and he jammed it into his pocket. He cleared his throat.

"I'm sorry, Tori. Really. I didn't mean the Fuss-'n'-Bluster bit." He flashed a rakish grin, causing the dimple in his cheek to wink at her. "Honest, I was only fooling you."

How could he be so maddening one moment and so charming the next? Forgiveness tugged at her heart, but she didn't want to give in, not yet. "Don't try to sweeten me, Charles. I'll not stand for your cajoling. Now go upstairs, if you think you can walk by yourself. You stink like a mule. I trow you've been lounging with more than a few."

"Aw, Tori, don't be angry—"

She pushed him toward the door. "Go on. I'll send someone up with hot water as soon as 'tis ready."

He grumbled under his breath but turned to do as bidden. He paused with his hand on the curved newel post. "You will be careful, won't you, Tori? Carlton's reputation with the ladies is legend." He paused, frowning as if fumbling for words. "You are . . . er, that is to say, you have heard of his relationship with Bawdy Be— er, Baroness Rowan, have you not?"

Tori blushed. *Bawdy Bess. Is that how the men of Lon-*

don refer to Carlton's paramour? How awful for her. Tori managed a swift nod.

Charles nodded, looking distracted. "Good, good. 'Tis perhaps best you know of that. Just . . . be careful."

Tori watched him go, confusion twisting at her heart. Perhaps she worried too much. Perhaps she should allow him his frivolous behavior. He was a man, or almost. A man's priorities were different from a woman's, at the same age. Perhaps if she left well enough alone . . .

But no matter how much she tried to convince herself of that, she could not. It was too dangerous. The streets were full of temptations that could lead a young man astray. Women and drink, crime and treachery, and all in the name of entertainment. Charles was young and foolish. Without her intervention, he would be ripe for whatever band of ruffians caught his eye.

The Mohocks, for instance.

Were the men who accompanied him an hour before part of that ruthless group? Was she already too late?

Tori bent down to pick up the discarded glass and decanter of claret, setting them on a huntboard with a sigh. Lord Carlton's caution of her need for protection sounded again in her ears, but she knew she would disregard it. She had to help Charles break free of his bitterness. She'd lost her mother—she couldn't bear to lose her only brother, too. And Lord knew there was no one else to care, with her father away. The task was her own. Time enough later for dreams of home and romance. And the earl of Carlton?

It was an unnecessary worry. If what the London gossips held was true, Lord Carlton was a rake of the first order, whose only cares were for women—many of them—and for himself. Whatever fleeting fancy he held for her would soon be forgotten.

She was far too settled for his exotic tastes.

Thank goodness.

Chapter Four

La Fantôme was a phantom no longer.

The morning visit had at least accomplished that much, Alex mused as his carriage stopped in the limestone-paved courtyard of Rawlings Hall. But little more. He now knew that her name was Victoria Wynter and that her brother called her Tori. He knew that she was, indeed, comely of face and figure, and he knew her hair was a long, shimmering blond, highlighted by strands that glinted like spun gold. Her eyes were the blue of the cornflowers that waved in the wind in the meadows surrounding his ancestral manor, his beloved Carlton. But he had no knowledge of why she chose to hide behind a mask. Neither did he know if she'd told the truth about her innocence regarding the dead courier.

Quite the mysterious one, she was.

But no ghost. No phantom. The near-kiss had done much to dispel that image from his thoughts forever. Victoria Wynter was as alive and vibrant as any woman he had ever met. Exasperating, aye. Stubborn, certainly. But without a doubt she was intriguing, and he couldn't deny wanting to know more.

Much more. *Dieu,* he could still feel her breath on his lips.

Alex frowned as he stepped down upon the rain-slicked flagstones. The wind caught his cloak and swept it wide, cooling his overheated body. He shouldn't be worrying about the woman. In truth, he should devote his full concentration to the queen's mission. Women and duty rarely mixed well.

The front door swept wide for him as he reached it, cutting short his ruminations.

"Hurry in from the damp, milord. 'Tis blowing fit for a midsummer squall!"

Alex's butler, Grimes, hastened him inside and took his cloak and tricorne. Standing inches taller than even Alex, Grimes often intimidated callers with his great height, but it was his haughty demeanor and cold stare that sent most uninvited guests hastening away. Alex smiled to himself, wondering what they would think if they could see his solicitous attitude toward his employer.

"Your mother asked after you, milord. She hopes that you come up, if you have time." Grimes inclined his head close and spoke in an undertone. "I believe she is lonely, milord."

A pang of guilt stabbed at him. Alex nodded. " 'Tis my fault. I've left her alone too often of late." *And will even more, by necessity, in the weeks to come . . .*

"Perhaps a companion would not be out of the question, milord?"

Alex shook his head with a frown. "I've spoken to her on the matter quite often, but she is opposed to the idea." He reached for his watch, found it missing still, and cursed under his breath. "Do you have the time, Grimes?"

The long-nosed butler snapped open his watch case, a gift from Alex's father. "Half past nine, milord."

Plenty of time to visit his mother and gain a bit more

sleep before his afternoon meeting. "I'll see my mother directly, but first I must speak with Mr. McDowell. Have you seen him?"

"Aye, he is in his quarters, I believe, sir."

"Thank you, Grimes."

"Oh, and milord, you had a visitor—"

"Not now, Grimes. Later."

Alex took the stairs two at a time, past leaded windows that stretched toward the high ceiling, past the paintings of ancestors long since dead. As he reached the second floor, he followed the east corridor toward his cousin's chamber at the far end.

It was not a customary situation to have one's valet sleeping on the same level as his employer, Alex mused, but then Rorick had never been a customary valet.

Alex knocked on the door. "Rorick?"

A muffled voice responded immediately from within the room. "Is that your croak, cousin?" The door opened. Inside stood Rorick, dressed only in breeches and hose, with shaving soap frosting the red-gold bristles on his lean cheeks. "Ye're up early. Or did ye no' go to bed at all?"

Alex shrugged. "I had things to do this morning."

His cousin gestured with the glistening razor he held in his hand. "Come in and close the door. I've nae wish for yer cleaning wenches to see me prancin' aboot half-clothed." He had turned away; now he stopped to cast a grin and a naughty wink over his lean shoulder. "Besides, ye know they arena happy with me since I spurned their advances."

Alex cast a spurious eye at the dual set of scratches on the back of his cousin's neck and on his muscled ribs. " 'Twould appear you have not withheld yourself from all of our English women, Rorick. Whoever gave you those marks must have given you quite the tussle."

Rorick dabbed the soap from his cheeks, then ran the cloth over his shoulders and chest for good measure. "Is this a ploy to learn the lass's name for yerself?"

Alex grinned at the jest, but said nothing.

"Along that vein of thinking, cousin, I understand ye had an unexpected caller this morn." Rorick watched him closely.

"Whoever it was can wait. I have not the time—"

"I have a feeling ye wouldna turn this one away, cousin. 'Twas your luscious baroness."

Bess. Ye gods. Alex closed his eyes and leaned back against the door. "Damn."

"Grimes told me she was in a fair bit of a tizzy." Rorick's tone was casual, conversational. "She vowed she would wait till ye returned, but she left half an hour ago. Perhaps she tired of Grimes's sour old face, eh?"

"I was to go to her apartments after the reception. I had business, but promised to meet her there afterward."

"But instead we were chasin' after yer mystery wench." Rorick thrust his arms into his shirtsleeves and cast a pitying look at Alex. "I doona think Baroness Rowan would understand."

Alex laughed humorlessly. Understanding was not one of Bess's better qualities. "It could not be helped."

Rorick peered at him with sudden intuition. "Come to think of it, 'tis been nigh a sennight since ye last visited her. Mayhap e'en a fortnight."

Alex shrugged and turned away. Rorick's perceptions rarely struck far from the truth. "I have something I need you to do today."

If he noticed the change in subject, the Scotsman had the good grace not to mention it. "Aye?"

"I have an appointment to meet Sir Julian Whittendon at the Wolf and Fox tavern at four o' clock this afternoon. Send a footman to confirm his attendance, would you?" Crossing the room to the small escritoire before the window, Alex withdrew a quill and a sheet of heavy paper, scrawling a message while he spoke. "When you're through, go somewhere and buy a gift for the baroness—something pretty—and deliver it with this note."

"A peace offering?" Rorick teased. "Ye get yerself in trouble and depend on my good looks to get ye out?"

Alex slanted an amused look at his bawdy cousin. "The gift will be the peace offering, ye randy Scotsman. I doubt if you would be an acceptable replacement."

And the gift *was* meant to soften her, Alex admitted to himself as he walked the paneled corridors to his mother's chambers. Though he knew his relationship with the sultry baroness was over, he had no wish to hurt her. Better to ease his way from the liaison and leave Bess with her dignity intact. She was not to blame. . . .

It was his own restless heart.

His mother's door was closed, as it always seemed to be. Alex knocked and called, *"Maman?"*

From within, he heard his mother's voice, *"Oui, cher!* Come inside!"

Alex entered the room his mother had inhabited since their move to London. A large room of grand proportions, it was dominated by the heavily carved bed she had once shared with his father during London social seasons long since past. Someone had drawn back the draperies from the tall windows, flooding the room with a gray light that somehow appeared warmer when it touched the cheery, claret-hued walls.

Garbed in a lace-bedecked dressing gown, a frilly commode covering her hair, his mother reclined on a chaise longue before the marble hearth. A book of sonnets lay forgotten on her lap as she gazed up at him, expectancy brightening her eyes.

"Alexandre! I am so glad you came to see me this morning." Even after twenty-nine years in England, Isabelle Rawlings had not lost the inherent French accent that flavored her speech. "You have been so busy of late. I have missed you."

Guilt gnawed at him. He should make more time for her. She was so frail of heart, so delicate, and he was her only child. In truth, except for the servants he was her only link to a world outside Rawlings Hall. Since his father's death she had become a recluse of sorts, rarely venturing from the safety of her private chambers. Alex worried about her—more than she could ever know. "I am sorry, *Maman.* I have been remiss as a son, have I not?"

"*Non,* nonsense, you are perfect. Your father would be so proud, could he see what you have become."

Wistfulness saddened her voice and shone in her soft brown eyes. Alex felt a lump form in his throat that had nothing to do with the dueling injury incurred in his youth. How he wished that what she said could be true. "I miss him, too, *Maman.*"

For one brief moment, their eyes met in mutual understanding—Jonathan Phillip Rawlings had been a strong influence in both their lives. Then Isabelle dragged her gaze away, looking down at the book in her hands—to hide sudden tears, Alex felt certain.

"I was just reading a bit before you came," she said tightly. "Reading, and thinking. I know I should go out for some air, but I never seem to have the time."

"Why don't you come downstairs, *Maman?* Have your tea with Rorick and me. 'Twould do you good. You stay hidden away too much."

"And you worry. Ah, *mon cher.* I am such a trial for you."

Alex knelt beside her and took her hand in his. "Nay, never say so. But I do worry for you, *Maman.*"

"I just cannot bear—well, I have been thinking. . . ." Her voice trailed away in hesitant uncertainty. Alex waited patiently for her to find her focus once more. "I have been thinking, Alexandre. Of Carlton. Do you remember how it was?"

"Of course I remember."

"It has been so long since we have been there, and it is so beautiful in the springtime. I know it was too painful to bear after your father's accident, but perhaps the time has come to put that behind us."

Seven years. Time enough.

"Alexandre? What think you, *cher?*"

She watched him closely, awaiting his answer. Feeling low and unspeakably selfish, Alex gave her the only answer he could. "Nay, *Maman,* not yet." He rushed on, unable to quite meet her eyes. "I want to . . . I just—"

He stopped, helpless to explain. How could he? Anne had sworn him to silence, and even had she not, he would never have involved his own mother.

Isabelle leaned back against her chaise, a vague remoteness haunting her eyes. "'Tis all right, *cher.* I understand."

"*Maman*—soon. I promise you."

Isabelle nodded. "I believe I shall rest for a time now, Alexandre. I am weary."

"As you wish, *Maman.*" Alex bent to her and kissed her cheek before he left the room, quietly closing the door behind him.

The look in her eyes haunted him the rest of the afternoon. Duty called to him from all corners of his mind—his duty to his country and to his queen, his duty to his mother, and most of all his duty to his family name.

Somewhere in the midst of it all came a call of a different sort, a sweet voice that conjured images of silver and gold and shining white. Alex awoke from his half sleep sweating, tense and achingly, inexplicably aroused. Remnants of his final dream stayed with him in his wakefulness, and he wondered without meaning to when he would see Lady Victoria again.

At three that afternoon, Alex left Rawlings Hall in his carriage, bound for the meeting with the unfortunate Sir Julian. The carriage's lumbering path through the afternoon traffic honed his anticipation to a sharp edge.

At last the coach turned from Newberry onto Pickway Street, and scant minutes later drew to a halt before the Wolf and Fox tavern. Edgy uncertainty bade Alex sit no longer, and he jumped down to the cobblestones, sinking up to his ankles in a drift of rubbish that had overflowed from its pile at the edge of the street. A stomach-turning stench met his nose almost instantly: rotting vegetation, dead fish, and an underlying putrescence that was as unidentifiable as it was insidious. His stomach muscles tightened in protest. Wrinkling his nose, Alex called up to his driver.

"I'll go in now, before I lose my breakfast. Burles, I don't believe I would wait here, were I you. Stop back in an hour. I should be done by then."

The heavy, florid-jowled driver nodded, nervously eyeing the seamy surroundings. "Aye, milord. And thank 'e." He clucked and sent the grays in motion, as eager to be away from that lowly hole as was his master.

Agilely leaping over the garbage, Alex stood in the tavern's front alcove, shaking his foot to dislodge the slime that had attached itself to his boot. Dissatisfied with the effort but unable to do more without water, he gave up and entered the tavern.

The dark interior stole his vision with the closing of the heavy door behind him. For the first ten seconds, Alex's only impressions of the place were rough laughter and the scents of ale and boiled cabbage. Gradually his eyes adjusted to the dim light and he could see once more.

Before him, three steps led down into a large room dominated by an enormous hearth and a long counter on the opposite end. An enormous fire roared in the hearth but seemed to illuminate only the circle of small, round tables closest to it. The rest of the tables hovered in crowded darkness, offering a place for patrons to sit with their wooden tankards of ale or grog but little in the way of elbow room. Only the dingy booths lining the room's perimeter offered a man privacy. Two doors led from the room, to where he knew not.

Alex scanned the tables, searching for someone who possessed the appearance of wealth, but of the men in the tavern none seemed likely. He lifted his gaze to each of the two doors leading off the main chamber and wondered which led to the harlots rooms above. Was that where Whittendon hid? Or had he never intended to honor the queen's demands at all?

With a sigh of resignation, Alex crossed the sawdust-sprinkled plank floor to where the barkeep stood with his stout arms leaning against the counter, watching him.

"What can I do f' ye, guv?"

"A pint of your best ale, if you please, and a table, good sir."

The barkeep guffawed. "Me best! 'At's a good 'un, m'lud. Now, which cask would 'at be in?" Chuckling some more, he wiped his palms on a stained apron and indicated a corner booth with an incline of his head. "Ye can sit at 'at 'un over there if ye mean ter be out of the way. Sally'll bring ye yer ale in two shakes."

Alex frowned. "Out of the way? Why would you say that?"

The stout man shrugged heavy shoulders. "Why else would ye be in my place this day, m'lud?"

Why, indeed? Alex walked to the booth and sat down, not bothering to remove his heavy cloak. A moment later, when he touched his seat, he was glad he had not. Crusted grime coated the plain wooden seat. Alex grimaced, wishing Whittendon would hurry if he meant to attend this meeting at all. Unlike many of his peers, Alex had never quite understood the urge to grace the East End's more notorious haunts. The sooner he left this place, the better.

A well-rounded barmaid stopped at his table and set a tankard before him. She brushed aside a hank of stringy black hair with the back of her hand. " 'Ere ye be, m'lud. Me name's Sally. If 'ere be anything else I can do fer ye, just let me know."

Alex nodded. "My thanks."

She stood back, hands on hips, and appraised him in silent appreciation. The brown corselet she wore laced about her waist raised pendulous breasts for perusal. Alex looked down into his ale and took a deep drink, lest she think him interested in her display.

"Don't get many o' yer sort about 'ere, m'lud," she stated casually. "Not at this time o' day, anyways."

Alex looked at her, wondering her purpose. "Nay? What time of day do you have my sort then?"

"Sally!"

With a swift, guilty glance over her shoulder, she whispered, "My husband." Her hand clapped down on the coin he had placed on the table and swept it into her pocket. "Aye, ye rowdy cur, I be comin'! Keep yer pants on!"

Left alone, Alex took another sip of the bitter ale and looked around the room. There was not much to look at. Two men whispered together in an opposite corner, earnest looks mirrored in each of their scruffy, bearded faces. A sailor sat at another table with a barmaid on his lap, his hand stuffed forearm-deep beneath her skirts while she giggled in his ear. At the counter, the barkeep and his wife bickered in low, good-natured tones, while a woman's shrill laughter could be heard from a room above. A few other men sat at odd tables, hunched over their cups. Alex scrutinized each in turn—the pale man with trembling hands, the black-faced charman, the man in the corner who slept with his head on folded arms. None looked right. He was beginning to believe Whittendon had misled the queen.

A touch on his arm startled him—he had heard no one. Alex looked up into the face of the sailor, sans the giggling barmaid.

"Lord Carlton?"

The smooth voice seemed oddly out of place coming from the shabbily costumed man before him. Its low undertone mingled discreetly with the myriad other tavern sounds.

"Aye." Alex paused, then, "Sir Julian?"

The sailor nodded. A sardonic smile twisted his lips.

"At your service, my lord." The ironic curl deepened. "Of course, you do realize that, had I any other choice, I would not be here."

Alex nodded. "Point taken. Please, sit down." He indicated the bench opposite him.

Whittendon glanced quickly around to confirm their continued anonymity, then took his seat, sitting tensely on the edge and resting his elbows on the worn tabletop. "We must be careful. Even here, we are not safe."

"Your concern tells me some of what I need to know. You *are* a member of the Mohocks."

Whittendon closed his eyes and took a deep breath. "Aye. I have been. But it was not like that in the beginning. Not—" He swallowed once, hard. "Not like it has been of late."

Alex stared at Whittendon, at his youthful face, so urgent, so strained. *Mon Dieu,* he could not be more than twenty. "And how was it?"

Whittendon shrugged. " 'Twas entertainment. A farce." He looked down at his clasped hands. "But people are being hurt now, and there is no way out for those of us who wish it."

"So the reports are true. The Mohocks are responsible for the recent attacks?"

"Aye. More than is reported, in all likelihood."

Alex leaned forward in his seat, his forehead furrowed in concern. "Then why not get yourself out, man?"

Whittendon gritted his teeth in frustration. "I cannot. The bloody Emperor—" He broke off.

He had to be careful. The last thing he wanted to do was to frighten Whittendon away. "You are afraid," he suggested neutrally.

The nobleman looked away. "Aye."

"But surely with the queen's protection, you—"

"Protection?" Whittendon gave a short, sharp laugh. "Anne can offer me nothing valuable beyond a pardon for my debts. That, at least, will offer some consolation to my family.'' Whittendon closed his eyes and shuddered. ''If they knew . . .''

''No one has to know. Your loyalty to the queen is worth at least that much.''

''Do not admire my natural goodness.'' Bitterness haunted the shadowed depths of the young man's eyes. ''I assure you, I have none.''

''Yet you are helping me.''

The palest hint of a smile played around his lips, but his eyes were sad. ''Self-preservation is a great impetus, aye?''

Alex appraised his informant critically. Whether he could truly help Whittendon, Alex knew not—but he was willing to try. He knew only too well the folly that traveled hand in hand with youth. ''Tell me when the next Mohock meeting is to be held.''

''Nine of the clock, on the morrow. 'Tis to be held at the Hound's Breath on Drover Street.''

The Hound's Breath. Remotely more reputable than the tavern they now visited, its reputation was still suspect, if not for the Mohock name, then for at least a dozen other transgressions.

Alex nodded grimly. ''Aye. I know it. But how do they maintain their anonymity when they meet in such a public place?''

''There is a private meeting room in back. The owner is well kept for his silence.''

''And the girls?''

Whittendon shrugged. ''They do not know,'' he said simply. ''A bauble here, a pretty there. They're happy enough with the arrangement.'' He rubbed his palm along a jaw scratchy with a day's worth of blond whiskers. ''You're sure you wish to go through with this, then? 'Twill not be easy. The Emperor is not a stupid man. If he discovers us, God save us both.''

Irony lifted the corners of Alex's lips. ''Like you, Whittendon, I have little choice in the matter.''

"Ah." Sir Julian's eyes met his in sudden comprehension. "Her Majesty has something on you as well, eh?"

"Never mind that now. Tell me of the Emperor."

"Little do I know to tell."

"Try! Who is he?"

"I don't know."

"Is he a nobleman?"

"I don't know," Whittendon repeated, shaking his head worriedly from side to side. "He has the speech of a noble, though."

" 'Tis possible, then. Will I meet him tomorrow?"

"The Emperor's ways are his own. You may . . . or you may not."

"Tell me what will happen at tomorrow's meeting."

"Ah, but that is part of the mystique, my lord. The anticipation, the unknown, is what drives much of the interest. One never knows what will happen until the night is upon us, full fury."

Later, as he replayed the scene over and over in his mind, Alex found little solace in Sir Julian's cryptic words. A warning, surely.

Until the night is upon us, full fury.

The night, Alex wondered . . . or the Emperor?

Chapter Five

From the safety of the hired coach, Tori watched in silence as her brother emerged at last from the Fox and Dove with three of his good-for-naught friends. Others of the same ilk preceded them, wobbling and drunk. Their raucous laughter carried easily over the sounds of the night.

If he knew you were following him, he'd never forgive you. . . .

The warning came again, sharp in her mind, but she ignored it. It was for his own good, after all. Her brother's penchant for self-destruction gained momentum with each passing day, and for what reason? She could not fathom. But she did know that in her father's absence the duty fell to her to remind Charles of his heritage and of the responsibilities it entailed.

The difficulty lay in his inability to hear her.

With a sigh of resignation, Tori secured the black cloak high about her chin and pulled the borrowed tricorne down low over her eyes. The breeches she wore felt odd, but were much less restricting than petticoats. She would need as much freedom as possible if she meant to keep Charles in her sights. It was her only chance to discover whether her suspicions were true.

Tori turned the latch of the coach door and stepped down. Her brother's oversize boots felt loose despite the cloth she'd stuffed into the toes, and the heels thumped clumsily against the cobblestones. She squinted into the night.

Hearing her descent, the driver rose from his stooped position beside the rear wheel. Tori turned to him.

"My thanks to you, sirrah. I do appreciate your willingness to aid me in my ruse."

"My pleasure, m'lady, but are ye sure ye don't want to go by coach?" His grimy face reflected his concern. "The streets aren't safe fer a man no more, much less a wee thing like yerself. I daren't send ye off to the devils o' the streets—"

"Dressed as I am, I'll meet with little trouble." Tori's gaze slipped past the man's shoulder. Charles had gained half a block already. "My party is leaving us. From here I go on foot."

"But m'lady!"

Tori dug into the one of Charles's purses she wore at her waist and withdrew another coin to add to the gold she'd used to secure the driver's cooperation earlier that evening. She tossed it to him. "Here's for your silence and cooperation, good man. Pray for me, if 'twill ease your mind. But please—tell no one."

Before he could protest again, Tori turned and walked swiftly in the direction her brother had taken. Somewhere ahead, the voices of the men hung in the night air like darting bats, but she could no longer see them. She quickened her pace into a half jog, trying not to think about the lantern she'd left in the coach. The completeness of the darkness unnerved her more than she cared to admit. At one point the toe of her boot caught against a loose stone and she nearly tripped. Bracing a hand against a rough wall, she caught herself and hurried on.

A swirling sea of fog had appeared from nowhere to hinder her. It thickened about her, disguising surroundings, distorting sounds, magnifying the apprehension creeping along her spine. Never had she felt as alone as she did now. As lost.

Nerves jumping, Tori peered into the mist for any sign of the men. Why couldn't she see them? At times their voices sounded to be only a few feet away, and her heart would jump as she searched about for an advantageous hiding place. Seconds later the sounds were barely distinguishable, and she knew she was losing them.

Until the crash of breaking glass met her ears from just ahead.

Tori broke into an all-out run, no longer taking care to muffle her steps. Fear beat fast and hard within her breast. God's mercy, what fool's mission were they up to? And Charles, in the middle of it.

A street sign emerged from the mist above her head, heralding a corner. She hurriedly rounded it of and came to an abrupt halt as she nearly collided with a man's broad back.

The involuntary gasp that ripped from her throat might well have been a scream. The man spun around, hands spread in readiness for combat.

The situation might have been comical, were she much less frightened. Beneath a tricorne, a black silk mask was tied about his head, pirate-fashion, revealing only the lower half of a pudgy face. Small, piggish eyes widened in surprise . . . then in interest.

A slow smile slashed his face. ''Well, now. Look what we have here.'' Raising his thumb and forefinger to his lips, he gave a sharp, earsplitting whistle.

From some distance away came shouts in response.

Terror snapped through Tori like the crack of a whip as the man lunged for her. The adrenaline gave her the impetus she needed. Pivoting in her overly large boots, she bolted.

Behind her she heard a rough curse, then the sounds of the man scurrying to catch her. Fear lodged syrup-thick in her throat. Could she outdistance him? Recklessly Tori dashed across the street, thankful for the fog that she had cursed earlier. If she couldn't see her surroundings, that meant he could not see her. It was her only hope.

Somehow her feet found the way. She passed by alcoves—no sanctuary there. Too soon her pursuer would be upon her and all would be lost. She could hear his footsteps. Slower now. Muted grunts. Aye, he was still looking for her. Her hiding place would have to be well disguised.

Half-blind, Tori ran with her fingers trailing along the nearby wall for balance and orientation. When her hand touched air, she thought at first it was another alcove and nearly passed it by. Intuition made her reach deeper into the space. Her fingers met nothing but air. It was a narrow alley, large enough only for human traffic.

She stepped into it without another thought.

The alley reeked with the odors of discarded rubbish and the stale, rank smells of sweat and something else, something unidentifiable but undeniably human. Faint rustlings skittered in the darkness. Rats?

A tremor of revulsion churned upward in her throat. Tori choked it down and inched farther into the narrow space.

Was he there? She pressed herself against the wall and stared wide-eyed toward the street. Her mind played tricks, showing movements in the darkness she couldn't be sure were false. She blinked once, hard, but the shifting shadows remained.

She'd heard once that a person could die from fear, but she'd never believed it until now. Tori shuddered, waiting. A cadence of terror throbbed in her veins. She pictured the masked man crouched just around the bend, hands ready to grab her the moment she braved the street again. She no longer heard his heavy footsteps stalking her. Was he there?

Somewhere close by, a pebble clattered along the cobblestones. Tori needed no further impetus. She turned and vaulted headlong into the blackness. She stumbled once, twice, but kept from falling and rushed on.

At the rear of the buildings, another alley crossed hers. Tori turned left in the hope that her path would take her near the Fox and Dove, anywhere she might find a hired cab that could deliver her to safety. She could feel a cramp beginning in the muscles at her side, and her breathing sounded like the rasping wheeze of a tuberculosis victim, but she didn't stop. If she stopped now, she'd be unable to go on at all.

In her blind haste, she didn't see the dark object on the alley floor before her. Tori sprawled, face-first, upon the hard ground.

It took her a moment to regain her bearings. Her bruised ribs felt as though a giant vise squeezed the breath from her. She lay there panting on the damp ground, desperate for air but unable to do more. Pinpricks of black appeared in the center of her vision. Gradually they expanded until they completely replaced the misty gray of the fog all around her.

How long she lay there, Tori had no idea. Seconds . . . perhaps minutes, perhaps more. The first conscious thought she had was of the cold. Shivers began at her fingers and toes and spread their way inward.

Her second thought was of the expensively booted feet standing over her.

A hand jostled her shoulder. "They will leave you if you cannot rise, Whittendon. You must hurry!"

The hoarse voice struck a familiar chord somewhere in her fuzzy brain. Tori frowned, trying to remember.

Hands were on her back, her arms, urging her to rise. Big, urgent, but not ungentle. With each second's passing, her thoughts became clearer. With clarity came the reminder that she must conceal her identity.

Tori leaped to her feet and jerked the tricorne down low on her brow. She jammed her hands into her pockets and began to walk away, the way she'd come.

The hand clapped over her shoulder. "Did you not hear me, Whittendon? Or did the fall knock the sense out of your wooden head? The others are this way." Enough light glimmered around the edges of a nearby shuttered window for Tori to see, the man pointing in the opposite direction. "Come. You know 'tis not safe for any of us to lose the others for long."

The raspy voice nudged at her fogged brain, urging her to remember. Tori lifted her head just enough to look at the man. She couldn't see his face clearly, but his height left her no doubt as to his identity. She'd met only one man in her life who towered over her enough to make her feel womanly. That combined with the voice . . .

It was the Earl of Carlton.

He reached for her again. Tori jolted back and tucked her chin down.

"Are you all right, lad?" She could hear the frown in his voice. "Does aught ail you?"

She shook her head, cursing her poor luck. Was it not enough that she'd lost her brother over the course of the night? That she'd barely escaped assault by an unknown miscreant? Now she had to deal with the earl, too. This was not her night.

"Whittendon, what's the matter with you?"

He took a step closer and alarm bells went off in her brain again. Tori backed away, pressing a hand to her throat and shaking her head in a pantomime explanation that her voice was gone. There had to be a way to escape.

"What do you mean, you can't speak? You spoke perfectly only moments ago." He released a lungful of exasperation and put his hands on his hips. "Bloody hell. You must have hit your head harder than I thought."

Tori's mind worked feverishly. If ever there was a time for a ruse, this was it. She had to find a way to escape, and the only way was to get him to leave her. But how?

Summoning every dramatic inclination she possessed, she pressed her hand to her forehead and stumbled against the brick wall nearest her, allowing it to support her.

The ruse worked. The earl edged closer to her. "Whittendon?" Concern gave his voice an urgent edge. "You are not well, lad. Shall I fetch the others?"

Renewed hope winged its way through Tori's heart. She nodded, slumping even more pitifully against the building in case he needed further convincing.

But the earl didn't rush off as she'd hoped. "I don't feel right leaving you injured, man," he said, uncertainty evident in his tone.

Still slumping, Tori waved him away with her hand. Just go, she thought in frustration. Then she felt her feet leave the ground as the earl's arms closed behind her knees and back.

His chuckle sounded close to her ear. "By God, boy, you're light as a feather. A bit soft in the rump, too. You must be younger than I thought."

Tori held her breath. Any movement at all might bring her deception to his attention. But how was she going to escape now?

"Ho, Carlton. Are you there, man?"

The whispered call rang out in the alley as well as if it had been shouted. Tori's heart sank as the earl froze in his steps. "Aye," he called back quietly. "Is that you, Whittendon?"

"Who else?" came the clipped reply. "You'd better come—the others'll wonder if we've deserted them." A pause, then, "Stay where you are and I'll come to you."

"Hold a moment," the earl returned. The easy calm of his voice might have reassured her in another situation, but not tonight. Tori twisted in his arms, desperation making her reckless. He tightened his grip, his arms banding around her like a snake's coils. "Look at me," he said in a hiss.

Feeling defiant and helpless, Tori shook her head.

"Look at me, or I'll be forced to call for reinforcements."

She turned her face away and he cursed under his breath. Adjusting her weight, he carried her over to the shuttered window. His arm fell away from behind her legs and her feet dropped to the ground. Before she could flee, she found herself backed against the wall.

"Who are you?"

Tori pressed her lips together and refused to look at him. It was a futile gesture. In the next moment, her tricorne was swept away.

He sucked in his breath. "*Dieu!* You!"

"Aye, my lord. Surprised?" Frowning, Tori lifted her gaze. The glow from the window revealed more than she expected. The Earl of Carlton stood before her, a black silk mask tied around his head. She gasped. "You—"

"What are you doing here?" he grated.

"What are you doing with that mask?" she whispered back.

The voice came again. "Carlton?"

The earl pressed his thumbs into her shoulders. "Aye, Whittendon. Worry not. I thought I saw someone, but 'twas naught but the fog."

"Best be getting on then, aye?"

"Aye. I'll be there directly, just as soon as I find a place to relieve myself."

His crudity brought hot blood to Tori's cheeks, but it had the desired effect on the unseen Whittendon. His laughter floated on the mist. "Do that, but be quick about it. The rest is sure to begin soon. We'll be missed."

With the threat of intrusion gone, the earl turned on his captive. "Thunder be damned, woman! If 'twas danger you hoped for tonight, you've found it. What in bloody hell are you doing out here?"

Tori jerked away from his pinching grasp. "You were gentler when you thought I was a man."

"No man feels like you do. My God, Tori, what were you thinking?"

"Don't call me that. I gave you no leave—"

"But you certainly take leave where you can. Was it your intention to risk your life tonight?"

Tori lifted her chin. "My life is my concern, not yours."

"Well, you can thank your good fortune that I made it my concern. Again." He shook his head at her like a patronizing father. "I'm beginning to think you possess a flair for this sort of thing. It's most unnerving."

"You would accuse me?" Tori put her hands on her hips. "I might remind you that you have been in the same places at the same times. And considering your current attire, I'm beginning to understand why."

"My—" His hand moved to his face.

"Yes. The mask."

He shrugged. "If you'll recall, you have a penchant for masks as well. In more ways than one, it seems."

"What do you mean by that?"

"Only that there is more to you than meets the eye, my Lady Mystery. You have more than a little explaining to do."

His overbearing attitude infuriated her. "I ask for no explanations from you, milord. Neither do I expect to be asked to explain my actions to a stranger."

In a fraction of a second, he grabbed her and pulled her against him without even a by-your-leave. His hand closed over her mouth before she could utter a protest. The scent of him filled her nostrils, tangy with spice. After the gamy odors of the alley, she found it almost unbearably refreshing.

His lips moved strands of hair by her ear. "Listen."

At first she heard nothing but the beat of her own heart. In the next moment a pair of voices came, so close that

Tori jumped in surprise. She never guessed they stood so near a crossroads.

"... nothing about for any of us," the first voice grumbled.

"A waste of a good night," a second agreed.

"Night's still young, though."

"Right. P'raps if we move on—"

When the voices had passed, Alex released her. "We must get you away from this place," he said urgently. "Luck was with us this time. With the next, you may not be so fortunate."

Tori shook her head. "Don't trouble yourself, my lord. I found my way here. I can find my way home."

The short laugh he gave was quietly menacing. "Oh, no. I'm afraid you have no choice, my lady. You will stay here until I return." He took a step nearer. "You will crouch down"—another step—"as close to the wall as you can. And you will cover your face with your cloak."

Tori stiffened at the arrogant display and lifted her chin. She stared into the mask's shadowed eye slits, hoping she looked more confident than she felt. The mask hid so much from her—she felt distinctly at a disadvantage. "And if I do not?"

"I know where you live." No humor levied what was without a doubt meant to be a threat. Tori shivered in spite of herself and did as she'd been bidden.

He left her there without turning back. Tori never found the time to defy him. Within what seemed only seconds he returned, so quiet she heard not a sound until he touched her shoulder.

"Let us go," he urged. "Quickly, before I am followed."

He held out his hand to her. Tori declined to take it, instead struggling to her feet on her own trembling limbs. The thought of his hand encasing hers left her feeling oddly unsettled.

Though she couldn't see his eyes, she felt his gaze upon

her, probing her, until she felt the very depths of her heart were laid bare to him. She lowered her gaze, focusing instead on the safer area of his hands.

"I could bring you home with me."

Alex spoke the words with quiet humor, but something made Tori think more than humor prompted the offer. Heat surged to her cheeks, and she drew herself up straight. "I think not," she replied archly.

"Then I shall escort you to your home."

He said it so smoothly Tori had no chance to protest. Grabbing her wrist, he dragged her behind him for five blocks, unerringly picking the way through the fog. When they were safely away from the ruffians' path, he hailed the first unoccupied sedan chair they encountered.

"A chair?" Tori gazed upon the small, human-powered conveyance with open skepticism.

"Unless you prefer to walk."

The three-mile journey to Maryleborn Court stretched before her in her mind, complete with blistered heels and stubbed toes. "All right. The chair it is."

While Alex gave the men instructions to her home, Tori climbed into the seat. The portion remaining appeared too small to seat a child in comfort. Alex looked at it, shrugged, and squeezed in beside her.

Tori groaned and squirmed in discomfort. "I don't think we fit."

"Of course we will. We simply need a bit of arranging." He shifted.

"Ouch! You're on my leg!"

"Your pardon." He moved again, then grimaced. "You wore a sword?"

" 'Tis but a dagger," Tori replied airily.

"Aye, well, it feels more like a sword. The hilt is bruising my thigh." He eased onto one hip in an effort to make room, but succeeded only in crowding her further with his wide shoulders.

Tori sighed. His elbows had caught her in the ribs not

once, but twice. The cushionless seat pinched her buttocks mercilessly, and her left foot was going numb. Gazing out the window, she saw they only now approached Charing Cross. "We'll never make it."

"Don't be such a pessimist."

"This will not work," Tori insisted.

"Perhaps if you sat on my lap."

Tori's mouth fell open. She promptly closed it. "I beg your pardon?"

A twitch played about the corners of his mouth, but he didn't smile. " 'Twould mean comfort for us both. And warmth. For practicality's sake, of course."

Tori shivered, as cold as she could ever remember being. But comfort? Hardly.

The thought of enduring a long ride confined in close contact with the Devil Lord intimidated her more than she cared to admit. Tori shook her head. "I . . . I don't think so."

"No?" The twitch became a full-fledged grin. "Unless you're afraid of me."

Half taunt, half insight, the earl's soft charge rocked the foundation of self-possession she'd relied upon since her mother's death. Stubbornness overpowered common sense. She stared into Alex's eyes. "How intuitive you are, Lord Carlton," she replied coolly. "You're absolutely right. Comfort is the primary objective. Prepare yourself, then."

Tori shifted; Alex lifted. With a flurry of cloaks and oversize boots, they had accomplished the impossible task of exchanging places within the diminutive space. At last able to stretch her legs into a more graceful position, Tori should have felt at ease.

Logic dictated it. Why, then, was relaxation farthest from her mind?

Heat seeped into her by slow degrees, through places she'd thought might never be warm again. The shivering stopped, allowing her to feel again. And feel she did—too much. Carlton's chest behind her seemed a bastion of strength, of power. With every breath he took, she felt the tensing and releasing of muscles against her shoulder blades. Each drew a wellspring of awareness from where had been only aggravation moments before.

Without rests for his arms, he had little choice but to brace his hands on his thighs. One rested on either side of her tensed legs. As they touched her only by fine hairs, she sensed their power more than felt it.

"Will you tell me now why I found you in such an extraordinary situation, Lady Mystery?"

His low words were a pleasant buzz in her ear. Deliciously distracted, Tori shook her head and felt her tricorne bump against something solid.

"Blast!" The hoarse curse blew hot air against her nape. "Then would you mind removing your hat?"

Before she could respond, his hand came up beneath the brim and knocked it from her head. The tricorne bounced to the floor onto the tangle of their feet.

Annoyance flared through her at the domineering gesture. Tori stiffened. "Lord Carlton," she bit out, "you do take much upon yourself!"

She crossed her arms tightly over her chest and leaned forward, anything to break away from the solid wall of his chest. Yet something in her lamented the loss. She ignored it.

"So you have told me," he said in his rasping voice, dry humor lacing the claim. "Twice. But please—call me Alex."

Beneath her, his legs wobbled. Her weight shifted off balance. In an effort to compensate, she brought one leg down. "Why should I do that? I hardly know you."

Was it her imagination, or did he move his right hand? His thumb and first finger now pressed snugly against her thigh.

He laughed softly. "We have met thrice. I've saved your life on at least one occasion. And I know intimate secrets about you. I should think that might prove that we are far from strangers.'' His leg muscles tightened along the length of hers. ''I should like to call you Tori. Or perhaps you prefer *Mademoiselle de Mystère.*''

''Please don't call me that.''

His knee lifted almost imperceptibly. Tori might not have noticed, but the movement parted her legs just enough to send shocks of nervousness flitting down her thighs.

Feeling as green as a miss in short skirts, Tori shifted one leg over both of his. Her feet now dangled six inches above the cabin floor, but at least her legs were locked safely together.

Small comfort. Now his face was but inches from hers.

Tori pulled back, but was determined to hide her discomfort. She arched a brow at him. ''A purporter of secrets? As though you are innocent of such things, Lord Carlton.''

''I have never claimed to be an innocent, *mam'selle.*''

''Nor could you,'' Tori retorted.

The grin that twisted his lips should have warned her. ''Nay,'' he agreed. ''Nor could I.''

His hand closed over her knee, warm and firm. In one silken movement, he trailed his fingers upward along her breech-covered thigh before she could utter a word of protest.

''Aye, secrets and mysteries become you, Tori.'' The whisper slid down her spine like a silken chemise. ''They shimmer about you, as haunting as your silver gown, and shadow you as surely as this cloak.'' His knuckles brushed along her ribs.

Tori struggled against the strange tide of emotion washing over her. She braved a glance at him. ''Lord Carlton—''

He touched a finger to her lips. ''Shhh.'' His gaze burned down into hers, his eyes glittering black in the shadow. His lips loomed before her suddenly. Close. So close.

Dear God, he meant to kiss her.

Tori lifted her hand to his chest, meaning to hold him at bay. But her hand fluttered uselessly against the hard plane of his chest as he closed the inches between them. She pressed harder, until she could feel the steady beat of his heart thudding under her palm. Strong and purposeful. Slow but insistent. And somehow she forgot her purpose in resisting. Whispers spun through her reeling thoughts.

One kiss.

He bent her back over his arm by slow degrees until she thought she could bend no more.

It would harm no one.

His lips hovered over hers, so close she could feel their warmth.

Just one.

Their forceful softness. Their . . .

Kiss him. . . .

Throwing caution aside, Tori yielded to the temptation winging through her heart. Without thought, without fear, without even a glimmer of worry for her brother, she felt her eyes drift closed. Her head tilted back ever so slightly. Her lips parted in anticipation of his touch.

Soft laughter broke the spell.

Tori's eyes flew open. Her surprise amused him even more. Alexandre Rawlings, the notorious Devil Lord, laughed at her with abandon, with delight. His amusement transformed his features into an almost supernatural handsomeness that took her breath away.

Embarrassment and confusion warred for control in her thoughts. Fury surpassed them both. Unable to bear his smug pleasure, Tori reacted without forethought, something utterly foreign to her nature. Both fists came up. With a snarl of anger, she pounded them, heel first, against his chest.

The force of the blows knocked her precarious perch aboard his lap off-kilter. Unwilling to join the tricorne in the narrow foot crevice, Tori clutched at his shirtfront with a gasp. The rending of cloth was clearly audible in the cabin.

Alex caught her with ease and pulled her to him, shifting her comfortably in his arms. "Your eagerness to show me your thanks is heartening, *mam'selle,*" he said, his voice full of good humor, "but 'tis not necessary to gain my cooperation."

Fuming and horribly embarrassed, Tori tried to enlarge the space between them. "You are not amusing, Lord Carlton. Not in the least. Indeed, I find you most offensive."

He smiled. "And I find you most captivating." The smile broadened, deepening the cleft in his chin. "A bit headstrong, perhaps. You still haven't told me your reasons for being in such a dangerous area of London after dark and without an escort."

"I told you, it's none of your business." She locked arms securely across her chest, then tossed a glare at him. "On the other hand, 'tis obvious why you were there, milord."

"Aye? Pray do tell, *Mam'selle Mystère.*"

Tori ignored the jibe. "When we first met, I thought you were no more than a rake bent on conquest. But I was wrong, wasn't I? Why the mask, milord? What are you hiding?"

His face betrayed nothing. "My mask has a simple explanation—I was playing a prank on a friend."

"I don't believe you."

He shrugged. "Believe what you like. It matters little."

"Oh, no?" Tori pushed back even farther, until the cabin wall pressed against her spine. At least she could see his eyes. "I saw them tonight. And I believe you're one of them."

"You're speaking nonsense. Who?"

"The Mohocks. I saw them. Do you deny it?"

Chapter Six

With the clatter of wood on stone and a bone-shuddering jolt, the sedan chair lowered to the ground. Tori looked out the window to see the ornate scrolls of a familiar iron gate.

"Never mind," she muttered hastily. "I don't want to know."

Grasping the cold metal latch, she pushed the door open and scrambled from his lap. Before he could follow, she slammed the door behind her.

"Good-bye, my lord," Tori said, backing away as she met his compelling stare. The urge to escape was especially strong within her, sharpened by the strength of her own heartbeat. "Maybe someday you'll realize the foolishness of reckless games."

She spun on her heel and fled across the courtyard, her boot heels beating her passage across the smooth flagstones. But before she could reach the house, a hand closed over her shoulder. His fingers bit into her as he spun her around.

He'd removed his mask, and his eyes held a deadly seriousness that made her throat close. "Not so fast, *Mystère.*"

Tori pried at his fingers, determined not show her fear. "Let me go!"

His husky laugh infuriated her. "Not again."

Increasing her efforts, she wriggled and twisted, using her body as leverage. He let her struggle for a while, then with a swift, efficient movement, he bent and hoisted her into his arms as if she weighed no more than a child.

Tori gasped. "Sir! You take too much upon yourself." She thrust against his chest with both hands. "Put me down."

"I think not."

"You must leave, before someone sees you!" she said in a hiss.

His cold laugh rang out in the courtyard.

"Or hears you," she added impatiently.

"Then stop struggling." One brow flared in a grand arch. "Or you'll force me to make enough noise to rouse the entire community."

Tori lifted her chin to meet his stare. A chill traced her spine, but not from cold. His eyes looked like chips of onyx in the night. A muscle clenched and unclenched repeatedly in his jaw. Dressed in black from toe to chin, he looked downright sinister. Tori had every reason to believe his claim.

How maddening. And how ill-timed.

No one must know of her night-time forays—nor of Charles's. She ceased her struggles but crossed her arms across her chest in a final play for self-protection. "Very well. If you insist upon forceful measures."

A slow smirk spread across his face. "That's better," he whispered. "I do."

She gritted her teeth as a fierce wave of dislike swept over her. How could she ever have thought him attractive? "What do you want?"

He ignored her and began walking with her toward the house.

"If you don't answer me, I'm going to start screaming."

He grunted. "I thought you didn't want us to be heard."

Tori made a face at him. "*You* are a brute."

His lips twisted. "Aye. And 'twould do you well to remember that."

As if to prove his point, he half tossed her into the air. The breath whooshed from her lungs, and she abandoned all pretense of indifference and threw her arms around his neck.

"Brute," Tori grated again through clenched teeth, but she locked her fingers together anyway. "Beast." Then, as though these weren't harsh enough, she said, "Blackguard."

On the doorstep of the west entrance, Alex set her to her feet, then bent low in a grand flourish. "At your service, lovely Tori." Straightening, he held her captive with a taunting grin. "You've accounted for the letter 'B' most successfully. What letter shall we try next?"

She would have left him on the doorstep if he hadn't been standing between her and the door. She turned up her nose at him. "Heathen."

"Your endearments warm my heart, lovely Tori. But be careful. Some others might not be quite so . . . forgiving."

"Oh? Do you dare threaten me, Lord Carlton?"

He shrugged a cloaked shoulder and turned his face away, staring off into the night. "I dare much these days, Tori."

Bold words, but they lacked the arrogance she might have expected of him. Tori frowned. "Aye, you and your barbaric friends."

His mouth hardened as he stared into her eyes, but he said nothing.

Thinking she'd struck a nerve, Tori pressed on. "You can't bully me, you know. Not when you're so obviously a part of those outlaws. The Mohocks, or some such club. Aren't you afraid I'll tell some—"

Her words fell short as he suddenly moved toward her with purposeful, catlike strides. Eyes wide with fear, Tori backed away, but he followed every step of her retreat. Two steps more, and the wall scraped her shoulder blades and she could go no farther. She could only watch as the earl closed the distance.

He stopped inches away, his bulk filling her gaze. His hand closed around her jaw and brought her chin up against her will. Her mouth went dry when she saw the fury blazing in his eyes. "You know nothing. Say it!"

Her will flagging, Tori swallowed and straightened her spine. She felt the bricks scrape against her woolen cloak, felt cold seep through, but nothing chilled her as much as the earl's expression. "You're afraid," she said, wishing she didn't sound so weak. "Why? Do you expect me to protect your identity, and theirs, too?"

His fingers squeezed her jaw, but oddly, it didn't hurt. "Tori . . ." A warning.

She grabbed his wrist. "Why do you wear a mask? Is it a symbol of the club?"

"Why do you?" he countered. "Lady Mystery, of the silver vizard. Your ploy was quite successful if you meant to attract attention. You certainly captured mine."

"Brute."

"You already said that." His fingers moved suddenly, the barest caress across her cheek, the mole at the corner of her mouth. "You don't want your identity known in connection with your actions. I'm sure you can understand why the same is important for me."

"If you think I'll protect your precious hide, you—"

His thumb brushed across the fullness of her lips, quelling her words. Tori shivered against her will and felt her stomach drop to the vicinity of her toes. Rational thought evaporated into the night.

"I've saved you," he said softly. "Twice."

The soft claim took her aback and raised a question for which she had no answer. ''Aye,'' she whispered. She held her breath and dared to look at him, to let him see her confusion. ''But I don't know why.''

He went still, gazing into her eyes. ''Don't you?'' His free hand came up from the folds of his cloak. Tori watched it draw near with a fascination that she found both compelling and frightening at once. ''Don't you really?''

His hands cradled her face and he closed the inches between them. Tori held her breath as his fingers traced the heights and valleys of her face, feeling every sense she possessed come alive for the first time. Gloriously so. And when he with the barest of pressures urged her mouth upward to meet his, she couldn't find the will to stop him.

At the first touch of his lips, lightning energy jolted through her. Sharp pleasure, shockingly distinct. Tori gasped and stiffened, but not for long. His lips plucked rousingly at hers, firm yet gentle, soft but with a delicious friction.

Tori felt herself relaxing by increments, until she felt pliant with the heady sensations. Warmth flooded her with each stroke, and a small sound of pleasure escaped her throat. She felt weak and light-headed and oh, so alive. She moved restlessly, wanting something more and yet not knowing what.

As though he sensed her surrender, Alex pressed closer and deepened the kiss in one motion. A low groan of conquest rumbled from his chest as he touched his tongue to her mouth in a sinuous slide along the sensitive inner flesh of her lip. The effect was as stunning as it was unexpected. Tori shivered, but her body felt on fire within the alien confines of her brother's clothes. She clutched at his shirt, needing an anchor as he deepened the contact. His kisses swept aside the last vestiges of her defenses, scattering them to the wind as his tongue slipped into her mouth. His arms tightened around her waist beneath the flowing cloak and lifted her against him until only her toes rested on solid ground. Over and over, his lips and tongue swirled and suckled, darted and beckoned, until she slipped her arms around his neck and held on tight. His body fit flush against hers, as if there were no end to her body and no beginning of his. And she didn't seem to care. Tingling sensations vibrated through her. They spread along her limbs like fire licking at dry kindling, seeming to culminate in her lower belly and beyond, where his body strained most against hers, oddly hard.

Alex broke the contact after several long, torturous moments, and rested his forehead against hers. Lord, she gave of herself with an abandon that defied inhibition, yet somehow also cried innocence. The contradiction seduced him, but unnerved him as well with its power over him. Aching, he stared down at her. His heartbeat caught as her eyes slowly fluttered open.

"Alex?" A dazed whisper.

He shook himself. *Dieu,* what was he doing? To bring this woman into his life, with danger on all sides, was unthinkable. Reprehensible.

Somewhere he found the strength to step back. Regret rose within him at the loss of her body, but he shoved it aside. "I, uh, apologize, Lady Victoria. I shouldn't have—"

The confusion in her eyes nearly undid him. Alex cursed the gruffness that was forever a part of his damaged voice. But damn it, it couldn't be helped. It was for her own good.

He straightened and took another step back. "I shouldn't have done that," he repeated. " 'Twas a mistake."

Alex watched as she drew herself up, her spine mast-straight and proud. "Yes. Yours, my lord. Don't ever touch me again."

He ached to hold her, to kiss her hurt away. But he couldn't allow desire for something that would never be to interfere with what he knew must be done. Duty must come first. "You shouldn't have been out, Tori."

She swept her cloak more firmly about her and refastened the frogs he'd loosened. "As I said once before, my movements are none of your concern, Lord Carlton."

His brows drew inward in a scowl. *Mon Dieu,* but she could be stubborn. What he found most aggravating was that she was right. "You're not a fool, so pray don't act like one. It's not safe for you to venture out at night alone, and well you know it. And for God's sake, forget what you saw!"

She turned away, placing her hand on the knob. " 'Tis far from your rights to tell me what to do, my lord. Don't even try."

Desperation could make a man do reckless things. Alex flattened his hand against the door and held it closed. "Little fool. Don't you know what they are?" His voice vibrated with fury through his clenched jaw. "They would slit your nose on a whim, or mark your pretty skin just for fun. And that's if you're particularly fortunate. 'Struth, they'd prefer to do worse—much worse with a sweet of your caliber."

Somehow the strength of his warning seemed to break through her haughty facade. Her eyes widened as she stared at him. "They are the Mohocks, aren't they?" she whispered. "I had thought, but I couldn't be sure, and—"

"They are devils." Alex let his hand drop to his side. He averted his gaze, knowing he'd said too much already. "Go, *Mystère.* Go back to the safety of your beautiful home. Seek excitement with a lover, if you must. But keep your pretty nose out of what is none of your business."

He turned and stalked into the mist, not waiting to see if she went inside or not. She was right. She was none of his concern. He had no responsibility toward her. None whatsoever.

But his body throbbed with tension, and his heart beat much too swiftly to lay claim to indifference. And he knew he would see her again.

* * *

Tori watched Alex recede into the fog. Then, slowly, she turned the knob to the servants' entrance and let herself in. Inside, the house remained in darkness, a sure sign all were still abed. She sighed, relieved that no one had heard them. No one knew about her foray into the city. And if she had any say in the matter, no one would know of Charles's actions, either.

She slipped the boots from her feet and padded through the empty rooms. Pale moonlight glimmered in long fingers down the hall, summoning her to the front of the house, where someone had failed to draw the draperies. She yielded to temptation and stopped there, searching the gray mist for movement.

Was he out there still?

Then she realized what she had been thinking. *Good heavens, Tori, what utter nonsense.* Stepping back from the window, she grabbed the heavy draperies and pulled them shut. Of course he wasn't there. He'd probably gone back to his friends.

She headed for the stairs and marched up them. Why couldn't she stop thinking about him? She meant nothing to him. The kiss . . . well, that was just an experiment by a man who had a lot of experience in experimenting. She mustn't allow schoolgirl fancies to persuade her it meant anything more.

Charles's room remained empty. Tori deposited his boots by his bed, knowing that if her foolish brother managed to make it home with his boots intact on his big feet, he'd be of no mind to wonder why a second pair lay beside his bed—if he made it home at all.

Her door creaked as she opened it. Tori winced at the loudness of it, and she shut the door more slowly. Closing it behind her, she made a mental note to advise Smythe of it in the morning. She didn't like the idea of being discovered skulking about the house because of something so inconsequential.

Stripping her brother's clothes from her body, she dropped them to the floor and drew on a shift, shivering as the cool night air raised gooseflesh on her arms. The high bed beckoned, promising warmth. Tori climbed into it, curling herself into a tight ball beneath the heavy coverlets. But the warmth seemed meager when compared with the heat of Alex's kisses. The feather tick seemed especially lump-ridden, affording the barest of comfort, and her gown felt overly rough against her skin.

And sleep eluded her. Images insinuated themselves before her closed eyelids. Hair as black as a raven's breast. Eyes that burned when they gazed at her. A smile that seduced as it threatened her comfortable existence. Grumbling, Tori squeezed her eyes tight and rolled her face into the lavender-scented pillow slip. From the deepest recesses of her mind, the taunts came, sharp and accusing.

He knows too much.

He knows nothing. Not really.

And he guesses even more. 'Tis why he follows you.

He did not follow me. 'Twas coincidence.

Coincidence. Aye.

It must be! He is but a scoundrel. A rake.

Are you sure?

Aye. Just like Father. Just the same.

Thinking of her father only made things worse. Her absent, selfish father. Before her mother died, she'd been too oblivious to realize the truth of his jaded existence. The womanizing. The drinking. His affection for throwing extravagant parties. He'd driven her mother to her death as surely as if he'd pushed her from a cliff. Death by a broken heart.

Her mother's diaries had provided ample evidence.

Now that she was gone, he hardly seemed to remember the daughter and son he'd left behind. He was too busy pursuing his business interests in Italy—or was it only another woman? And was it any wonder Charles had sunken to roistering?

Alexandre Rawlings was the same sort of rake. The evidence might as well have slapped her in the face. Handsome he might be, but he was no shining knight. No knight would consort with the company he kept.

Mohocks. He had admitted as much.

But what about Charles? Did he consort with Mohocks as well?

Terror choked her at the thought. Terror and something else, a resentment that her father had brought them to this end through his selfishness.

Not Charles! There had to be a way to get through to him.

And the earl. A man who could condone activities such as he'd described must be part savage himself. She'd expected violence from him. Brutality. But his kisses were nothing like that. Strong and masterful, aye. His touch had brought a trembling anticipation to her limbs, evocative and soothing. With each knowledgeable assault on her senses, her world had veered madly, then careened end over end with delicious abandon.

She'd been kissed once before, but never like that. Tori raised cool hands to her cheeks, remembering how much she'd wanted to bury her fingers in his hair and draw him down to her. But that was madness, wasn't it? Danger clung to him like an aura. Frightening and intriguing all at once. Hardly the kind of man who could fulfill her dreams of a kind husband, a happy home, a marriage of honesty and trust. A gentle love to give her happiness was what she wanted. . . .

Wasn't it?

Alex, he'd asked her to call him. . . .

Sleep was a long time in coming.

Chapter Seven

Alex wearily stumbled through the doors of Rawlings Hall as the first pale fingers of dawn touched the edge of a gunmetal sky. He'd been walking for what seemed hours—*was* hours—since leaving Tori on her doorstep. She was a distraction he could ill afford. He'd walked to rid himself of the feel of her body, to clear his mind of the sweet scent of her perfume. To think.

He closed the door and leaned his head against the casement. He'd succeeded in that. Too well. Unfortunately, he could only think of Tori.

Lady Mystery. *Mon Dieu.* She was more incredible than he'd imagined. And he'd left her without receiving any answers. Damn, he'd even left without his watch!

He stalked through his kitchen, his thoughts ajumble. What would make a respectable noblewoman risk her life by venturing into London's backstreets and alleys? At night. Unescorted. Dressed as a man, to boot. Not even the Middleham title her father held could protect her from the censure that would certainly follow should she be discovered by the wrong person.

Alex walked a silent path through the rooms, avoiding furniture and baubles with an easy familiarity. No lights, no sounds met his attentive ears. The household still slept. *Good.* Maybe he could get some sleep after all.

Pressing his fingers against his eyes, he mounted the marble stairs one by one. His legs felt like oak timbers, a thousand years old. Lord, he was tired. Mind, body, and spirit. Discovering Tori in the midst of the Mohock fray reminded him of his own vulnerability. If they discovered his identity . . . Tonight they had been mischievous, limiting their work to pranks—a shattered window, a stolen horse. Yet beneath their laughter and jibes flowed an undercurrent of something harsher, a brutality awaiting release.

How long before their actions changed directions again toward meting out pain upon the unsuspecting? Like the woman they had repeatedly tortured a week before his appointment with the queen. Alex grimaced and rubbed a palm against his stubbled jaw. Acting for the queen, he would be a party to whatever the Mohock bastards chose to do. For the first time tonight, he thought of what that might mean. Because of Tori.

Could he watch while they bedeviled an innocent passerby?

With a bitter sense of fatalism, Alex knew he had no choice. He would have to, if he meant to satisfy the queen. Thank God he was able to spirit Tori away in time. But what about the next time?

Alex paused with his hand on the doorknob. His jaw tightened. There wouldn't *be* a next time. Surely the lass would come to her senses, now that she'd seen how dangerous the London streets could be.

He slipped into his bedchamber and closed the heavy door.

"Ye're in rather late, cousin."

Alex spun around at the voice, his eyes searching the semidarkness. The rising dawn let enough light around the draperies for him to discern Rorick reclining on a chaise near the hearth, a book tented over his face. "Rorick," he muttered, pushing his fingers through his hair. "You nigh scared the life from me."

Rorick rolled to one side and leaned his head on his hand, facing him. The book dropped unheeded to the floor. "Jumpy, are ye?"

Alex gave a husky laugh. "Aye . . . a bit." He shrugged out of his cloak and dropped it on a wooden chair. "These stories of Mohocks and the like had me staring into the shadows."

"Late nights. A bit of nerves." Rorick tapped a finger along his cheekbone as he studied him. "Sounds like guilt to me."

Alex flashed his Scots cousin a sharp look. "What do you mean?"

"Och, mon, do ye forget who ye're talking to? Ye canna fool me. 'Tis a woman, aye?"

Alex felt his breath ease out as relief swept over him. *Of course he wouldn't realize. . . .* "Well—aye. A woman."

Rorick cocked a brow at him. "*A* woman? Or the one we trailed that night at the palace?"

Alex tugged at the ruffled jabot that was choking him. "My cousin you may be, dear Rorick, but I cannot see why you need to know my every move." His fingers at last managed to unravel the knot. He dropped the length of lace to the table and moved on to the buttons on his coat.

Rorick laughed. "Defensive, are ye? The lass must be quite the bit of skirt."

Somehow, the thought of Tori described as anything less than noble sent a sharp flare of protectiveness spearing through him. Yanking the coat from his shoulders, Alex flung it at his smirking cousin. "Mind your tongue," he grated.

Rorick pulled the coat from his face, and his laughter deepened. "Temper, temper, my lord," he mocked. "Protective, aren't we?"

Alex scowled, knowing any contradictions would be seen through at once. "What are you doing here, Rorick?"

He watched as his cousin stuffed his frock coat into a ball and shoved it behind his head like a pillow. An impish grin slashed his cheeks into deep dimples. "Why, I came to help ye ready for the evening, o' course." Rorick batted his eyelashes with all the innocence of a simpering miss, his eyes sparkling mischievously. "Is that no' obvious?"

Stripping the black linen shirt over his head, Alex dropped it purposely to the floor. "Then make yourself useful. A valet aids in his employer's grooming, you know. The wrinkles in that jacket will be the devil to steam out." He placed his heel into the iron bootjack and pulled steadily, watching his cousin. "Though I daresay if you endeavor to become helpful now, 'twill be the first sign I've seen of it yet."

"Aye, and I wouldna want to shock ye into an early grave." Fox-red eyebrows joggled up and down playfully. "Admit it, cousin. Ye're but angry because I got too close to the truth. Come, now. Confession is good for the soul."

Confession. If only he *could* confide in him—it would feel good to know he wasn't alone. He'd been alone far too much in this godforsaken city. And he could use his cousin's canny mind to aid his strategy. Even as a child when his family visited Carlton, Rorick had always prevailed during games of Seek and Find or King of the Wood. Always. Even when the others, with Alex in the lead, banded together to teach the young Scot a lesson when Rorick's attitude became too much to bear.

Mon Dieu . . . how he yearned for the simple pleasures of years long gone. For innocence lost.

Alex shrugged away the useless thoughts and turned his

back on his cousin. " 'Twould not be seemly to carry tales of the lady's . . . charms," he replied. "Nor her eagerness. I hardly think she would feel thankful for the interest."

Chuckling, Rorick stood up with yawn and a rib-cracking stretch. "True. But ye know I willna tell a soul." He paused and pinned Alex with a baleful stare. "If Bess found out, she'd have yer hide."

Bess. He'd hardly thought of her in days.

Alex sat on the edge of the bed with a sigh, wishing his cousin would leave so he could sink back into the soft mattress and yield to the needs of his body. "Did she like the gift? Whatever it was you purchased."

"Ye bought yer mistress an incredibly expensive pendant. And she appreciated it verra much, if the way she thanked me was any indication."

Alex gave him a tired smile. "If you are trying to get a rise from me, Rorick, I fear you've come at the wrong time."

"Ah. Then ye doona care that she kissed me full on the lips."

He should care. Any decent man would. Scowling at the sudden surge of guilt that filled him, Alex shook his head. "Mayhap you could oblige me in taking her off my hands, if you fancy her. But watch your step, cousin. Bess is like a summer storm. Sometimes she's warm and sweet and desperately seductive. Others, she's wild and sudden and utterly merciless."

Rorick cocked his head, a question in his eyes. "Ye sound as though ye're through with her."

"Aye."

His cousin nodded matter-of-factly. "I doona think she is done with you. Ha' ye thought of that?"

Alex grimaced. "I know. I need to tell her myself." He paused, considering this, then grimaced again, shaking his head. "I had hoped the gift would appease her."

"No' likely." Rorick walked to the door. He paused with his hand on the knob, then turned back with a half-cocked grin. "Doona trouble yerself, m'lord cousin. 'Tis no' the first time a man has thrown his mistress over for another."

Alex watched him leave from his place on the high bed. For long minutes, he turned Rorick's parting words over and over in his mind.

Not the first time . . .

But Alex felt certain it was the first time it had happened to Bess. For all practical purposes, Baroness Elizabeth Rowan had always been the one to do the leaving. Until now.

Alex groaned at the prospect of being first.

Regret spurred him to move. Stripping the last of his clothing from his body, he stretched back against the soft, woven coverlet and closed his eyes, hoping to forget for a time.

Yet, weary as he was, sleep eluded him. Images spun through his mind with the power of a cyclone on the open sea, sucking his consciousness along behind on a wild ride behind his closed eyes. The queen. Tori. The Mohocks. His obligation to his mother. Around and around they danced, taunting him to take action.

The urge to confront the Emperor and force the issue with the Mohocks burned in him, a fire made all the hotter by his feelings for Tori. He wanted nothing more than to spirit her away to safety, to take her with him and his mother to the stately manor that he loved so well. It appeared in his thoughts as it would in early summer, sweeping wings of golden brick and mullioned windows graced by tall trees green with burgeoning leaves, while all around cornflowers waved in a fresh breeze. Carlton Manor, his father's pride and joy. True, the house held painful memories of his father's death. But perhaps it was time to put them to rest. To get on with life.

Yet how could he, when the Rawlings name and his father's memory lay in the balance if he failed the queen? And if the Mohocks discovered the truth about him . . .

Death did not appeal to him. And he felt certain the queen would agree, most strenuously.

But what was he to do about Tori?

Nothing. You will do nothing. Her concerns are beyond your control.

The whispers of conscience arose in his mind, soft and insistent. Though a part of him recognized the chime of truth in the charge, still another part of him wanted her. He wanted, nay, *needed* to know more about her. Why she dressed *en masque.* Why she went out alone at midnight, dressed as a man. And yet he sensed that knowing the answers to these questions wouldn't quench his interest.

She is no concern of yours.

Alex scowled behind his arm. *Nay. No concern.* She as much as told him that herself. And as beautiful as she was, as bewitching as her kisses were, he had no right to become involved with her. He already had one mistress. He did not need another to distract him from what was, by necessity, his main purpose—spying on the Mohocks. The best thing he could do for Tori was not to drag her into the mess.

If she kept herself out of it.

Alex groaned and rolled over, dragging the heavy coverlet with him, and wondering why he should feel so uneasy.

After five hours abed, Alex could pretend no longer. Cursing aloud, he flipped the covers back and swung his legs over the edge of the bed. His head ached. His eyes felt as though burrs lay wedged beneath the lids. Grimacing, he pressed his fingertips to the inner corners of his eyes and massaged them.

No sleep. None.

Forcing his eyes to open, Alex let his gaze fall upon the tapestry bellpull. Alex reached for the robe that lay across the foot of the bed. Gathering it around his bare body, he stood and reached for the pull.

After five minutes and no response, Alex pulled again. After enduring another five-minute wait, Alex stalked to the door. Swinging it wide, he leaned his head and shoulders out into the hall.

The corridor stood empty. But not silent. Besides the comfortable, familiar sounds of the household staff performing their daily routine, he also heard voices. One man. One woman. Arguing.

Rorick . . . and Bess?

Alex squeezed his eyes shut as resignation rolled through him unchecked. Could his day get any worse? Somehow that didn't seem likely.

The voices were getting closer.

"Bloody hell," Alex mumbled. Without a moment's delay, he closed the door quietly but firmly, wondering what Rorick thought he was doing. He leaned an ear against the door, straining to hear.

Rorick's voice came, muffled but audible. "Baroness, ye canna barge into his lordship's chambers! 'Tis unheard of—he isna even awake as yet!"

Closer still, accompanied by the rapid clicks of her high heels, came Bess's more strident tones. "Barge? I am here to surprise him, Mr. McDowell," she claimed.

"Madam, he willna like it, ye comin' unannounced—"

"Are you hiding something for him, Mr. McDowell? Or perhaps someone?" She laughed. "What a loyal . . . servant?"

She placed an emphasis on the last word that made it an unmistakable slur. Rorick's response came too low to discern.

They had stopped in the hall, but their obvious proximity spurred Alex into action. His dressing gown would provide scant protection, he thought, knowing Bess's overt attentions. Alex scanned the room. His gaze paused upon his breeches, lying crumpled at the foot of his bed. He seized them and thrust first one leg in, then the other.

"Alex?" The doorknob rattled.

Thank God he'd thought to turn the key. Alex yanked his breeches up over his thighs, cursing when they tangled in the tails of his robe.

"Alex? Open the door. 'Tis I, Bess!"

Her knuckles rapped sharply against the oak. Grimacing, Alex hopped up and down, twisting and straining, until he had freed the robe from his breeches. With a sigh of relief, he fastened the laces.

"Alex, if you do not open this door, I swear I shall—"

Rorick's deep bass interrupted. "Baroness, if ye'd but let me announce ye properly. 'Tis early, and 'tis certain I am that his lordship is indisposed."

"Oh, do begone!" Alex heard her hissed command. "I'll not move even an inch until I see Lord Carlton. In the flesh."

Resignation bit into him. He had no choice. Not one. *Mon Dieu,* he was not safe even in his own home.

Straightening his robe, Alex tightened the satin ties, then squared his shoulders. The knob felt as smooth and cold as ice beneath his fingers. Clenching his teeth, Alex turned the key and swung the door inward in one abrupt movement.

As one, Bess and Rorick turned to stare at him, mouths agape. Bess recovered first. A wide smile sharpened her exotic features. "Aha! You *are* here," she said brightly.

Alex scowled, in no mood to indulge her. "Well? What is it?"

The smile slid away, to be replaced by a pretty pout. She sidled toward him. "Shame on you, Alex. Is that any way to greet a close friend?" She shook her head. "Really, from the reception around here, I might question your eagerness to see me." She watched him closely.

Alex exhanged a glance with Rorick. " 'Tis fine, Rorick. You may go back to your duties."

His Scots cousin raised an incredulous brow, then shrugged. "As ye will, yer lordship."

Alex waited until Rorick had disappeared around the

corner before he turned his attention back to the small woman at his side. He frowned down at her. "Was there something you wanted, Bess, that could not wait?"

The pout gracing her lush lips deepened. She dropped her hand away from him. "Do I need a reason to see you, Alex?"

Her question charged his uneasiness. It was as if she sensed his lack of interest, saw through every lie. Alex dropped his gaze, finding new interest in the pattern of the wool carpet. "Nay. Nay, of course not, Bess." Bloody hell, he sounded so . . . uncertain. He cleared his throat and tried again. " 'Twas only that I didn't sleep at all well. I'm not really in the mood to see anyone."

A satisfied smile curved her lips. "Well, as long as that is the only reason. Really, though, Alex, you might have answered."

Alex gave her a swift, nodding bow. "I stand chastised."

Long-lashed cat eyes boldly swept from his face to his bare toes, then back again. "Now that that's settled, will you let me in, my lord rogue?"

Alex groaned inwardly as his last hopes for an easy escape drifted away. He cleared his throat. "Bess, you know that is hardly proper. The servants—"

"When have we ever worried about servants?" She took a purposeful step toward him.

"And my mother," Alex emphasized, redoubling his efforts. " 'Tis her wont to visit with me toward the noon hour." The lie came easily to his lips.

Not to be deterred, Bess ducked under his arm and swept into his room. She turned to him, her green eyes glittering. "Oh, how nice. I've always wanted to meet your mother."

"Bess—"

The warning tone of his voice would have cowed most women. Bess only tossed her head in a manner that made her auburn curls bounce. She drifted toward the disheveled bed, a mischievous look in her eye. "Come in, Alex, and close the door. Or do you wish for your mother to see more than she bargained for?''

Alex cocked a brow at her, feeling dislike for her build within him. To think had he once sought her out daily. He must have been blind. ''Meaning?'' he asked coldly.

She slowly presented him the feminine curve of her back. As he watched, she reached behind her. Her fingers toyed with the laces of her gown. '' 'Twould be quite a shock for someone of her delicate nature to witness her son with his mistress. I could make it difficult for you, you know.''

The imminent arrival of his mother was just a pretense, but Alex decided to play along for the time being. A voice in him urged him to have it out with Bess, to tell her the truth. He knew he should. But by damn, no matter how much he disliked her now, even more abhorrent was the idea of purposely hurting her. He needed time to think of a way to ease her disappointment. Yes, he had tired of her, but he did not wish her ill.

He entered the room and closed the door, turning to her. ''Does that satisfy you?''

''It might if you came a little closer.'' When he did not, she moved toward him, the gentle sway of her hips an open invitation. ''Shall I come to you, then?''

And Alex let her, feeling the betrayer all the while. He had no understanding with Tori at all. But as Bess reached for the velvet lapels of his robe, as she pulled him down to her, all he could think of was his Lady Mystery.

Bess stretched up on tiptoe and tilted her mouth for his taking. When he made no move toward her, she surged upward, watching him all the while. She pressed sultry kisses along the flesh of his lower lip, nipping, biting, brazenly offering herself to him. Alex closed his eyes against the question in her gaze and waited for a surge of interest, waiting. . . .

But none came. Instead he remembered the way Tori had felt last night, encased in thin man's breeches, soft and warm and seductive against his thighs. He remembered the scent of exotic flowers and cloves that always clung to her, sharp and fresh. He remembered the sweet taste of her as even in her naivete she responded to his kiss. But most of all he remembered the fierce protectiveness she'd displayed toward her young rogue of a brother, a sense of deep caring and heart that he found most noble.

And he wanted her to feel that way for him. That way and more.

Bess's kiss became all the more cloying. Unable to bear it any longer, Alex closed his hands around her shoulders and pushed her away.

Her eyes flared wide. "Alex? What is it?"

Alex took a step backward. *Tell her,* the voice in his head insisted. He took a deep, steadying breath. "Bess, I—" He broke off again, uncertain how to go on.

She folded her hands against her skirt as she stood apart from him, as prim as a maiden untried. A small, knowing smile curved her lips. "Can you not say it? Oh, Alex . . ." With a breathless sigh, Bess launched herself at him, wrapping her arms in a stranglehold about his neck. She laughed and pressed boisterous kisses to his mouth, his face, his neck, his chest. "I have waited so long for this. If words fail you, I vow I can wait another day. But please do not make me wait for much longer!"

The question *For what?* hovered on the tip of his tongue, dangerously close to spilling free. Suddenly the full import of her declaration crashed over his head with all the power of a falling brick. He stared at her. "What do you mean?"

Bubbling over with laughter, Bess hugged him harder, bouncing with her excitement. The arms around his neck felt like a noose. "Do not pretend with me, love. I know you too well." She smiled, looking more vulnerable than he could ever remember. "I can hardly believe this is happening, at long last."

"Bess—" Reaching behind his neck, Alex tugged at her

hands until she loosened her hold and allowed him to draw them down. He held them against his chest to soften the blow. "Bess. I'm sorry . . . this is a mistake."

Her brow furrowed into a frown, and she shook her head. "Nay. You are only afraid. But I am willing to wait, love, until you are ready."

"Afraid? Aye." Alex touched her cheek, willing her to understand. "Of hurting you."

A fleeting glimpse of some unknown emotion appeared in the depths of her eyes. Bess stepped back, quickly, warily. "Hurt me? I told you, I'm willing to wait for you."

"And if 'tis not meant to be?" *Tell her! Now, before 'tis too late.*

Bess stopped short, watching him. "Is there something you're not saying, Alex?"

Before he could say anything, Rorick burst through the door without even a knock for advance warning. "Yer mother is coming," he blurted.

Alex frowned at his cousin, feeling dull-witted and confused. "My . . . mother?"

Rorick nodded. "She told Mary, the chambermaid, of her intentions but moments ago." He jerked a thumb at Bess. "What dae ye want me to do with her? Yer mum canna find her here."

"You needn't refer to me with such indifference, Mr. McDowell," Bess said through clenched teeth. One auburn brow had risen to lofty heights. "Think you that I am in some way blemished? That I'm not fit to greet your employer's mother?"

"Nay, madam," Rorick drawled as he crossed his arms in a stoic stance. His Scots brogue broadened, as it always did with the rise of his ire. "I think ye're perfectly fit to greet Lady Carlton—in the withdrawing room. But in m'lord's bedchamber . . . well, that is another story altogether."

Bess opened her mouth, a reply ready on her lips, but Alex stepped in. "What Rorick means," he inserted smoothly, "is that Mother has been possessed of a delicate nature of late, and finding you here would be a shock she can ill afford."

Rorick glanced at his watch and shifted his weight. "We must hurry, m'lord," he urged. " 'Twill be only moments. . . ."

Bess's eyes narrowed as she gazed back and forth between the two men. "I don't believe you."

But Alex heard the hesitation in her voice. "Please, Bess?"

She tilted her head to one side and peered at him. After only seconds, she sighed. "Very well. But promise you'll come to me," she insisted. "I said I would wait for you, but I don't expect to languish alone forever."

Alex gave her a lazy smile, trying not to count the precious seconds that filtered away like sand through his fingers. "Of course. A day or two—"

"Tomorrow."

Alex nodded, willing to do anything if it meant getting her out before his mother arrived. "Tomorrow it shall be."

Bess lifted her chin high as Rorick offered her his arm, instead grasping her skirts and sweeping imperiously past him. She paused at the door. "Do not disappoint me this time, Alex."

She left the room without another word, leaving Rorick to follow on her heels like a nipping puppy.

As soon as she was gone, Alex moved into action, wondering what could have gotten into his mother. She never visited him in his chambers, preferring instead to summon him to hers. Of all mornings to alter her habits, why today?

His shirt lay on the floor. He stripped the robe from his body and threw it across the bed, then grabbed the shirt. Raising his arms, he yanked it over his head. The seams of the black linen complained, but held fast with nary a tear.

A glance in the mirror displayed exactly what he'd anticipated. Red-rimmed eyes, dark shadows cushioning them. Hair hanging limp against his shoulders, fuzzed from sleep. A thickly whiskered jaw. Alex couldn't remember when his mother had last seem him in such a state of dishabille. Hoping to work some magic before she arrived, he pulled loose the ribbon that had secured his hair the night before and began to work a comb through the knots, all the while cursing the inheritance of his father's wavy locks.

Without warning, the door behind him swung inward. Alex schooled the sleepless night from his face and turned, ready to face his mother's inquisition.

Chapter Eight

Rorick stood in the doorway, his hands gripping the door frame on each side, his legs propped as wide as those of a sailor on a rolling deck. He grinned at Alex, one brow cocked mischievously. "Well, ye might thank me."

The smug humor in his tone brought instant comprehension. As the knowledge merged with relief in his head, Alex dropped the comb on the cherry chest of drawers. "*Maman* is not coming, is she?"

Rorick ducked into the room and closed the door behind him. "Now, ye know yer mum doesna often emerge from her quarters. 'Twas meant to be a hint, ye lughea."

Alex grimaced. If he weren't so fog-brained, he might have seen through his cousin's ruse. Still, Rorick's unabashed smugness grated on his nerves. "Bess was quite put out with you," he said tersely. "I could have handled her without your help."

Rorick snorted and leaned back against the door. "Precious little proof o' that did I witness. If ye wish, I could bring the lovely baroness back, just sae ye can prove yer manhood. She couldna be far.'' Seeing Alex's face, he relented. ''Och, ease up, mon. I wasna serious.''

Now that the conflict was behind him, at least at present, Alex felt almost relaxed, but also more than a trifle guilty. He turned away, staring into the waning coals in the hearth. ''I didn't tell her, Rorick. I didn't find the opportunity.''

''Ye found a way out instead,'' Rorick commented with his customary talent at observation.

Alex felt no need to search his heart—the truth taunted him with accusations of cowardice. He nodded. ''Aye. That I did.''

He cast a gauging glance toward his younger cousin. Rorick was shaking his head. ''Best rethink that, cousin. The baroness doesna seem the kind of woman who forgives easily. Better to cut it off quickly.''

''I know. I know!'' Alex shoved his fingers back through his hair, ruining his efforts of moments before. ''I just don't want to hurt her. I want to be free of her, but crushing her has neither appeal nor purpose.''

''Ye have nae choice. 'Tis the way of a woman. Nae matter yer intentions, she canna be anything but hurt.''

Something about his cousin's tone . . . Alex peered at him. ''You seem to know much about the baroness.''

A faint smile touched the young Scotsman's mouth. ''She is a woman,'' he replied loftily, as though that were explanation enough. He pushed off from the door. Coming to a halt by the hearth, he studied the coals that had absorbed Alex's attention moments ago.

''Ah. A woman. Of course. And just this morning, did you not tell me Bess had kissed you as thanks for my gift?''

An uncustomary blush touched the crests of Rorick's cheeks, but he betrayed no further unease. ''That's right.''

''Moments ago she behaved quite differently. Which is it, Rorick? Was it truth? Or only one of your games at besting your English cousin?''

The questions seemed to come from deep within him, as though he'd been pondering the situation for some time. Though perhaps he had. Rorick had been with him for two years, and still Alex didn't know the reason he had left his family in Scotland.

Nor much else about him, for that matter. The man had always possessed a great economy of words when faced with questions concerning his past.

Rorick shrugged, indifference making the gesture a dismissal. "She is but peevish that I wouldna rally to her invitation."

"If you are certain that is all . . ." Alex watched him closely. "Peevish. I see. I had no idea you and she were so close."

Rorick took a poker and stabbed it into the coals, stirring them energetically. "She is your mistress, Alex, not mine," he snapped. "I have nae need to be tied to your bloody England any further than I already am."

Alex frowned at the claim. "Tied? To England? What an odd choice of words, Rorick. If you like England so little, why do you not go back home? Your mother must miss you greatly. Your father. Why do you stay here, playing at being a valet, when all you love is elsewhere?"

Rorick thrust himself to his feet, still grasping the poker in his hand. He opened his mouth to speak. Then, as though he'd thought better of it, he clamped his lips together. After several moments, the tension in his face eased. "What ken ye of what I love? What ken ye of me at all?"

Alex sat on the high edge of the bed, wondering what had just passed through his cousin's thoughts. Such despair in his voice. Such resentment. "I know you're my cousin by blood. And I've counted you my best friend since we were children."

Rorick's shoulders slumped, and he exhaled deeply. "Well said, cousin. If ye doona know, that is why I came here."

They stared at each other for several moments, measuring each other. Then Rorick started, as if he'd just thought of something. "Och, I almost forgot." He shoved his hand in his coat pocket. "I did have another reason for aiding ye with the baroness's hasty departure."

Alex let the change of subject pass by unchallenged, now certain that his cousin would confide in him in time. "Aye?"

Rorick withdrew a many-times-folded piece of paper from his pocket and extended it forth in his palm. "This was left on our doorstep just moments ago while Baroness Rowan was making her impassioned plea for yer heart," he replied, the corner of his mouth twitching with good humor once more.

"Left on the step?" Alex took the scrap from him. It felt heavy, weighted from within. "Who delivered it?"

"That I doona know. Cavandish said there was a clamoring at the door, then naught but this. He thought ye should know."

Curiosity bested him. Alex began to unfold the small square of dirt-smudged vellum. The inner folds showed nothing as it opened—no handwriting, no message. But nestled at its center was a single, flat stone with a stylized *M* painted on each side.

Alex froze, scarcely breathing. The Mohock summons.

Rorick leaned close to view the contents. Immediately a deep frown furrowed his brow. "A stone."

Alex swallowed. "Aye."

"And the note?"

Alex closed his hand over the markings on the stone, but held up the wrinkled piece of paper in his free hand. "No markings. No message."

Rorick's furrowed frown deepened. He shook his head slowly. "What do ye think it means?"

For one tense moment, Alex interpreted the bemusement in Rorick's voice to be suspicion. Realizing that the summons had not been correctly interpreted, he breathed easier and gave an indifferent shrug. "My guess is, 'tis but a prank. It means nothing." He tossed the paper on a nearby table, but kept the stone hidden away.

"Or perhaps 'tis a signal," Rorick commented, peering at him askance. At Alex's sharp look, he gave a wicked grin. "That's it! 'Tis a sign from yer mystery wench that she wants to meet ye. The 'W' is for Wynter. That's it! But why hide it from me, yer own cousin?"

"A signal." Alex tried to laugh, but it came out as a rasping cough. "Don't be foolish, cousin. Secret signals? Next you'll be attributing other nocturnal peculiarities to me as well."

"Like bedding two women and hiding it from both?" Rorick grinned even wider, strong teeth brilliantly white against a tawny beard. " 'Tis nae wonder ye've been a wee bit jumpy of late. 'Course, if 'twas a good Scots lass, ye wouldna have a need fer more than one to weary yer bones."

Alex grinned weakly. "Is that so?"

"Aye. A tryst with yer milk-and-water English maids canna come close ter comparing to a tumble in the heather with a Scottish lass. No e'en wi' the fair baroness."

Alex had no intention of confessing that it was Tori's kisses that held the power to make his knees quiver. That it was her touch of innocence that fired a storm of longing more compelling than any brought about by Bess's casual seductions. Nay, he'd not confess it. *Dieu,* he could hardly admit it to himself. Were he wise, he would banish the dangerous lady from his thoughts. Were he a cad, he would accept every nuance of pleasure she felt inclined to yield him, then pass her by with nary a thought.

But for better or worse, he'd never claimed to be wise, and despite rumors to the contrary, the epithet *cad* had never fit quite right.

He grimaced, realizing at that moment that his life had come to be ruled by the whims of three women, or so it seemed. One wanted him. One did not . . . or so she claimed. And one ruled his fealty through duty.

His actions taken in Anne's name must take precedence over all else. God knew, he wanted nothing more than to leave the queen's intrigues to her sworn guard. To court Tori and convince her to marry him and leave London for the more peacful life at Carlton Manor. But he also knew that were he to disobey Anne's wishes, his downfall would come as swiftly as the Duke of Marlborough's own descent from favor. How many years had Marlborough served the queen, only to be banished from polite society when the queen's fancies changed?

Nay, Anne held too much over his head. He would not let the queen's whims destroy his father's memory, nor would he allow the Rawlings name to fall into ruin. It was the only thing he could offer a wife, when his French blood might cast a shadow over his suitability. Unless he kept his promise to Anne, all hope for the future might well be surrendered. Disgrace would surround the Rawlings name. The courtiers would whisper that the downfall, after centuries of loyal service to the Crown, had come about at the hands of one man—a single generation tainted by French blood.

The stone burned like icy fire against his palm. Alex clutched it, in anger, in frustration, in desperation. Aye, he would continue to do Anne's bidding. He would find her traitors. And when it was done, he would return to Carlton, his ancestral home, with a wife who could love him despite his blood.

And never would he set foot in London again.

With a contented sigh, Tori snuggled deep into the goose-down pillows and drew the woolen coverlet over her. Closing her eyes, she smiled to herself. Outside, a wicked wind whispered and moaned. The first drops of rain pinged against the windowpanes. But here she remained, cozy in her bed. For the first time in weeks, she would have a full night's rest, devoid of worry.

Peace, blessed peace.

Charles had stayed home for the evening.

Oh, not by choice. But having arrived home after the noon hour, falling-down drunk, and having spent the remainder of the afternoon raiding Maryleborn's stores of libations, Charles could hardly complain. He'd long since fallen into a stupor—it had taken Smythe and two footmen just to carry him up to his chamber. Charles was none the wiser.

Tori giggled to herself and stretched her arms over her head in delicious abandon. Charles and his complaints could wait until morning . . . when they would be met with her disapproval. Until then she would enjoy the blissful respite, and perhaps dream of a way to help him give up the hedonistic lifestyle he seemed so determined to maintain.

Still smiling, she rolled to her side, punched the goose-down pillow into an acceptable thickness, and rearranged the covers about her. She allowed her eyes to drift closed and, with a satisfied sigh, waited for sleep to claim her.

Seconds ticked by.

Minutes.

Long minutes.

Tori squirmed beneath the covers and screwed her eyes tight. Fingers of light escaped the hearth and pried at her eyelids from the cracks between the velvet bed hangings. With a disgruntled sigh, she kicked back the covers and yanked at the hangings. Lying down once more, she determinedly closed her eyes.

Minutes ticked past.

Long minutes.

Hours . . . or so it seemed.

Tori turned her face into the pillow and drew the covers over her head. She fidgeted, trying to get comfortable. She rearranged the coverlet for what seemed the tenth time.

And she froze when, minutes later, a crash of splintering

glass and a long, full-throated scream sliced through the stillness of the night.

Terror slithered along the length of Tori's spine. Her eyes flared open, wide. Another shriek came from belowstairs, seconds after the first. It served to pierce through the immobility that gripped her. Throwing back the heavy covers, Tori dropped to the floor and raced for the door.

Darkness gripped the halls, but she knew the house as she knew her own mind. She ran down the stairs with the surefooted grace of a cat at ease in the night. Sobs drifted up from the front of the house. From elsewhere came the sounds of opening doors, indications that the scream had roused more than just Tori.

In the foyer, she could just make out the open doors that led to the library. She hurried to them. Incoherent ramblings from within assured her she had located the right room. She peered in.

Pale moonlight shimmered through the tall, vaulted windows of the library. The patter of rain was louder here, almost drowning out the snapping sound of wet draperies striking the window frame. The reason became readily apparent as the moonlight revealed a gaping hole in the largest window. It also revealed a shape on the floor. Tori quickly recognized her young chambermaid, Phoebe, crouched there with her hands grasped about her knees.

"Phoebe? Phoebe, what on earth are you doing here? What happened?"

The girl sobbed even louder and began to rock. Tori moved beside her and touched her shoulder. Unlike Tori, Phoebe seemed to be fully garbed, her hair still dressed in the braided roll she wore every day.

"Phoebe, what happened?" Tori repeated. When she received no answer, Tori knelt beside her and took her by the shoulders. "Why did you scream? Please tell me."

Phoebe stared blankly up at her. Tears streamed from her eyes. Her shoulders shook beneath Tori's touch. "The window is broken, Phoebe,'' Tori said gently. ''Do you know why?''

The girl nodded, shivering violently. The wind that pushed at the draperies had taken hold with a bitter cold that nipped at Tori's bare feet.

''Blast, 'tis as cold as a barn in here,'' Tori muttered. ''Stay here while I stoke the fire.''

Tori stood up. The motion roused the girl enough to speak. ''Be careful, miss, not t' step on the glass,'' she quavered.

Glass. Of course. Tori peered hard at the floor, but could see nothing. Cautiously she inched her bare feet toward the hearth, relieved when she reached it without encountering any glass. A full coal basket rested to one side. Within seconds she had a small fire blazing.

The fire provided enough light that she could see the glass shards littering the carpet and a cluster of upholstered chairs placed before the windows. Brocade draperies billowed wildly away from the shattered panes and splintered wood as the wind whined through the gaping hole.

Tori turned back to the girl. Phoebe's face looked as pale as the moon. ''What the devil—''

''Aye! Aye!'' Phoebe recovered her voice full measure. She leaped to her feet. '' 'Twas the devil, miss! I saw 'im! I *saw* 'im!''

Sensing that the girl was on the verge of fleeing, Tori held up a hand. ''Hold, Phoebe. I would speak with you.''

''But miss!'' Indecision furrowed the girl's brow. Tears flowed freely from her pale eyes. ''What if the dark'un returns?''

''Dark one? Don't be ridiculous,'' Tori scoffed, having no patience for the girl's tendency toward ''visions.'' She was about to continue when an odd shape caught her eye from its resting place beside a glass-shrouded chair. *Now what?*

She crossed the room and bent at the waist to pick it

up. The weight of it surprised her—almost as much as the feel of what it came wrapped in.

" 'Tis a brick," Tori murmured, mostly to herself. "Wrapped in a cloth of some sort."

She turned it over in her hands. Something dropped to the floor from within the folds of silk. Glancing at the floor, Tori saw several gold coins winking up at her. The sight of them nestled against the expensive carpet added to her bemusement. *What on earth?*

Phoebe's hands scrubbed up and down at her arms as she stared at the gold. Her eyes looked wild. " 'Tis a gift from the devil. Lord Lucifer! Touch it not, miss, I beg ye."

"Oh, posh. Do not go on so, Phoebe," Tori admonished. She bent at the waist to gather the coins, then picked her way back through the field of glass. "You speak nonsense."

Phoebe shook her head. "Nay! I saw him, miss. I did." Her eyes fixed upon the brick as Tori approached. She backed steadily away. "I swear it."

"Miss Victoria?" Smythe's voice broke in from the doorway. "Are you quite all right?"

The thin-nosed butler peered warily around the door frame, his sleeping cap askew, a coat half-buttoned over a shin-length nightshirt. Tori nodded at him, her mouth set. "Aye, I am. But I fear our window is a bit worse for the wear."

Phoebe pushed forward eagerly. " 'Twas the devil himself, Mr. Smythe. I saw 'im. Rode up on 'is black stallion, bold as brass, 'e did!" Her eyes widened, then narrowed in turn as she remembered. "Looked straight through me with 'is wild, red eyes. Red like blood, they was. Then he laughed—horrible wicked!—and tossed a thunderbolt through the window. The devil! I swear 'twas him."

From the hall came a collective gasp from the servants who had gathered. Phoebe gave a short nod in affirmation of her theory.

Tori made a face and hefted the brick. *Devil, indeed.*

The weight of the brick proved the claim false. 'Twas naught more than miscreants bent on destruction.

She exchanged a look with the now relaxed butler. "It seems Phoebe has had a bit of a shock, Smythe. She was here when the window was broken."

"Here?" Smythe's voice rose in surprise. He looked at the young maidservant closely. "In this room?"

The girl stopped posturing for the others and seemed to shrink within herself. Her mouth worked repeatedly, but not a sound came out.

Tori gazed at the girl more closely. She frowned as she realized that Phoebe seemed to be the only person in the entire impromptu gathering who happened to be dressed. "Aye. She was here. She screamed when this came crashing through the window, I do believe." She hefted the brick with a wry smile. "The thunderbolt."

Smythe turned to Phoebe. "What were you doing here at such an hour, when you should have been abed?"

The girl's gaze darted back and forth between Tori and the butler. "Nothing. I could not sleep—I—" All of a sudden, she burst into tears and covered her face with her hands. "Oh, I'm so afeared I can't think!"

Though she suspected the girl meant the weepy scene to distract attention from her purpose, Tori saw no need to force the issue. She'd seen the way Phoebe had been looking at one of the male servants—likely this incident had interrupted what was meant to be a midnight rendezvous. She found some sympathy for the girl. "It does not signify, Smythe. Phoebe isn't at fault here. The window was obviously broken from the outside, not from within. Have Mrs. Pertwee take her to bed now."

"Aye, miss," Smythe agreed. "As you wish."

There was nothing more she could do. Eager to return to her chambers and the peace that had been disturbed, Tori left the securing of the room to the servants and carried the oddities to her room.

But once she was back in her bed, sleep seemed an

impossibility. She couldn't stop thinking, couldn't stop the questions circling her brain. Huddled beneath the covers, she stared at the silk-wrapped brick where it sat on a table by the door, the stack of coins a bewildering companion.

In the dimly lit room, the crimson scarf appeared almost black. What was its purpose? Had the miscreant thought it would muffle the crash of the brick, allowing him time to make his escape with less risk of being seen? And if so, why had he used such an expensive scarf? So impractical. So casual.

And why, in the name of God, had he then paid for the pleasure?

The brick called to her, dared her to draw near. Without understanding why, Tori found herself leaving her bed and walking over to the table. Cool air caressed her bare ankles, but she did not stop. She reached out a hand to touch the scarf. The ravaged silk felt smooth, pleasing beneath her fingertips. The ribbon that once secured the silk in place had been cut during the crash, loosening a portion of the fabric and exposing the rough, crater-pocked surface of the brick itself. She brushed her fingers over the brick. Touching it only served to heighten her curiosity.

Why wrap it in silk?

A timid knock sounded on the door, inches away from her. Tori felt her stomach leap, then drop to the vicinity of her toes. Swallowing to free the fear lodged in her throat, Tori called, "Who is there?"

" 'Tis me, miss. Phoebe." The maid's voice was little more than a whisper.

Phoebe. More than a trifle relieved, Tori opened the door. "Yes, Phoebe? Is aught amiss?"

The girl hovered timidly in the hall. She swallowed visibly. "Might I speak wit' ye, miss?" She dashed a gaze this way and that up each end of the dark hall.

The girl's preoccupation was obvious. Tori pulled the door open wider and stood aside. "Of course, please come in."

As Phoebe entered the room, Tori closed the door quietly behind her. She led the way to the dressing table and gestured for the young maidservant to sit upon the low, upholstered bench. Phoebe sank to the bench and sat there, trembling. As Tori lit several candles, she couldn't help but notice the nervous way the girl had of tucking her skirt about her knees.

Tori smiled, hoping to set her at ease. "Now, tell me, Phoebe. What is the matter?"

Phoebe bit her lip and cast her eyes down. Her hands worked together in her lap. "I don't . . . perhaps I ought not to 'ave come. . . ."

"You have come this far," Tori prodded gently. "Surely you have something on your mind. You need not fear me."

The girl nodded, miserably and swallowed hard. " 'M afraid ye'll be angry with me. But I could not tell ye afore—not with the others about." Phoebe's face reddened. She took a deep breath, then reached into her skirt pocket. She withdrew something white and held it out before her.

Tori looked down. A piece of paper trembled in the girl's palm, unsealed but folded in thirds.

" 'T must 'ave fell out of the wrap, miss. My hand touched it when ye went to went to stoke the fire."

A paper. Wrapped within the silk. Tori's stunned mind worked to grasp the meaning. "What is it?"

Surprise shone in Phoebe's pale eyes. "Why, 'tis a letter of some sort. I thought ye should 'ave it."

She moved forward, offering the message before her. Bemused and troubled, Tori took it. Limp with the damp of rain, the paper felt cool against her palm. Her first urge was to open it immediately. Uncertainty stopped her. Never in her life had she encountered something so out of place. But then, her life had once seemed rather normal . . . until Charles's recent behavior knocked her staid existence to pieces.

"Well? Do ye not wish to look at it, miss?"

Tori cleared her throat. "I suppose I should, aye?"

She took a deep breath to steady herself, then carefully, gently peeled apart the damp folds. Bold, black script leaped out from the pages. Her gaze darted to the signature at the bottom before reading the few sentences.

A gasp caught in her throat. She blinked, but the signature slashing the page did not change.

Alexandre Rawlings.

The eminent Earl of Carlton.

"What is it, m'lady?" Phoebe asked, sounding frightened but excited. "What does the devil's note say?"

Tori clutched the note to her bosom and frowned at her. "Did you not read it?"

Phoebe shook her head. "I cannot, miss. None ter teach me." The girl's pale eyes glittered with curiosity. "Is it a threat or the like? Is it vulgar and vile?"

Tori felt her lips twitch, but managed to smother the smile that threatened. Somehow she didn't think Phoebe was trying to be amusing. "Oh, aye, just so. But it can wait until morning." Or at least until you leave the room, Tori amended.

"Oh." Wistfulness drew Phoebe's wide lips down at the corners. "Well, I thought ye should 'ave it."

"And I do thank you," Tori reassured her.

As the young chambermaid drifted toward the door, a thought occurred to Tori. "Phoebe? I would prefer that you do not mention this to anyone. The less who know, the easier it shall be to capture the man."

"Nae man, miss," Phoebe said, poking her fingers toward her eyes in the ancient way of warding off evil. "The devil 'imself, ye cannot forget!"

The girl's vision again. How she wished she could tell her that her devil was naught but a scalawag in the flesh! "A devil on a black charger," Tori repeated dryly.

"Aye! Wit' fire flashin' in 'is eyes, and 'is black cape blowin' in the wind!"

Tori shook her head, laughing in spite of herself. "Phoebe. 'Tis raining, and so it has been for an hour or more. His cape must have been a sodden mess. It could hardly blow in the wind!"

The girl flushed, but staunchly clung to her convictions. "Well, it *looked* like a cape. Mayhap 'twas the gates of Hades clanging behind 'im." Before Tori could oppose her once more, Phoebe placed her hand on the doorknob. "I've o'erstayed my welcome, so I'll be goin', miss. But do be careful, please. The devil and 'is minions like not to be trifled with."

When she had gone, Tori locked the door behind her and checked the window latches. Feeling somewhat safer with that accomplished, she wandered to the dressing table and lit a candle. She spread the note flat on the table. The pool of candlelight glared across the white paper, illuminating every word, every loop, every perfectly wrought curlicue.

Her breath quickened.

Faith, his signature was as wickedly bold as his kiss.

The notion flared through her thoughts unbeckoned, taking her by surprise. Tori waited for shock to ripple through her. Shock that he had dared to kiss her. Shock that the kiss had elicited such sweetness in her heart. Shock that he had dared to destroy her property. Shock that he'd dared to claim responsibility outright. Shock that he'd dared to expect forgiveness for the action.

But in its place a sense of excitement boldly touched her, a tingling admiration of his carefree spirit . . . and more.

How ridiculous.

Absurd!

Yanking her wayward thoughts back in line, Tori scanned the sparse lines of explanation, now smeared across the damp vellum.

My dear Tori,

Please forgive my inexcusable intrusion upon your

home. Would that it might have been different, but you may at least take heart in the knowledge that the wreckage has been in pursuit of an honorable cause. The gold should cover the cost of the damage.

Regards,
A. Rawlings

From the dainty table across the room, the gold coins winked in the dim light, a merciless taunt. Tori stared at them, a frown pulling upon her brow.

Had he shattered the window to punish her? As retribution for not surrendering to his seductions more freely? And what did he mean, 'twas done for an honorable cause? A man in his right mind could not possibly believe destruction to be honorable.

The man, or devil as Phoebe claimed, was mad. Quite possibly dangerous.

She should alert the proper authorities.

She should . . . yet she knew she would not.

Not yet.

Berating herself for a fool, Tori crossed the room and sat at her dressing table. Her image stared smugly back at her from the mirror. Knowingly.

She lowered her gaze, instead opening the slim drawer at the front of the table. Just within rested the gold watch Alex had impressed upon her that first night at the palace. She slid her hand into the drawer and lifted it out. Just the feel of it brought to mind the events of that night and his seeming concern for her.

Tori shook her head. His concern was naught more than an attempt to find her alone for a time, away from prying eyes. Not for her protection, as he'd purported, but for his own unscrupulous purposes.

In that instance, Charles's warning rang again in her ears, a tolling of logic and reason.

Carlton's reputation with the ladies is legend. . . .

She'd heard rumors. Who in London had not? But never

before had it affected her enough to take notice.

What bothered her more—his notorious reputation or his scandalous behavior—she could not say. Why it should matter, she fathomed even less.

The watch ticked a steady rhythm against her palm. Maddening. Relentless. Taunting. She closed her fingers around it, squeezed it, willed it to stop. But like the childish daydreams of love and honor that had always bedeviled her practical ways, it continued on.

She couldn't stop thinking about the heat that had enveloped her when his lips touched hers.

Tori bit her lip and squeezed her eyes closed. *Blast! Blast, blast.*

Perhaps she could do nothing about foolish wishes, but she did have a choice in her dealings with the blackguard Earl of Carlton. At morningtide, she would pay a visit to Rawlings Hall. She would leave him to his watch, his womanizing, and his bloody roistering. And she would have no contact with the rake again.

Chapter Nine

The moment he'd heard the woman's shrill scream, Alex had wheeled his mount around and raced away from discovery. The last thing he needed was to be seen and recognized ere he could complete his mission. Two blocks away, the others joined him—men who had apparently been assigned to observe this latest test of loyalty. As one, they slipped through the night with only the clattering of hooves on cobblestones to drown out the sound of the woman's terrified shriek, still ringing in his ears.

By the gods, he hated this. What a night.

Within minutes they reached the fringes of St. James Park. Alex led the way through the gate in the Mall, slowing so as not to attract attention. But they met no one. Only the harsh blowing of the horses and the mournful call of a night bird broke the silence.

Beneath him, Alex felt his horse tremble and snort uneasily. Something, or someone, was nearby. He rubbed his hand in reassuring circles on the beast's neck and urged him along the path.

As they neared a large grove of trees, the man Alex knew only as Hawk let out a piercing, warbling whistle . . . once, twice. One by one, the entire Mohock band emerged with their horses from the shadows among the trees. Their black garb cloaked them well. Even now, Alex found it difficult to distinguish them until they stood, reins in hand, on the road before him.

A single man stepped forward. The rest of the band instantly drew back to allow him room, a respectful deference obvious in the gesture. Tall, burly, the man wore his cloak flipped back over his shoulders despite the chill, giving him a cavalier appearance that was almost congenial . . . until Alex looked into his face. At that moment, *congenial* was the last description he might have used.

Unlike the others, this man had chosen not to wear the silk mask that was the Mohock trademark. In a shaft of moonlight that wended its way through the tree branches, Alex could see clearly the scar tracing a crescent moon into the man's square forehead. A matching line slashed a hard jaw, marring a fashionably trimmed golden beard. Pale eyes stared at him, so intense and assessing that Alex felt certain the man knew both his identity and his true purpose.

The thought pricked the hairs at the nape of his neck.

"Well?" The man's voice sliced through the air as smoothly as a swordpoint through human flesh.

Hawk slid from his horse and stepped forward. With a frown and a meaningful jerk of his head, he indicated for Alex to do the same. "Emperor, this is—"

The man cut him off with the curt slash of one hand. "Don't be a fool. I know who he is. He's been with us before." His gaze flicked toward Alex. "Did he fulfill our little test?"

Hawk nodded. "Oh, aye. Aye." He nodded again. The nervous gesture conjured an image of a gobbling turkey in Alex's thoughts. "Right as rain, sir."

The Emperor turned to Alex. "Did you, now? And what test did you choose?"

Again Hawk answered before Alex could. "Broke a great window at the front of a grand house, sir. The Duke of Middleham's, I think."

A supercilious smile lifted one side of the burly man's mouth. His brows rose. "Oh, aye? How terrible. How barbaric." Tossing the reins to the nearest Mohock, the man folded his hands behind his back and began to pace before Alex. "Such a minor feat, young pup. I'm almost disappointed. I'd hoped for more from you. Still"—he gazed at Alex through narrowed eyes—"still, we did promise, did we not? And you have fulfilled your side of it, even though I had expected you might have chosen something more . . . lively, shall we say?"

Alex shrugged. " 'Twas among the choices quoted me by your man, Hawk. I but selected what I saw to be the simplest to accomplish."

"Ah, you do have a tongue. And a mind of your own, it seems. I was beginning to wonder." The man stopped pacing and squared his feet in a bold stance before Alex, fists on hips. "Now tell me, pup. Do you always choose what is easiest?"

Though he asked amiably enough, Alex could hear the challenge in the words. Another test. He squared his shoulders and stood taller. "Nay. Do you always question your men so bluntly?"

"Aye, I do . . . if it needs to be done. So you have spirit. That's good. That's very good. Can you be loyal?"

Alex knew he had to convince this man. "Can you ever be sure of any man's loyalty?"

The Emperor laughed, throwing his head back to expose a corded throat. "Well spoken, pup. You'll do. For now." Still grinning, he lifted his hand and snapped his fingers. Another man stepped forward to lay a heavy sword across his waiting hand. "Step forward, pup, and kneel before me."

The sight of that glistening length of steel sent a scurry of apprehension skittering down Alex's spine. Somewhere deep inside, Alex found the determination needed to force himself to move. He sank to his knees.

In the space of a few seconds, he'd absorbed the sensation of dampness and cold seeping through his breeches. A light breeze caught at the tree branches. The twittering sound drew a rasp along his nerve endings.

He heard a cold *swish* behind him and imagined the Emperor pulling the sword along his leather glove. He closed his eyes, concentrating on that sound, and wondered if it would be the final sound he ever heard.

The sword landed first on his left shoulder, then lifted and touched his right. A hand touched his head and removed his tricorne. Alex suppressed a shudder, waiting—for what, he knew not.

"Rise, pup."

Alex obeyed the command. His knees felt weak, but he stood tall and strong, refusing to show any fear. He lifted his gaze to find the rest of the Mohock band standing in a circle around him—like a flock of crows, he thought. He smothered the grin that threatened his equilibrium. *Aye, crows, ready to pick at my bones.*

The Emperor stretched out a hand. Alex could see the gold hairs peppering the thick fingers, a healing cut on the edge of the pinkie. A heavy ring in the shape of a goat's head with rubies for eyes. No pauper, this.

The man grasped the edge of Alex's mask, and with a surprisingly gentle tug slid the silk from his head. He stepped away and lifted the mask above his head. At the sign, each of the Mohocks followed his lead until the entire contingent faced Alex without their masks for the first time.

The Emperor turned to Alex. "These are your compatriots. Look at them. Remember them. 'Tis rare that you will see them thus."

The mask still raised above him, the Emperor turned so

that all might hear. "You've run with us the better part of a sennight, and tonight you become one of us. From this night forward, you will address us only by the names we've taken as Mohocks when we are together as such. You will choose your own now. I am the Emperor, your leader. You know Hawk. Bear . . ."

Rounding the circle, the Emperor named them all for Alex's benefit, pausing by each in turn. Alex studied each man closely, committing each face to memory. Some he knew by sight—Viscount Lynley, with his enormous feet and bearlike figure, who paraded himself as Fox; Justin St. Clair, young heir to the aging Earl of Huntington, with the trace of a scar at the corner of his mouth, was Troll; and the freckled visage of Sir John Abbingdon, who ran about as Crow, could not be disguised.

Such ridiculous names. And now he must choose one as well. *Sacrebleu.*

Once Alex had heard the introductions, the Emperor stepped back. "And how shall we call you? Pup?" He laughed raucously at his own joke. The others followed suit. "Or perhaps something so tame would not be to your liking. Come. Give us a name, pup."

Alex faced the cocksure leader without intimidation. The names Wolf and Ferret leaped to his mind, and just as quickly he discarded them. Too close to the truth.

Another image, this one more difficult to dismiss. An ominous presence. A predictor of doom. "I think perhaps Raven would suffice."

The Emperor's eyes glinted in the moonlight. He spun on his heel to eye the Mohock circle. "Behold, all of you . . . and witness the birth of"—his voice had risen with a dramatic flourish; now it dropped to a mere whisper—"Raven."

A volley of huzzahs arose in the still night air, and of a sudden Alex was surrounded and receiving congratulatory thumps on the back by all. He tried, but could not quell the burst of excitement that began in his belly and raced down his limbs at this evidence he'd been accepted into the fold. It wouldn't be long before they fully disclosed their practices to him. Their plans. Their allies. Soon this mission of Anne's would be complete, and no one, *no one,* would ever feel the need to question his loyalty again.

Not even Victoria Wynter.

Chapter Ten

Drinking had never been his forte. Drinking the rotgut served at the Hound's Breath might just be enough to kill him.

Alex groaned aloud as pain axed through his skull with increasing regularity. He'd been hungover before, but never like this. His head felt like something was yanking his brain out through an ever-narrowing gash in his skull, then stuffing it back in from the other side. 'Twas exceedingly unpleasant. Moving away from the hurt only made it worse.

All in the name of the queen.

Perhaps if he kept reminding himself of that, it would make the bloody headache worth it.

The night's events had passed with flawless ease. He was now Raven, a Mohock. After the ritual in the park, the Emperor had issued an invitation to return to the Hound's Breath for drinking, gaming, and celebrating, Mohock fashion. As the newest member, Alex hardly felt in a position to refuse. He had intended to stretch his libations throughout the evening and use the gathering to listen and learn what he could. What the devil had gone wrong?

Some spy he was proving himself to be.

Gritting his teeth against the pain, Alex braced his hands against the soft mattress and heaved himself to a sitting position. The room ducked and dove about him, but Alex ignored it and blinked blearily at the clock on the mantel.

Ten-forty. Surely not so late.

Though he wanted naught more than to collapse against the mattress again, to tunnel himself beneath the pillows and blankets and resume the more pleasing prospect of a dream involving the lovely Lady Victoria, Alex knew he must resist. It was his wont to lunch with his mother in her quarters. If he showed himself in his present condition, she'd think he'd taken leave of his senses, surely. Worse, she would require an explanation, something he could not give her. And she would worry.

He should send her back to Carlton Manor without him—she would be safer there, and happier. Yet he also knew she would not go alone. He would just have to finish this thing quickly.

Somehow he found the presence of mind to stand. On feet of lead, Alex shuffled to the pitcher and basin. Not a drop of water rested in the bottom. Muttering beneath his breath, Alex shambled to the bellpull beside the bed. Dragging his gaze away from the allure of the bed, he gave an irritable yank on the tapestry pull. When three minutes had passed with no response, he pulled on it again, twice, then once more for good measure. When yet another five minutes slipped by with no sign of Rorick, Alex heaved a long-suffering sigh and resolved himself to finding his missing valet himself. Again.

Bloody Scotsman. Alex drew a heavy robe on over his breeches from the night before. *Can he not even rouse himself long enough to bid a chambermaid draw me water?*

As he reached the bottom of the stairs, Alex nearly overlooked the door to the sitting room standing ajar . . . until a feminine voice brought his steps to a sudden halt. His heart thundered as he listened, hardly breathing, to a voice most recently heard in his dreams. Low in pitch but clear as a bell, it could not be mistaken.

Victoria Wynter?

Mon Dieu, *not now.*

Heedless of the pain that stabbed his head with each step, Alex skulked down the last steps until he could no longer see inside the sitting room, gaining comfort in the thought that if he could not see her, neither could she see him. He pictured in his mind his bedraggled hair, a day's growth of whiskers dark on his chin, and scuffed breeches peeking beneath the skirt of his robe. He grimaced. Not quite the image he wished to present to the loveliest woman he'd ever met. What in God's name was she doing here?

Curiosity gained the better of him. For a moment Alex forgot about seeking out a hiding place and edged along the foyer wall until he could peer through the crack along the door. His vantage point gave him a clear view of Tori and the room's second occupant. Alex frowned. *Rorick.*

He watched as Tori lifted her chin a notch in response to whatever Rorick had just told her. Her eyes sparkled with determination. "A delay is unacceptable to me, Mr. . . ."

"McDowell, milady," Rorick answered evenly. Only someone who knew him as well as Alex could discern the irreverence hidden within the seemingly polite response.

Tori acknowledged him with a graceful tilt of her head. "Mr. McDowell. I shouldn't like to challenge your authority, but I cannot wait for another time. Please fetch Lord Carlton immediately."

"I fear he isna of a mood for visits, milady. Might I convey a message to him for ye?"

Her cheeks flushed becomingly, and a sigh of frustration lifted her bosom. Alex let his gaze drop to play over the tempting curves. Not overly large, but perfectly formed. Just enough to fill his hand, warm and soft and—

Alors! Alex closed his eyes as sudden, voracious desire surged through him. With difficulty, he dragged his attention back to the conversation.

"Then I shall wait here," Tori was saying, her cornflower eyes blazing obstinately. "As long as I must."

Rorick opened his mouth as if to protest, then apparently thought better of it. He stepped back and gave a short bow. "As ye wish, milady. May I offer you something while you wait?"

"Nay, unless you mean to alert his lordship."

Rorick bowed again, but when he turned to the door, Alex alone witnessed his eyes rolling heavenward in a look of unchecked annoyance.

Too late, he remembered to move away from the door.

The oak portal slammed into Alex's forehead as he hurried to step out of the way. A solid thunk resounded through the foyer. Alex gasped aloud, but gritted his teeth against a growl of pain, determined not to give himself away.

His effort was lost on Rorick. "What the devil?" Rorick peered around the door. His mouth fell open, but then a wicked glint came into his gray eyes. "Well, yer lordship, I see ye're up. And just in time, too. How fortunate."

Quick footsteps sounded in the sitting room. "Lord Carlton?"

Alex grimaced and glared at his errant cousin. "Bloody fool Scotsman," he muttered in a hiss. "Could you not have held your tongue?"

Too late for escape now. He was trapped. Alex had just enough time to smooth his hair back with his hand before the door was pulled open and Tori peered into the foyer.

Her eyes widened as she took in the whole of his appearance. Inch by inch, her gaze touched upon his hair, his chin, the dressing robe that was tied off-kilter, his bare feet. At the sight of naked flesh she discreetly averted her gaze, but not before Alex witnessed the frown that pulled at the corners of her soft lips.

"Lord Carlton." Her voice melted his insides like sun-warmed honey. "You are looking quite . . . well this fine morning."

Dieu. How could he be burning with embarrassment and burning with desire all at once? Alex cleared his throat. "Please excuse me, Lady Victoria. You have caught me unawares."

"So I see."

At least she refrained from surveying the ruin of his appearance again. Alex took advantage of her averted gaze to do a little surveying of his own. She'd removed her cloak before he'd arrived downstairs. It lay with her muff and purse across a nearby chair. Her golden hair was twisted in an intricate mass of braids and curls that left her slender neck and throat exposed. She'd worn a gown the color of the deepest ocean that made her skin look as fair and rich as cream. Her beauty made him all the more conscious of his dishevelment, and all the more determined to resist her allure. This was no gentle, wilting miss. Beautiful, aye. Desirable, without a doubt. But interfering and dangerous all the same. He could not afford to let her get in his way.

She clasped her hands primly before her skirts. "If you have a moment, I would speak with you, my lord."

Now? She would speak with him now? Alex swept his hand back over his hair and ignored the meaningful look Rorick aimed his way with a slyly cocked brow. "I do not think—"

"I fear it is quite important and cannot wait," she interrupted. Her eyes, as clear and bright as blown glass, met his gaze, and tarried. " 'Tis imperative that I speak with you now."

"I'm hardly presentable at the moment, Lady Victoria. Perhaps you would permit me to return your visit at a later time," Alex resisted.

"Nay." No one could mistake the steel of determination in her velvet smooth tone. "Nay, I think not."

"If the lady doesna mind yer blighted appearance," Rorick interjected, "none will disturb ye here. If yer lordship wishes, o' course."

Alex glared at him, wishing he'd mind his own business. The look Rorick returned was one of pure, wide-eyed innocence, and wholly a sham. Tori watched with undisguised interest.

Seeing he had no choice, Alex resigned himself to the encounter. "Very well, my lady. Shall we sit?"

Rorick ducked out the door. "I'll just leave ye two to yerselves," he said, winking when Alex cast an accusing look his way. "I'll see that ye're no' disturbed."

The sound the latch made as the door closed brought a cold shiver to Tori's heart. Never had she heard a sound more ominous. She swallowed against a sudden surge of uncertainty and passed by the settee that Alex had indicated. Sitting beside him, sitting at all, was not in her plans. She needed to keep her wits about her. And she hadn't expected to find him dressed in naught but a dressing gown. The thought of what he wore, or didn't wear, beneath it made her cheeks burn.

"Will you not sit, Tori?"

The question came as she took up a stance behind the chair that held her cloak and purse. She shook her head. "Nay, I prefer to stand."

She closed her hand over the back of the chair as if he would take it from her. At least having it between them afforded her a small measure of safety—a measure she desperately needed when he used her given name with a familiarity that threatened to unnerve her. She must retain the upper hand in this situation!

He shrugged, his shoulders moving beneath the black velvet of his robe, and eased down on the settee. "As you wish."

Tori shored up her determination, needing to press on before she lost her nerve. "I take it my visit this morning came as a surprise to you."

A single, wicked brow arched upward as Alex favored her with a small smile. He leaned insolently back in his seat. "If you mean did I expect you to call, then the answer is nay."

Tori gripped the chair harder. His relaxed posture had caused his robe to gap open, exposing a smattering of chest hair and more flesh than she was comfortable seeing. She pinned her gaze to his face. "Nay?" she echoed. "Then 'tis your habit to break one's windows and pay for the damage in the same breath? It must happen often for you to worry about it so little." She didn't try to disguise the sarcasm that crept into her tone. "Or perhaps 'tis such a well-known fact that I am the last to know. How silly of me."

At least he had the decency to look chagrined. He cleared his throat. "I apologize for the inconvenience I might have caused you—".

"Might have? *Might* have?" Tori knew her voice had risen, and she didn't care in the least. "Know you, milord, what sort of damage a ten-pound brick causes to a large piece of glass? Especially since it was raining heavily enough to surpass the Great Flood last night, in case you do not recall."

A closed expression veiled all emotion from his eyes. They looked black and bottomless, and oh, so hard. "If you need more money for the damage, I—"

Offended, Tori lifted her chin. "That's not why I'm here."

A pause. "I see."

"Do you? I find that highly unlikely, Lord Carlton. In fact, I consider it almost laughable."

He leaned forward slightly, the expression in his eyes almost predatory. "Then why did you come, my dear Victoria? You obviously had some mission in mind when you arrived at my home this morning.''

The smug question infuriated her. *So bloody confident.* She wanted to strip that away from him, to show him that without honor and integrity, power meant nothing. It was precisely that same ruinous attitude that attracted young blades to the Mohocks and other clubs with similar agendas, that false devil-may-care freedom that seduced them into lives of depravity. And Alex Rawlings was one of them.

She met his gaze, righteous anger clashing with steely boldness. Then, ever so casually, she opened the drawstring closure of her purse. Reaching within, she withdrew the note Phoebe had brought to her the night before, and took painstaking care to smooth out the creases before displaying it to him.

''A letter of admission, signed by an eminent lord of the realm. A scattering of gold crowns. A witness who saw you, Lord Carlton, outside our window last night.'' She made the note dance up and down, an open taunt. ''The queen's men might be interested in information such as this, I should think. With public outcry against the Mohock club so great?''

His eyes assessed her carefully, but he did not speak.

Tori brushed her fingers across the wrinkled letter. ''Aye, I should think they'll find this most interesting. What say you, my lord?''

The scowl he wore spoke volumes about his own determination. ''Aye, they might,'' he admitted at last. His gaze never left hers. ''Would you do that?''

She'd expected lies, insinuations, anything but that calm, direct question. ''You are a scoundrel, my lord,'' she said, her voice pitched low with trembling emotion. ''A man who taunts the people of London for sport, hiding behind the protection of friends. You torment innocent women—''

''Nay.'' He sat forward with a suddenness that caused

her to recoil in alarm. His robe parted with the separation of his knees. "Nay, my lady, I do not," he said, his voice an insistent rasp. "If you recall, I saved you."

"That is not the point." Tori said with mild irritation. She refused to acknowledge the relief that sped through her with the realization that he wore breeches beneath the velvet robe. Not bare flesh, a thought she found utterly disconcerting. "You are a Mohock. You cannot deny what that means."

Alex looked away, an ominous scowl on his face.

Tori pressed on, gaining confidence. "A Mohock blackguard. Despoiler of property. Flouter of decency. And you are a nobleman by right of birth. How can you turn your back on that? Does your name, your family, mean nothing to you?"

He shot to his feet. "My family means everything to me," he said in a low growl.

Tori grabbed her purse and stuffed the letter inside, refusing to be intimidated by his roar of denial, nor the tight-lipped scowl that made his face a mask of anger. "Then how could you risk hurting them this way?" she persisted. "You dishonor them with your actions."

"What interest is it of yours?" he challenged in return. Emotion churned in the indigo depths of his eyes. "What difference does it make to you?"

Tori opened her mouth, but the answer that leaped to her mind was one that made no sense. Because he came to her in her dreams? Because she couldn't bear to think of her dark knight as anything other than noble and good? *Ridiculous.* "I . . . care about my brother," she said stiffly. "I care that he is being drawn into your world, and he deserves better."

"And that's the only reason?"

Was it only her imagination, or had he moved closer? Suddenly the room seemed terribly small as other reasons distracted her. Ridiculous impossibilities. Absurd, really. Like the way her pulse began to race the minute she saw

Alex. And the way she could not stop herself from noticing the sliver of lightly furred flesh descending from the throat of his velvet robe.

Tori lowered her gaze to his chin, unwilling to see if he recognized her confusion. "Of course. I would do anything to save my brother."

"Even risk your reputation with the likes of me?" Alex chuckled softly, mocking her. "How very sacrificial of you."

The jibe hit its mark. Tori left the protection of her chair and took an involuntary step toward him, her purse clutched tightly in her hands. "I should have expected you to be patronizing. A man without scruples, leading a life of reckless debauchery—"

"Bah!" Alex faced her, hands on lean hips, feet braced wide. One brow jutted upward. "You know nothing about me. And neither do the rest of your precious nobles."

"I have heard rumors."

"Ah. Rumors." Sarcasm bit through the curt repetition. "Are you a purveyor of tales, then?"

Tori stood her ground, clutching the purse to her breasts for protection as he took another step toward her. "Rumors often begin with a foundation of truth," she hedged loftily.

"Pray, do tell me what they say, my lady. I do enjoy a good tale."

"I need no rumors to see what you are." Tori lifted her chin in defiance, matching him taunt for taunt. "I've known from the first." She lowered her gaze to sweep the length of him. "Trouble. And my assumptions are vindicated at every turn. In the company you keep. Your womanizing. And in your incredibly insufferable arrogance."

Her breath caught in her throat as he closed the distance between them. He loomed before her, powerful and vital, his face a tight mask of fury. "Then answer my question, Tori. Tell me why you came."

All the explanations she had prepared fled before the onslaught of his determination. Tori stared up at him, too late questioning the wisdom of her venture. Speechless, she could do nothing but give him the truth. "I came to convince you to leave Charles be. To keep your Mohock friends away from him."

Some of the tension seemed to ease from his features as he watched her, searching her eyes for truth. "I have naught to do with Charles," he said quietly.

Desperation and dismay brought a catch to her throat. Tori swallowed against the sudden constriction, praying she would not humiliate herself with tears in front of him. "Do you mean to refuse me, then?"

"You cannot live his life for him, Tori."

Tori turned away from him before the tears formed in her eyes. " 'Twas not my intention to live his life for him. I want only to help him. . . . He does not seem able to help himself."

She heard him behind her before he touched her. Still, when his hands closed over her arms, a shiver swept through her body, powerful with an unexpected heat. Her breath left her in a rush. What was left of it snagged in her throat in a hiccuping sob.

"Tori . . ." With the gentle pressure of his hands, Alex urged her to turn toward him. She resisted, her stubbornness born of uncertainty and years of self-imposed control. "I did not mean to upset you."

Tori did not answer. Could not. Overwhelmed by her own inner turmoil, she could only wait with her heart in her throat—wait for the shivers to stop, for her breath to return, for the images assaulting her confused thoughts to dissipate back into the nether corners of her mind.

With exquisite slowness, his fingers skimmed along the sleeve of her gown. The barest of touches, yet the movement raised gooseflesh along her arms.

"Tell me"—the hoarse quality of his voice played over the surface of her nerve endings—"would you like to hear what the rumormongers say of *you,* lovely Tori?"

He was teasing her, trying to distract her. But his tone

was light, almost kind, devoid of malice. Hesitantly, knowing she should not listen, Tori nodded.

"Ah, good. You have courage." She could hear the smile in his voice. "When I first saw you, in all your silver glory, I sensed that. You were—are—*magnifique.*"

The hoarse rasp of his voice both lulled and thrilled her. Delicious warmth cocooned her. Breath-stealing awareness broke free of the restraint of her self-control. She felt free and trapped at once.

Unable to bear the confusion his nearness wrought within her, Tori pulled nervously away. She drew a shaky breath and spoke over her shoulder. "You were going to tell me—"

"Oh, aye. I shall tell you."

With distance between them, she felt safer. Tori turned to face him, needing to see for herself whether he told the truth or more lies. But in his eyes she discerned neither honesty nor falsehood, only an intent expression she found wholly unnerving.

"Tori. Lovely Tori." His mouth formed her name like a physical caress, whispery soft. "Your appearances at the various balls have caused quite a stir this season. Did you know you were the talk of the town?" Alarm careened through her as Alex took a purposeful step toward her. "Stories abound of your true identity. Hundreds. All of London wondered who you were."

He took another step toward her, then another, until he stood directly in front of her. The settee behind her barred her escape. Tori began to feel like a hare stalked by a hungry fox, cornered in its own burrow.

His lips curved slowly upward, his dark eyes glinting slivers of midnight. "Some say you are an escaped murderess, seeking in disguise the lover who betrayed you. Others claim you are a spy for a foreign king, though no one seems to know which royal house claims the honor." His gaze swept over her at a leisurely pace. "A pirate queen eluding customs authorities. A jewel thief. A clever bride-to-be watching over her groom."

He stood so close now that Tori had to tilt her head back to see him. Inches away. "So many stories . . ." His hand lifted. Softly, slowly, his fingers drifted along her forearm in the barest of caresses. Tori stared, transfixed. The sight of his hand upon her caused contradicting bursts of caution and excitement to ricochet along her spine.

"Please . . ." Her voice came out in only a whisper as the last vestige of logic arose, weak and without emphasis. "Do not touch me so."

Her protestations went ignored as one strong finger spiraled gently around a long loose lock of her hair. "Some even say your hair is the result of a pharmacist's concoction," he murmured, rubbing his thumb over the silken gold. "But I know the truth of it."

"Aye?" She tried to sound indifferent, but she could scarcely breathe. Her voice sounded as tight as his, falling strangely upon her ears. Unable to stop, she found her eyes moving from his long fingers, along a bare wrist lightly traced with fine black hair, to a wide expanse of shoulder and the open neck of his robe. His throat and jawline were dark with a night's growth of whiskers. But it was his mouth that mesmerized her. Full-lipped, but still vitally male, it brought immediately to mind the way it had felt when he kissed her. Lush. Sinful.

Extraordinary.

"Oh, aye," Alex whispered to her, "you are an innocent. No murderess would be careless enough to allow herself to be caught with her victim. Yet I found you just so. Neither are you a spy." His fingers stole to her chin to trace a featherlight caress along her jaw. "Nay . . . you seem far too trusting for that." With his free hand, he lifted the golden weight of her hair and let it fall in a shimmering arc over her right breast. His hand hovered along her shoulder, dangerously close. "Your lovely hair?

Only a fool could be so blind to think it contrived by medicinal spirits.''

His thumb smoothed gently over the full pout of her lower lip. ''Your kiss? Something so sweet could only be pure . . . though none but a lover could know for certain.'' Alex cupped her jaw with his palm, urging her to look at him.

Wondering why time seemed to have slowed its mad pace, Tori allowed her head to tip back. Something drew her gaze irrevocably upward, until it collided with his. His eyes smoldered like glowing coals, inches away. ''I would like to be certain, Tori. So very much.''

Chapter Eleven

Logic told her to push him away, but his dark gaze held her enthralled. Tori's eyes drifted closed as, by minute increments, Alex closed the remaining distance between them. Wonder and anticipation roared in her ears. And when his lips touched hers, gentle and soft, all reason deserted her.

Warmly, slowly, his lips played a sensual question over hers. Wanting, but not forcing; persuading, but not demanding. Instinct told her he was offering her the option to refuse. *Will you . . . ? Do you want . . . ?* How strange that the answer spinning through her head was, *Yes.*

As though he sensed her submission, Alex sought the response Tori found herself wanting more and more to give. His big hand curved around the back of her neck, urging her closer. His tongue flicked delicately along the soft carve of her mouth. Inviting. Inciting. It was heavenly.

A sigh of pleasure parted her lips. Alex needed no further incentive. Tori felt his strong, hard arm close about her waist, drawing her against the heat of his body, while his tongue dipped within to gently test the warmth of her mouth. Smooth and sleek, fiery hot his kisses were, and oh, so pleasurable.

Without thought, without fear, Tori found herself wanting to press against his hardness, to ply him with her softness. Daring much, she reached out and touched her tongue to his. A shock plummeted through her, and she gasped at the sensation.

At the first touch of her tongue, a deep growl rumbled from his throat and into her, vibrating throughout her pliant body. Instantly his tongue twisted to circle hers, engaging her in a teasing play that reminded her vividly of a dance. Gliding and darting, dipping and sweeping. Alex tasted; Tori gasped. Tori sought; Alex answered. Over and over again, until pleasure and want mingled in her heart, indistinguishable.

Feeling her world begin to collapse, Tori reached out. Her fingers tangled in soft, ebony velvet. Beneath her touch, Alex's heartbeat quickened, tempting her. Without a thought for the impropriety of her actions, she flattened her hand against his chest, marveling at the curve of man-hard muscle that flexed there. Light-headed, she slid her hands up his chest, seeking a support for her weak arms. Her hands found the solid line of his collarbone. His lean throat. Shoulders that were a curving mass of muscle and bone. Each new discovery tempted her to seek more.

His lips left hers to trail a devil's path along her cheek. Bright lights flared behind her closed eyes when the kisses opened hotly against her neck. Without realizing it, Tori tilted her head back. Her arms closed around his neck and she drew him closer, her fingers threading through the hair at his nape.

"Tori . . ." His lips touched her ear, his voice little more than a muttered groan. One arm tightened about her waist. The other hand slid to rest upon the rounded curve of her hips, pressing her close to him. "Ah, love. How desirable you are."

Fierce response rippled through Tori's body. Shaken, speechless, she tightened her fingers in his hair. Her lips parted in a soundless sigh. Awash with sensations and emotions she'd never before experienced, she could only wonder at the feel of him, the masculine scent of him, the way her body responded to the heat of his. At her abdomen, an alien hardness pressed against her, vibrantly alive.

Alex reclaimed her lips, and Tori's world tipped off-kilter. In an instant she felt the silk of the settee behind her back. Then Alex joined her, his weight oddly welcome as he covered her body by half. His kisses pressed deeper, storming her defenses with expert ease. One by one his fingers found the pins in her hair, and the heavy mass tumbled free over the edge of the cushion. He plunged his fingers deep within and cradled her head with a reverence that set her dangerously atremble.

"Ma coeur. Je t'adore. . . ." The whispered French should have rankled her patriotic pride, but instead the words left her breathless, aroused. Kiss-softened lips brushed hers with nibbling caresses. "You are . . . so very lovely."

Faith. She felt drugged. Weak, yet on edge. Helpless, yet all-powerful.

A gentle hand came up under her breast, stopping her breath entirely. Excitement shot through her like a shooting star bursting across the sky. Even through the woolen bodice, Tori could feel her nipple harden beneath the circling attentions of his thumb.

And she knew he could feel her response as well.

Sudden embarrassment shocked her out of her reverie. Tori tried to move away. "Alex, wait—"

"Shh. *Mon petit ange.* Little angel." He spread his hand over her breast. His long fingers drew inward, ever so slowly inward, to meet at the tightening nipple. So expert. "I will not hurt you. Worry not, my lovely Tori."

Somehow he had managed to unfasten a good portion of her bodice. His hand slipped within, shockingly hot against her flesh. Before she could protest, his head lowered over her, his lips tantalizingly parted. And she realized just where he meant to kiss her.

"Oh, no . . ." Why did her voice sound so odd? "Alex, wait!"

Her nipple reached ever upward beneath the thin silk chemise, burning for his touch. Begging. Wicked, betraying flesh.

In the next instant, heady sensation twisted through her body as Alex brushed aside her chemise and took her within the sleek heat of his open mouth. Tori caught her lower lip between her teeth as his tongue laved at the prickling flesh, stoking the odd fire that had begun in the nether regions of her body. Never had she felt so wanton, so alive, so much a creature of the elements. As hot as fire. As sultry as a sun-warmed pool. Flying free on currents of air only she could feel. *Faith. . . .* The sensations alternately frightened and enthralled her, confusing her entirely. She knew she should push him away, knew she should try to escape. Why did that seem so difficult?

She reached out to push him away, but her fingers tangled instead in his sleep-ruffled hair. Long and loose, it seemed to ensnare her, to draw her touch, until she yielded to her desires and flattened her palm along the hard curve of his head, holding him to her.

Over and over he took her breast in his mouth, then sinuously drew back so that her nipple all but left his lips, until she arched against him in mindless pleasure. His tongue did magical things. Wicked things. Circling. Licking. Tasting. Inch by inch, moment by moment, he stole her breath from her with his languid assault on her senses.

So caught up was she in the sensations raging within her inexperienced body, Tori did not notice the precise moment when his hands began to move. She knew only a spreading of the pleasure . . . delicious heat. His legs tangled with hers, pressing her down. The weight of her skirts constricted her. She shifted against them, and they lifted away, freeing her. Cool air bathed her hot skin; then she felt his hand at her center, touching her with an intimacy that shocked her out of her languid complacency. *Sweet heaven.* He was touching her *there?*

Tori's eyes flew open as burning accusations filled her with regret and she realized what she had almost permitted . . . *Nay! Invited.* What had she done? What was she thinking?

Outrage poured through her, chasing the heels of shame. Her hands met the hard width of his chest, shockingly bare—good Lord, had she caused that, too? But just as she prepared to shove him away, the unexpected happened. Alex pulled back of his own accord. And the look on his face froze the blame and regret in her heart into something far more painful.

Disgust marred the chiseled features. She was sure of it. Somehow that made everything she'd done seem so much worse.

He pushed his fingers through his hair and perched on the edge of the settee . . . as far from touching her as he could manage. "I'm . . . sorry," he began haltingly. "I should not have . . .'Twas a mistake. I—" Unreadable dark eyes swept over her, then quickly glanced away. "Oh, hell."

A mistake. Oh, aye.

A sob caught on a snarl in her throat. In one brutally clear moment, an image of how they must look together seared itself into her consciousness—all rumpled clothes and flushed faces, heated expressions and kiss-roughened lips. Tori's cheeks burned, and not from the scrape of an unshaven chin across them.

Mortified and furious at once, she thrust her hands against the voluminous folds of her skirts and, without thinking, lashed out with one long, stockinged leg. The force of the blow spilled the unsuspecting earl to the floor with a spine-jarring thump. "Get away from me, you . . . vile blackguard!"

Alex gaped at her as though he thought she'd taken leave of her senses. "Tori—"

She struggled to sit up, and jerked her bodice into place. "Scoundrel. Cockerel. Bloody, rotten, preening jackanape!" Tears of regret stung her eyes and vibrated in her throat. Tori pushed them away. She would not give in! Not yet.

In a moment the blank incomprehension in his eyes gave way to something knowing and amused. Alex rose slowly to his feet. His robe, jostled in the fall, had become unbelted. It winked open and closed with his every motion. Tori felt her gaze being drawn toward that tempting flash of flexing muscle and dark, silky hair. *Wicked, really. Sinful.*

Tori swallowed, more determined than ever not to yield to that kind of madness again.

"So now you understand, *petite.*" The rough rasp of his voice matched the expression in his blue-black eyes. *Cold. So cold.* "I am all of those things and more. Mayhap now you'll believe me when I tell you to keep out of this . . . for your own good."

It was all naught but a ploy. A means to manipulate her. Tori cringed at how willing she must have seemed to him.

Such an eager little pawn.

Humiliation ballooned within her. The desire for vengeance arose swiftly on its heels. Suddenly she wanted to hurt him as he had hurt her. She wanted to see within his heart. To know his secrets and throw them in his face. To puncture the billowing arrogance and watch it deflate, spent.

In the end, she settled for something far more obvious.

Behind her, her hand closed around something flat and padded. Without further thought, she launched it at him with as much strength as she could muster.

"Bloody, arrogant cur!" Six feet away, the pillow bounced from his chest without leaving a mark. Still, the effort made her feel better. "Cowardly guttersnipe!"

Alex threw his head back and laughed aloud. "A peculiar choice of weapons, *ange.*"

His endearments rankled her pride. Tori coolly met his gaze. "Do you mean the pillow or the insults, Lord *Bastard?* Both met their mark well enough."

A lazy smile turned the sensual curve of his mouth. "Ah-ah-ah. Temper . . ." Stepping close again, Alex waved a warning finger beneath her nose. He shook his head in mock disapproval. "Such language from a lady. Your epithets burn my ears, *ma belle.*"

Tori batted his hand away. "And your French ramblings do nothing to impress me, Lord Carlton. Or are you too simple to heed pointed warnings?"

Alex shrugged and walked to a cabinet to pour a drink from a crystal decanter. Arrogance etched the strong lines of his face with cool disdain. "I heed only what I deem necessary." He paused, gazing askance at her, then continued in a mock confidential tone. "That, of course, does not generally include empty fears of frustrated women."

Tori raised her chin as the insult found its mark in her already wounded pride. "I will not allow you to bait me, sir—"

"Bait?" Alex laughed, long and low. "Pray, be cautious with your claims, my lady. Some might infer it was my intent to catch you . . . and as I recall, you did a fair bit of the chasing this morning yourself."

"Liar!" Tori's shriek echoed off the plaster ceiling medallions. "How dare you!"

"I dare much, *ange.*" His lips twisted in a wry imitation of a smile. "I should have thought that was obvious."

"Your beastliness was obvious. Your total lack of any sense of propriety." Seething, Tori felt her fingers curl and unfurl around the purse that had somehow found its way into her hands. Tears blurred her vision. For the second time that day, she felt herself losing control, and she knew Alex to be the cause. The prospect frightened her, yet she could not help herself.

"What a fool I've been," she continued raggedly. "To think I actually hoped you might be different. That I might appeal to some vestige of goodness lurking in your heart. Goodness!" The word was bitter with the tears that thickened her throat. "You're no better than the rest of your Mohock friends. Well, mark this upon your memory, Lord Carlton. You shall never—*never!*—lay hands upon my brother. I swear it."

"Tori, your brother's life is his own. No matter the cost, you must allow him to make his own mistakes. The sooner you learn that the bett—Owww!"

Alex clasped a hand over his face as the full weight of Tori's purse swung through the air and collided with his nose.

"Bloody hell!" His free hand flashed out and caught Tori by the arm before she could retreat. With a ruthless disregard for causing her pain, he yanked her to attention before him, upsetting a small table in the process. A glass bowl crashed upon the floor. Wax apples tumbled about their feet.

Tori pried at his fingers. "Let me go!"

"Like hell I will!" he thundered. "Vicious wench! What the devil do you have in that thing?"

"Think you still that I cannot take care of myself, Lord Carlton?" she challenged.

He pulled her forcefully against his chest. Inches away, Tori could feel the warmth of his breath bathing her face. His eyes bored into hers. "Do you still not understand?" His voice was a harsh whisper. "Must I issue another lesson, sweet Tori?" His gaze held her captive as his hand swept the length of her body in unspoken warning.

"No further lessons are needed. Believe me, I understand. Perfectly." Trembling with anger and the precariousness of her situation, Tori still managed to lift her chin a notch in direct defiance. "I understand that you are a criminal in the eyes of the queen. I understand that all I have to do is whisper in the proper official's ear to see you rot in the Tower forever. And I understand that all you have to do to prevent that is to cooperate with my wishes. You need my silence as much as I need your help. So the question becomes, do *you* understand, Lord Carlton?''

Blue-black eyes narrowed dangerously. ''Do not deceive yourself, *ange.* You have no control over me.''

''Nay?'' Desperation made Tori bold. Without his help . . . ''Mayhap your mother would be interested in your nocturnal activities, then. I understand she is staying in London. Here with you, as a matter of fact.''

Alex scowled at her for long moments before he responded. ''You would not be so rash,'' he hedged.

''Would I not?'' Tori twisted her wrist in his grasp, hurting herself in the process. She grimaced at the pain, but did not relent. ''Release me and find out.''

As though he sensed her pain, Alex eased his grip slightly, but his manner changed not in the least. ''How would you explain your knowledge? Not to mention our . . . questionable association. Consider the scandal, were word to get out.''

Tori stared into his eyes, determined to convince him. ''Scandal can be averted. And I would do anything to save my brother and to shield my family's name. If you will not help me, I will find another way.''

''Bah!'' Alex flung her wrist aside and began to pace in front of her. Glass crunched under his slippered feet. Rubbing her abused wrist, Tori watched him run his fingers through his tousled hair. Abruptly he stopped before her. Frustration had transformed his features into a fierce mask. ''Do you not understand that courting danger so carelessly could well find you killed?''

''At the hands of your friends, Lord Carlton? Or would *you* claim that particular honor?'' Tori watched his expression carefully. The flippancy in her tone could not quite veil the insistence of the query. She could not help herself; she had to know.

Alex stared at her, shaking his head slowly from side to ide. "You know the answer to that."

A field of energy hovered in the space between them. elt, but not seen, it gave tangible proof that the spark that ad ignited into a grand fire only moments before still emained, smoldering in silence. Tori swallowed uneasily nd shifted her gaze to the wall behind him. "Do I?"

Warning bells began to toll an insistent rhythm in her ead. *Careful, Tori. The man is more a danger than you ad even suspected. You came here to obtain his help . . . nd you've yielded far too much to him already.*

Alex resumed his pacing. "And what exactly do you ntend if I don't cooperate with your plan?" he demanded. 'To dress as a man and take part in the sport yourself?"

"If I must." With Alex's attention averted, Tori vatched him unabashedly, intrigued by this man's comlex appeal. His clenched jaw gave clear evidence of the xtent of his ire. Perhaps now would be the time to play er last card. "But your Mohock friends seem to be a selferving lot. Mayhap 'twould not be difficult to find another vho would be more amenable to my plans . . . for the right rice."

Alex halted and whipped his head around to glare at er. "The hell you will!" he said in a growl. "You could ot be so foolhardy."

Tori crossed her arms beneath her breasts. "For my rother? I would do anything."

They stood at odds, fear and desire set aside, risking all n one last, daring effort to triumph, each knowing in their earts what losing might mean to their lives. With a sinkng heart, Tori feared the worst. Just as she was wondering vhat she could do to further convince him, Alex sighed.

"Foolish woman." His voice sounded flat now, reigned. "I suppose it cannot be helped, then. Bloody hell. Vhat is it you want me to do?"

The sudden offer shocked Tori to her toes. Her gaze

flew to his face to find him scowling at the floor, his eyes hidden. "What did you say?"

Alex shrugged one muscular shoulder. "My life is so far from my own just now that being beholden to one more person will not change much." Eyes as dark as a starless sky lifted to hers. "But I shall accept your offer to pay for the deed, sweet Tori."

Secure in the relief that she'd met her purpose, Tori waved off his explanation and his warning without concern. "Whatever your cost, my brother is worth a thousand times more, Lord Carlton. Name your price."

A slow, cynical smile curved the sensuous line of his lips. "I believe you mistake me, *ange*. I do not speak of gold."

The full import of his words swept through her with all the power of gale-force winds across the moors. Tori stiffened in an instinctive gesture of self-protection. "I beg your pardon?"

He gazed flush into her eyes. "One night with you."

"Nay!" Tori's thoughts dashed in frantic circles, seeking a viable escape. "You have no right—"

"The choice is yours, *petite*. One night with you in my arms. Think you the price too steep? I hardly think any other Mohock would ask so little."

Stone cold eyes surveyed her closely. In an instant the certainty struck her . . . it was another ploy. A means to be rid of her. Tori decided to call his bluff. Gathering up her cloak, she swept it around her shoulders in a broad flare of fur-trimmed velvet before she bothered to answer. She met his stare with quiet dignity. "Very well. I did not come to yield to you, but yield I will if 'twill save my brother from certain ruin. Just see to it you are completely successful."

Finished fastening the silk frogs on her wrap, Tori headed for the closed portal and the safety beyond it. She could feel Alex's regard upon her back, a heavy weight. His voice stopped her as she reached for the knob.

"I trust you will keep your pretty nose out of business that does not concern you. I have no intention of risking my life safeguarding you because of some foolish whim of yours. I shall contact you when I have accomplished your goal . . . and to claim my prize."

She would not turn around. By God, she would not! But she also could not resist a last, parting stab. "Aye. And I trust you'll have thought of suitable tortures that I may repay you in full for your trouble."

Not waiting for a response, Tori fled the room, feeling affronted, haughty, and yet hopeful all at once.

Alex clamped his lips together as he watched her leave, wanting nothing more than to call her back, to apologize for his boorish behavior. But that would be foolishness. He could not allow sentiment to ruin the emotional distance he had fought so hard to achieve. By playing the mannerless rake, he could keep her safe, away from the trouble she had entered so heedlessly.

He shook his head in rueful admiration as he thought of her protectiveness toward her brother. Such staunch devotion. She would risk all for her wastrel brother, with nary a thought for herself. It was a rarity to find such a woman in London. She was so different from Bess.

Bess. Alex frowned. Yet another problem that needed tending.

Sighing, he knelt and began to gather the pieces of glass.

"Quite the hellion, eh, cousin?"

Rorick's amused burr came from the open doorway. Still annoyed with the Scotsman's earlier disloyalty, Alex refused to look at him. "That hellion is a lady. The daughter of a marquess. 'Tis best you remember that."

"Aye, cousin. How thoughtless o' me to forget."

"You seem to have forgotten much this morning," Alex retorted caustically. "Such as how to be rid of guests when I am otherwise occupied."

Rorick's thick brows stretched upward in feigned surprise. "I didna think ye'd mind a visit from such a bonny lass, cousin. But if ye'll recall, I did try to send 'er on 'er way. 'Twas hardly my fault ye stuck yer nose in when ye did." Rorick picked up the pillow from the floor and grinned down at Alex, his teeth a white slash in the thick auburn beard. "The wench has quite an arm, eh, cousin?"

Alex cocked an annoyed brow as he dropped the last piece of glass into his palm. "You should see her aim," he said wryly. He rose to his feet.

"It couldna be as sturdy as her temper. She twitched from this room sae swift, the front door blew open tae keep out o' her path." One red brow quirked above twinkling gray eyes. "A rare fine site, those swingin' skirts."

A surge of possessiveness overwhelmed him with Rorick's offhand comment. Alex turned away under the pretense of finding a container for the broken glass before his observant cousin could see his response. Rorick meant nothing untoward. And Alex knew he had no right to feel jealous. Tori was a beautiful young woman, a prize for any London blade. For her own safety, that was all he must be to her. A carefree scoundrel. A lusting rake. No more.

The sting of jealousy gave way to more substantial pain as Alex heedlessly squeezed his hand into a fist to punctuate his thoughts. "Damn!"

"Here." Rorick took a square of cloth from his pocket and spread it open to accept the shards from Alex's hands. A single sliver had worked itself into the fleshy base of his thumb. With uncharacteristic concern and a dexterity that seemed out of place in his meaty hands, Rorick gently pinched it between thumbnail and forefinger. The glass slid from Alex's skin, leaving only a tiny droplet of blood to mark its intrusion.

Alex pressed the blood to a corner of the white cloth. "My thanks, cousin."

Rorick's short nod of acceptance was surprisingly humble. "Ye should take more care, cousin. But I am e'er here to serve ye." He turned to leave.

His words struck Alex as odd. Humility rarely touched the young Scotsman's tongue. It was not the first time he'd seen some quality in his cousin that he couldn't reconcile in his mind. It would certainly not be the last. The man was an enigma. Once again Alex found himself wondering why Rorick had chosen to leave Scotland, his family, and his friends, for the lonely life of a valet to his Sassenach cousin.

As Rorick left the room, he tossed a parting shot over his shoulder, proving that humility didn't sit well with him, after all. "By the way, cousin, 'tis brazen yer women are becomin'. Ye may wish t' reconsider yer habit of retirin' in the altogether. Two visits in as many days doesna bode well for the tranquillity of yer chambers."

Rich, rolling laughter followed Rorick down the hall, echoing in the drawing room long after he was gone.

In a rare panic, Tori leaped down from the carriage and raced up the front steps of Maryleborn. The door swung inward for her as she approached. She brushed past a surprised footman without pause for thanks and swept through the hall, glancing into the rooms she passed for any sign of her brother. Not seeing him, she hurried back toward the young footman.

"Thomas, have you seen Lord Charles?"

The pale, bewigged footman swallowed nervously as he stood at attention. His Adam's apple gave a convulsive wobble. "Aye, milady."

Impatient with his reticence, Tori waited for his response, but received none. "And . . ." she prompted at last, "where is he?"

Crimson seeped between the extensive freckles covering his cheeks. "I, er . . . well, I . . . that is to say—"

Tori set her hands on her hips. "Spit it out, Thomas, if you please. I have no time to waste."

Thomas took a deep breath. "In the pantry, milady."

His mottled complexion colored further. "At least, 'e was a little while ago."

Bemused by the footman's vague explanation, Tori gave up, nodded her thanks, and made her way through the corridors toward the back of the grand home. Coming to a closed door across the hall from the kitchen, she stopped.

Muffled noises came from beyond the portal. Even amid the clattering and laughing from the kitchen, the sounds of giggling were unmistakable. Stealthily, she placed her hand on the knob and pushed the door open far enough that she could peek within.

A single window spilled meager light into the crowded room. Tori could see nothing but tall shelves amassed with dry goods and other foodstuffs, all necessary to the running of the manor's kitchen. But she knew she was not alone. Whispers and low laughter came intermittently from some hidden space within the room. Catching her lower lip between her teeth, she hesitantly eased into the room.

The hushed sounds became stronger as she moved toward the final aisle created by the ceiling-high shelves. Peering into the gloom, Tori's eyes widened at the sight of Charles seated on the floor, legs outstretched, fervently kissing the buxom young maidservant who sat across his lap. If the sighs and groans that met her ears were any indication, they appeared to be enjoying themselves immensely.

"Charles!"

The two on the floor separated with a guilty jump, red faced and disheveled. Recognizing their spy, Charles relaxed visibly against the wall. The smug, bleary-eyed expression on his face was as much an affront as the unlaced shirt that framed his meagerly furred chest to his navel. Worse yet, the sharp scent of brandy clung to him, strong enough that she could smell it from her position across the aisle.

With an impudent grin, Charles waggled his fingers at her. "Hullo, sis."

The girl Tori recognized as one of their scullery maids. She shifted uncomfortably in Charles's lap as Tori's attention shifted to her. Her fingers fumbled at her bodice, trying to shift the material back in place. Her eyes looked as round as those of a startled horse. She could not seem to look away from Tori's penetrating stare.

Faith, she was perhaps all of fifteen. Perhaps. Tori's lips pressed tighter together. The girl was little more than a child. What servant would think to resist her employer's advances?

Understanding the girl's fear, Tori's heart softened. "Mary, is it not?"

Tears formed in the maidservant's brown eyes. Pushing away from Charles, she knelt before her mistress, nodding her head miserably. "Aye, milady," she quavered.

She looked as though she expected to be flogged. Tori sighed. "Mary, would you please return to your duties now? I believe I heard Cook calling for you."

Risking a sideways glance at Charles from beneath lowered lashes, the girl nodded again, then scurried from the room faster than a pup chasing its tail.

Alone with Charles, Tori turned back to him and crossed her arms. With less and less amusement, she watched as he lolled his head back against the wall and gazed at her through slitted eyes. His mouth had the bold and puckish look of their father. What would he say if she told him that? "For heaven's sake, Charles, the least you can do is close your shirt."

His grin widened. One eyebrow waggled up and down. He resembled some fallen angel, golden and perfect, but with deviltry in his eyes. "Offending you, am I, sis?" He made no attempt to straighten the widespread neckline.

Tori threw her hand in the air in exasperation. "Your attitude offends me. Your manners offend me. Your actions of late offend me." She shook her head with a weary sigh. "How could you, Charles? Playing love games with our own servants."

His laugh ridiculed her. " 'Twas simple, and 'tis far from love. I wanted to. She was willing. Is that not usually the way of things?"

" 'Tis irresponsible. She is a part of our household. You cannot use her for your enjoyment, then discard her when you are through! Think how that appears to others."

The arrogant turn of his mouth fell downward in a self-indulgent pout. "Such a prude you are, Tori."

Tori planted her hands on her hips. "At least I do not waste my life with alcohol and loose women! Not to mention the unspeakable things you do with your friends."

His eyes, mirrors of her own, blazed beneath golden brows. "My friends are just that. They do not question who I am, nor do they ask what I do."

"They are barbarians!"

"You have no idea what they are!" he denied.

"I have seen them. I have heard of their exploits in the *Spectator*. They are a pox on the face of London."

"They are men, as am I. Men who know what living is about."

Tori shook her head, her mouth a grim line. "They are animals. They live a lie. Charles, you are so much better than that."

"Why?" His blue gaze delved into hers, reflecting an odd, angry sort of puzzlement. "Because I am the son of the Marquess of Middleham? Because I have ancestors who can be traced back to the times of the Normans?"

"Nay. Because you are you." Tori took his hand into hers, noticing for perhaps the first time how big it was. Physically, Charles was almost a man. When had that happened? She met his gaze, begging him to understand. "Charles, it breaks my heart to watch you do this to yourself. The drinking. The carousing. I know what you are. Do not let our father's mistakes ruin your life."

"Father!" Charles spat. "Our father does not deserve the respect that title implies."

Such hatred. Yet Tori knew he would have a change of

heart in a moment if their father returned a new man. "You miss him, don't you, Charles." A quiet statement, not a question.

He shook his head with a vehemence that tore at her heart. "Nay. I mean nothing to him. Just a means to an end. An heir." His mouth twisted in an angry sneer. "He did his duty."

"Oh, Charles. You mustn't blame him for his weakness. He had not the strength to face what his actions did to our mother. Please don't allow yourself to fall into that same trap."

He gave a curt laugh. "Blood is blood. Much as I hate it, he is a part of me."

"Nay, Charles! You cannot think that way—"

With a growled curse, Charles slammed his fist against the wall, then stalked toward the door. "Do not waste your time on me, Tori." He turned to her, his face like stone. "Worry about yourself. You're his daughter. You're a Wynter, too." The door crashed on its frame behind him.

The impossibility of the situation overwhelmed Tori. For one brief moment, she allowed herself the tears she hated. They burned at the backs of her eyes, blurring her vision. She had no choice. God be willing, Lord Carlton would be able to dissuade Charles. But how?

The promise she'd made to him loomed again in her thoughts, as brazen now as the moment it had left her tongue. *Brazen, aye, but necessary. A small price to pay in exchange for Charles's safety. His future.* But would Carlton truly hold her to her vow? He could not be so dishonorable. *Oh, surely he would not!*

Yet she could find no conviction to reassure her flagging confidence. As she left the small room, she felt his presence with her. Dark as sin. Hounding her steps. Never letting her forget that he would claim his prize.

Closing the door behind her, she could not decide whether the prospect frightened her . . . or intrigued her.

Chapter Twelve

Rain slashed down in steady sheets from the lowering afternoon sky as Alex stepped down from the carriage. Grim anticipation undermined his determination and halted his advance. Heedless of the rain that drenched his clothing, Alex stood rooted in place beside the open carriage door, staring up at Bess Rowan's fashionable town house while rainwater sluiced down the neck of his cloak. Hardening his heart, he prepared himself for what he knew he must do. The time had come. In all good conscience, he could delay no longer.

A flicker at a leaded window caught his eye. As though she had sensed his presence, Bess had pulled aside a heavy drapery and peered out at him. The brilliant smile that curved her full lips drove an arrow of guilt through his heart.

And now I do what I do best, Alex thought with a grimace as he lifted a hand to her in a halfhearted greeting. He knew it was right. He knew it was necessary. Why should it be so difficult? He'd only hurt her more if he stayed.

At the window the draperies dropped into place. In the next instant the door was flung wide.

"Darling!" The exuberance of her greeting tied his innards in knots. She stood in the golden light from the doorway and clasped her hands together before her, suddenly displaying all the prim poise of a maiden. "Whatever are you doing, standing there in the cold? Come inside, darling, and warm yourself by my fire."

Alex had no need to see her face to recognize the double edge to her invitation. Hunching his shoulders against the tension gathering there, he turned to his driver as he closed the carriage door. "Wait here, Burles. I will not be long."

The portly driver raised waterlogged brows, but only murmured, "Aye, m'lud." He turned his gaze discreetly away.

Trudging up the steps, Alex felt the weight of his guilt bearing down upon him. He'd known for quite a while that Bess' feelings ran deeper than his own. Her eyes, green as a cat's, shone with honest pleasure as she watched him. Her smile only grew brighter when he stopped before her.

Bess stepped close to him and pressed her cheek to his. "Alex," she said softly against his ear. "I just knew you'd come tonight."

Alex stiffened. By the gods, he felt like a condemned man approaching the hanging tree.

Taking a hasty step backward, he cleared his throat. "Hello, Bess."

"Oh, pox. Such a cool greeting. Has it been so very long?" Bess tossed an indulgent smile his way and met his gaze full-on. "Will you not come inside, milord rogue? I feel certain I could find something to warm your blood a trifle."

Before he could refuse, she took his hand and pulled him inside. Behind him, the door closed with a quiet click of the latch. The sound echoed in Alex's ears, so final, so daunting. At once, Bess reached for the fastenings of his cloak, her fingers swift with an ease bred of experience.

Drawn by the sounds of Alex's arrival, a footman emerged into the foyer from a rear corridor. Bess swept the wet cloak from Alex's shoulders and tossed it to the young man without a word. A pointed frown dispatched the footman discreetly back into the shadowed hall, leaving Alex alone with her once more. With a low, sensuous laugh, Bess pulled Alex relentlessly across the cool, white and gold foyer toward the stairs . . . and her bedchamber.

Not this time. Alex braced his feet against the slick marble floor. "Bess, wait."

Bess paused, then turned back to him. Delicately arched brows stretched high in disbelief. "Wait? Whatever for?"

The time had come. Alex took a deep breath. "May we sit down? In the withdrawing room, perhaps?"

A flicker of suspicion surfaced in her eyes, only to be chased away a moment later by a confident smile. Bess inclined her head slowly. "If you wish. We have all the time in the world." She released his hand and crooked her finger at him with a coy smile. Her hips swung with a fluid, come-hither grace as she led the way. Her purpose was as clear as the moon in the midnight sky.

Watching him, Bess seated herself upon a small settee in the room Alex had selected for its neutrality, and patted the seat next to her. Swallowing his misgivings, Alex lowered himself gingerly to the edge of the cushion, his back stiff, a hand perched on each knee. He cleared his throat, preparing to speak.

Immediately Bess slid over next to him. Her proximity put Alex even more on edge. He cleared his throat again. "Bess."

The smile that curved her lips seemed almost predatory in nature. "Aye, darling?" Her hand found his thigh and she leaned into him, nuzzling her nose against the curve of his neck.

Alex grimaced and shifted uneasily. "Bess, stop that. I have something I would speak with you about."

Her teeth grazed his earlobe. "Speak all you like, my Devil Lord."

" 'Tis serious, Bess. Please."

Her husky laugh sounded in his ear, low and teasing. "My. You do sound serious. How deadly dull." Her lips and tongue closed about the fleshy lobe, suckling wetly. "I daresay I can provide a cure for that," she purred.

Her hand crept high on his thigh. Alex halted it with his own. "Bess, cease this foolishness. Damnation! Listen to me!" She laughed and redoubled her efforts. Suddenly her number of hands seemed to have quadrupled. Exasperated, Alex broke away and thrust himself to his feet. "Bloody hell, woman! I did not come for this!"

Her mouth dropped open, then snapped shut as outrage and disbelief merged over her fine-boned features. White lines pinched inward at her full lips. Behind the fire of anger in her eyes lurked a more elusive vulnerability. "And just what do you mean by that, Alexandre Rawlings?"

Alex thought he saw fear reflected within the hard green depths of her eyes, and he wondered if she already knew. The thought unleashed massive waves of guilt and tension from the fringes of his consciousness. Distracted, Alex pushed his fingers through his hair in an attempt to gather his thoughts. "I . . . came because we need to talk."

An uneasy laugh burst from her, a short, choked hiccup of mirth. "Talk? Darling, conversation has never been a mainstay of our visits. Or has it been so long that you've forgotten?"

"I will not be staying, Bess," Alex said gently.

Her eyes narrowed. In the space of mere seconds, realization transformed her features into a mask of stone.

"Who."

It was not a question. It was a demand.

Alex blinked. "I beg your pard—"

"My pardon?" Bess leaped to her feet and began to pace before him. "You have the utter gall to request my forgiveness?'' Her voice rose higher with each sharp word.

Alex tried to placate her. ''Bess, be reasonable.''

''Who is it, Alex? Just who the hell have you found to replace me in your bed?''

She had every right to be angry. Still, Alex felt an unreasonable rise in his own temper. ''There is no one.''

''Then why?'' Tears glittered like ice in the corners of her eyes, but she dashed them angrily away. ''Why are you leaving me?''

Alex heaved a sigh and let his head fall back. With his stomach churning, he stared at the ceiling, wishing he could block out her voice, wishing he could rid himself of the guilt, wishing he did not have to see his own betrayal reflected in her eyes. Why, she'd asked. How could he answer when he'd evaded that question in his own thoughts? ''Don't make me do this, Bess.'' *For both our sakes . . .*

''You cannot answer me, can you?'' Bess stalked across the room. Stopping before him, she planted her hands on her hips and pinned him with a furious stare. '' 'Tis because I was right. You have found another.'' Her nostrils arched unbecomingly.

Like it or not, his thoughts leaped unbidden to Tori. Protective anger reared within him and raced headlong, untethered by conscience.

''Who is it?'' Bess demanded. ''That preening biddy, Lady Caroline?'' She laughed at her own joke, baiting him. ''Nay, you would never be satisfied with a lover so old and fat. The widow Ashton, mayhap?'' She wrinkled her nose and tossed her long, hennaed curls. ''Hmph. She has been without a man for so long, 'tis likely she does not remember how.''

Disgusted by her cruelty, Alex turned away, shaking his head. ''Your charity never ceases to amaze me, Bess,'' he snapped.

''So 'twas my *charity* that turned you away from me, then? Ha!'' She grabbed his arm. Her nails bit into his flesh even through his coat. "Do you think me that stupid? I watched you for months. I watched as you went from one woman's bed to the next. Your feet rarely touched the ground between them. I *know* you, Alex. Your faithlessness. Your roving. And I wanted you anyway."

Alex wrenched his arm away. "You know naught of me."

"Aye, I know you. My only fault was in thinking I could tame your wandering ways."

"You know a mask. A shell of a man."

"I loved you. In spite of what I knew."

The simple, bitter words took him by surprise. *Bess? Love?* It hardly seemed possible. Yet he saw the truth of her claim reflected as hurt in her eyes.

"Does that surprise you?" Bess choked a caustic, humorless laugh. "Bawdy Bess, capable of love? Or is it only that you do not want to hear that I might be human?"

He did not know what to say. He did not know what to think. He knew only that he'd hurt her more than he would ever have expected. "I am sorry, Bess."

But even to his own ears, the words sounded but a weak excuse.

Her eyes blazed a new, encompassing hatred. "Spare me the platitudes, and spare me your pity, Alex. Sorrow shares nothing in common with your selfishness. Relief shines on your face as brightly as a candle in the night."

Sudden doubts undermined the clarity of his decision. Was the blame his alone? Was he incapable of the love and loyalty he'd convinced himself was missing from his life? The thought frightened him more than he cared to admit. Desperate to find evidence to the contrary, Alex purposely conjured a mental image of Tori. Tori, innocent and caring and beautiful. Noble to the end in her selfless endeavors to save her brother from ruin, she seemed everything that Bess was not. Sensual and passionate, she fired his imagination in the dark hours of the night. Soft and womanly, yet with a core of determination, she filled his every waking thought with dreams of family and home. Companionship. A lifetime of warmth. But was it only a fantasy? And was it more than he deserved?

And Bess. *Ye gods.* He'd never wanted to hurt her. He just didn't love her.

"I'll go," he said, hoping to cut short her pain. He cast about for his cloak, but could not see it anywhere in the room. With an inward groan, Alex realized where it would be found. The footman had absconded with it during his retreat in the face of his mistress's brazen overtures.

Bess crossed her arms across her breasts. "Oh, aye," she jeered, "do leave, you French bastard." She tossed her head at him. "I would expect no more from you."

Before he could complete his exit, she headed him off, barring the closed portal against him. She pressed her spine against the white door and spread her arms wide. "No kiss farewell, Alex?" she taunted.

Alex breathed a weary sigh. "Bess, I think we both know 'twould be best if I left now."

Her pout curved into a lush, predatory smile. Stretching like a cat, she arched her back, a purposeful motion that thrust her breasts into full prominence. "I see. No kiss. In light of that, I think the least you can do is tell me my competition for your favors. Do you not think it only fair?"

Her words rubbed along his nerves like a cat's silken purr, but Alex's jaw hardened as she unwittingly confirmed what his conscience had been telling him all along.

His favors. Not his love. To Bess, they were one and the same.

She ran the glistening tip of her tongue along her upper lip. With bold purpose, she stretched out a hand to slide it along his chest. Her fingers toyed with each of the buttons in turn. "Can she give you as much pleasure as I?" She raised her chin slightly, and allowed her lips to part in invitation. "Shall I remind you?"

In an instant Alex became acutely aware of a slender

finger sliding along and beneath the waistband of his breeches. With the precision and speed of a cracking whip, he snatched her wrist away. "Nay."

She twisted her wrist so viciously that Alex knew he must have hurt her. She did not seem to care. Her arm felt like a writhing snake beneath his grasp. All the while, the vicious smile never left her lips.

"How will she compare, Alex? Will she kiss you in all the places you love so well? Will she touch you beneath a duke's dinner table whilst conversation flows about you?" Thrusting herself away from the door, she forced her breasts against his chest and locked her free arm around his neck. Try as he might, Alex could not break free. "Tell me, Alex, and tell me true. Will she ride you so hard in your carriage that you can scarce step down for the weakness in your knees?" With a savage laugh, she began to move her hips against his, tainting with her coarseness an act they had once both enjoyed. "Will she writhe in mindless pleasure beneath your rutting body?"

Disgusted, Alex let go of her wrist and braced both hands against her shoulders. He pushed hard, anything to break the contact. "By the gods, woman! Are you mad? Why are you doing this?"

Her pale cheeks flushed crimson. Her breath came harsh and swift, her breasts heaving with the effort. "Damn you, Alex Rawlings! Damn you to hell! Because I want you, and because you do not want me!" She clenched her hands into fists and struck at his chest over and over again. And Alex let her, stoically withstanding the blows until her anger was spent. At last, with a sob, she presented him her back, clutching her hands protectively over her arms. "Damn you to hell," she whispered dully. "I still want you. Even now, if you touched me, I'd burn for you. I'd melt in your hands."

Conflicting emotions of pity and disgust waged war in his mind. The depth of her passion surprised him more than he thought possible. What desire he once felt for her was gone. Now he felt only regret. Alex shook his head slowly. "In time, you will feel differently—"

"When?" She spat the question as though it were laced with alum.

When you take another lover? When you have attended a dozen more balls, a hundred more teas . . . Even in his own mind, the suggestions sounded feeble and inane. He could think of no answer to console her. He could only shake his head like an idiot. He felt . . . ineffectual, and more than a trifle guilty. "I am sorry, Bess. Truly sorry."

He opened the door, but the empty foyer told him no servants hovered near. *No matter.* Better to face a cold carriage ride than to prolong this disaster a minute longer. The tavern would warm him well enough.

With a last apology, he walked toward the outer door, not stopping as her final words followed him.

"You will be back, Alex. Make no mistake in thinking otherwise. No one can give you pleasure like I can. You'll be back before a fortnight is done. We are two of a kind, you and I. Oh, aye—you will be back."

He closed the door silently behind him. Immediate relief flooded through him. It was over. At long last, it was over. He was free!

A sudden desire to go to Tori overwhelmed him, uplifting his battle-worn emotions. By the gods, he wanted nothing more than to yield to that seductive urge. He needed to see her. To hold her. To believe in her innocent code of honor, for in her presence he became honorable himself. A gentleman, as befitted his title. A man his father would have been proud to call son.

But the tavern called to him, an incessant summons.

Duty.

He must see it through.

"Yer lordship?"

Alex lifted his head slowly from the scarred tabletop. For a long, uncertain moment, he swayed on his bench.

His eyebrows stretched upward with the herculean effort of opening weighted eyelids. Achieving moderate success, he squinted upward through a haze of blue pipe smoke and the curtain of his own disheveled hair to find the serving woman who had been watching him from across the room the evening long. *Ye gods.* The barkeep must have thought him too far gone to notice that the woman possessed the bulging shape of a barrel and features more equine in nature than human. Her smile displayed a gap where her front teeth should have been. ''Uh, aye?'' he said hoarsely.

Her smile brightened now that she had gained his attention. ''Would ye be likin' aught more ale, m'lud?'' She lifted the wooden pitcher she carried and swirled the contents within. ''I 'ave a fresh, cool jug right 'ere.''

Around them, the laughter and drunken shouts of his fellow Mohocks shook the walls and floors of the Hound's Breath tavern. In this haven, they were free to do as they pleased—as long as the tabs were paid in coin—and the men were in fine form this night. Their restlessness reaffirmed the need to further his masquerade.

Careful to maintain the charade of bleary-eyed drunkenness he'd promoted the evening long, Alex slanted a lopsided grin at the barmaid and propped his chin on his fist. ''More? Aye. I've a thirst cannot be quenched this night, m'lady,'' he slurred. Lifting his free hand, he tapped the rim of the tankard with one shaking finger. ''Pray, pour away.''

Horse Face flushed with pleasure. ''Oh, sir. I hain't a lady.'' The pleased smile remained on her face as she leaned purposely before him to pour a steady stream of brown ale. Alex quelled a grimace. She smelled as strong as the beverage she carried, ripe and unwashed. When his cup was full, he waited for her to move away.

Instead, work-roughened fingers slid up the length of his arm, then toyed with the loose mass of hair falling over his shoulders. ''Nay, I hain't a lady,'' she murmured. ''But

I do know 'ow to please a gennulman such as yerself, m'lud.''

The invitation was bold in her eyes, unmistakable. Alex shifted uncomfortably on his bench. The last thing he wanted was to fend off the advances of a gold-seeking female. Yet caution must be his first consideration if he were to get close enough to the Emperor to divine his secrets without exposing himself as a fraud.

Then, too, there was his promise to Tori. Bracing himself, Alex patted the woman on her bottom before giving the plump flesh a hearty squeeze. The woman squealed in delight.

Alex flashed her a silly grin, then allowed his body to list southward on his seat. If anyone knew of Tori's brother, a woman likely would. Possibly this woman.

Sliding his fingers into his purse, he withdrew a coin and held it up so that it caught the light. ''I wonder if you could tell me . . .'' He let his voice drift off in invitation.

Fixed on the flash of silver, the woman's eyes gleamed. She licked her lips. ''Sir?''

Reaching for his cup, Alex made his voice conversational. ''Tell me, love. Have ye seen a blond about tonight?''

Her gaze snapped back to his. ''Now what might ye be wantin' with a washwater miss, when ye 'ave me at yer service, m'lud?'' she asked harshly.

Alex brought his cup to his lips. ''A boy, love.''

Her face fell faster than a stone dropped from the Tower. Her hand fluttered to her throat. Odd, he never would have guessed her to be a flutterer. '' 'Tis boys ye fancy, then?'' she finally managed.

The question caught Alex unawares. ''Nay!'' he spluttered into his ale. He felt a ridiculous urge to explain, as though his answer to her might make a difference. ''He is a friend. I had hoped to share a table with him. He—'' Alex clamped his lips together. *Dieu!* He sounded like an idiot.

The lines between the woman's brows eased. "Golden 'air, then? Young? Face like an angel from 'eaven?"

Alex smiled in spite of his discomfort. "You know him?"

She shrugged. "I seen 'im around, but not tonight. Not yet, anyways." Horse Face leaned close to him until her breasts hovered before his eyes. Her breath washed over his face, fetid and moist. The space where her tooth had been winked obscenely. "P'raps yer lordship 'ud be int'rested in a bit of fun with the boy and myself? If the boy was willing, o' course." She flashed him a coy smile.

Before he could protest or retreat, she surged forward to press a wet kiss on his mouth, then backed away with a lift of an eyebrow and a gleam in her eye that made him very glad of his pretense. Surely, were he as drunk as an alemaker's apprentice, he would hold less of a charm for her than his gold.

He hoped.

Left to his cups, Alex settled back on his bench and resumed his performance. The hour was still young for the revelers, too soon for secret plans to be made. All around him, Mohocks made merry. Alex watched their progress from behind the rim of his tankard.

Rabble-rousers, the lot of them, roaring and dancing about a room that was as damp and miserable as the night. Alex turned a baleful eye toward the rough-hewn beams above his head as yet another series of drips found its way through his hair and runneled down his back. No one else seemed to notice the inconvenience, least of all the men who quaffed their drinks with hearty good cheer, who laughed and roared and guffawed at their own bawdy jests, who danced clumsy-footed jigs with each other as readily as they did the wenches who fawned over them for the favor of a trinket.

Pretending to drink deeply of his ale, Alex allowed his attention to drift about the room, taking in every person, every deed. Near the barman stood Hawk, the Mohock who had been assigned to him that first night. Next to him was Troll, the Emperor's randy sidekick, sporting a wench on each arm. At least fifteen others suffered various levels of inebriation at the tables. One even lay on the floor.

But no Charles Wynter. Yet.

A couple closeted in a secluded corner snared his attention. Away from the dusty light emanating from the great stone hearth, both man and barmaid seemed oblivious to their audience. With single-minded intensity, they grappled, touched, and grinded, managing all but the final act in lusty abandon. The sight drew Alex's gaze with a perverse compulsion that soured his stomach. Though he wanted to, though he knew he should, Alex could not look away.

Behind the man's head, Alex could just make out the dull glint of gold dangling like a medal from the wench's hand.

A gold watch.

Thoughts of Tori crashed in upon him. It was not the same! He had not tried to purchase her as he would any common tavern Judy. Yet he had not resisted the urge to bait her, to force her hand in return for his cooperation.

Resisted? He'd leaped at the chance.

Alex clenched his jaw at the pain of self-recrimination. His mind rebelled. It was not the same. He had changed.

Had he not?

Ye gods. As much as he'd prattled to her of the price of his cooperation, it seemed irony would have the last laugh at his expense. It would seem his own cost would be the greatest in the end. He had paid with his heart. And Tori would never know. Must never know.

Groaning under his breath, Alex slumped over the table, resting his head on his arms. It was hopeless, even if he was successful in his mission for the queen, even if he managed to learn the identity of those who would plot against her to gain the power of the throne, even if he could save Charles from ruin and convince Tori of his feelings for her. To many he would still be nothing more than the tainted Devil Lord, a half-French insult to the integrity of the English nobility. And Tori was the only daughter of a marquess, a man of more than enough power and wealth to command an untainted suitor for his daughter. Never would he agree to her pairing with an earl of modest wealth and property, whose ancestry would contaminate the bloodline of the house of Middleham. Assuming Tori would accept him, of course.

Marriage to her . . .

Alex shook himself from his musings. Whatever happened to his plan to find a sweet country miss to bear his children? Someone who could accept him despite his past? Better to return his attentions to the task at hand rather than entertain futile yearnings, however delightful the dream.

Relegating the thoughts to the back of his mind, Alex used the advantage of his disheveled hair to risk a study of the one man who might hold the answers to the queen's quest. Unlike the others surrounding them, the Emperor remained separate from the fray, preferring instead to sit alone at a quiet table, flanked by two personal guards. Power emanated from him, a visible entity. It radiated from his enigmatic regard, the aloof curl of his lip, the deceptive calm of his posture. Everything about the man elicited a tingle of warning along Alex's spine. He reminded Alex of a falcon, keen of eye, canny in its perceptions. A dangerous adversary, were he to discover the truth of Alex's purpose.

Closing his eyes once more, Alex affected a rattling snore designed to attract the man's attention. Beyond ensuring his disguise, he could do little until someone made a move. He could only wait . . . and watch.

The room grew dark as the fire burned low in the hearth. Eventually the barkeep retired, the tavernmaids having long since disappeared into the nether reaches of the inn, the Mohocks of choice on their arms. The only sounds in the darkening tavern were the faint rustling of bodies, an occasional snort, and the rippling of gas through a flatulent backside.

An ache brought on by his hunched position settled between Alex's shoulder blades, but he resisted the urge to stretch his muscles. Still, he had to do something. Scarcely breathing, he allowed his eyelashes to part and risked a glance in the Emperor's direction.

Damn. The man's body formed a curve over the rough-hewn table, but he did not sleep. The Emperor was writing. Or sketching, Alex amended as he watched him. A deep frown caused a crescent between his brows as he worked, the quill scratching continuously over the paper. What could be so important to require his attention at such a late hour? Even his thugs had sought rest while the man toiled at his writings.

Alex sighed and slammed his eyes shut. The man appeared disinclined to make a move on so foul a night. The evening was a complete loss. Grumbling under his breath at his luck, Alex resigned himself to a cramped sleep up on the hard table and tried not to think about Tori.

Sometime later, a chance sound swept Alex back from the verge of slumber. Opening his eyes, he blinked in confusion as the room around him slowly came into focus.

The first realization to slam into his numbed brain was that the Emperor had disappeared. But before Alex could jump to his feet, a low voice sounded from the dark void.

"I see ye made it, lad. About time, too."

The Emperor. Who was he speaking to?

"Aye, yer eminence. Late I may be, but ever diligent."

The rough voice responded from nowhere, and its hoarse quality tinged with a sharp edge of rancor traced fingers of familiarity along Alex's spine. *Dieu,* it could be his own!

Alex narrowed his eyes, straining to see. As they adjusted to the darkness, he could just make out the outline of a man seated at the Emperor's small table. His bulk hid the leader from Alex's view.

"Ye do not want to be late for our associations, friend. I might think ye . . . ungrateful."

A short laugh. "Friend? I fear that term hardly applies here, yer eminence. Ye're a mercenary, and well paid for the task we require."

The stranger tried hard to disguise the fact, but Alex had spent enough time with his cousin to recognize the Scottish subtleties of the man's accent. And the rasping tones were assuredly affected.

The Mohock leader responded with a snort. "Cocky, are we?"

"Nay. Just practical." There was a sound of a bench sliding back. "Have we a bargain, yer eminence? Or must I find another to—"

"Hold." Silence, followed by a huffed sigh. "Very well, friend. Ye have need of a strong force. I have need of yer gold. And my men . . . well, let us just say they have need of a bit of sport."

"Then ye'd best remember that." The stranger's tone allowed no room for denial. "The contract is for this one deed only. Ye will know none of us. And ye will be paid upon completion of the task. No' a tuppence before."

"Agreed. The queen—"

"No particulars," the man interrupted swiftly. "No' here."

The Emperor chuckled, low. "Ye're safe, friend. The tavernkeep is well paid. Even were he about, he'd keepsafe our confidences to the grave."

"Aye, well, I have no wish to be dispatched to my grave so soon. No names."

By unspoken agreement, the two men lowered their voices, enough so that Alex could no longer make out their words. But one thing was certain—the plot of which they spoke in some way involved the queen. The rumors must be true.

What were they saying?

All too soon the discussion ended. Disengaging from the shadows that sheltered him, the dark shape rose and prepared to depart. Alex followed the shape with his eyes, watching, waiting for the man to face the light. Too late he realized his error. As he passed by Alex, the stranger slowed, then stopped altogether. Still cloaked in shadow, he turned back to stare directly at Alex.

Alex froze, not daring to move. His skin went cold, prickling with caution. Sweat beaded beneath his clothing. Could the man see him? Blessed Christ, should he close his eyes? Should he turn his face away? Yet Alex knew that any movement now, however slight, could expose him.

Through his eyelashes, Alex saw the man take a step toward him. He bent closer, his movements measured. Alex felt his breath clot in his throat.

"What is it?"

The cloaked man took a hasty step backward at the Emperor's inquiry. He shrugged. "Must have been a rat. Ye seem to have an abundance of them here." Without further comment, he spun on his heel and started for the door.

The Emperor observed his departure, a watchful expression on his face. Slowly, his gaze swept over the dark room. Curious. Suspicious. "Aye," he murmured. "A rat."

Alex relaxed as the Emperor turned back to his work, yet he could not rid himself of the unsettling feeling that had come over him at the Emperor's agreement.

Chapter Thirteen

Plink.

Tori opened her eyes.

Plink-plink.

Her eyes widened as the sound settled further into her consciousness. What was—

Plinka-chink.

The window.

The window?

The predawn air felt cold as she swung her legs over the edge of her bed. Tori shivered, thankful for the thick carpet that covered the floor. Across the room, the moon stared at her through the window like a giant eye—she had forgotten to close the draperies before retiring. Stealthily, she tiptoed across the floor, half expecting to see a dark figure looming there as she reached it. No matter that her bedroom was on the third floor. Rationality had no place in nighttime fears.

A barrage of pebbles smacked against the window as she drew near. Tori clapped her hand to her mouth, stifling the scream that clambered up her throat. She sucked in a lungful of air through her fingers and released it, then drew another. Her heart started beating again. Within moments, good, clean anger chased away the fear.

It could only be Charles. Blast him! If he'd forgotten his key again . . .

Tori freed the catch and pushed the window open, wincing as frigid air rushed down the neck of her thin nightgown. She leaned her head out and looked down.

A figure stood in the courtyard, to be sure, but well cloaked. And dawn was still too far off to provide more than a faint glimmer—certainly not enough to illuminate his face. She could not identify him. Tori cleared her throat. "Charles, is that you?" she half called, half whispered. It *must* be him. "Blast you, Charles, if you intend to go out at all hours, you might remember to carry your key!"

"Would that I possessed a key just now, my lady." The amused voice that rumbled up to Tori stilled her, then stirred her. "Think you that I would be down here taking aim with pebbles, had I a key?"

"Lord Carlton!"

"The very same. Though I thought we had dispensed with titles and formalities, Tori."

Tori sniffed her reproval, remembering his demand to be paid for his assistance. "Lady Victoria to you, sir."

"Ah, Tori. You wound me."

She could hear the smile in his voice. "And just what are you doing here?" she demanded, feeling annoyed and foolishly delighted just the same. "Skulking about our courtyard like a common thief."

A pause. "I had to see you."

The quiet declaration made Tori's blood go still all over again. *Don't be foolish, Victoria Wynter,* she cautioned herself. *Wily he is, but not so clever as he thinks.* Missish fancies were no reason to attribute notions of gentility to him. His actions proved his true nature time and again.

She took a deep breath. "You have information for me?"

"Aye. And more than that."

That stopped her. She didn't know what to think.

"You look beautiful tonight, Tori."

Was this a jest? A game to him? Self-conscious, Tori ran her fingers through her hair. " 'Tis morning, almost. And you must be blind, Lord Carlton. I'm a sight."

"Aye," he purred. "A sight a starving man might feast upon. Your beauty far outshines the moon in the sky, Victoria Wynter."

Heat filled her cheeks and her mind. Tori ignored it. "You are most complimentary, my lord. But surely you must realize that I know you cannot see me. If I cannot see you, then—"

"Oh, but I can, *petite.*" His voice was a low growl that stroked along her nerve endings with purposeful seduction. "You are as clear to me at this moment as if you stood but inches away. You are the dawn in my moonlit sky."

Tori shivered, but only in part from the cold night air. "Why did you come?" she whispered.

He ignored her question. Perhaps he'd not even heard it. "You are my Juliet, fair and pure."

Tori squinted through the dark. He seemed to be holding a hand over his heart. The other appeared to be spread wide in response to his avowal. A smile tugged unexpectedly at her lips. She smothered it. "You must be drunk."

"And you are the blush of a rose, full with the nectar of the morning dew. I'd like to drink from you—"

"Drunk, or mad!" Tori spluttered, blushing feverishly. Merciful heavens, had he any idea what his words were doing to her? If only she could believe him.

Correction. He was not mad. *She* was.

She tried again, waving him away. "Begone from here, unless you bring news. Someone will see you."

His laugh twirled about her, heady and deep. "And what

will they see? Naught but a man smitten, paying court to his lady."

His lady. And all the connotations that went with that.

Tori closed her eyes against the vision. "We both know that is a lie."

"Is it?"

Her thoughts were spinning wildly. She no longer knew what to think.

"Fair and pure. Lovely and sweet. You are everything I cannot have, *ange.* And everything I want."

The urge to go to him pierced through her reticence, sharp and compelling. *Madness.* Tori's breath eased shakily from her lungs. "Stop."

"I cannot."

"You must!"

"I want to see you."

"Nay."

"Tori. I do have information for you, but I do not wish to shout it for all the world to hear."

That sounded rational. But what if he . . . ? What if she . . . ?

He sighed at her hesitation. "If you will not come down, then at least permit me to call on you."

If he did, indeed, have information for her, she would have to see him sometime. At last, Tori nodded. "Very well. I will be home today, but I have no idea that Charles shall be. Considering his habits of late, I think we may safely assume he'll not be receiving visitors. 'Twill be safe to call upon me then."

Alex laughed again. "Will it, now? Until then, my lady."

Removing his tricorne, he swept it before him, bending low in a jaunty bow. And then he was gone, blending into the shadows with an ease she found startling. As though he were a part of the night itself.

And perhaps he was. The Devil Lord, gossipmongers

would have it. And yet she did not fear him.

He was not half as dangerous as her own longings.

Tori shifted on the watered-silk chair and glanced toward the mantel clock for what must have been the twentieth time since her aunt and uncle's impromptu arrival.

"Will you not have a scone, dear?" Lady Knowlton, Tori's aunt and temporary guardian, held out the plate that Mrs. Pertwee had left for them. "I say! You are looking rather peaked of late. Does she not, Alfred?" Lady Knowlton gazed worriedly at her husband. "Thin as a rail."

Tori sighed inwardly. "I am quite well, Aunt Margaret. I but had a sleepless night. Something I ate, no doubt."

Lord Knowlton dragged his eyes from the broadsheet he was perusing and turned an approving eye upon his niece. "She looks ravishing to me, Maggie. Stop pestering her."

"Nonsense! I vow, she is quite pale. You really should eat something, my dear."

Tori gritted her teeth against the retort that leaped to her tongue, instead curving a chiding smile at her aunt. "Really, Aunt Margaret, I ate no more than an hour ago. I couldn't possibly eat anything else."

Why had they chosen this morning to visit, rather than their usual teatime arrival? Why, when she couldn't think at all for the flutters of anticipation setting her stomach awhirl? She'd not slept a wink since Lord Carlton left her hours before.

Alexandre Rawlings. Earl of Carlton.

Devil Lord.

He was a mystery to her, to be sure.

And she was the biggest fool there ever was. How often had she accused Charles of being a John-o'-dreams when she could hardly claim better? Allowing herself to daydream about a man too dangerous to share the stable life she envisioned. She should never have agreed for Alex to come.

"Victoria. Victoria, dear."

Tori gazed blankly at her aunt for several seconds before she came to the realization that she'd been speaking to her for some time. "Aye, Aunt Margaret?"

Her aunt's mouth puckered into an annoyed moue. "Victoria, dear, I was just saying that I think perhaps if you and Charles came to stay with us during your father's absence—"

"We've discussed this before, Aunt Margaret," Tori cut her short. "Although I appreciate the offer, I cannot see invading your home while we have a perfectly good home here in London. And surely our father shall arrive home soon. 'Tis very kind of you to offer, but—"

"Kind? Did you hear her, Alfred?" Tori cringed. Her aunt's shrill voice held all the power of a gale-force wind. "Why, we would love to have you and Charles at Evanleigh with us. 'Twould almost be like having a son and daughter of our own. Is that not, so, Alfred?"

"Hmmm?" Lord Knowlton's expression was that of a man who had listened to his wife's chattering for too many years—blank, but tolerant. "Did you say something, my dear?"

Lady Knowlton stared at him in open irritation. "Aye. I fear I shall be deemed a windbag for the number of times I am forced to repeat myself, dear husband. Put down that broadsheet and help me convince Victoria that she and Charles belong with us while their father is"—she slanted him a meaningful look—"traveling."

"Charles, did you say?" Lord Knowlton showed his first sign of interest. "Where is that young rapscallion?"

Tori's heart sank. "I— He—" She broke off. She could hardly tell them that Charles spent his nights on the streets, and his days either drunk or sleeping. She must try to convince him of the error of his ways herself, before her relatives discovered the truth and took action. And by God, she must succeed! Aunt Margaret meant well, but were she to discover the truth, their father would be the first to hear. Then she could only imagine what would happen. "Why, Uncle Alfred, Charles is—"

The metallic clank of the brass door knocker resounded heartily throughout the foyer and the entire house, cutting short her declaration. Tori went very still, scarcely able to breathe, as she waited helplessly for the announcement she knew would come. Time seemed to slow as the footman's steps marked his stride across the floorboards, relentless in their regularity. Voices sounded without, inaudible to her ears. It mattered not. There was only one person it could be.

Lady Knowlton straightened in her chair and gazed expectantly at Tori. "Were you expecting someone, my dear?"

Tori shook her head, unable to speak for the lump that had lodged in her dry throat.

A light rap sounded at the withdrawing room door. Tori swallowed hard, then took a deep breath. "Yes?"

The liveried footman stepped within the room and clicked his heels together. Inanely, Tori found herself focusing on his shining boots, where a scuff marred the toe. *Mustn't have that must we?* A nervous giggle tickled her throat. She choked it back.

The footman cleared his throat. "Excuse me, m'lady. Lord Alexandre Rawlings, the Earl of Carlton, to see ye."

He bowed and backed away, allowing Alex to enter the room. Tori's heart gave an irrational leap at the sight of him.

Was it fair for any man to be quite so handsome? All dark edges and taut lines. As always, he dressed almost exclusively in black from head to toe. She had to admit the color suited him, serving only to accentuate his dark appeal. Masculine power surrounded him like a suit of armor. Intensity burned in the depths of his eyes as they met her own. Darker than indigo, they were today. Startling. Feeling quite faint, Tori watched as he smiled pleasantly at her aunt and uncle, then stopped before where she sat.

He took her hand gently and bowed over it. The heat of his skin warmed her from the inside out. Tori's breath left her completely as she met his gaze. "Your pardon, my lady. I didn't realize you had callers. I'll call at a more convenient time."

Lady Knowlton held up a delaying hand. "Pray, milord, do not leave on our account. Will you not take refreshment with us?" She reached over and patted Tori's hand. "Victoria, will you not present us to your caller, my dear?"

With a sinking heart and conflicted feelings of anxiety, pride, and roweling embarrassment, Tori applied herself to her duties. "Lord Carlton, may I present my aunt, Lady Knowlton, and my uncle, Lord Knowlton. Aunt Margaret, Uncle Alfred, the Earl of Carlton."

Alex stepped before Lady Knowlton and took the hand she proffered. "I am charmed to meet you, my lady. And Lord Knowlton." He inclined his head in the direction of Tori's uncle. "A pleasure, sir."

Gazing into his eyes was a torture Tori could ill afford. She fastened her gaze to his chin instead. Smooth shaven. The cleft there beguiled her to touch it. *Oh, do stop, Victoria!*

She cleared her throat. "Will you not sit with us, Lord Carlton?"

His smile deepened the shadowy cleft. "Only if you are certain I am not intruding . . ." he hedged.

Lady Knowlton quickly stepped in. "Indeed, nay, milord! Sit with us, do. You may tell us how you know Victoria."

Alex sat on the settee opposite Tori and her aunt, looking very much at ease. "Ah, but that *is* a tale. I have quite a fondness for good tales, you know." He directed the comment to Lady Knowlton, but by the twinkle in his eyes, Tori had the distinct impression he meant quite a different type of tail. *The cad.* "Shall I relate it to you?"

Tori squirmed in her seat. "I'm certain that—"

Her aunt leaned forward eagerly. "Of course! Please, do tell." She gazed fondly upon her niece. "I am always interested in Victoria's acquaintances. Am I not, Alfred?"

"As you say, my dear," Lord Knowlton responded, right on cue.

"There, you see?" Lady Knowlton nodded, satisfied. "Lord Knowlton agrees with me, so it must be true. Please proceed, Lord Carlton. We are all ears."

All nerves might be more to the point, Tori thought, making a sour face her aunt couldn't see.

And Alex's smile teased her without mercy. " 'Twas at Lord Rutherford's ball last month."

Tori frowned. That was days before she met him, she was sure of it.

"Lady Victoria outshone every woman in the ballroom with her brilliant smile and gracious nature. Your niece is indeed a toast, Lady Knowlton."

A small frown appeared between Lady Knowlton's brows. "Lord Rutherford's, you say?" She turned to Tori. "My dear, I didn't know you attended the Rutherfords' gala. Your uncle and I had prior engagements that evening, I'm quite certain. Surely you didn't go unchaperoned?"

Tori smiled to distract her aunt. "Of course not, Aunt Margaret. Charles accompanied me."

"But my dear, I'm sure you told me that you did not desire to go out that evening. We did invite you to attend the theater with us, did we not? Alfred?"

Lord Knowlton barely glanced up. "Aye, my love, I believe we did."

Alex stepped in smoothly on Tori's behalf. "Your niece was the noblest of creatures attending, I assure you, Lord and Lady Knowlton. Never did she behave with anything but the utmost of propriety. And you would have been proud of Charles. He performed his duties as chaperon most admirably."

Tori gazed upon Alex in utter amazement. Why in

heaven did he bother making excuses for her? For Charles? He must know that Charles was not her chaperon at the Rutherfords' if he had seen her that night. And they had not met that night at all—she had been *en masque.* By rights, no one should have realized her identity. And he knew more about Charles's habits than anyone in this room. Compliments seemed highly irregular, considering that.

Why did it seem the more she knew about Alexandre Rawlings, the less she understood?

Lady Knowlton seemed more eager to accept Alex's comments without question. "Oh, milord, you are indeed gracious to say that about our dear nephew. And I am very glad to hear of Charles's acceptance of his duty. Oh, he is a good boy. A welcome heir to the Middleham title, I assure you."

"Aye, I am quite familiar with Charles's qualities," Alex managed smoothly. *And those of his sister,* the light in his eyes seemed to say. Tori looked away, absurdly pleased.

Lord Knowlton set his newspaper aside and placed his hands upon his knees. "I say. Did you say where Charles is, Victoria, then?"

"Ooh, you are quite right, husband. Lord Carlton arrived before Victoria could tell us." Lady Knowlton nodded her head so hard that her periwig tilted. Without a pause, she lifted a hand to right it.

Pained by the necessity, Tori opened her mouth with a ready lie, only to be interrupted once again by Alex.

"Actually, 'twas Charles I came to see." Alex ignored her raised brows. "I had planned to invite him for a tour through the park on the morrow."

"Charles is . . . indisposed this morning," Tori interjected, trying not to blush. "I should be glad to convey your message to him at his earliest convenience, however."

Lady Knowlton leaped to her feet, shuffling to and fro

as might a banty hen. "Charles, ill? Shall I go up to check on him—"

"Nay!" Tori checked herself as all eyes swung her way. She lowered her eyes, fearful her aunt might have seen too much. "I do not think it necessary for you to do that. Neither do I think he would welcome the attention. 'Tis best to just leave him be when he is like this."

What urged her to meet Alex's gaze, Tori knew not. Suddenly it was as though a powerful magnet drew her irrevocably to him. And the deed, once accomplished, proved too strong to reverse. A single fragment of time stripped away all the vestiges of civility—his polished manners, his pretenses, his benign good humor—exposing the desire burning deep within him. For her. All for her. Had she any doubts regarding her own interests, they were eliminated by the surge of feeling that consumed her in return. Never had she felt such an overwhelming response toward a man. Breathtaking. 'Twas as though it had been brewing within her for quite some time, and had just then come violently to fruition.

With a strength of will born only of years of devotion to duty, Tori crushed the emotions vaulting within her and dragged her gaze away.

Lady Knowlton seemed to notice none of it. "But Victoria, dear, if Charles is not well, he needs someone to take care of him," she protested. "At the very least, we could send a servant to market for a remedy. Alfred, tell her."

Lord Knowlton opened his mouth obediently, but Alex managed to jump in. "Lady Knowlton, your concern for your nephew is indeed heartening. But as I recall from those years, young men do not wish the coddling hand to soothe them. 'Tis considered unmanly, you know." He slanted an engaging smile her way.

Lord Knowlton stared at him in quiet assessment, then let out a hearty laugh. "By jove, you are correct, milord. I had almost forgotten. Let the lad be, Maggie."

Lady Knowlton pursed her lips in disapproval. "Victoria, surely you must agree with . . . Victoria, is aught amiss?"

Tori endeavored to appear as innocent as possible. "What do you mean, Aunt?"

"You are pale as a ghost. And I believe you are trembling. What betides you, child? Is it possible that you are coming down with some illness as well?"

A rush of heat filled Tori's cheeks, and she ducked away. "Nay, Aunt Margaret. Do not worry so."

She would not look at him. She would not!

Unsatisfied, Lady Knowlton touched her palm to Tori's brow. "You do not feel warm."

She had to look. She had to! Risking all, Tori dashed a glance at Alex. The hint of a smile tugged at his lips, toying with them much as his lips had toyed with hers. Remembering proved fatal. It was as though her insides were melting over a low flame. Slowly. Insistently. Tori caught the inner flesh of her lip between her teeth and stared down at hands she suddenly could not hold still. *Blast it, Victoria! Stop being a fool!*

Lady Knowlton withdrew her hand slowly as she gazed back and forth between Tori and Alex. She cleared her throat. "Aye. Well. I imagine I am just being overprotective. You know how I can be. I will think no more on it." Before Tori had a chance to question her aunt's sudden change of mind, Lady Knowlton turned to Alex. "So, you say you met Victoria at the Rutherfords', Lord Carlton?"

Alex nodded. "Aye, madame."

"Madame? How curious! Have you taken a journey to France of late, sir?"

Alex laughed, but did not meet her eyes. "With England and France at war? Nay, Lady Knowlton. 'Twas a slip of the tongue, truly. I do apologize."

Lady Knowlton watched him. "Aye. Quite possibly a

dangerous slip, milord. I beg you, have caution with your words."

"I bow to your wisdom, milady."

"Good." Tori cringed to see a small smile curve Lady Knowlton's lips. She knew that smile. "I say, I have not seen Estella Rutherford in ages. I shall have to pay a call on her soon, I think."

"In truth, we were not formally introduced then, milady," Alex replied with an equable smile.

"Oh?" A look of careful interest stretched Lady Knowlton's brows. "And may I ask who did introduce you?"

" 'Twas Charles," Tori interjected quickly.

"Aye, we have been acquaintances for quite some time," Alex added.

A bold lie, but a welcome one. Tori breathed a sigh of relief, glad for his intervention this time.

"I see." Lady Knowlton nodded, but a thoughtful frown knitted her brow. "Another thing, Victoria. Smythe informed me upon our arrival that the household suffered an attack by those dreadful Mohocks a fortnight past. Is this true?"

Smythe. That halfwit. Tori frowned. "Mayhap 'twas Mohock deviltry, mayhap not. I cannot say for certain."

Lady Knowlton exhaled an exasperated sigh. "Victoria, dear, who else would leave a kerchief of brass door knockers in your courtyard? The watch?"

Tori blushed, but shrugged. "Smythe should not have worried you over such a trifling incident. I certainly have thought no more on it." She was an adult. When would Aunt Margaret acknowledge that?

"Of course I worry. I see no other alternative, dear. I must insist you come to stay with us, Victoria. I had hoped to convince you, but if I must insist, I will do just that. 'Tis just not safe for you here alone."

"But Charles is here—"

"Charles is but a boy," Lady Knowlton interrupted. She held her hand up to ward off Tori's protests. "Nay, I am afraid I cannot take no for your answer, my dear."

Lord Knowlton nodded as he peered at her over thin spectacles. "I must concur, Victoria. You should not be about London without an attentive chaperon, and I fear Charles does not quite qualify. Why, only yesterday in the *Spectator,* another victim of the Mohocks stepped forward with a tale of woe and misfortune. And as we are your guardians in your father's absence, I must insist that you listen to us in this regard. 'Twill be best for you to be at Evanleigh."

"There, you see?" Lady Knowlton appealed to Alex as if for support. "Another attack. What is this world coming to? Why, I've a mind to take Victoria and Charles and remove ourselves to our country house in Devonshire. At least there we need not fear for our lives."

"Charles will not leave." Tori voiced her certainty with a calm that gave little evidence of her own desperation. She could not leave. Without her, Charles would certainly fall prey to his horrible friends. And then their father would return. What would he say when he found his only son sunken in the depths of a debauchery even he himself had never achieved? Charles would be disowned, and their family would fall into ruin. And marriage, her one hope for escape from her solitary London existence, would cease to be a prospect.

What to do?

Lady Knowlton waved a dismissive hand at Tori. "Charles is a male, Victoria. Do not pretend to understand him." She ignored Alex's amused snuffle and her husband's indignant grunt. "At least I will know *you* are safe."

Tori lifted her chin. "I'm afraid I shall not leave without Charles."

Tori expected a tirade, and Lady Knowlton did not disappoint her. She flushed crimson, all the way to her pale periwig. "Oooh, but you are a stubborn girl! Alfred! Alfred, talk some sense into her!"

"I am afraid there is nothing you can do to change my mind," Tori replied evenly before her uncle could comply. A pang of guilt stabbed at her, but she ignored it. If her aunt only knew the seriousness of the situation, all would be forgiven. Charles must be brought to heel. "I will not leave Charles."

"Victoria, you must see reason—" Lord Knowlton began.

Tori leaped to her feet and began to pace. "If reason means that I must abandon my only brother while running away to secure my own safety, then nay. I shall not be reasonable."

Alexandre watched Tori set her jaw with a single-minded determination and staunch devotion he had long since come to admire. This was not some milk-and-water miss—but then, he'd never owned that opinion of her. Fire such as hers could not exist in milk or water. And Tori possessed the fire of a thousand volcanoes. That had been evident from the first moments of their acquaintance.

He smothered a smile as he observed her persistent exchange with her aunt and uncle. Too often he had found himself the object of her ire, ire that heated her eyes into molten blue glass, and caused her skin to glow with a cool inner light. How could a man think when faced with beauty such as this?

Ah, but Tori meant more to him than beauty. It had not taken long to discover that loyalty and intelligence clung hand in hand with her loveliness. She was unlike any woman he'd ever met. Once, he had searched for carnal appetite and design in his women. Women like Bess, and a hundred others. Before him stood a woman he could need—nay, love—and know his faults were forgiven, his inadequacies overlooked, his bloodlines forgotten. With Tori, he could be the nobleman he was intended to become from birth, rather than the jaded courtier that had been his existence since his father's death.

But was it all a dream? Surely 'twas no more than a

desperation born of his miserable existence. Hopeful desperation. Her father would never allow it. And were he the gentleman he wanted to become again, he'd not be sitting here in her withdrawing room, chatting with her relations. Contemplating the thousands of ways he wanted to kiss her, until he thought he would die for want of her. Watching her respond to him in ways that made him want her all the more.

Such a lovely dream. But his duty came first. And so did hers. So his conscience whispered. Yet he could not find within himself the desire to leave. Not yet.

"What of you, Lord Carlton?"

The high, reedy insistence of Lady Knowlton ripped his attention back from the verges of impropriety. Alex cleared his throat, suddenly very aware that all three of them were staring at him—Tori, tight-lipped, with her arms crossed beneath the upthrust of her breasts; Lady Knowlton, exasperated and red faced; and Lord Knowlton, grimacing visibly. "I do apologize. What did you ask?"

"I asked—" Lady Knowlton began.

"Maggie, let us not involve Victoria's guest in a trifling squabble," Lord Knowlton pleaded.

"Please," Tori agreed. "I have made up my mind. You can say nothing that will alter my opinions. I will remain at Maryleborn Court for four more weeks. If my father has not returned by that date, then I shall bow to your desires and reside at Evanleigh until such a time as he arrives. Will that satisfy you, Aunt?"

Lady Knowlton's lips resembled a puckered prune. "Nay," she replied stubbornly.

"Well, I am afraid that shall have to do. I am a grown woman, Aunt Margaret. Mayhap someday you shall see me as such."

Alex shifted uncomfortably as the tension in the room became quite palpable. He cleared his throat again.

Tori's anger suddenly dissipated as she realized what Alex must be thinking of her. How he must see her! "Oh,

Lord Carlton, do accept our apologies. I did not mean for you to witness our disagreement. 'Twas an unpardonable sin."

Alex rose to his feet, and Tori's heart plummeted. Stepping before her, he took her hand. "Do not feel required to apologize, Lady Victoria. I am not at all offended. In fact, I much enjoyed our visit."

"You are taking your leave of us now, then, milord?" Lady Knowlton inquired.

Alex gave her a small smile and nodded. "Aye, milady. I fear I have another engagement." He turned slightly to Tori, and his smile deepened. "Lady Victoria, I do hope to call on your brother again? If it does not inconvenience your household too greatly."

Call on her brother, indeed. His meaning was perfectly clear to her. The intensity of his regard unsettled her, but Tori found she could not look away. "Nay, indeed," she responded, scarcely able to gather breath. "Charles will be happy to receive you, milord."

Breathing was no easier as he lifted her hand to his lips. Before Tori could absorb the stirring aspects of the warmth of his breath on her hand and the tender grasp of his fingers, his lips touched her skin. Her heart threatened to pound its way out of her chest with the wing beats of a thousand birds. She felt warm and cold at once as she remembered the few kisses they'd shared, the feel of his body as he'd crushed her to him. So fleeting. So rare. Was it wrong of her to want that again?

His eyes softened as he lowered her hand. His gaze passed briefly over each of her features, delved for truth in her eyes, then dipped to rest momentarily upon her mouth. "You are too kind, my lady. But I do appreciate the honor."

Flustered, Tori began to pull away, but the press of his thumb against her palm halted her movement, her surprise increased by the distinct slide of a scrap of paper within her sleeve. "What—"

Without another word, Alex released her hand and turned to her aunt and uncle. ''Lord Knowlton. Lady Knowlton. I was honored to make your acquaintance. 'Tis my fondest hope to meet you again soon.''

Lady Knowlton smiled and dipped in a slight curtsy. ''The wish is reciprocated on our parts as well, milord.''

''A pleasure, milord,'' Lord Knowlton assured him.

Tori made a motion to follow Alex to the foyer, dreading his departure more than she could admit. He stopped her with a gentle hand. ''Nay, do not trouble yourself. I shall see myself out. Until next time, Lady Victoria.'' He nodded to her once, bowed, then backed out of the room.

When they'd heard the click of the front door, Lady Knowlton broke the silence brought on by his departure. ''A strange young man.'' Her gaze fastened upon Tori, relentless.

Lord Knowlton frowned. ''Seemed harmless enough to me.''

''What do you make of that French way of speaking?'' Lady Knowlton's thin brow arched mercilessly. ''Quite unusual. I hardly liked it. Seemed rather . . . unpatriotic. What do you know of this man, Victoria?''

Tori shrugged, able to think of little but the note scratching at her wrist. ''Very little, Aunt. He seems very amiable. Charles likes him very much. I admit I know him less than it may appear.'' *There. That should satisfy her.* She could hardly tell her aunt that his French words often had a breathless effect on her. Hardly an announcement Aunt Margaret would find reassuring.

Lady Knowlton squinted at her in obvious suspicion. ''Indeed? He seemed rather familiar with you, Victoria, by way of his actions and his regard.''

''Did he? I hardly noticed.''

''Hmmph. We shall see.''

* * *

It seemed hours before Tori was allowed the privacy of her own bedchamber. 'Struth, it *had* been hours. Tori sighed as she closed the oak portal behind her, feeling much as though she'd taken part in a physical struggle. Aunt Margaret meant well, but her inquisitiveness bespoke a concern that could be deemed smothering. Her visits were exhausting at best, exasperating at worst.

Tori slid her fingers up her sleeve and withdrew the note Alex had so mysteriously deposited there. Not wanting to take the time to light a candle, she crossed to the window. The light clearly defined the heavy script scrawled across the paper.

Secure invitation, Hallifield Ball, two nights hence. Meet me, Venus statue, garden. Nine o'clock. You are lovely.

The last he'd underscored twice for emphasis, with bold slashes. So like him. The thought made her smile. Smile and laugh, throw her arms about her waist and twirl around the floor, only to collapse at length, breathless upon the bed.

Lovely. He thought she was lovely.

But as she lay there, staring at the velvet draperies above her head, the levity of the situation slowly, irrevocably drifted away.

Foolish heart, she chided herself, closing her eyes. *Foolish, simple, wishful heart.* He was a rogue. A man the gossipmongers delighted in. And he was a Mohock.

Yet he had also sheltered her from their sport thrice over.

Realization speared through her as the full import of his message settled upon her. Tori jolted upward, wide-eyed. He must have some news for her of Charles! And now she must wait two days before he would tell her. *Wretched man.*

A second realization followed close behind, one that disturbed her even more than the first. For with the imminent fulfillment of his end of the bargain, the small matter of Alex's payment could no longer be ignored.

Chapter Fourteen

Until a nobleman she didn't recognize lurched past her to vomit into a potted plant, Tori had thought the Hallifield ball could get no worse. Obviously, she had been wrong.

Wrinkling her nose and trying not to breathe, Tori eased away from her corner and hastily skirted the dance floor. Safety loomed in the form of a marble column. She ducked behind it and made a fervent wish that time could somehow move faster.

Two hundred guests overran Hallifield Park's grand ballroom. Two hundred tippling, giggling, stumbling guests. The exquisite decor so labored upon by the come-lately Lord John Hallifield, first Viscount Lydon, could scarcely be seen through the crush of wide-skirted ladies and satin-coated bloods. Not that they would have noticed.

Poor Lord Lydon. 'Twas obvious the man had spared no expense. Thousands of candles provided a genteel glow over the assembly, showing the ladies and their escorts to best advantage. An eight-piece orchestra played a rousing country dance from the colonnaded rotunda, shielded from the guests by enormous potted plants and a few well-placed screens. Tubs of ice hidden at intervals throughout the room kept temperatures amenable without the drafts brought by open windows.

What a shame that she was likely the only guest sober enough to notice.

Even Hallifield Park with all its modern accoutrements could not fascinate her this night. Neither could the bucks with whom she'd declined to dance—seven in all. From the moment her brother had deposited her in the ballroom and swiftly disappeared, she'd thought of little beyond her meeting with Alex, and what he would tell her about Charles.

When the hands on her watch at last approached the appointed hour, Tori left the ballroom and stepped out onto a brick gallery. The chill of the night air wended its way through the silk of her gown in an instant, but she would not be swayed from her mission so easily. Standing on the edge of the gallery, she surveyed the sloping grounds.

Yew hedges, ten feet tall and closely planted, drew intricate paths throughout the garden farther than her eyes could see, filling the air with their tangy scent. Somewhere in their midst resided the statue—and Alex.

Somewhere in the dark. Along a path she could not see.

A shiver trailed along Tori's spine. Mazes in daylight could be a pleasant enough diversion. But the prospect of entering the overgrown labyrinth before her, alone, without benefit of a candle or even a rushlight, chilled her more thoroughly than the night air. Yet, if she hoped to discover the truth about Charles, then enter she must . . . and would.

Tucking away her reservations, Tori plunged forth into the maze on leaden feet, clinging to the hope that the search for the Venus would not take long.

Within minutes she came to the conclusion that she was hopelessly, helplessly lost.

Hedges loomed about her like ancient monoliths, sinister

in their ability to chase light from their midst. Overhead, a quarter moon flirted behind a veil of lacy clouds, but afforded her little help. Wrong turn after wrong turn thwarted her progress. Only the muffled laughter and music emanating from the nearby Tudor mansion prevented her complete disorientation.

Tori gritted her teeth and stalked onward, wishing she could rail her frustration to the heavens. *The Venus statue? Bloody funny.* She couldn't even find her way out of the hedges.

"There ye are. Ye might ha' thought of a more convenient spot to meet than these blighted gardens."

Tori's heart leaped to her throat as a sour voice came from behind her. She spun around. No one trailed her.

"Feeling a bit womanish tonight, are ye? Night too cold for your dainty sensibilities?"

The second voice came from her right, beyond the hedges, but very close. Two men.

Tori hurried up the path, but the next cross lane turned away from the voices, not toward them. The path behind her was useless. She caught her lip between her teeth, considering. Perhaps she should call to them.

Yet how could she be certain of their trustworthiness? They could be thieves—or far worse. Rather than announce herself, Tori wedged herself into the closely planted yews. First an arm. A shoulder. A knee. Branches caught at her hair, brushed her face, poked into her ribs, and held her fast. Certain the sharp-scented yews would never release her, Tori redoubled her efforts. At last the branches relinquished their hold, and she burst free to the opposite side with the swishing of boughs and a few crackling twigs to herald her.

"What was that?" The first man's voice rose, just above a whisper. Caution prickled the length of Tori's spine. She held herself very still, listening. Waiting.

"Come on, man. Ye're stalling. 'Twas naught but a rabbit."

"I've never heard a rabbit sound like that. I'm telling you, it was something." The hedge to Tori's left shook. She backed away slowly, her gaze drawn by those swaying branches.

"Well, 'tis gone now." As though to prove his claim, the second man raised his voice to a more audible murmur. "Quit poking that bush, ye bloody worm. It's gone, I tell ye. Now, what have ye found out?"

"Oh, nay, mate. Ye've not paid for that privilege yet."

"Paid," the man scoffed. "The Emperor won't like it that you want to hold the information for your own gain. Best reconsider, man."

Pale light glimmered through the dense yews. Curious now, Tori searched for a space to peer through. She leaned near, holding her breath. In the dim glow of a covered lantern, she could clearly see the shapes of two men, one tall with bearlike bulk, the other slimmer, almost willowy for a man. In the darkness, she wasn't sure but wasn't that . . .

In the next instant, a hand clapped over her mouth. Shock ricocheted through her, stomach-churning in its intensity. Before she could react, an arm closed over her chest and dragged her back.

A scream ripped upward in her throat, but the hand smothered it so completely that all that emerged was a whimper too faint for anyone else to hear. Fear sluiced through her, swift, torrential. Tori struggled to free herself, twisting and straining against the ironlike arms that held her captive with flagging ease. As a last resort, she struck out with her slippered heel. The kick brought a muffled grunt of pain.

Her captor pressed his lips against her ear. "Hold," a familiar whisper commanded. "Don't . . . move."

Relief shuddered through her body and weakened her knees. *Thank God, Alex.* Tori clutched at his arms, now grateful for his strength. Speech was impossible—even should the situation warrant it. Her pulse swelled in her veins like a river thick with spring rain. She nodded to let him know she had heard.

His hand loosened, but did not drop away. It settled on her shoulder, his forearm a protective tether across her breasts. His breath touched her ear, the barest whisper of wind. "Speak not. They cannot know we're here. Listen."

As though to accommodate them, the men's voices raised enough to hear without straining.

"The Emperor knows my loyalty. But I would be a fool not to expect recompense for my troubles."

"Ye *are* a fool, I vow." The sneer in the second man's voice was unmistakable. "Ye were on guard duty that night at St. James. 'Tis your fault we had to leave the queen's spy there. Had ye been doing your duty, he would have been sunk in the Thames with none the wiser."

"The hell ye say! I was not the only guard that night, as well ye know. I say if Plunket and the Scotsman had not lost their tempers, the spy wouldn't have been killed at the palace at all!"

Tori clutched her hand to her mouth before her gasp could escape. The dead man at the palace! Then these men—

Alex shifted restlessly behind her. Tension poured from every inch of him, enveloping her, until she thought she could feel his heart beating within her, strong and vivid with life. Tori knew he was remembering, as she was.

"Bah. The queen's man should not have been there. You should have seen him coming. Had the man not come when he did, we could have had her, and none the wiser until it was over."

"And the woman in white? Whose responsibility was she?"

Tori straightened. They mean me, she realized faintly. Behind her Alex went as still as a stone.

"The woman was . . . an error. A minor one," the second man hedged, his tone grudging.

"Minor? Ye and I both know the plan was premature.

The queen's man. The woman. No telling what might have happened, had we gained the queen's chamber."

A defensive cough. "That matters not. The new plan is infallible, as well ye know. And the Emperor sent me to discover your offer. If you have nothing for him, best tell me now."

Long silence answered him. At last, the first man spoke. "The fires are to be set one fortnight hence?"

"Aye. Eight in all, unless the men get carried away. That should be enough to distract the queen's men."

A pause as the first man considered. "I have a way of knowing the queen's whereabouts at the appointed time."

"For a certainty?"

"Aye." The man gave a rough laugh. "I'm free with one of the ladies who attend her. My Abbie will answer any question when in the throes of pleasure."

"I think," the second man said slowly, "the Emperor will be interested in your claim. But be warned—if 'tis naught but air and vapors—"

"Sir!" The word punctured the air with an indignant little squeak. "I pray you, take care with your accusations!"

"Plague me not with your ego. Too much is at stake with this plan to bear that as well. The Emperor will see you get what you deserve. Are you with us? Or not?"

"Aye. With you. Am I not a Mohock? I would never flout the vows of the club."

"See that you don't," the second muttered coldly. "Now, we must return to the ball. We have new members to recruit. With the Emperor's plan, we'll need all the hands we can get."

The truth slapped Tori with painful clarity. The Mohocks were responsible for the death of the man at the palace. But what was that bluster about the queen? And fire?

Sounds of their retreat reached her ears. She made a

motion to follow them, but immediately found herself encircled by Alex's strong arms.

"Let go, Alex!" she whispered fiercely. She turned her head, and her nose bumped into his chin. "We must follow them!"

"Nay. *We* will do nothing of the kind. I will follow, and you will find your carriage and leave."

"But they are getting away!" Tori fought against his restraining arms. Then a cold thought sliced through her urgency, and she froze. "Unless . . . unless you want them to escape."

"Don't be ridiculous."

She swallowed. "You're a Mohock. You're one of them."

"Go home, Tori. Let me do what must be done."

"And what is that?" Tori tried to turn in his arms, to confront him. "Deceive me to protect your compatriots?"

He loosened his hold so suddenly that Tori lost her balance and fell into him. His hands closed about her wrists, locking her tightly against the solid bulk of his chest. "Don't try to understand, Tori. You shouldn't be involved in any of this."

She lifted her chin. "You involved me."

His eyes looked like black coals in the faint moonlight. "Aye, and I regret it daily. You need to do as I say. Trust me."

Trust him? She had long suspected that his involvement with the Mohock band was not what it seemed. But was it only wishful thinking, or truth? Could she trust him?

His lips were inches from hers. Firm, yet supple. She could feel the warmth of his breath on her face. Heat sped along her nerve endings at the realization. Tori transferred her gaze to his chin, determined to overcome her weakness for him. "What exactly is 'this,' Alex? Why were they speaking of the queen?"

"That's not important just now. You—"

"They killed the man at St. James," she persisted. "Did you know?"

"Nay."

"The queen's own man, Alex! Have you taken complete leave of your senses? How can you call these men friends?" She wrenched at her wrists, hurting herself but not caring. "They're Mohocks. They hurt people for the delight of it, for God's sake!"

His hands fell away from her. Unease and concern mingled on his face as he stared at her. "Tori. You cannot understand."

She was free, but could not make herself leave. "Then make me understand," she said softly. "Help me trust you."

Alex pushed his fingers through his hair. Torn between the urge to confide in her and the desire to keep her safe, he felt her nearness more than ever. Scant inches separated her from him, not enough to stop the mounting need that tempted him to touch her. *God, not enough.* "You must believe me. I . . . Ah, Tori. Lord, what a mess."

"Of your own making." Sadness tinged her voice, not the accusation he might have expected. "Charles is just like you . . . and just like our father. God help him."

"Tori, look at me. Please." When she would not, he cupped her jaw in his hand, gently urging her chin upward. Her skin felt like sun-warmed satin against his palm. "I knew none of what happened. I promise you I did not."

Slowly her gaze lifted until she looked into his eyes. Into his soul. And for the first time in his life, he felt the urge to bare all to a woman. To let her see him for who he truly was. To trust her with his heart.

"I want to believe you," she admitted at last. "But they escape even as we speak."

"Nay, not escape." Unable to stop himself, Alex brushed the pad of his thumb over her lips, wanting to test their softness with his own. "Did you not hear them? They'll be looking for new blood for some time."

"And how will you know who they are? Did you see them?"

The question halted him. Alex frowned. "Nay."

The look on her face was one of expectancy. "Then how will you find them?" she asked simply.

Alex dropped his hand to his side.

"Well, *I* know them." Triumph glowed in her eyes. "I saw them. You need me if you want to catch them, Alex. That is what you want, isn't it?"

Alex smiled and stepped closer to her, doing his best to distract her. "You're a very determined woman, Victoria Wynter."

She hugged her arms close to her body, but stood her ground with a lift of her chin. "I've had to be."

Alex nodded and lifted his hand to her shoulder. She didn't even blink. "Aye. I can see that. But Tori, I cannot like you being exposed to danger."

" 'Tis far too late to worry about that. And it's not your choice. If you go back in, you can do nothing to keep me from following you." Her eyes appealed to him in the darkness. " 'Tis more than Charles now, Alex. And you need my help."

To his surprise, he found himself agreeing with her. Without her, the Mohocks inside looked the same as any other men in Hallifield. If he ever wanted this charade to be over . . . "Very well. But only until you point out to me the men we heard. Then I take you home."

She nodded and held out her hand to him. "Agreed."

Taking her hand felt like the most natural thing in the world. Alex led the way back through the maze, savoring the feel of her fingers intertwined with his own, wishing he could prolong the moment. But the manor soon loomed before them, golden light spilling from its tall windows. Pausing on the flagstone terrace, Alex turned to Tori for one last unguarded moment.

"Are you ready, then?"

She nodded slowly. "Aye."

''Scared?''

Her fingers tightened around his hand. ''Not when I'm with you. I mean . . .'' She colored slightly and bit her lip. ''You . . .'' She pulled her hand from his grasp. It fluttered up to her throat. ''Oh, I don't know what I mean.''

A leaf clung to her hair. Alex lifted his hand and brushed it away. He couldn't stop himself from touching the honey gold strands. She'd come as herself tonight, not as *La Fantôme.* Perhaps that was why she'd left the periwig at home. ''I do,'' he said simply.

He allowed himself one last touch along her cheek. Her lips parted as she gazed at him, waiting, trusting. His heart leaped to his throat as the need to kiss her crushed through him. Dragging in a shaky breath, he stepped back and cast her a lopsided grin. ''Well. Shall we go in?''

The lights inside were bright enough to hurt his eyes. Alex paused in the entrance, waiting for the blindness to dissipate. He heard the French doors close behind him and knew Tori had followed. He turned his head. She stood beside him, close but not touching, her eyes wide as she scanned the room's nearby occupants. ''How shall we do this?'' she murmured.

They could hardly stroll the perimeter of the room. For Tori to limit herself to the company of one man for too long would be more than enough to invite rumors of their association. And that sort of invitation never needed to be issued twice. Alex grimaced. Having been the brunt of such gossip all his life, he knew only too well how swiftly it could spread. ''This is too dangerous,'' he whispered without turning his head.

She smiled. *Smiled!* ''Nonsense. I'm perfectly safe with you.''

''If you stay with me, you're bound to be ruined.'' He swept the room with his gaze to punctuate his meaning.

Her lips curved upward again, drawing his attention to them. ''Shall we dance, then?'' She waited until he found her gaze. Her eyes sparkled like sunlight glinting across a deep lake. "They can hardly villify me for one dance, can they?"

One dance.

God, what he wouldn't give to hold her in his arms.

Hold her without guilt.

It would be in the name of duty.

All in the name of duty.

Right.

Alex cleared his throat. "A dance might be . . . a suitable diversion," he managed to say. His hands tingled at the prospect.

Her smile held all the pleasures of the universe. "Ask me."

He looked into her eyes and was lost. "Would you honor me with this dance, Lady Victoria?"

He held out his hand and watched as she placed her hand in his. His skin burned at the light touch. He closed his fingers about hers and led her to the dance floor where two rows lined up for a country dance. Reluctantly he released her hand and took his place in the row opposite her with the rest of the men.

The music swelled. Alex felt his feet begin to move in the steps of a dance he could perform by rote. His attention was wholly focused on the woman opposite him. Her hair glowed like polished gold in the bright candlelight as she circled and turned to the music. Her expression was relaxed, as if she took pleasure in the dance she performed. Perhaps only he could see the watchfulness in her eyes, the wandering of her gaze as she watched for the men she'd seen.

The lines merged and turned, and then he was facing her. As the dance dictated, he took her hand and raised it above them, the motion bringing their bodies together, not quite touching. All at once, her breath hissed out between her teeth. An intense excitement came into her eyes. "It's them," she whispered urgently.

At that moment, he wasn't sure he cared. Awareness

buzzed like a swarm of bees between them, setting his body on edge. Then she stepped back, extending their arms between them, and he turned her around in a slow circle. The slight inclination of her head told him where she'd seen them. He forced himself to look where she indicated.

It was not difficult to spot them. He recognized them immediately from the introductions that night. The burly one with the thick beard had been called Mars, and the thin-nosed, tall one had been dubbed Weasel. *One god of war, one nocturnal rodent. Hmmm. How fitting.* They prevailed over a small number of men in a corner behind a potted fern. One of the men was Charles Wynter.

The music brought them together once again. "Did you see them?" she whispered. "There, in the corner."

"Aye," he murmured. The attentive smile he flashed at her was more for the sake of the witnesses all about them, or so he told himself. He turned her about, and they moved together down the line of dancers. Their arms barely touched, their hands not at all, but he felt her to the depths of his soul. "I know them."

She nodded once. "Charles is with them." She said it quietly, but Alex could hear the despair in her voice. He swallowed the words of comfort he wanted to give her, instead returning to his place at the end of the long row of men.

At last the music stopped and Tori dropped into a low curtsy with the rest of the ladies. Alex's height gave him an eagle's view of her breasts curved invitingly above her bodice, her skin creamy pale against the rose pink silk. He bowed before her, and made a show of taking her hand for the rest of the assemblage. "I thank you for the honor of the dance, my lady," he said, his voice several notches too loud. "You will save another for me later this evening, won't you?"

She straightened and stepped away, primly reclaiming her hand. "I'm afraid my dances have already been claimed, my lord, but I do thank you for honoring me with the request."

He escorted her to the edge of the dance floor, doing his best to keep from touching her. "I'm brokenhearted, my lady. Another day, perhaps."

He left her there, knowing full well she'd find a way to meet him in the hall.

Bess Rowan narrowed her eyes as she watched Alex leave the room. He'd actually danced. She could hardly believe her eyes. In all the time she'd been with him, and in all the time she'd pursued him, she'd never seen Alex dance. Never cared for it, he'd told her. Hated the pomp and pageantry of it, he'd claimed. Why tonight? Had it just been that he'd abhorred the thought of dancing with her?

Ignoring her partner, Bess sought out the woman he'd been with. A pang of jealousy shrieked through her when she found her. Tall. Willowy slender. Her rose-hued gown must have cost a small fortune. And the color of her hair could be likened to spun gold. *The bitch. The usurping bitch.*

. Dawning realization drifted through her as she watched the woman meander, almost purposelessly, around the room and then escape through the same door Alex had used. And suddenly she knew.

He was meeting her.

He'd found a new lover.

He was never coming back.

Spitting mad, Bess turned to the young nobleman who'd been clumsily courting her off and on all night. She put on a simpering smile. "I say. Who was that dancing with the Devil Lord?" she asked innocently.

A lazy grin came over the lad's face. He leaned an insolent shoulder against a marble pillar. "I know . . . but I think I'll not tell you."

"Why ever not?" Bess edged forward until she stood indecently close to the boy, not against using her body to get what she wanted. "I'm sure 'tis all over London that we are no longer together. The poor man." She shook her head in mock concern. "I hope he can forgive me someday for setting him aside. It just wasn't meant to be."

The lad's eyes hooded over as he gazed down at her breasts, so close to him. "Oh." His voice sounded tight. Distracted. He licked his lips. "I thought perhaps you meant something else."

Sensing triumph just within her grasp, Bess smiled and only leaned closer. "The lady?"

His face flushed. Tiny beads of perspiration broke out on his forehead. "Actually, 'tis my sister."

Her brows shot up, but she managed to otherwise hide her surprise. "Your sister? How curious."

Charles Wynter looked confused. "How so?"

Bess smiled her most seductive smile. She stepped closer to him and took his arm. His Adam's apple bobbed as he swallowed forcefully. "Why, because. Just think of the happy coincidence. Alexandre Rawlings has perhaps found your sister . . . and I have found *you.* 'Tis almost as if it was meant to be," she finished.

The confusion left his features entirely, and he grinned back at her. "Well, if you put it that way . . ."

Smiling to herself, Bess led him away toward the hall. "Tell me more about yourself, Charles. And your family . . ."

Alex waited a full ten minutes before he claimed his coat from the staff and ordered his carriage brought up. Still no Tori. He was about to venture back into the ballroom when he spotted a surreptitious flare of pink skirt darting behind his carriage. His heart pounding, Alex clapped his tricorne down on his head and hurried to meet her.

The door to the carriage stood closed. Brushing away the doorman who rushed to assist him, Alex waited until the man had returned to the entrance before he slipped into his carriage.

Inside he could make out nothing in the darkness. "Tori?" he said.

"Aye. I'm here," came the hushed murmur.

With no further ado, Alex rapped on the ceiling, signaling Rorick to drive on.

The carriage lurched into motion. When they'd safely left Hallifield grounds, Alex lit a single lantern. The glow barely illuminated the pale oval of Tori's face as she huddled in a corner. A carriage blanket obscured her gown and much of her presence from the world outside.

Alex leaned back against the upholstered seat, allowing himself a brief moment of joy that she'd chosen to accommodate his wishes. At least he would know she was safe. "You can relax now. No one saw you get in."

She nodded, but didn't lower the blanket. "You realize I'll have to sneak into my home."

"I could climb the rose trellis and carry you up to your bedroom, if you think skulking would help," he joked with a smile.

She didn't smile back. Her lashes fluttered down, her expression all seriousness. "Are you going to tell me what's going on, Alex?"

Always questions. She already knew too much for her own good. "This subject again?" he asked with a weary sigh. He squeezed a measure of sarcasm into his words. "Why are you so certain something underhanded is—"

Her eyes whipped to snare his with a sharp glance. "Don't insult my intelligence. I have eyes."

"Aye. Beautiful eyes."

"And don't think flattery will distract me, either." She leaned forward in her seat. The blanket parted enough for him to see she wore no cloak beneath it over her ball gown. "I'm not a naive little girl in need of protection, Alex."

"I never said you were—"

"And you're no Mohock."

Chapter Fifteen

The declaration hit him like a fist in his belly, knocking the starch from him.

Her gaze never left his. "From the beginning, I've wondered about you, you know. About the truths behind your actions and your supposed loyalties. You are a complex man, Alex."

He tried to shrug off her suspicions. "You don't know what you're talking about."

"Don't I? Don't I, indeed?" Her beautiful blue eyes held him in their sway. He felt powerless to look away. "Tell me, what will you do if you catch up with these men? What care you of their designs, if Mohock you are in truth? What care have you for silence in their presence?"

Alex bit back the excuse that surged to his lips. Anything he said now would only make her hate him more in the end.

"Shall I tell you what I think?" She didn't wait for him

to respond. "I think you're hiding the truth of your association with the Mohocks."

She knew too much already. "I don't—"

"Don't you?" Her lips curved in a tiny smile that drew his gaze. "Don't bother to deny it. Your expression speaks for you. You have some reason for pretending to be loyal to them. What is it?"

With herculean effort, Alex turned his face away. The candlelight reflecting against the glass prevented him from seeing anything but darkness, but it didn't matter. At least he wouldn't have to look at her when he lied.

For a moment she was quiet, and he allowed himself a brief flare of hope that she'd given up. Then he heard a rustle of silk. A moment later, he felt a brush against his knee. He looked down against his will, and his breath caught in his chest.

She was on her knees beside him, the blanket pooled around her hips on the floor of the carriage. Her hair, streaming over her shoulders, glowed like spun gold in the glow of the candle. Sunlight and honey. Her face was turned up to him, irresistibly, hauntingly beautiful.

She placed her hand on his knee. Heat burned a devil's path to the heart of him. "Please tell me, Alex. Please don't turn me away."

Maybe it was the innocence of her entreaty. Perhaps it was only the moment. Despite his intentions to keep her safe, he found himself wanting to tell her, to bare his soul to her.

To love her.

Ah, God.

"Tori . . ." Her name crept from his lips like a secret. With dreamlike clarity, he watched his hand reach out as though it belonged to someone else. His fingers brushed her cheek, and the sensation robbed him of his will to resist. Suddenly the hand was his, and so was the desire, the need, the blazing urge to be one with her.

He cupped her jaw in his palm, drowning in the full flush of warmth that invaded his body. Her lips parted as she gazed up at him. Inviting him. Asking. Asking . . .

"I was right. You're not a true Mohock, are you . . . ? Say it, Alex. Say it."

"Nay." The word shuddered through him with the force of his love for her, bringing with it a surge of relief in the admission. "Nay, I'm . . . not a Mohock."

Then his hands were on her shoulders, lifting her, touching her. The blanket fell to the floor, and somehow she was reaching for him, too, coming against him with an eagerness that took his breath away.

Alex took her mouth, savoring the rise of her desire as it made her lips part for him. With the touch of her tongue came a greedy dizziness that spun through him with increasing intensity. He clung to her as he leaned back against the seat, clung to her as if he could never let her go. And by the gods, he didn't want to let her go.

Her body felt as soft as he remembered, like clouds in a summer sky, so perfect it was almost unbearable. Her mouth tasted of the wine she'd drunk at the ball. The scent of citrus and cloves wound through his mind, filling him, drowning him. It didn't matter. Only Tori. Touching Tori. Kissing Tori. Loving Tori.

Tori knew she should pull away. Her mother's warnings about the capricious nature of men needled her from somewhere in her memories, but they faded in the face of the bright lights and colors streaming behind her closed eyelids. Pleasure overpowered her ability for rational thought. Heady, intoxicating pleasure, heightened with each sleek sweep of his tongue against hers. Sweet sensation, made all the more heavenly by the feel of her body crushed against his. It was like nothing she'd ever felt before.

Somehow her world seemed to be turning, and she found herself beneath him on the velvet seat. The blanket she'd used to warm herself only moments before had disappeared, but she wasn't cold. Heat expanded rapidly through her as his hand found her breast. Slowly his fingers stroked and caressed, drawing inward toward her nipple until it ached to be touched, its tight crest foreign but oh, so pleasurable.

The sound that crept from her lips evaporated as he deepened his possession of her mouth. There was no thought, no reason. Only the wondrous touch of his tongue, the heat of his fingers as they stroked the bare flesh above her bodice, the hard feel of him aligned against her in the dark security of the carriage. That, and the rush of her blood thundering in her veins.

She wanted to . . .

Even before she finished the thought, she found herself touching him. She ran her fingertips over the hardness of his chest, then upward to the taut muscles of his throat. Marveling at the myriad textures she encountered, she traced along the faint scratch of his jaw and stroked her thumb along the softer curve of his lower lip, feeling it undulate with their kiss. The growl that came as his response could have been mistaken for nothing other than pure pleasure. The sensations she felt in her abdomen inched downward, deliciously unknown.

"Ah, God, Tori. *Ange.*"

Angel. Something about his French pronunciation only served to make the sweet sound more precious to her. Or was it only because it was Alex uttering the word?

Her breath caught as his lips slid down the column of her throat, his mouth working magic against her. She reached for him, and her fingers caught in the hair at his nape as she drew him closer. When his kisses drifted lower, she found herself holding her breath entirely, helpless against the excitement fluttering with butterfly wings within her as she wondered what he'd do next.

"Ah, Tori. Let me love you as I long to." His breath seared her skin as his lips hovered at the lacy edge of her bodice. "God forgive me, I need you so."

From the depths of a dream, she opened her eyes to

look at him. The sight of his mouth on her skin made the butterflies soar higher, faster. "Alexandre."

And then she didn't have to wonder any longer. His hand pressed her breast upward until the low-cut bodice barely contained her. Fascinated, she couldn't help but watch as his lips closed over the peak. Even through the costly silk, she could feel the flicker of his tongue, the suckling pressure of his lips, a lush, encompassing heat, and the prickling pleasure-pain as her nipple tightened, reaching out to him. Overwhelmed by the sight, she squeezed her eyes closed. The flutterings within her grew breathless and wild.

She'd never felt anything like it before, had never done anything like this before. All she knew was that she wanted to be there beneath him, she wanted to touch him, needed to be touched the way he was touching her. Needed more . . .

Too much?

The thought niggled at her, distracted her with its meaning. She frowned against it, pushed it away, but it wouldn't yield. For the first time in her life, the nebulous dreams of her future paled in comparison to her reality. And all because of a man.

This perfect devil of a man.

Needing an anchor for her reeling world, Tori closed her fingers over his shoulder and held fast.

He must have sensed her uncertainty. He dragged his mouth from her and lifted his head, raising his gaze to hers. Waiting. When she didn't speak, he pulled back even more, propping himself on his elbows. "Tori, love, if you . . . that is, if you're . . . you know you don't have to . . . I mean—Oh, hell."

It was the opportunity she needed. Reason should have leaped to the fore then, rallied by his offer of reprieve. But suddenly the nigglings of logic fell aside, stunned into silence by a heady realization. He cared for her. This notorious Devil Lord, this supposed ravisher of women and reviler of all things society held dear, cared enough about her to offer her escape.

And if she'd been honest with herself, she might have recognized her own growing feelings for the man who hid behind the Mohock mask.

Blowing out a shaky breath, Tori pressed her hand against his chest, trying not to notice the thud of his heart beneath her palm. "You make my head spin, Alex."

His gaze softened. He caught her hand in his and pressed it to his lips. "You make my heart beat, *ange.*"

Something in her melted. "Oh." The word squeezed out of her, but just barely. "I don't feel much like an angel."

"No?" He pressed her hand tighter against his heart. Tori closed her eyes as need assaulted her again. "My heart was dead until I met you. Naught but an angel could have made it whole again."

His fingers drifted down upon her breast again. She couldn't help herself. She arched against his touch. "Nay, I am not an angel," she whispered. "At this moment, I confess I feel quite sinful."

Surprise registered briefly in his eyes. "Do you?" She could hear the smile in his voice. His fingers slipped beneath her clothing—she could feel them working at her back. "Tell me to stop, and I will. Will you tell me?" Her bodice shifted, and she felt a rush of coolness at her breast that was replaced a second later with his palm. His dark gaze burned her as he stared down at his hand on her bare flesh. "So innocent."

The need she felt could hardly be termed innocent, no matter how little experience she possessed. Biting her lip, she watched as with his thumb he drew a light circle around the aching crest of her nipple. She stared, transfixed, knowing he was watching her and shamefully caring not in the least. With a patience she didn't possess, his thumb slid teasingly up the peak, circled once at the very tip with a motion that made her gasp, then continued down the other side. Her gasp sharpened with a funny hitch when his head dipped down toward her. At the first touch of his tongue she closed her eyes as heat and sensation radiated outward, consuming her.

There was a tug at her skirts and then warmth against her leg as his free hand slid up her calf, above her gartered stocking to the smooth flesh of her thigh. When it drifted higher, she stopped breathing entirely. The sensation of his fingers parting her shocked her, but not as much as the realization of how swollen she felt, how hot, how wet. Inexperience brought the first flush of embarrassment, but she barely had time to recognize it before he began to stroke his fingers along her cleft. Pleasure rippled with each sleek movement, stronger, more defined, heightened by the way he was kissing her breast.

She flattened her hands against his shoulders and held on tight. Her world seemed ready to explode into a million bright lights and colors—indeed, she could see them behind her closed eyelids already. Something was happening to her, something wonderful and unknown. Something . . .

And then it happened, a jolting sunburst of purest pleasure, startling in its intensity, wondrous in its unexpectedness. A cry ripped from her lips, the sound unrecognizable to her as her own. Her body arched against him, seeking his weight, his warmth, his hardness. The sensation clung to her, racking her body in waves, compounded by each additional stroke of his fingers. "Alex . . ."

He ripped his mouth from her breast with a groan. Breathing harshly, he gathered her close against him, holding on to her as if she were his last bastion of hope.

She felt wonderful. Glorious. She'd never guessed, even in her wildest dreams, that her body was capable of such a mystery. With a sigh, she twined her arms about his neck and pressed closer to him, turning her face into the warm curve of his shoulder.

He smelled of bayberry, fresh and clean, and something more, something that brought a new tingle of awareness, something wholly Alex. She pressed her lips to him, felt his pulse race beneath his skin. Daring much, she opened her mouth against him as he had done to her. The answering groan made her smile.

"I have to leave."

She'd not expected that. Then she remembered the events of the evening that had led them on this merry chase. "I know."

"I don't want to. *Dieu!*" He pressed his hands to her face, staring down at her, his expression ferocious. "I want to take you inside, up to your bedroom, and make that happen for you again."

That was a thought. Heat rose in her cheeks, but she asked anyway. "Can it happen again?"

His expression softened and he gave her a half smile. "Aye. Would you like that?"

"Can it happen for you?"

The question made all the air leave Alex's lungs at once. *Sacrebleu,* didn't she realize what her suggestion did to him? He was straining so hard against his breeches, it was a wonder he hadn't worn a hole clear through. He wanted nothing more than to lift her skirts and pull her astride him, there in the carriage, to move in her until he attained the release for which his body was screaming. But he wouldn't. He needed it to be love he made with her, not just physical release. "Aye," he admitted shakily.

Her hand slid along his thigh, then covered his aching flesh, shocking him. She watched him, her eyes curious. "Here?"

Even through the silk breeches, her touch was intoxicating. Too much so.

Before he lost his resolve, he pulled her hands from him and set her away. "Aye," he repeated, swallowing hard. His composure had fled with her touch. He patted her hands in place, then felt like an ass for doing so. "But you need know nothing of that yet, Miss Victoria Wynter."

She didn't seem to take offense. Perhaps she sensed the reason for his denial. "When?"

Lord. "I shouldn't have done as much as I did. You're young and innocent . . .'tis not my place to—well, you will marry, and your husband will expect to—"

"I want you to teach me, Alex."

He stared at her. What she wanted was impossible. A dream, one with which he'd indulged himself too often of late. Marriage to Tori came too close to that image of a long, happy life he'd been hoping for. He knew it would never happen. His luck wasn't that good.

It took every ounce of strength he had to say the words. "Go up to bed, Tori."

With a quiet dignity he loved, she drew herself up. Retrieving the blanket from the floor, she wrapped it around herself and left the security of the carriage. Alone.

His heart heavy, Alex watched until she disappeared inside her home.

He knew what he had to do. Opening the window of the carriage, he leaned his head out. "Rorick."

To his ears came the sounds of stretching, a yawn, and the crackling of joints. "Aye. Thought ye'd never end that one, cousin. 'Tis cold up here."

"Never mind that now. Drive on to the Guardhouse."

There was a long pause. "What for?"

" 'Tis time to bait a mousetrap."

Chapter Sixteen

After Alex's swift consultation with one James Halloran, captain of the guard, a team of soldiers were dispatched to accompany him back to the party. While they covered the exit, Alex slipped back inside to locate the two men Tori had identified.

It was not a difficult task. They had moved from the fringes of the ballroom to a gaming room just off the main corridor, still with their contingent of recruits. Cards had been dealt, and the expressions on their faces were intent, but not on the game.

Without a word, Alex slipped back to wait, and to watch.

Sooner than he'd expected, the game broke up. The one called Weasel paused inside the doorway and turned back to say a few words that had them all laughing as they left the room. The group dispersed, going their separate ways. Mars and Weasel made their way toward the front exit.

His blood running faster with anticipation, Alex managed to get there before them. Claiming his coat from the footservant, he gave the two a polite nod before he walked out the door.

As he walked down the front steps, he raised his fist in the air, giving the arranged signal to the guardsmen lying in wait.

Bess Rowan couldn't believe her eyes when Alex appeared back in the Hallifield ballroom. He walked with purpose, turning his head this way and that. It was obvious he was searching for someone.

Probably that blond bitch, Bess decided, pressing her lips together at the thought. Lady Victoria Wynter. A nobody in London circles. No one could even remember meeting her. An unremarkable nobody.

When Alex had covered the dance floor, he paused in the doorway of a gaming room, the one where the bitch's brother was holed up with some of his cronies. The look on his face was one Bess had seen hundreds of times. Alert with anticipation, the expression was one of discovery, like when Alex was about to pounce. Only when *she* had seen it, he'd always pounced on her.

She watched in silence as he retreated to a corner, his gaze never leaving the gaming room. After a short time, the group dispersed. To her amazement, Alex hurried toward the exit, nodded to two of them, and then walked out. *Hmmm.*

Curiosity killed the cat, Bess reminded herself, drifting to a window nonetheless. Alex had already disappeared, but the two men were just climbing into their carriage. There was nothing further to see.

She was about to turn away when several men wearing the uniforms of the queen's guard surrounded the conveyance. Three entered the carriage. One took the reins from the wildly gesturing driver. Two claimed the place of the dispersed footmen. The carriage started off into the night, the remaining guardsmen following in a separate carriage. . . .

One that belonged to Alex.

* * *

Alex let out an exasperated breath. The hands on his watch had just reached six and twelve. Six o'clock in the morning, and still the men had not broken down. Though he and Halloran had been relentless in their questioning of the captives, Lord Albert, second son of the Earl of Huntley, and Lord Mobley, heir of the Viscount Sommersby, each had betrayed nothing but resigned silence.

Smothering the anger before it reached his face, Alex walked slowly around the dank room, his hands casually folded behind his back. Lord Albert, the Mohock known as Weasel, stood with his back resting against the damp stones, supporting his chains with ease. The irons had been a threat more than a necessity—the man hadn't moved a finger once he saw the number of guardsmen surrounding his carriage. A model prisoner—but a poor informant.

According to Lord Albert, he'd heard of the Mohock band only through the writings of the *Spectator*. He knew none of the members of the club, he knew nothing of their plans, he knew nothing of their political agenda. He knew nothing of why he'd been identified as a Mohock—it was surely a case of mistaken identity.

The man was steady as a rock in his denials.

Think, Carlton, think! Alex continued his meandering path. He had to think of a way to make his captive nervous. The man held the secrets of the Emperor in his hand. He needed that information. If what he'd overheard was true, the queen was in imminent danger, and far sooner than he'd expected.

There had to be a way to make him talk.

Alex turned on his heel and reversed his path once more. Even in the dim light of a single guttering candle, he could see the man's eyes. He had been following Alex's progress with his gaze. As soon as Alex had turned, the man snapped his gaze forward.

Alex stopped directly in front of him. Beneath his unwavering stare, Weasel dropped his gaze. Even in the cool air of the dungeon, sweat began to bead on his upper lip. And was that a tic that worked at his temple?

Perhaps he was wearing down after all.

And perhaps now, the best thing he could do was leave the man to his thoughts. And wait.

One hour passed. Then two. Alex marked the passage of time with a yawn. As the hands reached the third hour since he'd left Weasel alone, he rose to his feet with a bone-weary stretch. Time to put the rest of his plan to the test.

It had occurred to him that the best possibility lay in the fact that Weasel and Mars were being questioned separately. Neither knew what the other was being asked. Neither knew what the other was saying.

Neither knew if he was being betrayed at that very moment.

Alex planned to use that uncertainty to his advantage. Halloran would do the same.

Straightening his shoulders and assuming an air of knowing arrogance, he nodded to the guard at the door. The guard opened the door for him, and Alex stepped through.

The man's fear was palpable, a cloying energy that Alex could sense the moment the guard closed the door behind him. Weasel no longer rested with his back against the wall. He strained at the end of his tether, the chains creaking as he tested the strength of the bolt that tied the links to the wall. The look on his face was feral, desperation stretching the skin over his cheekbones into a gruesome mask. Raw circles of red flesh surrounded the iron bracelets that held him prisoner.

"You can't keep me here!"

Alex betrayed no emotion as he leveled the man a stare. "Ah, but that's where you're wrong, Lord Albert. Or should I say, *Weasel?*"

Shock registered in the man's small eyes. "How did—"

The Mohock name was a key card in the game, and he knew it. Thank God he'd waited until now to use it.

"That is what they call you, is it not? The Mohocks?" Without waiting for an answer, Alex shrugged. "There has been a new turn of events."

The indifferent tone of his voice made the man's face pale. "What do you mean?" Albert demanded, his question ending in a womanish squeak.

Alex said nothing while he set a chair to rights and sat down upon it, reclining against the ladder back with a smug smile that was becoming easier the more he saw Albert's fear. At last, he laid down his next card. "Your friend has been talking."

Emotions flitted across the whip-thin man's face, shock, anger, denial, fear, one after the other. "He . . . he's lying. I don't know anything about the Mohocks! He's one, of course. Boasts of it all the time."

"Really?" Alex leaned his head back against the chair and closed his eyes, feigning indifference.

"It's true! I swear it." When Alex said nothing, Albert hurried on to fill the silence. "Did he tell you of the raids they make? The way they attack the unsuspecting in dark streets?"

"No." Alex opened his eyes into slits, watching him. "He told me about the queen."

"He—" Albert's mouth dropped open, his lips working with shock. A low moan escaped him. He closed his eyes. "Oh, my God."

"Aye." Alex sat up in the chair, every muscle in his body taut and alive. "Perhaps 'tis best you call upon God. But I'm not certain even God could save you from Anne's wrath."

All the strength seemed to drain from Lord Albert's limbs. His knees crumpled and he dropped to the stone floor. His eyes opened, but he stared dazedly at nothing.

"He talked. I can't believe it. After all his prattle about loyalty to the Emperor, he talked." A chortle burst out of him that was almost like a cry of pain.

Now was the time for the trump card. Alex leaned forward on his knees, assuming an expression that he hoped exuded concern. "Perhaps all is not lost, Lord Albert."

Precious seconds passed before his statement registered. The precise moment it did was obvious—Albert's head snapped up, desperation making his eyes glitter with hope. "What do you mean?"

"If we knew the details of the plans against the queen . . . if we could thwart the Emperor's game without disrupting the queen too greatly . . ." Alex gazed off into space, pretending to be deep in thought. He nodded sagely. "Aye, I think the queen might be grateful enough to grant you pardon. 'Tis certainly better than the alternative." He paused delicately, then whispered, "Death and dishonor."

Albert closed his eyes again, his whole body trembling as he considered the consequences.

"Lord Mobley said you had a contact in the queen's household," Alex prompted, hoping his ruse had been strong enough.

"Abbie," he said, his eyes closed, his voice faint. "Abigail Masham."

"The queen's confidante?"

"Aye. But she knows nothing of any of this. She just . . . talks . . . when we . . . that is, when she—I—"

It was almost comical. The queen's confidante, a married woman, was bedding a young, randy scoundrel who plotted against the queen. And being indiscreet, to boot. What a scandal. "You're sure she knows nothing?"

"Aye."

"Good. Still, the queen should know that her consort has been, shall we say, free with information?"

The man seemed to shrink within himself, his head hanging between thin shoulders. "Aye."

"What else?"

Long seconds passed before the man mustered a voice. "The fires."

The word sent a shiver zinging up Alex's spine. "Tell me."

Albert's brow furrowed. At that moment in time, the young lord seemed to have aged fifteen years beyond his twenty-five. "They mean to set fires to create the chaos needed to get close to the queen. Eight in all." His voice grew fainter. "The Emperor believes if enough fires are set, the ensuing panic will divert attention from the queen. Even the most stalwart guardsmen will lower their guard and allow us access to the queen."

The palace was near Tori's home. It was certain the fires would be in the vicinity. And the spring rains had not been strong enough to halt the progression of a large blaze. And fire could spread out of control so quickly. "He is mad," he whispered aloud.

"Aye. Mad." Albert rubbed his hands over his eyes. "God save us all."

Fury sped through Alex, sudden and fierce. He gripped the edge of his seat. "Who is he?"

Albert shook his head, his eyes wild. "I don't know. I don't know!"

"Then tell me who he is working for." Alex shot to his feet and began to pace. "He cannot be working alone."

"I—He—" The man's tongue worked frantically as he stared fearfully at Alex. " 'Tis a foreigner. A Scot, maybe. The others are Jacobites, but I've only ever seen the one. I know not who he is!" he cried, holding up a hand as Alex spun toward him. "I swear it!"

It wasn't much more than he already knew. The Emperor might be mad, but he wasn't stupid. He'd covered his tracks well. Just now, Alex needed as much information as possible. *Fires and murder, holy God.*

He looked at the man on the floor, whose anxiety had turned him into a blubbering mess. "When does the plan go into effect? When will the fires be set?"

Albert sat with his knees to his chin, his arms wrapped tightly around them, his face white as he rocked back and forth like a child trying to comfort himself. "Three days." His voice was little more than a whisper now. "In three days, he's to send a signal to all Mohocks. We're all to meet at the Hound's Breath before noon to receive our instructions. The fires will be set that evening. Anne will be dead before morning."

Three days. Not long. But with any luck, it would be long enough to get Tori and his mother out of the city before all hell broke loose. And time enough to get Anne to safety.

Chapter Seventeen

When will he come?

Tori wrapped the woolen shawl tighter around her shoulders and squelched the urge to rise from the chaise to pace the floor for what must be the hundredth time. The hours of the night had passed with excruciating slowness. Worry and fear dominated her every thought, holding tight to her imagination with an iron grip that made sleep impossible.

It had taken every ounce of her strength to let Alex go. She'd watched from the door as his carriage departed, guilt clenching her heart until she finally closed the door and slowly mounted the stairs to her room.

He'd promised to come to her when he could. That hope alone soothed her as the clock ticked away the hours. It kept her from wondering if something had gone wrong, if the captives had somehow turned on their captors. What if . . .

But she couldn't allow what-ifs to torment her for long. She had other things to fret about. Though she'd been home for hours, Charles had not returned for the evening. Didn't he realize what anxiousness his irresponsible actions caused her? She felt helpless—so helpless. Seated comfortably in her bedroom, the rest of the world held at bay, she knew she was safe . . . but she could do nothing to help those she loved in their travails—except pray. And pray she did in earnest, for Charles, for his safety, for Alex, for the queen, and for herself.

Yet it did not seem enough. Prayer would not deflect the slash of a knife aimed at the queen. Prayer would not make the differences between her and Alex disappear. Prayer would not make Charles return to his lighthearted and easygoing but sensitive old self. Alas, her sweet baby Charlie was no more. Charles would not change unless he wanted to.

She missed him, but perhaps it was time for her to let him go. Perhaps it was time to get on with her own life.

Could that life be with Alex?

If only he would come . . .

She was considering going down to the kitchen to ask for a cup of cocoa to calm her nerves when the door to her room crashed against the plaster wall. Tori jerked upright, her eyes wide.

Her breath left her in a noisy rush of relief. "Charles! Good heavens, you scared the life from me. What on earth are you doing?"

For once, her brother stood steadily on his own two feet without support of any kind. Tori allowed her gaze to travel over him. Nay, he was not drunk. Not a single popped button nor missing shoe marred his appearance. His cloak remained knotted around his throat, carelessly flung back over his shoulders, and his hair, golden even in the meager light peeping through the open draperies, was still smooth and tidy.

But the expression on his face arrested her survey. "Charles, what have you been doing? What's wrong?"

An ominous scowl twisted his handsome face. "What have I been doing? What have *I* been doing?" Blustering, he came into the room and began to stalk across her rug, not bothering to close the door behind him. "The question I would like to pose is, what have *you* been doing?"

Guilt immediately began to gnaw at her as she wondered what he knew. She'd flouted more than a few of society's rules of late, and any one of them could see her reputation in shreds. Resisting the urge to bite her lip, she decided to brazen it out and leveled at him a direct stare. "I'm sure I don't know what you mean, Charles. Couldn't you be a bit more specific?"

Anger suffused his face with mottled color. He thrust clenched fists to his hips and glared at her. "Oh, you don't know what I mean. Huh. First I hear that you've been snooping about my private affairs, asking questions that are none of your business. Then you leave the Hallifield party without my knowledge, without a thought that I might worry about you. And then!" His voice rose measure for measure with his indignation. "*Then* I have to defend you to the gossipmongers who insist upon spreading rumors about you and the Devil Lord! That, my dear, is what I mean."

With an arrogant lift of his brow, he crossed his arms over his chest and waited. Tori folded her hands in her lap, feigning innocence. "And what is it that has you so upset?"

"What has me—" He broke off, clamped his lips together, and turned away from her, his nostrils flaring. For several moments he continued to pace until he regained control. "You had no right, Tori, to ask questions like you did," he gritted out tersely. "My affairs are none of your concern. I am seventeen years old, a man—"

"Then why don't you start acting like one?" she returned. Flinging her shawl away, she leaped to her feet, coming around to face him. "You moan about being a man, yet you behave like a petulant child who has been caught doing the very thing he's been warned against."

Blue eyes flashed at her. "And you do so like to warn, don't you, Mother Victoria?" he said with a sneer.

That hurt. She bit back the response that leaped to her tongue. It would serve no one to yield to the petty bickering of childhood.

Charles rocked back on his heels and crossed his arms over his chest. "If I've told you once, I've said it a thousand times. This is *my* life, not yours. I will do with it as I please. So keep your nose out of my business."

He turned and stomped toward the door. Tori reached for him, but missed. "Charles, wait. Charles!"

Catching up her dressing gown from the end of the bed, she yanked it on as she hurried down the corridor toward the front of the house. She leaned over the balustrade to peer down into the entry hall. "Charles!"

It was no use. He was gone. Tori wandered back to her chamber, worry slowing her steps. Things between them only seemed to be getting worse.

Restless, she rang for her lady's maid, then stood in front of the window to wait.

No chance for slumber now. How could she sleep when she'd lost her brother to monsters? Her attempts to protect him had come to nothing in the end. She could berate and chide and shame, but short of locking him in his room, she could not force him to abide by her wishes. She could not force him to grow up. It was a painful lesson, but one she had learned well.

The only course of action she had left was to help eliminate the temptation from Charles's life. The Mohocks were clearly plotting something terrible—she had to stop them before her brother became too seriously involved.

And to eliminate the Mohock temptation, she needed Alex. But was that all she needed him for?

So many things had happened in the short time she'd known him. So many reasons not to trust him, not to believe in him . . . and yet she'd been doing just that for weeks.

But was it the man who inspired such faith in her, or was it naught more than a reaction to the tense situations she'd become embroiled in?

"Yes, m'lady?" Phoebe, her superstitious maidservant, peeped her head in the doorway.

Tori nodded. "Good morning, Phoebe. I'll require you to help me dress this morning. Now, in fact."

Phoebe stepped inside and closed the door behind her. "Aye, m'lady."

The young maidservant, for all her talk of visions and superstitious ways, made short work of the fastenings and underpinnings of her dress. Tori submitted to her ministrations, grateful for the distraction. Phoebe's chatter usually annoyed her. This morning it filled the empty minutes as she ran a brush over and over through Tori's hair in long, soothing strokes. Too soon, she gathered her brushes and curling tongs together. A knock at the door interrupted her progress.

Phoebe paused, her hand on the knob. "Aye?"

Smythe's timid tenor sounded outside the door. "A visitor for milady."

Tori felt a surge of anticipation, knowing the answer before she asked, "Who is it, Smythe?"

"Lord Carlton, my lady. He's waiting for you in the blue room. Shall I tell him you're not at home to visitors—"

He got no farther as Tori brushed past a surprised Phoebe and burst into the hall. Smythe stumbled back, but she ignored him and all semblance of modesty as she raised her skirts above her ankles and ran to the stairs. As she neared the bottom, she slowed to a more dignified pace.

Her pretense of decorum evaporated as soon as she saw him.

"Alex . . ."

His name burst free from her lips in a heated whisper, like a bird taking flight. The door clicked shut as she ran to him, scarcely able to draw breath until she felt his arms close around her.

He held her as he did in her dreams, cradling her against him until she no longer knew where her body ended and his body began. His scent filled her mind, alien and yet familiar and compelling. She shivered as his lips brushed against her neck; he whispered to her, over and over, holding her so tight her toes lifted from the fine carpet.

"Tori. Ah, Tori, sweet *ange*."

Emotion, heady and pure, surged in her breast, threatening to overwhelm her heart. Reluctantly she pressed her hands against his chest and looked into his eyes. She had to know. "What is it, Alex? What's happening? What were those men about?"

He kept his hands around her shoulders, his fingers tightening convulsively. Emotion darkened his eyes as he gazed down at her. "Treason. Murder and betrayal, plain and simple."

As if murder were ever a simple thing. "The queen?"

"Aye. The queen."

Tori shook her head, unable to comprehend what kind of person could be capable of such a plan. "But why?"

Taking her hands in his, Alex walked to a settee and sat down, pulling her down next to him. "I don't know. But I do know that you need to get away from London. You could go to your aunt's house. She's been wanting you there; we both know that. At least at Evanleigh you'll be safe." His fingers squeezed hers. "Promise me that. Promise me you'll go."

"I-I can't." As soon as she spoke the words, a tension as tangible and real as an oak door wedged its way between them. Tori could sense it in his sudden hesitation, could see it in the way his eyes grew distant and shuttered, could feel it in the way he loosened his hold on her fingers and slowly pulled away. "Don't look at me like that, Alex."

His lips tightened. "You won't leave London, even knowing how much it means to me to keep you safe?"

Her heart lurched within her breast. "Does it?"

His gaze met hers. "Aye."

"How much?" She could barely breathe.

Her throat went dry as he lifted a hand to her cheek.

His fingers trailed along her cheekbone in a caress as gentle as the brush of an angel's wing. Her lashes fluttered, then closed as emotion surged through her, burning in its intensity. She sensed more than felt him move closer to her until she felt the tease of his breath on her mouth, tantalizingly warm.

"More than I ever dreamed possible, *ange.*" The whispered words winged their way to her heart as his lips came down on hers. The kiss they shared was sweet and urgent, desperate with the underlying threat of separation and uncertainty over what the future might hold.

Alex broke away first, turning his face into her hair. "You won't leave London, will you." It was not a question.

Tori slowly shook her head. Her temple nudged his jaw; she could feel the rasp of a day's growth of beard. "I can't leave Charles. God help me, I should be able to let him go, but I can't leave him to those . . . those blackguards!"

Alex said nothing—he didn't have to. Tori could feel his reproach in the way he'd stiffened against her. She rested her forehead against his cheek, willing him to understand. "My father—our father—as much as abandoned us after our mother died. Charles was devastated," she explained. Lifting her head, she gazed into his eyes, so intensely dark, and said softly, "I can't do that to him, too."

Her words tugged at Alex's heart. Combined with the lethal weapon of her guileless blue eyes, the effect was devastating. He wanted nothing more than to throw her over his shoulder and carry her away to safety himself, but he knew that by doing so he might lose her forever. "I know," he said quietly.

The expression in her eyes sent hope whisking through his veins. Gratitude, yes, but more than that, her gaze held an emotion he might believe to be . . .

But that was ridiculous. Tori was innocence and light

and family duty. To even hope that she could have come to care enough to marry him, a man she thought of as a blackguard of the darkest order, was . . . well, laughable. She might be grateful that he had helped her; she might even feel some semblance of fondness for him. But not *love.*

She was too innocent. She didn't even realize how associating with him could affect her status among her peers.

The urgency of the situation had brought on a false sense of closeness. No matter how much he wanted to believe otherwise, the intimacies they'd shared were a direct result of that.

Not love.

Beneath his close scrutiny, Tori flushed, but did not look away. "Thank you. For understanding."

Now it was Alex's turn to feel heat flooding his own cheeks. He'd not blushed in years, but when she looked at him like that . . .

He swallowed and inched away from her, hoping the space would give him some much-needed perspective. "Aye, well," he blustered, "if you knew how much I'm tempted to cart you off to your aunt's house myself, I suspect you'd not be thanking me."

Her lips curved in a smile that made him feel like he'd swallowed the sun. "That sounds more like you."

"Bold and stubborn?"

"Opinionated," she agreed.

Alex grinned in spite of himself. "Aye."

He glanced down and realized she'd linked her fingers through his. His heart turned in his chest. *Ah, God.*

For a few moments he basked in the peace and pleasure of the moment, knowing it would end all too soon.

"Alex?"

"Aye?"

"I want to help you."

The thought struck terror in his heart as he pictured her at the hands of the Emperor. Defenseless. Alone. "Nay."

"Alex, we have to bring these men to justice."

"Not *we*. 'Tis *my* duty, and mine alone."

She frowned at him. Pulling her hands from his grasp, she clenched them together in her lap. "You can't do it alone, Alex. They are too many. You will be killed!"

Alex rose from the settee and crossed the room. Resting an elbow on the mantel, he stared down into the low flames in the hearth. "Nay, I think not," he said at length. "They have no idea who I am, or even that there's a traitor in their midst. I'll be perfectly safe, and with luck, the queen shall be as well."

Behind him, he heard her come to her feet and knew she stood there, arms akimbo, frowning at him. "But—"

He would not stand by and let her endanger herself.

"I don't need your help, Tori." He turned to face her, steeling his heart against what he knew he must do. He stared back at her, forcing down the emotion that rose in him at the sight of her confusion. "I don't need a helpless woman under my feet. You can't help me. For God's sake, we'd both end up dead." He paused for effect, hating himself, but the words came forth as bidden—cold and callous. "I won't be responsible for you again."

The harsh words cut through Tori like a heated blade. She stared at him, comprehension refusing to come. The words came from Alex's mouth, to be sure, but they didn't sound like Alex. And when she stared into his eyes, she saw nothing of his heart, his soul.

It was as if the man she knew was gone, and in his place was but a cold reflection. All in the blink of an eye.

She tried to reason with him. "Alex . . . I-I want to help you. I couldn't bear to see you hurt. You can't do it alone. You need me."

"No." He stared at her a moment longer, then turned back to the fire. "No, I don't."

Confusion and hurt barreled over her as the import of his words registered. How could he say such things, after the sweet way he'd held her earlier? After the words he'd whispered. She'd almost believed him. Was it really only moments ago?

She lifted her chin, determined to hold back the tears that threatened at the back of her eyes. "I don't believe you. And I don't think you believe it, either."

He shrugged. "Believe what you like, *ange*. The truth of it is, I . . . I've been trying to find a way to tell you. It's just not meant to be with us, Tori. I think you sense it, too. It's not you," he hastened to assure her. "It's me. I don't think I'm the kind of man who could make you, or any woman, happy for long. You'll see the truth of it in time. Find yourself a man worthy of you—I am not that man."

Stunned, Tori watched him turn toward the door, all her daydreams and happiness filtering away with each second that passed. Anger welled up inside her, sudden and swift. She drew herself up with as much pride as she could muster. "You can't tell me what to do, Alex. Charles is my brother, and I will help him if I can. I will not leave London." No matter how painful being near you might become, she added silently.

His hand on the doorknob, Alex had paused. Now he nodded agreeably. "As you wish." He hesitated for only a moment longer before he said, "By the way, Tori—I release you from your obligation."

Completely frustrated, Tori crossed her arms over her breasts and glared at him. "What obligation?"

His smile was cold and cruel. "I release you from your obligation to spend the night with me. I think now we both realize that would be a mistake."

Only when she heard the front door click shut behind him did Tori close her eyes, her only concession to the pain tearing her heart into shreds.

Alex slumped against the leather seat of his carriage, hardly feeling the bumps and jolts as the driver picked their way down the street. He was tired, bone tired. Of scandal, of indiscretions, of lies. Tired of the whole masquerade of life and its hidden faces. Soon this farce with the Mohocks would be over and he could get back to his life as scheduled. Such as it was.

But somehow, without the hopefulness Tori gave him, that prospect gave him no pleasure.

He'd never wanted to hurt her. He'd wanted anything but that! But when she insisted upon joining him in any way possible, when she seemed willing to risk her life to help him, he knew he had to do something. They'd gotten too close, and somehow her persistence had knocked his mask askew. Or had she pulled it free altogether? She'd seen too much of him, the real Alex, and her giving nature could only get her into danger. Breaking off with her was the only way to ensure that she wouldn't want to come near him again.

The carriage stopped before Rawlings Hall, and Alex stepped down. Before he'd even set foot on the steps, the front door was flung wide and Rorick rushed out to him, his expression grave.

He thrust something into Alex's hand.

Alex looked down. In his palm rested a weighted piece of paper, tied with string. His pulse began to race. He looked at Rorick.

His cousin's stare was intense. " 'Twas left on the doorstep this morn," he said slowly.

Grasping the ends of the string, Alex made quick work of the knot. He unwrapped the small parcel.

Unlike other Mohock summons, the stone was insignificant this time, a weight only. Instead, scrawled in a bold hand, he read:

Today
Twelve o' the Clock
Hound's Breath

Alex squeezed the paper into a tight ball.

"Ye're in trouble."

He looked up at his cousin's perceptive statement. "What do you know of this, Rorick?"

Rorick shrugged. " 'Tis as I said. Smythe heard a knock at the door. 'Twas there when he opened it." He made a disgusted face. "Smythe's knees were knocking when he bade me give it to ye. Auld pussy willow."

Alex nodded, trying not to sound impatient. "What is the time?"

"Ye still doona have yer watch, cousin?"

Alex raised a brow. "The time, cousin?"

With a knowing smirk, Rorick flipped open his watch case. " 'Tis half past ten. Why?"

Ignoring his impudent cousin, Alex turned on his heel and strode into the house. Rorick followed on his heels, refusing to be left behind.

"Do ye mind if I ask what—"

Without slowing his ascent of the grand stairs, Alex said with a grunt, "I mind."

"—yer doing?" Rorick continued, undaunted. "I hate to be a pain in the arse—"

"Then don't be."

"—but if ye'll tell me yer trouble, p'raps I can be of some assistance."

Alex opened the door to his chamber and stepped inside, and Rorick followed. "If you want to help, Rorick, then ring for some hot water. I only have a few minutes—"

"Until what?"

"I have to go out."

"That I gathered." Rorick yanked on the bellpull, once, twice. "What was on the paper?"

Alex jerked at the laces of his shirt. "Don't ask questions, Rorick. You don't want to know—"

Rorick caught his arm. "Alex." He kept his gaze steady as Alex gave him a questioning look. "You can trust me."

Alex stared down at the hand gripping his forearm. Broad, wide-knuckled. Kind. "I . . . I don't know, Rorick."

"Alex." His cousin's voice was gruff. " 'Tis obvious ye're troubled. I willna tell a soul."

Alex felt his certainty wavering. Rorick, for all his cocksure ways, had always been a true friend to him—perhaps his only friend. And if ever there was a time he needed to trust a friend, that time was now.

Shirt in hand, he waited while six footmen brought in heavy wooden buckets of water, while another two followed with the copper tub. Readying the bath seemed to take forever. Steam rose in pale tendrils from the water, a seductive invitation to soak his weary muscles. Yet when the footmen were one, he remained motionless.

At last he lifted his gaze to Rorick. "All right."

Alex dug in his coat pocket. He held the note out for Rorick to take, and watched as his cousin read the short missive.

Frowning, Rorick looked up at him. "What is this? A joke?"

Alex arched a brow. "Do I appear to be laughing, cousin?"

"Nay." Holding the note gingerly in his hand, Rorick sat on the edge of the bed. "Do ye wish to tell me what it means?"

Wrapping his shirt around and around his hand, Alex frowned and tried to focus his thoughts. "You've heard of the Mohocks?"

Rorick cocked his head. "The men who've been terrorizing London? Aye, but—"

" 'Tis a summons from them." Alex jammed the shirt into a ball and tossed it into a corner.

"And . . . the connection would be . . . ?"

Alex closed his eyes, trying to form in his mind how one event had led to another. It had all happened so swiftly. A ball, a meeting with the queen, yes, but the rest of it . . .

"For some time now," he began slowly, "I have been a member of the Mohocks." He waited for the flare of recrimination, but instead found stoic acceptance on his cousin's face. ''You don't seem surprised.''

Rorick cleared his throat. ''Well, your recent, er, behavior has been a wee bit odd. At least everything is beginning to make sense.''

Alex watched him closely. ''There's more.''

The Scotsman's fox-red brows flared. ''Aye?''

''I joined the Mohocks on a secret mission for the queen.''

''The queen,'' Rorick echoed, his voice flat.

Alex nodded.

Rorick blew out a long breath that rustled the ever-present curl of hair that flopped willfully over his forehead. ''Well. Would ye like to tell me how this all happened?''

Briefly Alex related everything from the queen's request, to meeting the Emperor, to overhearing the men in the Hallifield maze.

''But the Emperor's plan is coming to fruition much sooner than I had thought,'' Alex explained. ''I'd not expected that note for days. Something must have happened.''

''Mayhap someone discovered the capture of the two men.''

Alex nodded at the logical suggestion. ''Perhaps.'' He leaned over the washbasin, scooped his hands in, and brought warm water up over his face. ''I have to hurry if I'm to finish this.''

''Ye're not going alone?''

Alex seized a brush and began to stroke shaving soap across his cheeks. He picked up a razor. ''I don't have a choice. I have to go alone.''

In his shaving mirror, Alex saw Rorick cross his arms over his chest. ''I will go with ye.''

Alex set the razor down and turned around to face him. ''Nay, cousin. I can't ask you to do that.''

Rorick walked to the oak armoire without a reply. Retrieving a fresh black shirt, he laid it out on the bed. "Ye didna ask. I offered."

They regarded each other solemnly, Rorick determined to succeed, and Alex equally determined to deny him.

Alex reached for his shirt. He would not draw his family into danger, but perhaps . . . "There is something of grave importance to me," he offered slowly, "if you truly wish to help."

"And that is?"

"Take a message to the queen's guard. Then take Tori and my mother away from London."

Without a word, Rorick took the razor, rinsed it in the basin, and began to stroke it against the leather strop. "Yer woman, and yer mother."

Stuffing his shirttail into his breeches, Alex reached for his waistcoat. "Aye." He could sense his cousin's reluctance in each harsh stroke of the razor. Placing his hand on Rorick's shoulder, he said, "Rorick, 'tis the best possible use of your strength. I haven't the time to carry the message to the queen myself. And I can't go into this not knowing whether Tori and my mother are in danger. Take them to safety. Please."

No emotion at all passed over Rorick's features. At last he turned to the door, and Alex's heart sank.

He almost didn't hear Rorick as he said, "Aye, m'lord," before he closed the door.

Chapter Eighteen

Tori curved her fingers around the fragile china cup, letting the warmth from the cocoa seep through her as she leaned closer to the window to watch the courtyard and street beyond the iron gate. Behind her the clock on the mantel kept up a relentless pace, driving the morning on. Laughter, clunks, and scrapes could be heard from all over the mansion as the house servants carried out their duties, while outside, carriages passed by on the cobblestone street, their clattering wheels and polished exteriors pleasant reminders of friendly visits and drives through the park. A cerulean sky promised a glorious spring afternoon.

Incongruous details. A normal day, by all appearances. Yet, inside, her heart clenched with each progressive *tick-tick* of the clock.

Charles's withdrawal from her was now complete, and Alex . . . something dreadful must have happened. His cold words had struck a crippling blow to her trust in him. Yet she couldn't bring herself to believe what he'd said. Alex's actions—the way he held her, the soft rasp in his voice as he spoke her name, the look in his eyes—all these things belied his claim that he no longer cared for her. Whatever his reason for trying to drive her away, she was equally determined he would not succeed. She had to find a way to make him see reason.

A black coach and four with its shades drawn rambled up the gravel drive into the courtyard, startling her from her reverie. The coach door crashed open, and a man burst free and raced on long legs toward the front door. Even before she heard Smythe answer the rapid knock, Tori recognized the coat of arms that graced the coach door.

She ran to the door and flung it wide. "Alex?" she said breathlessly.

But the tall man in the foyer was a stranger to her, his face hidden beneath a low-pulled tricorne. He gesticulated wildly as he spoke with her whey-faced butler.

Smythe turned to her and issued a brisk bow, doing his best to retain a measure of decorum. "Lady Victoria, this man says he—"

The man stepped forward, trying to edge past Smythe. "My lady, I must have a word with ye. 'Tis of the utmost importance."

Belatedly, he swept the hat from his head to reveal a shock of red hair and a square face she might have described as handsome, in a rough sort of way. A square-cut jaw, a hawkish nose. High, prominent cheekbones, delicate, yet the face was the kind that might have seen a few tavern brawls. Sleek, well-formed brows. Generous lips that at the moment looked grim. For some reason he seemed familiar.

His eyes fascinated her. Gray, but lit by an inner light that made them appear wild. Almost . . . hunted.

Recognition settled upon her then, and she felt rather foolish for not recognizing Alex's valet straightaway. "Mr. McDowell, isn't it?"

He gave a short nod and brushed past the sputtering Smythe. "Aye, milady. I have a message I promised to convey to ye.'' He cast a mistrustful eye toward her butler. '' 'Tis a message for ye alone.''

''Please.'' Tori gestured toward the open door to the blue room. ''Come in and sit down.''

Her heart raced as she preceded him into the formal withdrawing room, leaving Smythe to mutter alone as he made his way into the bowels of the house. A message—it could only be from Alex.

Before she could sit, he grasped her arm and turned her back to him. She stared up into his eyes, arrested by the intensity she saw reflected there. ''No time for social niceties, milady. Ye must come away with me immediately.''

The urgency in his voice made her heart clench in her chest. His fingers were cold through the light wool of her sleeve. ''Sir?''

''Alex sent me to fetch ye. Ye must come with me—*now.*''

Alex was in trouble. She felt it, as certain as if she'd witnessed it herself. In the space of an instant, the heartless way Alex had dismissed her drifted away, the pain meaningless now. He needed her. ''What has happened?'' she asked. ''How—''

'' 'Twill all be clear shortly, milady. I canna explain now. Will ye come?''

Swallowing the lump of uncertainty that had formed in her throat along with the thought of what might lie ahead, Tori nodded and stepped to the door. When she opened it, she found Smythe lurking in the foyer, frenziedly dusting the paintings that lined the walls. She had the distinct impression he'd been there all along. Eavesdropping, no doubt, but there was no time to speak with him about it now.

''Smythe, have someone fetch my cloak. I'll be going out for . . . for a drive. I'll be back shortly.''

The butler darted a look behind her and opened his mouth as though he might say something. After a pause, he pressed his thin lips together and clicked his heels, bowing with a flourish. "As you wish, my lady."

Tucking her chin into the thick warmth of her cloak to ward away the chill spring air, Tori walked to Alex's waiting carriage with the enigmatic Scotsman by her side. Neither the driver—whom she couldn't recall having seen before—nor the liveried footmen paid them heed—indeed, they behaved like wooden statues, staring off into the distance as though arrested by the greatest of sights to behold. The peculiarity of their behavior made her pause.

McDowell tugged at her arm. "Come."

She waited as he opened the coach door and folded down the step. He held out a gloved hand to assist her, and she placed her own within it.

His fingers closed around hers, solid as English oak and just as strong. It should have made her feel safe. Instead, for some reason she couldn't explain, she felt an odd fluttering of trepidation.

Stuff and nonsense. He was taking her to Alex.

She placed her foot on the step. As she stepped upward, she saw something completely unexpected inside the coach.

The mass of a woman's skirts were spread out over one of the seats, tiny black leather half-boots peeking from beneath. In the blink of an eye, she noticed the dress was claret; the ribbon that trimmed the skirt, satin. Details, again, but suddenly they didn't seem so unimportant.

The flutterings in her stomach grew stronger. She tried to turn around, but before she could back away, she felt a shove against her rear. She pitched forward, falling, falling. Instinctively she put her hands out as the coach floor rushed to meet her.

She landed in a clumsy heap, pain exploding in her face as her cheekbone met the corner of a bench. More pain zigzagged like lightning up one wrist. Dazed, Tori blinked at the stars clouding her consciousness. She tried to turn over, but felt her legs being bent and pushed forward, heard the coach door bang shut like the crack of a whip.

The carriage lurched into motion.

Pain swept through her in sickening waves with each jolt as they clattered over the cobblestones. She tried to get to her knees. "What are you—"

Hands closed around her arms. Big hands. Alex's cousin's hands.

Tori swallowed a lump of nausea as the hands hauled her up to her knees. Her arms were yanked cruelly, painfully behind her. She cried out, wriggling and straining to get away.

"Shut up," he said in a growl, yanking her hands around to in front of her.

He had ropes around her wrists in the blink of an eye. Tori bit her lip against the excruciating pressure as he tightened the knot around her injured wrist. "Mr. McDowell," she begged, panting, "listen, please. I don't know why you're doing this, but—"

"Shut up, I said!"

High, tittering laughter bounced off the inner walls of the carriage. "Oh, come now, Rick. Let her talk. 'Tis ever so much fun witnessing her discomposure."

Tori froze at the cold voice.

McDowell hauled Tori up onto a seat. Her world righted, Tori stared across the carriage into the hardest pair of eyes she'd ever seen. The woman was beautiful, her skin as pale and rich as clotted cream, her lips full and sensual. Golden-red hair escaped from the hood of her cloak in long, curling tendrils. But her eyes were as cold as shards of ice. They raked up and down her body as McDowell secured her ankles with rough rope.

Tori didn't need to strain against her bonds to realize she was quite at their mercy.

No one knew where she'd gone, or with whom.

Fear threatened to overpower her, but she wouldn't let them see that. Tori returned the woman's measuring stare. "Now that you've accomplished your goal, I know you won't mind telling me who you are and what you want of me."

An icy smile tipped the corners of the woman's lips. "I'm surprised you don't know who I am, Lady Victoria. I certainly know who you are. Is that not so, Rick?"

The burly Scotsman scowled as he sat down next to his female partner. He leaned his face close to hers, his eyes hard, his mouth grim. "The name is Rorick, and I'll thank ye to remember it, Baroness."

So she was a gentlewoman. Hardly a surprise, considering her expensive clothing and high manner. Tori arched a brow, deciding she should be just as haughty. "I fear you have me at a disadvantage . . . Baroness?"

The red-haired woman laughed again, unmoved by the Scotsman's efforts at intimidation. "That, my dear, is quite the understatement. Eh, Rick?"

The Scotsman grunted and stared out the window. A muscle worked in his cheek.

"Don't mind him; he's quite ill-humored today." The woman studied her with narrowed eyes, then smile as she came to a decision. "Very well. I suppose it wouldn't hurt for you to know my identity—you won't be much of a threat to anyone after today anyway."

The implication loomed over her, but Tori felt oddly unafraid. She felt only a grim need to understand. "Go on."

The woman sat straighter in her seat, staring down her nose as she said, "I am Baroness Rowan. You've heard of me?"

From somewhere in her memories came Charles's warning: *You've heard of his relationship with Bawdy Be— er, Baroness Rowan, have you not?* "Bawdy Bess," Tori whispered, remembering her horror at her brother's indiscreet mention of Alex's mistress. It seemed a lifetime ago.

Rorick brayed a laugh, white teeth flashing a wicked smirk at the baroness. Bess flushed a mottled red. She lifted her chin and haughtily raised a single brow as she focused her attention only on Tori. "I see you have."

"As has most o' London," Rorick quipped.

The baroness glared at him. He slanted a sly smile her way, an obvious challenge. Stiffening, she shifted on the bench they shared, turning away. Never taking his eyes from her, the Scotsman inched closer, a self-satisfied smirk playing about his lips.

Tori watched the silent exchange, amazed by the river of animosity flowing between the two cohorts. Alex's cousin and his reputed mistress. Something linked them, but it was clearly not love. If she could discover what that link was, she might just find a way out of this mess.

She cleared her throat to gain their attention. "Aye, I've heard of you, Baroness. But perhaps you could explain how you know me."

Her ploy succeeded. With a cold shoulder angled toward the Scotsman, Bess turned her interest back to Tori. "Did Alex not tell you about me?"

She looked concerned . . . almost hurt. Tori shrugged, ignoring the stab of pain the movement sent through her shoulder.

"Well, did he?" Bess pressed, her voice growing shrill. She continued without a pause. "I suppose it does not signify at all. We both know what I am to Alex, don't we?"

Tori bit her lip, trying to ignore the tiny nagging doubt sparked by the older woman's claim. Rumors were the lifeblood of London society, and gossip about the Devil Lord's exploits with his mistress was among the favorite to be whispered. Yes, she knew of the relationship Alex had shared with the baroness. What she didn't know was whether Alex was still involved with Bess. Or had he thrown her over, as other gossipmongers had suggested?

"Yes. I see you do know." A pleased smile curved Bess's lips. "Good. Then there is no reason for further games between us."

Tori stared at her coolly. "What do you want with me, Baroness?"

Bess tittered again, a laugh that scraped Tori's nerves like shattered glass. "Oh, 'tis not you I want, Lady Victoria. I want Alex."

It was the answer she'd expected. Somehow she sensed that everything this woman did and thought and felt revolved around Alex. "I see," she said with a hint of wry humor. "And Mr. McDowell? Does he want Alex as well?"

The Scotsman turned four shades of red. His mouth opened and closed; his nostrils flared. At long last he mastered his wits and muttered, "Och, aye. I'd love to get my hands on my dear cousin Alex." He paused and looked at her. " 'Tis why ye are here, milady."

His voice held a tone of respect that rang especially false considering their situation. But she understood his meaning immediately . . . as well as the purpose behind their illicit partnership.

They meant to set a trap—and they meant for her to serve as bait.

For Alex.

Sharp, fierce panic arrowed through her. *Think, Victoria, think!* Forcing a quietude she couldn't feel into her voice, she said carefully, "You plan to use me to lure your cousin to you?"

"Aye."

She let her laugh ring out, hoping against hope that she sounded convincing. "Oh, you poor, poor man. If you only knew." Rorick's head whipped around; his brows crashed down into a dangerous vee as he stared at her. Before he could comment, Tori plunged on, casting a sympathetic glance at the baroness. "And you. If only you knew! We should be forming a sisterhood of women thrown over by the Devil Lord."

Bess lost her hauteur as her mouth dropped open. "What?" She grabbed Rorick's arm with both hands, her knuckles turning white. "What is she saying? You told me—"

Their earlier animosity forgotten, Rorick patted Bess's hand in an attempt to soothe her. But he raised a brow at Tori. "Nice try, milady, but I'm afraid yer ploy willna work. Ye see, I ken verra well Alex's regard for ye."

"I'm afraid you're mistaken, sir," Tori replied. " 'Twas no more than three hours ago that Alex told me he no longer wished to . . . see me. That our association was a mistake."

"Mm-hmm. But ye see, 'twas but an hour ago that Alex bade me see ye clear of the city before the fires begin. Desperate to see ye safe, he was. Of course, he doesna realize 'tis far too late for the two of ye."

Fires. The two Mohocks in the park at Hallifield's had been bickering about fires. She frowned. "I don't understand."

"Oh, come, come, milady. Will ye pretend ye doona know of my cousin's plan to rid the city of the Mohock scourge?"

"She knows, all right," Bess interjected. "I saw them together at the Hallifield ball, just before the guard took your associates away."

Tori studied the two of them, knowing she'd at last found the link. Somehow Rorick McDowell was involved with the Mohock club, and he was using Bess's desire for revenge to help him foil Alex's plan. "I don't know what you're talking about," she said carefully. "I know nothing about Mohocks, and I know nothing about your associates, and I know nothing about fires. You're both making a terrible mistake. I must insist that you take me back immediately."

The carriage rattled to a jarring halt, and Tori slowly became aware of the world beyond the conveyance. The scent of fish and the calls of street hawkers and carters told her they were somewhere near the river, far from the fashionable boulevards of her peers. But there were people, and where there were people, there existed the possibility that she would be seen. Perhaps rescued. Or at the very least, those people might provide her with the distraction she needed to escape.

The carriage rocked as Rorick rose to his feet, reclaiming Tori's attention. "I'm afraid we canna do that, milady." He paused, his hand on the brass handle, and gazed back at her, his expression inscrutable. "My associates await."

The door swung slowly open, and her hopes for escape died. She had a brief vision of a smattering of men standing outside the coach, their tricornes pulled low to shade the fact that they all wore masks.

Mohocks.

Desperation propelled her into action. She scrambled back on the seat until she was as far away from the door as possible. The men looked on, amusement in the smug lines of their mouths. In a split second, she grasped for the shade pull. It snapped free and rolled high, exposing her to the street opposite.

That single action brought on a flurry of reaction. McDowell and two of his compatriots lunged toward her, but only managed to wedge themselves tightly in the narrow opening. Aware that every second was a precious gift, Tori reached for the window latch, cursing the ropes that bound her so tightly. Small fingers grabbed her wrist—the baroness. With a snarl that came from deep in her soul, Tori brought her feet up and shoved hard, taking great pleasure in watching Bess's skirts fly up as she landed rump-first on the bench.

She turned back to her task, and had just managed to free the latch with her numb fingers when she was hauled backward. She opened her mouth to scream, but someone stuffed a handkerchief into her mouth and she was dragged from the coach. A circle of black formed about them to hide her struggles. Tori had only a glimpse of a sign waving in the wind against the worn brick facade of a tall building before a heavy cloak was tossed over her head and she found herself thrown over a burly shoulder.

She felt all nine jolting steps the man took to reach the building, each step driving his shoulder farther under her ribs until she thought she'd never breathe again.

She felt ill the moment they entered the building with the sign of the drooling dog. A hundred smells assaulted her, dominated by the choking fumes of stale beer and unwashed flesh. Her throat closed, her jaw squeezing tight against the lump of dry, salty cloth. Her stomach lurched and bucked in protest, and her eyes began to water uncontrollably.

The arms locked around her knees dropped away, and she slid down to the floor. "Stand just there, m'lady." The voice was low, but cultured, without the coarse quality she might have expected from a brigand.

The cloak was yanked from her with a snapping flourish. As her eyes began to adjust to the dim interior of what could only be a tavern, she could see that the circle of men dressed in black had not diminished. They were watching her, leering smiles flashing beneath their masks.

She forced herself upright. "What now? What do you want of me?"

By the way their leers spread, a different question might have been prudent. One man stepped before her, too close for comfort. He reached for her, his hand sliding along the curve of her neck. "I'll tell you what I'd like from you, luv."

The voice of a gentleman—but not, unfortunately, the heart of a gentle man. Not that the rest of them were any better, she amended with an insulted gasp as someone behind her cupped his hand around her buttock.

She jerked away from them both, but succeeded only in backing into yet another stout male form. And the circle was closing in. She felt the press of their bodies all around her. A touch here. A pinch there. Her breathing came faster as fear clenched around her heart.

A gruff voice chuckled near her ear. "Here now, Weasel. Yer scarin' her off. Not treatin' her nice enough."

Tori looked up into a face that—what she could see of it—only a mother could love. He had yellowed teeth, several of which were missing. Pocked skin covered his jutting jaw. Quick as an eel the man slipped his arm around her to hold her in place. He closed his free hand around her breast, grinding his palm in circles. Revulsion shuddered through her as his lips and hot breath touched her ear.

"She likes it easy, doncha, lady? Nice and slow and—Oof!"

She rammed her elbow into his ribs, and his breath expelled in a fetid rush. Before she could inflict further pain, hands grabbed her upper arms on both sides and she was yanked away with enough force to make her teeth clack shut.

Yellow Teeth glared at her, his jaw clenched. "Bitch!"

Tori lifted her chin. "Touch me again, *sirrah,* and I shall see the revulsion I feel revisited upon you as pain, ten thousandfold."

"Oooooh, listen to her!"

"Feisty little wench, ain't she?"

"Quite superior," said a third, grinning.

Tori turned on him, fury at the situation she found herself in making her bold. "Be not so sure of yourself, Lord Allenby. You're not so anonymous as you might think, despite the mask."

The grin fell from the man's face, and he clapped a hand over his mouth as though to hide the distinctive gaps between his teeth.

"And you . . ." Tori pivoted in a circle, glaring at each of the men in turn. "And you . . . and the rest of you. Do you truly believe you can hide behind a flimsy scrap of silk for long? If I can recognize one of you, how long will it be before someone else recognizes the rest, one by one?" She laughed caustically, hoping to instill a little doubt where only bravado reigned. "What help will your noble families be to you then? Will they support you? Protect you? Or will they close their eyes and let the queen have her way with you?"

A deep voice came from behind them, so clear and distinct that she felt it reverberate up her spine. "The lady is quite right, of course. We cannot go unknown forever. 'Tis impossible. But"—an enormous man emerged from the shadows near the hearth, his square face unadorned by the trademark black pirate's mask—"think of the glory we can create in this one night of chaos." His pale eyes gleamed with a fire she feared—it held both insanity and purpose. "And the lady is going to help us."

Tori lifted her chin. "I'll never help you."

The big man jerked his head toward the hall. "Take her upstairs."

Alex paused outside the Hound's Breath tavern. Judging from the whoops, bellows, and laughter emanating from within, the Mohocks were well on their way to building their courage through drink. Anticipation and doubt gnawed at him as he thought of the night ahead. He wouldn't have the benefit of drink to assist him—but then, he'd need all of his wits about him if he meant to succeed.

He had to succeed.

His hand closed around the scrap of silk in his pocket, the mask he'd wear. With any luck, the anonymity of the mask would serve a dual purpose. Besides the obvious result of hiding his identity from passersby, with luck it would also make it difficult for the Mohocks to identify any traitor in their midst—unless they caught him red-handed. And he meant to see to it that no one got close enough to catch him red-handed.

He entered the tavern and was immediately stunned to see the swelled ranks of the Mohock club. It seemed their efforts at recruitment had been wildly successful. Hovering in the doorway, he retrieved the mask from his pocket and slipped it over his head. With it tied securely in place, he walked down the steps and joined the crowd.

The Emperor held court at the hearth, participating in the revelry but standing apart with the reserve his position demanded. He held his hand up as he saw Alex approach, motioning for quiet.

"Ah, and here we have our Raven at last." *So much for anonymity.* "Come, join us, Raven, while we discuss the sequence of events that will take place today."

Alex made his way through the jovial men until he stood before the Emperor himself. As tall as Alex was, the Emperor stood even taller, an intimidating presence. Alex suffered an instant of doubt. What if the queen had chosen the wrong man? What if he failed her after all?

He couldn't let that happen. He would succeed.

He had to.

The Emperor's eyes flashed cold and gray as he told them what to expect. "We will work in groups of twelve. I'm sure I don't need to remind you that we will hit St. Alban's Church first. The rest will follow, one by one. You all know your sites. See to it that the fires are strong and enduring. We can't have the flames going out before we're ready. Remember, we need these fires to distract the attentions of the queen's men—"

Alex found his thoughts drifting as the Emperor's voice droned on. St. Alban's Church was only two blocks from Tori's home Maryleborn Court. Thank God he had sent Rorick to her in time. At least he had the security of knowing that Tori was safe, far away from London.

He hadn't wanted to confide in Rorick, either, but he'd had no choice. And if he were honest, by telling Rorick he had ensured that his mother would know the truth, were something to happen to him tonight. The minimum of comforts, perhaps, but at least it was something.

Hearing his name drew him back from his reverie.

"And you, Raven, have been chosen to receive the highest of honors."

Alex blinked. "I'm sorry, what did you say?"

The Emperor smiled slowly. "You will have the distinction of wielding the knife that shall take Anne's life. You shall assassinate the queen."

He held up his hands again, and a roar burst from the men, rising high on wings of ale and enthusiasm.

Alex froze, unable to believe his luck. He licked his lips. "Er, perhaps another Mohock would be a better choice. I'm still a novice at this, and—"

"Are you refusing us, Raven?" Without appearing to move, the Emperor suddenly appeared next to him. He studied Alex with an intensity that made sweat break out on Alex's forehead. "Are you refusing *me?*"

"Of course not. It's just that—"

"I don't brook refusal lightly, Raven. It isn't an attractive quality in a compatriot."

"I wouldn't exactly call it refusal—"

"I would." He snapped his fingers. "Bring out the girl."

Within a matter of seconds, Alex heard a scuffle on the stairs. Muffled grunts. A feminine squeal of indignation.

Nothing could have prepared him for the moment he saw Tori being led around the corner. Her hair was disheveled, her hands bound by tightly wrapped ropes. His heart lurched, and he took a step forward before he caught himself.

Tori locked her hands together and swung at the man pushing her through the crowd. "I said, don't touch me again!" She straightened her shoulders and walked toward the Emperor with all the courage of an experienced warrior. "How dare you have me locked away for hours, without water, without food, without daylight! When my father discovers your treatment of me, your names won't be worth the cost of inscribing them on a gravestone."

"Patience, my dear. Patience. All in good time." The Emperor paused, as though he was about to say more. Then he looked at her askance. "Tell me, my dear. Look about you. Are there any others you recognize?'' When Tori gave him a look of impatience, the Emperor smiled slyly. ''As a matter of curiosity, of course.''

Alex watched as Tori slowly turned to her left. Dread built to a fever pitch within his chest as he waited, higher, tighter, each second excruciating. Her gaze passed from man to man, paused, then went on again.

As he waited, a surreptitious movement at the far end of the room caught his eye. Alex watched as a man edged behind a taller figure standing nearby, his movements so slight as to be almost imperceptible to the casual viewer. As with the rest of the men in the room, the man was disguised by the Mohock mask, but something about the slim man's stance struck a chord of familiarity in him.

Before he could pursue that thought, he heard a tiny gasp and knew that Tori had seen him at last.

Chapter Nineteen

Their eyes met for one interminable moment, hurt and fear and desperation mingling painfully before she schooled her expression and continued on. But the dread in Alex's heart only continued to build.

Tori gazed at the Emperor, imperiously lifting a brow. "I see no one else I recognize. Does that satisfy you? Do you feel secure now?"

The Emperor began to pace, his hands behind his back. "You see no one."

"No."

"Ah." He circled the room, slowly, almost leisurely, pausing to look in one man's face, then shaking his head and moving on, the expression on his face thoughtful. "Not even one?"

Alex waited with dread in his heart, knowing it was only a matter of time. Somehow the Emperor knew—and he intended to use Alex's feelings for Tori to force him to do his bidding.

Tori shook her head. "I told you, no."

Like the attack of a snake, the Emperor turned on her, his face only inches from hers. "Lies!" he roared. The color drained from Tori's face. "What do you say to this?"

Raising his hand, he snapped his fingers. In an instant, Alex was surrounded, an ogre on each arm. They wasted no time in bringing him forward.

"What say you, madam? Know you this man?"

Alex held his breath as she turned her gaze on him. She glanced away. "No. I do not."

But the Emperor had heard the slight hesitation in her tone as well as Alex had. "I see. Oh, yes, I see." He turned briefly to another Mohock. "Call out the Scotsman."

Alex saw Tori stiffen. More surprises, then. He schooled his expression into neutrality and waited.

He heard ancient hinges squeal as a door opened, then closed again. He took a breath, wondering what the Emperor's surprise was. Footsteps crossed the uneven plank floor, slowly but inevitably coming closer.

"Hello, cousin."

Alex froze as the familiar voice crushed through him, shock and disbelief quick on its heels. He turned as if in a dream, seeing the concern on Tori's face, the victory on the Emperor's, the curiosity of the gathered band as they watched the drama unfolding before them. And when he'd turned far enough, he saw his cousin walking toward him.

"Rorick?" he said hoarsely.

"I see no introductions are necessary." The Emperor crossed his arms, waiting. His rough features showed he was enjoying himself immensely. "This woman says she doesn't know our Raven, McDowell. What say you?"

Rorick looked at him, a thousand unspoken thoughts shadowing his eyes. For one brief, breathtaking moment, hope flared in Alex's heart as he sensed his cousin's hesitation. They were friends, goddammit. Rivals at times, yes, but mostly friends. Surely he couldn't do this. But that hope died when the emotion he'd seen in Rorick's gaze hardened and Rorick turned his face away. "There was nae mistake. He loves her. He asked me to take her away from London before the fires began, and he's trying to protect her now." Rorick paused, nodding, but refused to meet Alex's gaze. "Aye, he loves her."

Alex darted a glance at Tori and found her studying him, tears glittering in the corners of her eyes.

"Love." The Emperor laughed. "Oh, so noble of you, Raven. And wanting to protect her. So very sweet. I have a proposition for you to that end. Would you like to hear it?"

"Aye," Alex said, gritting his teeth.

"I thought you might." The smile on his face could have turned boiling water into ice. "If you do what is asked of you, your lady will be allowed to live."

"And if I don't?"

The Emperor shrugged. "Then she'll die. And then you'll die."

Tori moved a step toward him. "Alex, don't do it. It's not worth it, I'm not worth it, don't—"

The Emperor snapped his fingers. "Take her upstairs."

"Alex, don't listen to him! Alex!"

Her screams echoed in his ears long after she disappeared around the bend in the stairway. Alex forced his fingers to unclench, knowing his actions now would decide everything. Tori's freedom, her very life, depended upon his ability to convince them he meant to fulfill their demands.

Turning his head, Alex looked at Rorick. "Why?"

His cousin moved toward him. He had the look of a warrior, tall, strong, immovable. All he needed was a certain angle of light to transform the planes of his face into the countenance of a Viking. "Why?" he murmured for Alex's ears alone. "Why does the wind blow? Why does the rain fall? 'Tis my destiny, cousin. Surely ye feel it, too."

His words were strong, but something about them did

not ring true. Destiny? Aye. But not this way. "We create our own destinies, Rorick—as you so often reminded me when we were children. Do you remember?"

The words seemed to take his cousin aback. "Doona let yer mother hear ye speak such blasphemy," he said with a light shrug.

"Leave my mother out of this."

"I can do that, cousin. But only if ye fulfill yer end of the bargain."

"I've made no bargain."

"But ye did take the Mohock vow."

"Just tell me why this is all happening, Rorick. You owe me that much."

Rorick stared at him, his eyes distant. "Aye, I suppose I do." He moved to stand beside the Emperor, handing the big man a tankard of ale. "Ye've heard of the Jacobites, have ye not?"

Alex raised a brow, but said nothing.

"But ye ken only England's side," his cousin insisted passionately. "Ye havena seen the way the Sassenach forces uphold the so-called 'peace' in the countryside. Ye havena seen the destruction. The misery of my people at what amounts to being held prisoner against their will—prisoners of a government we doona agree with. Ye doona ken no' having a real voice against these things."

"And yet the men you've chosen to trust are Englishmen."

Rorick froze at the softly spoken jibe. "Like you?" he countered.

"You could have trusted me, Rorick."

His cousin had the decency to look chagrined before answering. "It doesna matter now.

Scotland wants what is rightfully theirs, and that means restoring James to the throne upon Anne's demise—no' the Hanoverian sausage-eater whose only claim to England stems from a shirttail relation!"

Alex raised a mocking brow. "I had no idea your interests were so political, cousin."

"Aye, and there are more people who share my interests than ye can imagine," Rorick swore. "My compatriots are many. We shall prevail."

"You always were one to adopt a cause."

"Enough," the Emperor interrupted. "You've heard your cousin's reasons. And as for the Mohocks—money and excitement are reason enough. Now give us your answer."

Long moments stretched the tension levels in the room to the farthest limits while Alex thought through how he should proceed next. His answer was, at last, simple and inevitable. "Aye. I will do as you wish."

Someone in the crowd let out a long-held breath.

The Emperor allowed himself a small smile. "Very good, Raven." With a wave of the Emperor's hand, the men holding his arms released their grip, though they kept their positions. "For your cooperation, I offer you a gift—to show *my* good faith. I give you your ladylove."

Rorick gasped. "What are ye saying?"

Hope spiraled through Alex. "You mean—"

The Emperor laughed. "Oh, no. I'm not so stupid as that. Nay, I believe we shall keep your lady until we have proof that you have accomplished our mission. However, I shall give you an hour or two with her—to say good-bye."

If he'd had any question in his mind regarding the fate they had planned for him, it was no more. For his part in the assassination, he would be allowed to say good-bye to Tori . . . and then he would be killed. If he could manage to find a way to see Tori clear of this mess, it might be worth it.

Alex took a deep breath and nodded slowly. "I accept."

Tori had been using her fingertips to pry at one of the planks nailed over the shuttered window when she heard the scuffle in the hall. Scraping footsteps, a few unidentified thuds, a grunt, a groan, a few muttered curses. Within a matter of seconds she heard a key in the lock. Uncertain of what was in store for her, she moved back until her shoulder blades touched the wall. She stared intently at the door, waiting, waiting. The doorknob rattled, turned, and the door crashed inward as Alex fell through the doorway and tumbled to the floor.

Disheveled, he leaped to his feet in a warrior's crouch of readiness and faced the door where his Mohock captors stood, dark grins on their faces. One cradled his wrist, and the other's grin was red with blood.

"Two hours, Raven. That should give you plenty of time with the woman. Then we'll be back for you. We have another lady who'll soon be calling your name."

The second man guffawed, slapping his friend on the back. "Good one, Wolfie, ol' boy!"

Still laughing, the two men slammed the door shut and locked it. The jarring noise propelled Tori into action. Her heart in her throat, she ran to Alex and watched his arms open as he turned to catch her. They felt like heaven around her as he held her tight against his body. Closing her eyes, she slid her arms around his neck and held on tight. He plunged his fingers into her hair and cradled her head in his shoulder. His breath was warm and sweet as he buried his nose in her hair and breathed deeply. "Tori. Thank God, Tori."

"Oh, Alex." She pressed her lips to his collarbone, his neck, his jaw, everywhere she could reach. "I thought they would kill you. I can't believe you're really here."

Here. It was the last place she wanted him. She'd hoped he'd save himself, find some way to get away. But oh, God, she needed him so.

She leaned back in his arms and gazed up at him. Her breath caught in her throat. "Alex, you're hurt!"

Blood oozed from a cut over his eye, coating a good portion of his face, but still he smiled at her with tenderness in his eyes. " 'Tis only a scratch." He touched her face, pressing his palm along her cheek. "I'm so damn thankful they didn't hurt you."

"I'm fine, except"—she held up her bound wrists—"for this. Untie me so I can help you."

When he saw the red, raw skin framing the ropes, his face darkened and he made a strangled sound in his throat. His fingers made short work of the tight knots. When the ropes fell away, he held her hands, his gaze drawn by the circles of rubbed-away flesh. "I'll kill them for hurting you. I swear it!"

"Never mind that now. Sit down on the bed." Lifting her skirt, she tore away a piece from her underskirt. Holding his face steady with a palm along his cheek, she dabbed carefully at the blood marring his face. "I'm sorry we don't have water, but this should help."

"What care I for water?" A slow half smile tipped one corner of his mouth. He placed his hands on her waist and caressed her ribs with his thumbs while his eyes flashed at her with something far different from pain. "I'm enjoying your ministrations too much to complain."

Smothering a smile, she pressed the wad of cloth firmly against the cut until the flow of blood had stopped. "There, I think that'll do."

"Good."

He grabbed her hand and pulled her down on the bed with him. Ancient ropes creaked as he shifted his weight to lean over her. Beneath them, the straw tick crackled and pricked through the thin sheets, but it mattered naught. She was with Alex.

The sight of him hovering above her, devilishly handsome and just a little bit rakish, made their situation seem somehow less dire. His fingers toyed with her hair, sending shivers down the backs of her legs, but it was the look in his eyes that made her pulse begin to race. "Well," she murmured breathlessly, "what are your intentions, sir?"

He slid his fingertips down the line of her throat, traced

her collarbone, then skimmed lower until they rested where bodice and flesh met, but his eyes never left hers. The darkest of indigo, but simmering with an inner fire, they made her feel vibrantly alive, but . . . waiting. "My intentions?" He laughed huskily, shaking his head. "Loveliest Tori. *Belle ange.* I would like . . . you make me . . . *Dieu!*"

His struggle with his feelings, and with the words that would express them, conjured the emotions and thoughts she'd only that morning supposed to be her undoing. Tori forced those feelings down now, and forced herself to put voice to the questions in her mind. She cleared her throat. "Alex, this morning, you . . . the things you said . . . and you left me, and . . . Oh, I'm making a wretched start of this. What I mean is, and perhaps you already know what I'm going to say, but why did you say those things to me this morning? I mean," she hurried on, watching his eyes for clues to his feelings, "I know why you said them, or at least I think I do, but I'd like to hear it from you."

His lips twisted in a bittersweet smile, and he traced her skin above her bodice very, very slowly. "I'm sorry for that. I didn't want to hurt you. I thought . . .'twas the only way to keep you safe. The expression on your face." He squeezed his eyes closed, remembering, and shook his head. "The hurt in your eyes . . . your beautiful eyes. All I could think of was getting you away, and you were so determined to stay."

Tori thought for a moment, giving his words a chance to heal the hurt they had only that morning caused. At last, she lifted a hand to his cheek, and he pressed against it. "Thank you," she said softly. " 'Twas as I thought. I was only afraid to believe it." Her emotions refused to be muffled forever. They flared again, demanding recognition, and she yielded to them with abandon. Lifting her other hand, she framed his face, her fingers trembling. "I love you, Alexandre Rawlings. They may come and take me away from you, they may abuse me unmercifully, but whatever comes, I am yours . . . forever."

A muscle worked in his throat, and he stared at her for long moments without speaking. His troubled gaze touched on her eyes, her hair, her breasts, her lips, then slowly, inevitably, he lowered his mouth to hers, claiming her for his own. His tongue teased at her lips and she opened for him, inviting him into the depths of her mouth and more. He tasted of forfeited dreams and bittersweet promises; a future lost, perhaps forever. Her arms crept around his neck, and she pulled him down to her, loving him with a wholeness she'd never known possible.

And might never know again. The possibility of losing him, of dying or watching him die, urged her to go where society demanded she should not. But society meant little to her now.

There was only Alex.

He broke off the kiss, his breath ragged in his throat as he stared down at her with a frown that was not a frown. Then, closing his eyes, he touched his lips to hers with a kiss that was butterfly soft and yet monumentally powerful. ''God help me, Tori. I have loved you so well in my mind for so long, it doesn't seem real to be saying the words.''

She pulled him down to her, gazing into his eyes, the eyes that had haunted her soul. His lips hovered over hers, a breath away. ''Then tell me without speaking. Kiss me, Alex, please.''

With a groan that seemed to come from the very depths of him, he swept her into his arms, taking what she offered so shamelessly. Except she didn't feel ashamed. His kiss was hot and powerful, deeply satisfying, and the taste and touch of him made her feel a part of the elements themselves. With his tongue he conquered and submitted, delved and ebbed, incited and invited, accepting all she had to offer and giving back even more.

Tori clung to him as the outside world melted into a thousand brilliant lights behind her closed lashes. Sensation flooded her body, things only Alex could make her feel. Tingles. Waves of awareness sparked by the lightest brush of his body, with each sleek swirl of his tongue against hers. Heat in places she had never understood until Alex.

His mouth left hers and traced a leisurely trail of kisses along her cheekbone to below her jaw. Tori arched against him as his mouth opened against her throat, heat and sensation radiating from that single point outward. She reached for him, pressing him closer to her, and gasped when he responded by lightly grazing her neck with his teeth.

His hand came up beneath her breast, lifting it high. Her nipple began to tingle within her bodice, and she realized he was teasing the crest between his fingers, splaying his hand over her and then drawing his fingers inward until her nipple contracted into a single point of pleasure, pertly begging for more. *Oh, yes.* And when he loosened the laces behind her back and slipped her bodice down, she knew again what she was begging for.

Desire—aye, a woman's desire—exploded within her, full-blown as his lips teased the hard peak. Tori opened her eyes, compelled to watch as his mouth opened and he took her inside his hot mouth, his tongue doing wonderful things to her. She bit her lip as pleasure and need spun a silken web between her breast and low in her abdomen, connected in a way she never realized.

''Ah, God, Tori, you are so lovely,'' he whispered. The rasp of his voice shivered over her flesh. ''I could do this to you forever.''

But forever wasn't to be, it seemed certain. Tori touched his cheek. ''I want you to do more.''

He stilled against her. ''You—''

''Yes. Everything.''

''Nay.'' But he didn't sound certain. His body was rock hard against her, rigid with need. Oh, yes, he needed her—as much as she needed him. And Tori was determined to convince him.

She reached down and slowly slid her hand up his thigh.

Wonder coursed through her as she felt his muscle tighten and release in response to her touch. The mild sense of shyness she felt evaporated, replaced by a blazing curiosity to know more, to experience all. Holding her breath, she curved her hand around the tense roundness of his buttock.

He groaned, closing his eyes.

The sound captivated her, reverberating along her nerve endings in a most delicious way. Tori closed her eyes, relishing the twitches and tingles she felt throughout the whole of her body. Pressing her lips to his throat, she thrilled to the faint rasp of his whiskers. Beneath his skin, she detected the throb of his pulse beneath her lips, swift and strong. Each unique sensation urged her on. Summoning all the boldness she could muster, she opened her mouth against his flesh, and instantly his breath caught raggedly in his throat. He tasted of salty male heat and smelled of bayberry and cloves, and it was all she could do to keep from sighing in pleasure.

Tilting her head back, she opened her eyes and looked up at him. "Alex?" She let her hands stray to his waist, marveling at the play of muscles beneath her palms. "Your body betrays you, as much as mine cries out for your touch—"

He rolled, shifting his weight onto one hip until he looked down at her. Determination etched his face as he caught her roving hands and pinned them against the mattress by her head. "You don't need to do this, Tori. If you're thinking of the promise I was so brutish to extract from you—"

"Oh, but I'm not."

"—then you may eliminate such thoughts from your head. I will not take advantage of you. You are distraught. You're not thinking clearly. And I assure you, I am not so much a cad as to force myself upon you in your confusion and fear."

The uncharacteristic formality of his speech only served to demonstrate his determination to convince her. Tori smiled, knowing it was but further evidence of his love. He loved her. "Is it wrong of me, then, to want your touch? Is it wrong of me to desire all of the things a woman feels when she is with a man? Oh, Alex." She gazed softly at him, letting all the emotions in her heart shine in her eyes. "Neither of us knows whether we shall see tomorrow come. I fear naught but dying without knowing you completely, in every sense of the word. Don't deprive us of what might be our last hours together."

He closed his eyes, his desire and his need for honor warring for control of him. His hold on her hands slackened. Slipping from his grasp, Tori slid her arms about his neck. "Love me, Alex," she whispered. "Love me now."

Alex opened his eyes as he allowed her to draw him down to her. As he hovered above her, he paused, his lips a breath away. "I do, *ange.* I do."

In the space of a single second, he closed the distance between them. His tongue parted her lips, tasting her in the way one might sip fine French wine, and she opened to him, inviting him inside with a depth of need that should have shocked her. But she was beyond shock. She was beyond the strictures of a society that assumed women didn't want, didn't need, didn't hunger. She returned his kisses with all the urgency of a woman fully sensible of her desire. Pleasure rippled through her with every brush of his hand, every stroke of his fingertips. And she wanted it all.

He pressed her onto her back, half covering her body with his own. His mouth ravaged hers, and she moaned at the tug it evoked deep in her stomach. He'd made her feel it, and the deeper, coiling pleasure that soon followed, once before. She'd thought of him in that same way many times since, in the nights when she had only a pillow to hold. And oh, she'd wanted to feel it again.

"Ah, God, Tori, what you do to me." The rasp of his voice had faded to a harsh whisper that touched her as surely as his hands. He moved down, his lips opening against her throat with a burst of heat and sensation that made her feel as though she were melting for him. His hands tugged at her loosened gown, pulling it away from her until the cool air kissed her to her waist. "Look at you. You are more lovely than I could ever dream."

His mouth closed over a taut nipple, his tongue swirling, laving and suckling on her tingling flesh until she cried out with mindless pleasure, her fingers tangling in his hair as she clutched him closer to her. His knee pressed between her legs, and she realized faintly that her legs were bare, too, and his thigh was riding that most private part of her. His hand closed behind her thigh, just below her buttock, and he pulled her closer to him, lifting her hips so that with every movement his thigh grazed her intimately.

He kissed her everywhere, between her breasts, on the soft curve beneath her nipple, the indent between her ribs, her navel, his mouth creating a wet path of interconnected pleasure. And yet Tori knew the best was yet to come.

Her hands skimmed his shoulders, and she grew impatient with the cloth withholding him from her. Pulling him up to her mouth, she kissed him deeply while her fingers fumbled at the ties of his shirt. When she had them undone, he rose on his knees above her, his eyes the darkest of midnight as he gazed down at her; then he stripped the shirt from his body and discarded it with a careless flick of the wrist.

The sight of him stole her breath away. He looked like nothing she'd ever seen before, or even dared to imagine. The dusky hue of his skin stretched taut over muscles that shifted with his every movement, and was traced with a shading of dark hair that began between his flat nipples and led down beneath the placket of his breeches. Her mouth dry, she stretched out a finger to touch a nipple, so different from her own. Slowly she traveled the path of hair, down, down, until her fingertip rested at the edge of his breeches.

His hand closed over hers, holding her there. "You are sure?" he asked hoarsely.

She locked her gaze with his as she slid her hand lower, brushing her fingers across the hard length of him. "Never have I been more so."

He closed his eyes, his breath squeezing slowly from his lungs, his hand issuing light pressure over her hand until she thought she could feel the very life pulsing within him. Curiosity surged within her. She yielded to it, knowing the time for missishness was long past. Sliding her hands around to the ties of his breeches, she began to tug them free.

With the laces undone, Alex stood up from the bed. His hands fumbled as he struggled with the close-fitting breeches, but within moments he stood free of them, and her curiosity was appeased. Her first sight of him surprised her, but she soon forgot as he rejoined her on the bed.

Gathering her into his arms, he found her mouth again, kissing her deeply as his hands slid down her body, along her hip, up the inner length of her thigh. He touched her then, as he had before, and she gasped into his mouth as she felt the heat of his touch expanding in her belly. His fingers slid along the hidden cleft, slickening her, at last settling upon a nub of flesh that sent sensation shuddering through her with each delicious stroke. With her eyes closed, she drifted into a dream of lights and pleasure, the stroke of his tongue in her mouth keeping rhythm with the play of his fingers, until she thought she could bear no more.

As if he heard her thoughts, Alex shifted against her, his knee parting her thighs easily as he moved over her. His chest brushed her breasts, the fine hairs teasing the tips. She felt the weight and heat of his hardness on her thigh; then he brought his other knee between her legs as well. Poised above her, he held his weight on his hands as he kissed her, then slowly settled down upon her.

The blunt tip of his shaft brushed against her intimately,

then glided along her folds with a rush of sensation that made her gasp. She held her breath, waiting on the brink of discovery. He didn't make her wait long. Rocking his hips, he caressed her with his full length, acquainting her with the feel of him. Then he reached between their bodies to touch her, his thumb moving in beguiling circles that made her thighs quake and tremble.

So good, this bliss. He slipped a fingertip inside her, one, then two, then three, a fraction at a time. In the back of her mind, she knew he was preparing her, knew that soon he would enter her body with his own. Growing up on their Middleham estate had given her at least that much physical knowledge. What she was unprepared for was the pain as she felt him slowly enter her.

She drew a sharp breath. ''Alex—''

He slipped his arms beneath her shoulders and cradled her head in his hands, but his hips continued the unhurried invasion of her body. His mouth hovered over hers, a breath away. ''Shh. 'Twill be over in but a minute, love, no more.''

Tori bit her lip against the burning and felt her body expand to accommodate him until he stilled his forward movement, his hips flush against hers. Gradually the pain subsided into a dull ache, but the pleasure was over for her, she was certain . . . until he sought her mouth and began to move within her body once again.

At first she thought the burning sensation had returned. Heat began to spread from the heart of her outward in deep, shimmering waves. She closed her eyes as he leisurely took her mouth and body. But soon it was not enough for her to feel, to submit, to savor. The urge to move was overwhelming. She lifted her hips forward to receive his thrusts—nay, to welcome them. Over and over, again and again.

Need spiraled higher within her, coiled tighter, as she raced toward the release her body craved. Driven by instinct, she gripped his hips with her tensed thighs. She uttered a low-ran pitched moan and held tight to his damp shoulders. Her breath came in soft gasps, and behind her closed eyelids, bright colors gathered. She felt so good, so alive, so wholly, deliciously female. Each time he moved, he stretched something deep within her; each time he withdrew, his shaft stroked again that nub of flesh that sang with blessed sensation. It was so good. . . .

And then it happened, a soaring, stunning sunburst of purest pleasure that began in the heart of her and exploded outward, casting her aloft in a void of lights and colors. Tori bit her lip against the cry that threatened to rip free, held tight as her inner muscles gripped and clenched around his flesh, again and again, until the intense sensations gradually subsided into a weary sense of wonderment and awe. Weak with pleasure, she could do no more than hold on to him as he charged toward his own release. His hoarse groan rang through the room but a minute later and he arched hard against her, spilling himself within the secret, welcoming depths of her body.

Peace drifted over her consciousness by minute increments, like the stillness following a thunderstorm. Minutes passed, then more, the only sound his ragged breathing in her ear. Still they did not move, but lay completely quiet, each twined about the other. His head rested in the crook of her shoulder, and his fingers twisted in her hair, still gripping her head as though to prevent her escape.

She felt wondrous, so vibrantly alive, as if her life had only just begun with this single act of love.

Tears misted her vision, and she smiled to herself. She ran her hand down the indentation of his spine. "Alex?"

"Mmmm?"

"Thank you."

The breath rushed from Alex's lungs as the tiny words lodged in his heart. She was thanking him? He had taken her virginity in a lowly tavern, he couldn't guarantee that he would even be alive at dinnertime, and if she could manage to stay alive, it was possible she might find herself with child. And she was *thanking* him.

"Tori . . ." His throat squeezed tight with emotion. He pulled away from her, just a bit, so that he could look down at her. She gazed up at him, her beautiful blue eyes shining with trust. Alex swallowed the apology that had leaped to his lips. He would not hurt her that way. "I should be the one to thank you, you know. But we don't have much time now. 'Tis time to prepare."

Her gaze touched on each part of his face in turn, her eyes soft. Lifting a hand, she caressed his cheek, her palm as warm and tender as the kiss of a summer breeze. He would never forget that touch—he would treasure it forever. "I know," she said quietly. "Whatever happens, Alex . . ."

He held her tightly one last time, memorizing the feel of her body against him, holding her dear. At last he forced himself to withdraw from the solace of her body, regret twisting his heart unmercifully. Slowly he adjusted his clothing, then took her hand and helped her to her feet.

She huddled close to him while he straightened her chemise, then tightened the bodice behind her back. Alex smoothed his hand ineffectually over her hair. "I don't think I can do much for this."

Tori backed away, running her fingers through the tangled mass. "It doesn't matter."

"I suppose not."

She separated the pale strands into three sections and began to work them into a long braid. Alex watched, fascinated by even this commonplace action. She finished and secured the plait by winding a few strands of her own hair around the end.

He cleared his throat, knowing there were things that must be said. "I will die before I allow them to hurt you."

She took a deep, shuddering breath and curved her hands around his arms, holding him tightly to her breast. "Keep yourself safe, Alex, please. For my sake."

He found himself nodding, if only to reassure her. "If we can manage to get you away—"

"A hopeless fantasy, I fear," she interceded.

"We must try! Should you get free, the first thing you must do is go directly to the queen's men. Tell them everything you know, and warn them that an attack on the queen is planned for this very evening. They must be forewarned, if at all possible. The queen's life depends on it."

"And then?"

He gazed into her eyes, losing himself in depths of deep, cornflower blue. "Wait for me at Maryleborn. I'll return if I can."

Raising on tiptoe, Tori pressed her lips to his in a fervent kiss, breathing in his scent, his warmth, his very soul. "No regrets?" she whispered against his lips.

With a groan that began deep within his chest, he wrapped his arms around her and crushed her to him. "Nay. No regrets."

He held her that way for a long time, until they both heard noises in the hall. Together they waited, not touching, hardly breathing, as they heard a key rattle in the old lock.

Slowly the door swung inward.

Chapter Twenty

Tori blinked, once, twice. Her breath rushed out with a mixture of relief and absolute shock.

Charles—Charles! stood on the precipice, his face partially covered by a Mohock mask. But she would know her brother anywhere.

"Charles! What on earth are you doing here?" A thought struck then, with lightning force. "You're not . . ."

Garbed in the black of the Mohock uniform, Charles stepped over the threshold and closed the door quietly behind him. "I would have come in earlier, but you were, uh, *busy.*"

Tori felt the heat of abashment rise in her cheeks—his meaning was only too obvious. "Charles," she began, "you don't understand. I . . . we . . ."

But her brother turned away from her. He lifted a tense jaw and stared Alex down. "I should call you out, you know . . . but I won't. 'Tis obvious what you mean to my sister. But for your own sake, you'd better hope your intentions are good.''

''Really, Charles!''

But Alex returned his gaze without blinking. ''The best, I assure you,'' he said solemnly.

Satisfied, Charles nodded and tossed a pile of dark clothes at Tori. ''Best get into these, then. We don't have much time.''

Digging through the pile, Tori found a pair of men's breeches, a shirt, a quilted waistcoat, and a long black cloak. ''Where did you get these?'' she asked, slipping the breeches on beneath the cover of her skirts.

Charles held a finger to his lips and opened the door just enough so that Tori could see the sprawled forms of two men on the hallway floorboards. Beside them lay several dark green bottles, turned over on their sides. The absence of puddles told her they'd been drained of their contents.

''Grog,'' Charles confirmed. ''And much of it. I told 'em I couldn't bear to think of them missing out on the festivities just because they had to guard you two.'' His lips twitched into a saucy grin. ''They were much obliged.''

''Oh, Charles.'' Tori shook her head, smiling broadly. ''To think I always reproached you for your knowledge of liquor.''

He winked. ''Quickly, now.''

Alex helped Tori dress while Charles watched the hall. When the last lace had been tightened, Tori called, ''Ready.''

Charles glanced at her. ''Not quite.'' He dug in his pocket and pulled out a scrap of black. ''Tuck your braid into the shirt and put this on. The collar on the cloak is a high one—perhaps 'twill hide enough.''

They slipped into the hall. By now, Tori reasoned, it must be late afternoon. The deep shadows that had gathered in the windowless corridor corroborated her assumption. "Which way?" Tori whispered.

Charles took her elbow. "Not that way," he muttered, indicating with a nod of his head the way she'd been brought up. "They'd see us for sure. There's another set of stairs at the back that the staff uses. We might have a chance there."

She didn't need to ask what would happen if they were seen.

Apprehension crawled slowly down Tori's spine as she followed Charles down the darkened hall. Alex had been hasty when he'd placed a hat on her head and tied on her mask, and its eye slits shifted ever downward, impeding her vision and making their surroundings seem even more sinister. Alex's bulk behind her reassured her somewhat, but she couldn't help imagining the enemy behind every closed door.

A second corridor branched off from the center of the first, and Charles led them down it. She wondered where he had gained his knowledge of the building's floor plan, then decided she didn't want to know. It was enough to follow him to safety.

After precious minutes of tiptoeing, they arrived at the back stairs. The noise rising unmuffled from the main rooms below served as an urgent reminder of the precariousness of their situation—any second their absence could be discovered. That thought kept up a thrumming litany in her head as they crept down the stairs, down and into another darkened hall that led to the rear of the building.

Holding his finger to his lips, Charles pointed to the door at the end of the passage. Her heart pounded as they approached the way to safety, faster, harder with every step.

Twenty feet. She held her breath.

Fifteen.

Ten. They were so close, it was a struggle not to run.

"I say, where are you three going?"

The voice came from behind them, casual yet curious. Tori froze, while in front of her Charles turned slowly around to face the intruder, a grim smile pasted on his face. "Oh, hullo. Just out for a bit of, er, air." He gave a wink that with the mask showed only as a twitch of his cheek muscles. "You know."

The door was but eight short feet away. The heavy oak planks, scarred by years of rough usage, beckoned. Her fingers burned to feel the cool wood beneath them as she swung the door wide, and—

"The Emperor won't like it, you know. Best return to the main room."

Tori heard the man's footsteps approach, closer than before, and her throat clenched with nervousness. Behind her, tension emanated from Alex like a cloud, surrounding her, filling her.

Charles moved a step closer to her. His face looked like a funeral mask, his smile stretching tightly over his bones. "Nonsense, man. A minute will make no difference to the Emperor."

"Ha! You're new. You don't know the Emperor." The unseen man paused then, oddly. "Er, who is this with you? Do I know—"

His voice cut off on a sharp intake of breath. The world seemed to be spinning too slowly as Tori turned around, unable to stop herself. She saw surprise registered in Charles's expression, the door again, a spiderweb of cracks radiating from a fist-sized dent in the plaster wall, each detail stunning in its clarity, until at last the sight of Alex met her seeking gaze.

Alex, with his arm clenched tight around the intruder's throat, his hand over his mouth.

The man's face was turning red and his eyes were bulging behind the eye slits of the black Mohock mask. His hooked fingers clawed at both the hand over his mouth and the forearm choking the breath from him.

Alex jerked his head toward the door. "Go," he said urgently. "I'll take care of him."

Tori let out a long breath, and realized she'd been holding it the whole time. "Alex, no!" She took a step toward them, then stopped when the intruder flailed his feet at her. "You can't manage this alone. It's too risky!"

Charles gripped her arm, his eyes watching the far end of the corridor. "We have to get out of here, Tori."

Tori set her jaw. She'd not come this far only to abandon Alex to the wolves. "Not without Alex."

The Mohock managed to work free enough to sink his teeth into Alex's finger. Growling a curse, Alex tightened his arm around the man's neck, tighter, harder, until the man opened his teeth. The man strained against his captor, trying to gain purchase. "Tori, get the hell out of here. Now!" Alex said in a hiss.

"I'm not going to leave you here alone!"

From the head of the corridor came sounds of approaching footsteps. Two men rounded the corner and halted as they spied the scene before them.

"Hey!"

"What—"

More Mohocks. Dieu. Alex dashed a meaningful look Charles's way, but the lad was one step ahead. His mouth tightened into a grim line as he pulled at Tori, obviously trying to edge toward the door. Stubbornness etched a tightness all over Tori's face as she dug in her heels. Alex gritted his teeth and groaned inwardly.

"Stop where you are!"

The second man turned back. "Get the Emperor!" he shouted behind him.

Alex could see his last chance to get Tori to safety slipping away before his very eyes. Behind him, he could hear rumblings of upheaval in the main room, and closer, stealthy shuffling as the two new intruders stole up while his back was turned.

With a last desperate glance at Charles, Alex steeled

himself to wait until he knew they were directly behind him. Then, with a growl that came from the very depths of his belly, he swung the straining body of his captive, fiercely launching the man into the approaching Mohocks.

He heard Tori's breath catch in her throat.

The three men went sprawling, then scrabbled about as they tried to find purchase among the writhing mass of arms and legs. In a moment they'd be up and upon their quarry—*him*—again. There was no time for escape.

A swarm of men came running around the corner to join the three in the hall. It was too late for him, but maybe . . . just maybe not for Tori.

Alex locked eyes with Charles. After only a brief pause he saw his small nod, and he knew he'd understood. A wave of relief swept through him, but all was not over yet.

From the corner of his eye, he saw Tori try to take a step toward him. He must make his move now, or it would be too late for even Charles to save her. Sucking air into his lungs, he drew himself up and then, in an explosion of motion, pivoted and launched himself at the approaching mob.

Tori gasped. Through a hazy veil of disbelief, she watched Alex sacrifice himself, and she knew it was on her behalf. Her mouth dropped open, but she could force neither breath nor words from her lips. Four Mohocks reached for Alex, but as determined as they were to take him, he meant just as much to resist. One leveled a kick into his ribs, and he grunted, sinking to his knees. She bit her lip hard, wanting to call out to him, to go to him—but instinct told her she should do neither of these things.

Feeling a tug at her arm, she turned to look directly into a pair of serious blue eyes—Charles, urgency and tension lining his young face. She knew what he wanted. "No."

His fingers tightened around her arm. She dug in her heels, ready for the fight. But without warning, Charles seized her and threw her over his shoulder, heading for the door.

She kicked her feet, wriggling. "Charles, no. Charles, stop! Alex—"

"Get them!" an angry voice shouted.

Somehow he managed to get them out, despite the blows she rained upon his backside. The last thing she saw was Alex, buried beneath a wave of black. Then darkness again as the door closed behind them.

Charles zigzagged quickly through the streets, never flagging, even when shouts from behind them made it clear that they were indeed being followed. His knowledge of their wending path both amazed and infuriated her. Each step pounded his shoulder into her ribs. Her breath came out in jerking huffs that kept rhythm with his footsteps against the cobblestones. She gave up fighting him, resigning herself for the moment to being at his mercy, but all she could think of was Alex.

It seemed an eternity before he set her on her feet. The shouts came from farther away now. It was almost certain they had lost their pursuers. She should feel relieved, certainly; triumphant, perhaps. They were safe, after all. But all she felt was loss.

"Tori?"

She couldn't look at him. He had taken her away from Alex when he needed her the most. They had just left him there to die. . . .

He touched her shoulder, hesitated, almost drew away. Then all of a sudden he pulled her into a crushing bear hug. "I'm sorry, sis, I'm so sorry. But you must see we had to. 'Twas the only way."

Tears burned her eyes, but to her surprise she found herself hugging him back. "B-but Charles . . . I l-love him. We can't let him die! We c-can't just leave him there! We have to go back!"

He wrapped his arms tighter around her and rocked her as if she were a child. The incongruity of their situation struck her. When did he become the comforter and she the needy? "He won't, Tori. I promise you. He won't die."

His tone was odd, strangely adamant. Taking a deep breath to compose herself, she pulled away and looked up at him. Charles seemed so different somehow. So tall, suddenly, his face grim. Even his shoulders seemed broader. He was growing up.

Before she had time to digest these changes in her brother and in herself, he took her hand. "Come. We must get help."

Help. Alex's words came rushing back to her. "The queen! Alex said we must get word to the queen. She'll know what to do."

"Then that's what we'll do."

Gritting his teeth, Alex tested his bonds once more while the Emperor and his followers watched and laughed. They'd knotted the ropes around his wrists, then tethered the ropes to a timber. Escape appeared unlikely.

"You'll not be absconding so easily this time, my friend," the Emperor said, a malicious grin lighting his eyes.

Alex glared at him. "You won't get away with this, you know."

"No?" The man laughed. "We get away with this all the time. Killing the queen will be a new game, nothing more." He paused, then added slyly, "Like your woman. Sweet bit of skirt, she is. Of course you won't mind if I—"

Alex hit the end of his tether, making the ropes sing. "You bastard!"

"Oh, come, what does it matter? You'll be dead. Your woman will need comforting." His eyes flashed with evil intent. "I'm very good at comforting young women."

From the back of the room came a familiar voice. "Alex, Alex. You should have listened to your dear cousin. He *told* you to stay away."

Alex looked up. Rorick moved forward, preceded by . . . Bess?

"Nothing to say, my love?" She sauntered forward, dodging men and tables as she went, her hips swinging in her signature come-hither walk. All eyes in the room followed her. "You really should have listened. Now your ladylove is at risk, your life is forfeit, and the queen is as good as dead. Surely that's not the end you sought." She stood in front of him, pouting her full lips, and arched an auburn brow. "We could have had everything, Alex, but you chose to betray me instead. How fitting that I betray you as well, don't you think?"

Alex turned his face away, refusing to answer.

She didn't seem to mind. Instead she turned to Rorick and the Emperor and asked, "Do you have the boy?"

Rorick shook his head. "He . . . well, escaped with the woman before anyone knew who he was."

Her full lips pressed into a hard, flat line. "Find them. Find them both."

Changing her demeanor abruptly, she slipped against the Emperor and clutched his arm, pressing her breasts against him. "You will find them, won't you?" she simpered. "I *must* have my revenge."

The Emperor slid his fingers up her arm as he stared into her eyes. "You shall have your fun, my sweet. And when this business with the queen is done, we shall have ours together."

Alex watched the exchange with a grimace. Could she have been so crushed by his rejection that it had driven her to these men, or had she been this way all along? Ye Gods, he must have been blind. "You seem to have forgotten one thing," he interrupted coldly.

The pair turned to him, their smiles fading. "And what might that be?" the Emperor asked.

Alex returned the Mohock leader's cool, unblinking stare. "Who are you going to get to kill the queen?" When he saw a flicker of hesitation in the Emperor's eyes, he continued, "Lady Victoria was your only hold on me. Now she's gone. It appears you'll have to find someone else to carry out your plans against the queen."

The Emperor studied him, while whispers arose from the ranks around them. Then he smiled. "As you wish, my lord. Whether you do or whether you don't does not signify. The queen will die tonight."

"Not by my hand."

The Mohock leader shrugged. "Perhaps not, in truth. But with the blood of your mother—"

"*French* blood," Bess interjected, wrinkling her nose.

"—coursing through your veins, you'll make the perfect scapegoat for our little . . . adventure."

Clenching his teeth, Alex glared at his captor. Before he could bite out a comment, two black-garbed men burst into the tavern room.

"The first fires have been sighted!"

"It has begun, sir!"

Bitter words died unspoken on Alex's lips. God help them all. It had begun.

"You must let us in! We have to get a message to the queen!"

Tori stood by, gritting her teeth, as Charles argued with the gate guards. *The fools!* Couldn't they see that they meant no harm to the queen, that they were there to help?

"G' on wit' ye!"

"Don't ye see the queen don't have time fer yer shenanigans? Look around ye, man! The whole city's gone mad."

The guard was more right than he knew. All about the castle, in every direction, she could see the red-gold glow of fire stretching greedy fingers into the sky. The guards couldn't possibly understand that the fires were the responsibility of the scourge of London midnights.

"Do you know who I am?" Charles asked, straightening his shoulders and puffing up with importance. "I am—"

"We don't care if ye're the Prince of Hanover himself.

No one gets into the palace. Now, get on wit' ye."

Muttering under his breath, Charles returned to the edge of the courtyard where Tori waited for him. "Imbeciles."

Tori patted him on the shoulder. "They're just performing their duties."

He scowled. "Aye. And only too admirably. There *has* to be a way to get inside!"

Tori nodded. "Why don't you walk around the wall and see what you can find? I'll stay here and talk to these lovely gentlemen."

He hesitated, looking as though he'd like to refuse, but he eventually saw the logic in the suggestion. "All right. Just don't let them near you. And stay out of trouble!"

As if *that* would be a problem, she grumbled to herself.

Hmmph.

On second thought . . .

Charles crept through the darkness, his nerves stretched taut. Perhaps 'twas only the fires and the distant shouts, but something felt wrong—very wrong.

Ahead he saw another gate. He approached it cautiously, waiting for a sign that the guards had seen him. But when he was allowed to approach without a cry of recognition, he shivered with apprehension.

The guards were gone. The gate was completely unprotected.

A sharp crack came from behind him.

He froze.

Before he even had a chance to turn around, something soft dropped over his head, twisted, and then he felt himself being pulled backward off his feet to the sound of laughter.

Tori studied the two guards for several moments before she approached them. They watched her approach, their expressions wary but curious.

One slapped his compatriot on the shoulder. "Ha! I told

ye!—Ye owe me a crown, Hobbs. It *is* a woman.''

''Aw, ye had a better look at 'er, 'at's all.'' He jutted his chin out at Tori. ''What do ye want, miss?''

Tori moved closer. ''I am with the man you would not allow in to see the queen. I am Lady Victoria Wynter. It is imperative that I speak with the queen.''

The two guards began to laugh. ''Lady Victoria Wynter? Sure ye are, dove. Now, what would a lady be doing dressing up as a man?''

The shorter one nudged his companion with an elbow. ''Well, Hobbs, ye know, they do say some ladies have . . . unusual tastes and habits.''

They leered at her.

Tori grimaced. She hoped Charles was having better luck.

Chapter Twenty-one

From where he had been led bound and flanked by two guards, Alex saw a lone figure being hauled through the unlocked palace gate, a cloak pulled tight around the person's head. For a moment he thought his worst nightmare had come true—that Tori had followed them and had been captured. He tensed, and immediately the hands gripping his arms on each side tightened. His Mohock captors had no intention of letting him escape.

To his surprise, the captive was led before him. The Emperor smiled as he pulled the cloak from—

Charles.

"I thought you might like to see this," the Emperor said. A cold smile contorted his face into a mask of evil. "He escaped once, and we reclaimed him. Your woman will be next."

The tension left Alex's body in a rush. Tori was still safe. They didn't have her.

He met the Emperor's gaze head-on. "Do you really think Charles would bring his sister to the palace, knowing that you would be here? She's miles from here by now,'' he said with a sneer.

''Really?'' The Mohock leader cocked a thick brow. ''Wolf? Where is she?''

A paunchy man stepped forward. ''At the north gate. The guards there are holding her at bay. She's just the distraction we needed to keep them in their places. They'll have no idea what is going on right under their noses.''

Charles strained against the hands pinning his arms to his sides. ''You bastard!''

Raising a brow, the Mohock leader stared down his nose at the lad, his expression cold steel. ''Excellent. I couldn't have planned it better myself.'' He turned to Alex. ''You see? Your efforts to expose us are meaningless. We have you and your traitor friend both in our possession. 'Twill be a simple thing to reclaim your woman later. And the queen will be dead before midnight.'' He nodded at Charles's captors. ''You two—truss the traitor up against that tree over there. Raven comes along with us.'' He raised his fist into the air. ''You know your positions. Let's finish this.''

If he didn't do something soon, it would all be over for the queen, for Tori, for himself. But what?

Passing beneath the twin towers, they gained admission to the palace. It soon became clear to Alex that the Mohocks had achieved their initial purpose only too well. Naught but silence met them as they moved stealthily down the wide corridors. The palace was deserted. In the rooms they passed through, hundreds of candles flickered in their holders, but they betrayed not a single servant or guard to interfere with their passage. It was overwhelmingly eerie, as if the rooms had been inhabited only moments before and the occupants had disappeared into thin air.

The Emperor seemed to know exactly where to go as he led the pack toward their final destination: the queen's private quarters. Alex's tension mounted as they climbed the last staircase and edged their way up the hall. There should have been sentries posted here, if nowhere else—the queen's personal guard.

"No use hoping for salvation, dear Raven." The Emperor's voice broke into the darkness, his almost normal tone speaking volumes about his confidence that his plan was fail-safe. "I'm afraid we've dispatched all of the queen's men. She is asleep as we speak—and that sleep will, unfortunately, be a permanent one."

Fury throbbed in his veins. Alex gritted his teeth. "Go to hell."

The Mohock leader gave him a small smile. "So idealistic," he chided. He shook his head.

Without waiting for an answer, he jerked his head toward the queen's bedchamber, motioning for the others to take their places on either side of the door. Alex's escorts tightened their grip to ensure he could not break free.

The Emperor stood quietly just outside the double door, his hand poised on the gilded knob. Alex could feel his heartbeat rushing in his veins, faster, faster. Time seemed to slow, or perhaps it was only his own awareness growing by leaps and bounds. He stopped breathing as he watched the Emperor's hand squeeze the doorknob, then ever so slowly turn it. The door should have been locked from the inside; but then, there should have been guards. He could have sworn that he heard the faint squeal of metal rubbing metal, the click of the tumblers giving way in the latch, the gentle whir of well-oiled hinges as the door swung silently inward. The Emperor entered the queen's apartments, followed by several of his black-clothed henchmen.

Apprehension joined with anger in a slithering dance up his spine as Alex steeled himself for what he knew must come next.

The one called Hobbs stood even taller and crossed his arms in his best attempt to look imposing. "I told ye, I don't care who ye are; ye're not gettin' in."

Tori planted her hands on her hips and stood her ground. "This is of the utmost importance, I assure you. Life and death—"

The short, round man nudged forward. "Begone with ye. Come back in the morning if 'tis so bloody important."

"If I wait until morning, the queen will be dead!"

Hobbs threw his head back and laughed. His Adam's apple bobbled like a chunk of ice in water. "And 'ow could that be, milady? The palace is a bloody fortress! If a pretty lady like yerself can't wile 'er way in, 'tis certain no one else can."

His compatriot nodded. "Go 'ome, lady."

Tori racked her brain as hysterics threatened her composure. She had to get in. She had to!

It suddenly occurred to her that Charles had not returned. She had been so caught up with the two guards that she'd completely lost track of time. How many minutes had passed? She looked around, but he'd disappeared around the bend of the wall long ago. She bit her lip.

"Well, go on wit' ye!"

Standing her ground, she raised her chin, planted her feet in a bold stance, and crossed her arms. "I demand that you search the grounds, just to be certain all is well."

The heavyset man rolled his eyes. "Crimminey."

Hobbs cleared his throat. Placing his hands upon his belt, he puffed out his skinny chest importantly. "Never you mind, Bates. I'll see to it."

Tori had hardly time enough to feel triumph before the gangly guard came running around the corner of the wall. Sheer terror contorted his face into a mask of almost comical proportions.

"Bloody hell! She's right!"

Thud.

Alex opened his eyes. The sound was definitely not what

he'd expected to hear as the worst of his nightmares came true.

There it was again. Another thud, followed by the unmistakable sounds of a scuffle. Good God, she was still alive, and she was fighting for her life. He began to feel physically ill, thinking of what might be happening within those walls. Growling with the strength of his fury, he flung his arms up against the hands holding him.

To his surprise, the hands fell away with ease.

That was when he knew something was very right. And before a minute had passed, his so-called escorts did the unthinkable.

They fled.

Astonished, he stared after them. Now certain of the rightness of the moment, he took advantage of his sudden freedom and kicked open the door. Plunging into the queen's chamber, he fought to see through the darkness, but the pale light from the hall failed to illuminate more than a foot or two.

Someone seized him from behind, pinning his arms to his sides. He felt the cold bore of a pistol press into his side, but he would not stop, even at his own peril. Not when he was this close to saving her. Wrenching and twisting, he tried to fight his way free.

A female voice rang out in the dark room, its tone imperious and irritable at once. "Is that all of them?"

"Aye," a male voice answered.

"Good. Then can someone *please* have the good sense to light some candles, now that the diversion has passed."

Even before the sudden flare of light, Alex knew that somehow, some way, Anne had triumphed.

The scene that met his eyes brought amazement and confusion. The queen sat, regally garbed and very much alive, in a delicate wing chair in the far corner of the room. Between Anne and himself, Alex counted twenty-four Mohocks in various states of confinement, a great many more of the queen's men in their brilliant red uniforms, and one frightened woman in a white nightdress and frilly mobcap cowering in an adjoining doorway. The man holding the gun to his side, he saw to his great relief, wore red, not black.

Anne's lips tightened as her eyes met his. "Take them all to the blue assembly room. I'll deal with them there."

"Your Majesty, wait." Alex tried to step forward, but was stopped with a jab of the pistol. It was beginning to annoy him. "I—"

She looked away. "All of them."

The noise in the assembly room had risen steadily over the hour-long wait the queen forced them to endure. Guarded by an armed brigade of the queen's men, the number of Mohocks had risen from twenty-four to nearly a hundred as they were captured, one by one. With the masks stripped from their faces, the number of men he recognized astonished him. Charles huddled next to Alex, his face white with fear. Even Rorick appeared some time later, captured at one of the many blazes.

Alex found himself shackled with the rest of them, in spite of his protests. At last an aide, resplendent in satin, swept through the double doors with all the pomp of a peacock and announced her presence. Shadowed by a meek lady-in-waiting, Anne shuffled painfully into the room with her head held high, still every inch a queen despite the gout that was beginning to cripple her movements. The aide helped her up onto the dais.

The Mohocks, rogue nobles all, fell silent.

She sank into the thronelike chair and heaved a loud sigh. Her lady-in-waiting fussed about her until Anne held up a hand. "Thank you, Abigail. That will do just fine."

Her eyes cast down, the lady-in-waiting nodded and stood back.

"Now, then. I'm sure you all know why you've been assembled here." Seeing their confused expressions, Anne laughed at her own wry joke. ''Yes. Well. Let's get on with things, shall we?''

She snapped her fingers, and her aide brought forth a rolled piece of parchment. Anne took it.

''I hold in my hand a list of your crimes. As you can see, the list is quite long. The most serious, of course, is the betrayal of your queen. Treason is a crime upon which the Crown cannot look favorably.''

Most of the men had the good grace to stare at their feet. Two men stood out, their heads held high, their expressions cold—the Emperor and Rorick.

Anne whipped her head around, pinning Alex with a direct stare. ''Carlton. It pains us to see you here like this.''

Alex frowned. Did she think . . . ? He swallowed once, trying not to focus on the apprehension making lazy circles in his belly. ''I was told the attack was planned for another date, Your Majesty. I learned only this afternoon that the plans had been changed, and before I could warn you, I myself was captured.''

She nodded, her expression calculating as she digested his claim. ''We see. And yet you appear here, in the midst of the attack itself.''

He forced himself to nod. ''Aye. I was to be blamed for your assassination. I was . . . much relieved to find that their plot did not work.''

''Were you?'' She raised a single brow. ''We imagine so. Relieved that you could not be blamed for our death, eh?''

He met her gaze directly. ''No, my queen. Relieved that England would not suffer what they had planned for it.''

She considered his words in silence. At last she nodded at her aide. From his pocket he withdrew a ring of keys and walked toward Alex . . . and past him. Confusion filled him as the aide removed the shackles from one of the men he did not recognize. His confusion grew as the man joined the queen at the dais. When she extended her hand to him, he knelt and kissed her ring.

Sweeping the Mohocks with her gaze, Anne indicated the freed Mohock. "We have had among you not one informant, but two. Allow me to present Mr. Jonathan Sikes, who has been in our service for many a year. Is that not right, Jonathan?" At his smiling nod, she continued. "Of course, you all have known him as Wolfhound, we believe." She paused delicately. "Quite a fitting name, if we do say so ourselves. Sniffing out prey, eh, Jonathan?"

He laughed and bowed to her. "Quite so, Your Majesty."

Anne squinted in Alex's direction. "Is that young Lord Charles Wynter we see out there beside Carlton? Good God. We attended your christening, young man. Your father would be quite put out to know you were here. What is your involvement in all of this?"

Alex stepped forward, ready to defend him, but Charles stopped him by placing his shackled hands on his arm. "Nay," he whispered. "I got myself into this. 'Tis up to me to get myself out." He took a deep breath and faced the queen. "I don't mean to be disrespectful, Your Majesty, but you're wrong if you think Alex, I mean Lord Carlton, was involved in this scheme. He did everything he could to get word to you. He even saved my sister and me at risk of his own life." He nodded thoughtfully, his expression grave. "I admit to an overabundance of arrogance in being lured to the Mohock meeting. The fault is mine, and mine alone. But you're wrong if you blame Alex."

Anne continued to stare at him, her expression betraying nothing. "And which is the one called 'the Emperor,' Jonathan?"

"The tall one with the scar on his forehead, your Majesty."

"Indeed?" She looked down her nose at him. "What excuse do you have, sir, for your involvement in this act of treason?"

Alex watched as the Emperor stood taller. He straightened his shoulders. But he said not a word.

Anne slapped her hand down on the cushion beside her. "Pah! Perhaps time in the Tower will loosen his tongue." She struggled to her feet. "Perhaps 'twill loosen all their tongues."

"Nay." Rorick lurched forward, startling everyone. He looked straight ahead, his back straight and tall. "Ye doona want Lord Carlton, Yer Majesty, if ye have nae wish to punish the undeserving."

Anne paused, supported on the arm of her spy. "And who are you?"

Alex watched his cousin click his heels together and stand even taller. "Rorick McDowell, Yer Majesty."

Anne raised a haughty brow. "And what is your part in all of this?"

Shadows of emotion flickered over his hard-cut features. In the end, he only shrugged. "I just . . . wanted ye to know that Lord Carlton is innocent. That's all. The Emperor, on the other hand, ye can throw in the Tower with the certainty that ye've done the right thing."

Ignoring the Emperor's sudden growl, Anne pressed, "And why should we trust your perceptions?"

He turned his tawny head and met her gaze directly for the first time. "Because I am the man who hired the Mohocks to kill ye."

Her brows, already raised, stretched higher. "Then you shall die first of all." Her gaze shifted momentarily to the Emperor's proud figure. "Well, perhaps second."

"I amna—" Rorick's voice broke, but he struggled on. "I amna proud . . . of what I felt must be done. But I am verra proud to be a Scot. And p'raps, on the day ye stretch my neck, ye will at least understand. I will be a Scot, no' an Englishman, no' a Brit, until the day I die."

Blinking rapidly, his face rock hard with the strength of his control, Rorick took a single step backward, a part of the crowd but ever removed from it by the grace of his actions. Tears burned at the back of Alex's eyes, but he would not shame his cousin by shedding them. Rorick had done him right.

Anne seemed to agree. Gazing directly at Rorick, she nodded in what Alex could only deem acceptance, then began to shuffle toward the door, supported by Sikes.

Just before she reached the door, she halted and patted the man's arm. "Oh, Jonathan. The young man's speech must have affected our senses. See to it that Lords Carlton and Wynter are released. They are free to go."

Charles let out a great sigh of relief.

"On the understanding," Anne continued firmly, "that we will hear of no more trouble associated with either of their names. We assume we are rightly understood?"

"I believe," Alex said dryly, "that I can safely promise you never to take part in such doings again."

Charles nodded, bobbing his head repeatedly. "Absolutely, Your Majesty. Never again."

Anne appeared to be smothering a smile. "Good. See that—"

From the corridor beyond the double doors came a high-pitched shriek of indignation. Though a trifle muffled, a female voice could be clearly understood. "Oooh! Unhand me! You have no right whatsoever to keep me from that room when I have evidence the queen must hear to make her decision!"

Alex and Charles exchanged a glance.

A male voice responded. "Lady, ye have been a thorn in my side for the last two hours— Aaargh!"

With that, the double doors burst wide and crashed into the wall on either side. Looking vaguely like a black-clad banshee in men's clothing, Tori stood triumphantly in the doorway.

Alex grinned at the sight of her, his heart swelling with relief and love. Her beautiful, fierce face reflected uncertainty only once—when she saw the queen standing only a few feet from the crashing doors. Then she dropped into a low, graceful curtsy that would have made any mother proud. "Your Majesty."

A guard appeared in the doorway, his coarse face as red as his uniform. "I tried to 'old 'er—"

Anne waved him away, then turned to Tori. "Well. I see you know who we are. Stand up, then, child, and let us have a look at you." She indicated the battered tricorne, still in place on Tori's head. "Without the hat, please."

The hat? Tori lifted her hand to the brim and swallowed hard, trying to gather her courage. Beneath the hat, her braid was a rat's nest of straw bits and leaves and tangles. Hardly a fitting way to be presented to the queen. Unfortunately, she had no choice. Taking a deep breath, she swept the tricorne from her head, and her hair tumbled down.

"Good heavens." Anne looked up at Sikes. "Jonathan, escort me back to the dais while we listen to this young lady's tale. We have a feeling this is going to be good."

Seated once again on her chair, Anne motioned to Tori. "Come forth, my dear."

Tori walked past the long line of Mohocks, pausing only when she came to Alex and Charles. Her heart in her throat, she let her gaze drift over the two men she loved most. She caught her breath when she saw the iron shackles. Furious, she stalked to the dais.

"Why the long face, my dear? Tell me why you are here."

She took a deep breath. "Your Majesty, I must protest. With the Mohocks, you have shackled Lord Carlton and Lord Wynter, two men who worked against the Mohocks, who did all that they could to foil the plan against you. Indeed, this treatment of two *heroes* is unworthy!"

The queen appeared to be studying her. "And how do you know the worthiness of these two men in what took place this night?"

"Because I was there. The Mohocks stole me from my home this very afternoon. 'Twas only through the efforts of these two men that I escaped.'' Tori glanced at Alex, and her voice softened. ''Indeed, Alex risked his life to be sure that we got to safety. He is an honorable, noble man.''

The queen actually smiled. ''Then, my dear, how can we possibly hold them? Jonathan, release the two men.''

Wings of joy lifted Tori's heart as she watched the shackles fall away. She ran to Alex, and he caught her in his arms and swung her around, heedless of the countless eyes witnessing their embrace.

He cupped her cheek with his hand, his dark eyes glowing as he gazed down at her. ''Ah, Tori. My angel.''

She looked into his eyes, hoping he could see all the emotion she felt, everything that she was, reflected in her own. ''I love you, Alex,'' she whispered. ''I will love you until the day I die.''

He tipped up her chin, and their lips met in a sweet breath of a kiss filled with hope and promise.

Someone cleared her throat.

They both looked up to find Anne watching them, a queer, dreamy expression on her face. ''We trust,'' she said mildly, ''that this means only one thing?''

''Ask her!'' Charles hooted, grinning like a madman.

Alex smiled down at her, and Tori's heart lurched as he dropped to a knee before her, touching only her hand in a soft way that bespoke reverence and love, but looking at her in a way that made her remember their impassioned hours at the inn. ''In the absence of your father,'' he said, ''I hope that I have the queen's blessing in asking for your hand in marriage.'' He pressed a swift kiss to her palm, then looked up at her again. ''Marry me, Victoria.''

Blinking tears away, she whispered, ''Aye.''

Whispers arose as he rose to his feet and pulled her into his arms once more, crushing her until she thought her ribs might break. Victoria found that she didn't care.

Until a familiar voice boomed, ''Sir! Unhand my daughter!''

Tori's eyes flew open. Stepping back from Alex, she

turned to find her father standing in the doorway. ''Father?''

Anne looked up at Sikes. ''Oh, good, another intrusion,'' she said wryly.

Standing two inches over six feet, James Charles Andrew Wynter, the fourth Marquess of Middleham, still cut an imposing figure at the advanced age of forty-nine, but it was his eyes that had the ability to make Tori feel as if she were eight years old again. As blue as a cerulean sky, they held power and wisdom in their depths—or they had until her mother had died.

Glowering fiercely, he stalked toward them. ''Sir, I demand to know what you were doing just now with my daughter.''

Alex returned his fierce look with a level gaze of his own. ''Why, I was embracing her, my lord.''

''And just who the devil do you think you are?''

''We do believe we can shed some light on that,'' Anne interrupted. ''James, allow us to present Alexandre Rawlings, Earl of Carlton. He has just asked your daughter to marry him, and she has accepted, with our approval. Carlton, this is your future father-in-law, James Wynter, the Marquess of Middleham.''

''I gathered that,'' Alex replied dryly.

''I'd like to know what the devil is going on,'' Tori's father demanded stiffly. ''I come home from a tour of the Continent only to find my household in an uproar because my daughter, my eldest child, has been kidnapped from our very doorstep, and all of London is in chaos. And when I come here to ask for assistance, I find that not only is my daughter safe and sound, but she is also about to be wed to a man I do not know, and to whom I did not give my approval.''

''We gave *our* approval,'' Anne reminded him.

The pointed admonition had the effect the queen intended. Straightening his shoulders, the marquess turned to his children. ''With the queen's permission, perhaps we should continue this conversation elsewhere."

With an enigmatic smile, Anne gave a vague wave of her hand. "By all means, James." She was still smiling as the door closed behind the motley group.

The Marquess turned to Tori and Charles with an ominously raised brow. "You couldn't wait until I arrived? I've been telling you for the past two months the date of my return. What kind of a man is he—"

Tori frowned and crossed her arms, breaking free of her childlike awe of her father's authority. "I've received no notice of your return, Father. And furthermore, Alex is a wonderful man! The very best of men."

All eyes turned to the marquess, who frowned. "I've written you four letters in the past two months, and each one stated the date I would be returning home," he insisted.

"I've received no letters."

Sudden suspicion made her turn to Charles, who had stood by her throughout the entire debacle. His face was red with embarrassment, but only anger showed in his eyes as he faced his father without fear. "I burned them," he said simply.

Pain crossed the marquess's noble features. "You . . . burned them? Charles, why?"

Tori reached for Alex's hand as the remembrance of Charles's pain swept through her. Charles only shrugged. "It doesn't matter."

Suddenly her father looked old and tired. "Well." He cleared his throat and glanced briefly at his daughter. "I suppose this isn't quite the right time to tell you that I've arranged for your marriage."

"What?" Tori's heart dropped to the vicinity of her toes. "Father, you can't mean—"

Charles stalked over, planting himself between Tori and the marquess. "You'll do nothing of the sort. You go off"—he poked their father in the chest—"and leave us here"—another poke—"to suffer our grief alone—"

Tori placed her hand on his arm. "Charles, calm down."

"No, I will not calm down!" He began to pace. "What you don't seem to understand, sir, is that we have done quite well without you. Tori has done quite well without you. And I daresay that her choice for a husband is five times the man your choice might be." He brought his chin up, his jaw tight with barely suppressed anger. "I know Alexandre Rawlings. I have, quite frankly, never known a better man. And he loves Tori." He met Alex's gaze and shook his head. "I've never seen a man more willing to die for the woman he loves," he said softly. "You have taught me much, my friend. I owe you for that."

With tears clouding her vision, Tori hugged her brother and softly kissed his cheek. "Oh, Charles." Sniffling, she turned to the marquess. "Charles is right. I love Alex, Father. I'm afraid I could not be happy with anyone else. I don't wish to be disrespectful, but there is no way on earth that you could force me to marry another."

The marquess cleared his throat. "Well. I see."

"Well? Is that all you can say?" Queen Anne's imperious voice came from the doorway behind them, surprising them all. Turning as one, the four saw the queen standing in the now-open doorway on the arm of her aide, quite obviously observing their exchange. Jonathan Sikes followed close behind. We want to hear your answer. If this is because Carlton's mother is French—"

The marquess raised his brows at Tori. Tori shrugged innocently.

"—then the least we can do is avow his patriotism. He's a good man, James."

"A very good man, Father," Tori echoed. She edged close to the marquess and tucked her hand through his arm. Gazing up at her father, she could feel the precise moment when he relented.

The Marquess of Middleham had learned to admit when he was wrong. "My only thought was for your happiness,

Tori. But I can see now that I need not worry in that regard. Your brother is quite right. You have done well without my help.'' He glanced, almost shyly, in Charles's direction. ''You both have.''

Tori hardly dared to breathe. ''Then you give your consent?''

''Aye.'' At her whoop of delight, he grinned down at her, then extended his hand to Alex. ''Welcome to the family, son.'' After a manly shake, he leaned closer to Alex. ''She has her mother's eyes, you know, and the same generous spirit. I always loved that best about her.''

''Excellent!'' Supported by her aide, Anne began to make her down the corridor. ''Mr. Sikes, you know what to do with the men. James, so glad to see you back in England. We trust we shall be invited to the wedding.''

''Of course, Your Majesty,'' the marquess replied as the four of them followed her. Charles lagged behind only slightly, while Alex boldly held Tori's hand.

As the queen left them, Tori's father whispered, ''I always have loved the sound of the French language. But I would never admit that to the queen.''

Epilogue

Eight months later

Tori sighed and stretched as the last vestiges of pleasure dissipated from her body in languorous waves. Running her hand down her husband's back, she smiled as her hand came away damp. "Hard labor, my love?"

Alex groaned against her neck. A second later she giggled as his teeth nipped her earlobe. "Vixen," he muttered. "Use my body most selfishly, sap my energy, then make jests about it."

"Selfishly? Hmmph. I seem to recall you—"

He covered her lips with his, his tongue stealing her words as he kissed her long, hard, and deep. "Vixen," he said again against her lips.

"Hmmm."

He slid to one side and nestled her body against his. Tori nuzzled her nose against his neck, breathing deeply of his scent. She loved these moments best, when time had no meaning and they could cherish each other as they could not during the day, when family, servants, and obligations occupied the majority of their time.

He flattened his palm against her rounding belly. His fingers made swirling patterns against her flesh. "The little one is active tonight."

Tori smiled and covered his hand with her own. "He is more and more each day. Sometimes it feels as if he's swimming inside me, kicking and wheeling his arms."

He wrapped his fingers around hers, squeezing them. "It won't be too long now."

"Two months, no more. I can't imagine what it will be like to see him at last."

He held her in silence for quite some time, the movements of their baby close against his side. Her breathing had become slow and steady; he thought she'd fallen asleep.

"Alex?"

"Aye?"

"Today I overheard Charles discussing returning to Oxford with my father."

He kissed her forehead. "That's wonderful, *ange.*"

"Father tried not to show it, but he's so proud of Charles. He's grown up so much. I think . . . I think Charles is going to be fine."

"Of course he will be."

She raised herself up on an elbow and gazed down at him. "I guess I just feel so blessed. I keep waiting to wake up from this wonderful dream."

He'd felt the same way at times, but if this was naught but a pleasant dream, it was the kind from which there was no awakening. The very best kind of dream.

The nightmare of the Mohocks was long behind them, and the Emperor had been executed. Rorick, he'd discovered, had received the queen's mercy and had been exiled. Even Bess could not hurt them, having disappeared after the fires. Some said she'd been seen cavorting around Austria with one of the Hanover princes.

His days were filled with sunshine and happiness beyond compare, and his nights . . . well, Tori had filled them with love and acceptance and mind-numbing passion. He no longer felt alone, and he'd learned that he was the sum total of his past, good and bad combined. And he thought his father would have been proud of what he'd become.

He touched her cheek, loving the way her eyes lit up when he did. Smiling at her, he murmured, "I think we may have another announcement soon forthcoming."

"Really? What?"

He grinned. "I've, uh, been noticing a lot of whispers and giggling going on between your father and my mother."

"Father and Isabelle?" she said in a squeak.

"Aye." He laughed. "He always did say he loved the sound of the French language. I have a feeling . . ."

She smiled and snuggled against him again. "I would love to see him happy. Oh, Alex, everything is so perfect."

"Aye. That leaves only one thing."

"What one thing?"

"We haven't decided what to name the baby."

"How about Atticus?"

"Atticus!"

"I had an uncle named Atticus," she said with good-natured defensiveness.

"Hmm, no. How about Josephine?"

"Josephine is a girl's name!"

"And what makes you think it's not a girl? Besides, I had an aunt named Josephine."

She started to laugh. The sound bubbled through him, lifting his heart. "I think we're just going to have to call him Phillippe," she said softly. "I believe it's the only name we've both liked."

"In that case, I guess it had better be a boy."

Conquer the Mist
Susan Kearney